An Amish Summer

Other Novels by the Authors

SHELLEY SHEPARD GRAY

LONE STAR HERO LOVE STORIES

The Loyal Heart

An Uncommon Protector

Love Held Captive (Available October 2017)

CHICAGO WORLD'S FAIR MYSTERY SERIES

Secrets of Sloane House

Deception on Sable Hill

Whispers in the Reading Room

AMY CLIPSTON

THE AMISH HEIRLOOM SERIES

The Forgotten Recipe

The Courtship Basket

The Cherished Quilt

The Beloved Hope Chest

THE HEARTS OF THE LANCASTER GRAND HOTEL SERIES

A Hopeful Heart

A Mother's Secret

A Dream of Home

A Simple Prayer

THE KAUFFMAN AMISH BAKERY SERIES

A Gift of Grace

A Promise of Hope

A Place of Peace

A Life of Joy

A Season of Love

A Plain and Simple Christmas

Naomi's Gift

THE HEARTS OF MIDDLEFIELD NOVELS

A Man of His Word

An Honest Love

A Hand to Hold

OTHER NOVELLAS

A Miracle for Miriam included in *An Amish Christmas*

A Place of His Own included in *An Amish Gathering*

What the Heart Sees included in *An Amish Love*

Flowers for Rachael included in *An Amish Wedding*

A Gift for Anne Marie included in *An Amish Second Christmas*

Heart Full of Love included in *An Amish Cradle*

KELLY IRVIN

THE AMISH OF BEE COUNTY NOVELS

The Beekeeper's Son

The Bishop's Son

The Saddle Maker's Son

EVERY AMISH SEASON NOVELS

Upon a Spring Breeze

Beneath the Summer Sun (Available January 2018)

An Amish Summer

Four Novellas

Shelley Shepard Gray, Amy Clipston,
Kathleen Fuller, and Kelly Irvin

THOMAS NELSON
Since 1798

An Amish Summer

© 2017 by Shelley Shepard Gray, Amy Clipston, Kathleen Fuller, Kelly Irvin

Published in Nashville, Tennessee, by Thomas Nelson. Thomas Nelson is a registered trademark of HarperCollins Christian Publishing, Inc.

Thomas Nelson titles may be purchased in bulk for educational, business, fund-raising, or sales promotional use. For information, please e-mail SpecialMarkets@ThomasNelson.com.

Scripture quotations marked NKJV are taken from the New King James Version®. © 1982 by Thomas Nelson. Used by permission. All rights reserved.

Scripture quotations marked NLT are taken from the *Holy Bible,* New Living Translation, copyright © 1996, 2004, 2015 by Tyndale House Foundation. Used by permission of Tyndale House Publishers Inc., Carol Stream, Illinois 60188. All rights reserved.

Publisher's Note: This novel is a work of fiction. Names, characters, places, and incidents are either products of the author's imagination or used fictitiously. All characters are fictional, and any similarity to people living or dead is purely coincidental.

Library of Congress Cataloging-in-Publication Data

CIP data available upon request.

Printed in the United States of America

17 18 19 20 21 LSC 5 4 3 2 1

CONTENTS

GLOSSARY OF PENNSYLVANIA DUTCH WORDS

*THE GERMAN DIALECT SPOKEN BY THE AMISH IS NOT A written language and varies depending on the location and origin of the settlement. These spellings are approximations. Most Amish children learn English after they start school. They also learn High German, which is used in their Sunday services.

ach—oh

aenti—aunt

appeditlich—delicious

bedauerlich—sad

bopli—baby

bruder—brother

bruders—brothers

bu—boy

buwe—boys

daadi—grandpa

daadihaus/dawdy haus—grandparents' house

daed—father

danki/danke—thank you

dat—dad

dochder—daughter

Englischer—English or non-Amish

fraa—wife

freind—friends

freinden—friends

froh—happy

gern gschehne—you're welcome

Gmay—church district, community

Gott—God

gut—good

haus—house

Ich liebe dich—I love you

jah—yes

kaffi—coffee

kapp—prayer covering, cap, woman's head covering

kind—child

kinner—children

lieb—love

liewe—love, a term of endearment

maedel—girl, young woman

mamm—mom

mammi—grandma

mann—husband

mei—my

mudder—mother

narrisch—crazy

nee—no

onkel—uncle

rumspringa—period of running around

schee—pretty

schweschder—sister

suh—son

schweschder—sister

sohn—son

Was iss letz?—What's wrong?

wunderbaar—wonderful

ya—yes

A REUNION IN PINECRAFT

SHELLEY SHEPARD GRAY

This novella is dedicated to the wonderful group of ladies who joined me on my first 'girlfriend getaway' in Pinecraft. It was an amazing weekend, and your kindness and enthusiasm always leaves me speechless. Bless you all!

*Do not judge others, and you will not be judged. Do not
condemn others, or it will all come back against you.
Forgive others, and you will be forgiven.*

LUKE 6:37 (NLT)

*Things turn out the best for those who make the best of the
way things turn out.*

AMISH PROVERB

PROLOGUE

Dear Graham,

Thank you for replying to my letter. What a nice surprise! It was so thoughtful of you to send me those packets of lavender seeds. Since it's only January, I've planted them in a little pot in my room. And months from now, when they're filling our back patio with a lovely scent, I'll think of you.

Sherilyn Kramer

Dear Sherilyn,

Thank you for your sweet note and get-well card. It cheered me up when I was suffering from the flu. I'm happy to tell you the flu has now left our house and none of us is too worse for wear. Only my sister-in-law, Katie Jo, was bedridden more than two days. But she is with child and my brother does dote on her, so that's a blessing in itself.

I hope this letter finds you still feeling well. Take heart. Winter is almost over! I'll write more soon.

Graham Holland

Dear Graham,

I know I sent a long letter earlier this week, but guess what! I talked to my sister, Sharon, and she wants to go to Pinecraft too! She said she rarely gets a break from her job baking, so this will be a great opportunity for her. That makes four of us able to go, including our two friends. We're going to purchase our bus tickets tonight and will call tomorrow morning to get a room at the Orange Blossom Inn in Pinecraft.

Sherilyn

Dear Sherilyn,

Wow, your sister's name is Sharon. I bet that created quite a bit of confusion when you two were growing up!

Anyway, when I talked to Beverly Wagler at the inn, she said she hosts an afternoon tea around three o'clock every day. Let's plan on meeting then. I would come down to greet your bus since my friends and I will arrive in Pinecraft earlier than you will, but I've heard there's always quite a commotion and swarm of people there. I doubt we'd get more than a moment to talk.

I can't wait to continue our acquaintance in person. Just think, soon we won't have to wait days for replies to our questions. There's no telling the things we're going to find out about each other. Ha!

Graham

Dear Graham,

This is a quick letter I hope you'll receive before you leave. I wish you safe travels and lots of sunscreen.

I'm for sure bringing a whole bottle for myself. Yes, I'll see you for afternoon refreshments at the inn. And just in case you've forgotten what I look like in the last six months (ha!), I'll be the girl with the red hair and freckles!

See you in person in Pinecraft. I honestly can't wait.

Sherilyn

CHAPTER 1

❧

"Huh," Sherry said, disappointment thick in her voice. "I thought Pinecraft would look different."

As Sharon Kramer followed her little sister out of the Pioneer Trails bus in the center of the small vacation community, she hid a smile.

She supposed, for someone as lovely and full of life as Sherilyn—or Sherry to pretty much everyone who knew her—Pinecraft, Florida, was somewhat of a letdown. From here, it wasn't all that picturesque or darling. It looked a bit weather-beaten and stuck in a time warp.

Then, too, they weren't near the beach or even Pinecraft Park. They were standing in the middle of a large, crowded parking lot next to a tiny post office. Another bus was parked nearby, idling listlessly, casting off noxious fumes and no small bit of heat. That extra blast certainly wasn't needed, given that the hot July sun was already beating down on them all.

"It sure is hot," Sherry continued. "Really hot."

It was so hot and humid Sharon could practically see steam rising from the pavement. But her main concern was that her sister sounded so disappointed, especially after all the exciting letter writing she'd been doing with her secret pen pal for six months. Sharon decided to try to console her a bit.

"Even the best vacation spots have parking lots. I bet the rest of Pinecraft is just as charming as everyone said it would be."

"Maybe. I don't know, though."

As Sharon scanned the great number of people who had come out to meet the bus, she added, "Oh, who cares? I know you don't. We both know you didn't come here to take in the sights."

Stretching her arms out in front of her, Sherry nodded with a sheepish smile. "You're right. I'm sorry. I think I'm just tired. And *neahfich*."

"*Nee* apologies needed. I feel nervous too. And it was a long trip. I didn't sleep more than a few hours of it."

"I'm exhausted too," Sharon's best friend, Vera, said as she tumbled out of the bus. Her arms were full of the two dozen items she'd claimed were necessities for the hour drive from their Amish community in Adams County to Cincinnati and the sixteen-hour bus ride from Cincinnati to the center of Sarasota, Florida. "I can't wait to get unpacked, organized, and take a nap."

"There's *nee* way I want to do any of that right now," Carla declared. She was the fourth and final member of their group. "I'm excited to see everything. And to get a peek at Sherry's mysterious pen pal." She turned to her best friend. "*Now* are you going to tell us his name . . . finally? All we know is that you met him at the wedding in January."

"Oh, all right," Sherry said. "His name is Graham Holland, and he's from Sugarcreek."

Vera frowned. "That name doesn't ring a bell."

"Maybe you'll remember him when you see him. We met a lot of people those couple of days in Shipshe."

"I remember meeting Graham, but I don't remember exactly what he looks like," Carla said. "Do you, Sharon?"

Sharon shrugged. "The name sounds kind of familiar, but there were over four hundred people there. I don't think I could match any of their names with faces. They've turned into a blur in my brain."

"It's *nee* wonder. Six months ago you were still getting over your breakup with John Marc," Sherry said. "You didn't pay much attention to anything."

"That is kind of true." Less than two months before that trip to Indiana, she and John Marc had called off their relationship. It had been obvious that, although they were both nice people, a future together wasn't meant to be. Sharon had supposed they were both disappointed about how things worked out in the end.

That belief evaporated when, just a week before leaving for Indiana, Sharon saw John Marc flirting with Viola, one of her good friends. Then, days later Sharon learned the two of them had been quietly flirting with each other behind her back even before Sharon and John Marc broke up. Neither had wanted to hurt her feelings, they claimed, so they hadn't said a word.

Which, honestly, made no sense at all. John Marc had still cheated.

She'd been so embarrassed—and angry too. She'd alternated between fuming and crying the whole journey to Indiana. Watching that happy couple recite their vows had felt excruciating. Though she had nothing but good wishes for them, witnessing their ceremony was a reminder that she was a long way from celebrating her own wedding day. She'd been so melancholy and hurt she'd barely talked to anyone.

The only person she remembered in any detail was a man

with sandy-brown hair and blue eyes. He'd been so nice and kind, and a little flirty. Handsome too. And for a few minutes, he'd helped her forget her disappointment and hurt. Ever since then she'd wished she could remember his name. But she couldn't remember anyone's name from that day, and she'd never even mentioned the incident to Vera, let alone to Sherry.

Sherry, on the other hand, had been her usual self, making friends right and left. She'd come home with a list of people she wanted to correspond with, having boldly asked the host family for all their addresses. As the months passed, Sherry told Sharon about some of her pen pals, including the mysterious man she'd just identified as Graham Holland. But Sharon had never paid too much attention since they all seemed like strangers to her.

As they waited for the bus driver to open the luggage compartments under the bus, Sherry scanned the area nervously. "Do you think he's here? He said he wouldn't come on account of the crowds. And I told him in my last letter, assuming he got it, that I'd see him at the inn. But maybe he's here."

"If he said he was going to skip this zoo, I bet he did," Vera said in complete confidence. "There must be over a hundred people here, all milling around. I'd avoid it if I could."

Sharon said nothing, but she nodded at Vera, letting her know she privately agreed with her.

Sherry shook her head in exasperation. "You girls have *nee* sense of adventure. I shudder to think what's going to happen to you when I'm settled and you have *nee* one to organize adventures."

"We'll miss you prodding us. For sure," Sharon said, thinking she really did need to start being a bit more like her little sister.

It was all because of Sherry's strengths as a correspondent that this whole trip had gotten off the ground. She and her mysterious man had begun writing letters to each other, and soon they were writing every week. Five months later, the two of them set up this trip for July, with Sharon, Vera, and Carla joining Sherry. Two of his friends were accompanying him here, too, as well as some others from his circle. Now they also knew they all hailed from Sugarcreek.

Everyone had rented rooms at the large Orange Blossom Inn, and they were going to spend the next two weeks enjoying the beach and all the sights the area had to offer.

Of course, Sharon also knew her twenty-year-old sister was privately hoping her many months of letter writing to Graham Holland were going to blossom into a summer romance.

Although their parents had at first not wanted them to go, in the end they encouraged it. They knew both their daughters needed this trip to Pinecraft, giving them some time away to figure out what to do next in their lives. Sharon was completely over John Marc's betrayal and was eager to meet new people. And though several men they knew had been attempting to call on Sherry, she wasn't interested in any man except the one she was writing letters to.

As the four of them walked to the side of the bus, where the driver and two burly men were unloading the luggage stored underneath it, Sherry was looking over her shoulder, scanning the thirty or so people standing closest to the new arrivals.

Suddenly Sherry gripped Sharon's arm and whirled them both around. "I think that's him! He must have decided he couldn't wait to say hello at the inn. Isn't that something?"

"Well, I think that means he's smitten," Sharon said, teasing her sister with a smile. She really was happy for Sherry. She had such a good heart, and it was so romantic to imagine that she and this Graham had fallen in love through a series of letters.

Still staring across the parking lot, Sherry gave a little squeak. "Oh my heavens . . . It looks like he's trying to find us." When she turned to Sharon, a dozen imagined insecurities flickered across her face. "Do I look okay?" She ran her hands over her apron.

"Of course. Even after our long bus trip, you look perfect." Sherry was animated—like she always was, especially when she was excited. Her dark-auburn hair was falling out of its pins. Her green eyes were sparkling. And her slim, athletic build was showcased in her clothes. She looked like she was ready for anything.

"You look *wunderbaar*," Vera said with a wink. "I'm certain this Graham is going to be real excited to spend more time with you. Why wouldn't he want to?"

Sherry brushed her fingers down the skirt of her pale-yellow dress. "I hope you're right. I'm going to be so embarrassed if he's disappointed. You know how some memories are distorted. He might have remembered me being prettier."

"He won't be disappointed," Sharon said. "Please don't think such things. You are lovely, and more fun and vibrant than most girls we know. Just be yourself. You're a wonderful-*gut* person."

Looking marginally more optimistic after that little pep talk, Sherry turned to Carla. "Will you walk over there with me?"

"Try to stop me," Carla teased as she grabbed Sherry's hand and led her through the crowd.

As they snaked their way through—Carla's coral dress and Sherry's yellow one mixing with the vivid colors of the other Amish summer dresses—Sharon smiled. Carla and Sherry were best friends and set off each other in the best ways. Carla was boisterous yet looked like a timid, perfect doll. Sherry, on the other hand, looked like a modern-day Amish Anne of Green Gables, ready to experience all Pinecraft had to offer.

Sharon laughed. "What I would give for even a tenth of their exuberance."

"We're only five years older than our sisters," Vera said, "but they make me feel old as the hills."

"Hardly that."

"Well, older and stodgier. Look how cute and fresh they look too. I, on the other hand, feel like a wrinkled mess."

Pressing her hands on her hips, Sharon leaned to one side. "Me too. And I'm stiff and sore. Sleeping on a bus is not comfortable."

"Sharon, tell the truth," Vera said a minute later as she returned from retrieving her and Carla's suitcases from the bus. "Were we ever that impetuous?"

"I know I wasn't. Maybe you were?"

Vera laughed. "Maybe I was when Stefan and I first started seeing each other."

"If you were, he must have liked it. After all, you *are* an engaged woman now."

Vera stood a little straighter and smiled. "That I am. And you are a maid of honor."

Sharon smiled back. She didn't want to do or say anything to spoil Vera's happiness, but being only a maid of honor wasn't exactly what she'd been hoping for a year ago.

She helped Vera locate the rest of their bags, said good-bye and thank you to the bus driver, and then the two women put all their belongings in a neat grouping so no one would accidentally walk off with them.

The hot Florida sun felt as though it was toasting her skin, and she was already sweaty and in need of a shower and a change of clothes. She also needed a couple of hours' sleep in a real bed.

"Now that we have all our bags, let's go see if we can round up those girls and get to the inn," Vera said. "I need a nap."

Scanning the thinning crowds, Sharon smiled. "You read my mind."

"There they are. Boy, Sharon," Vera murmured, "I didn't remember those guys looking like that. Did you?"

Sharon turned her head and followed her friend's gaze. And then she felt like gulping.

Sherry and Carla were standing with two men. They were chatting with them like they were long-lost friends. Long-lost best friends.

And the man standing closest to Sherry was not only smiling at her, but appeared to be intently listening.

He was easily the most handsome man Sharon had ever seen.

Her stomach dropped. He was also *that* man! The only man she remembered meeting at the wedding.

"Vera, you remember them? Do you know their names? I talked to one of those guys for a while the morning after the wedding."

Vera adjusted her glasses. "Really? Which one?"

Sharon realized the meeting that had been blurry for months was slowly becoming clearer. "I think he was that man with the sandy-brown hair. The man standing closest to Sherry. Do you by any chance remember his name?"

"Sure I do, now that I've put the name and face together. I *did* meet him at the wedding. That's Graham Holland."

His name was Graham. For a few minutes he'd made her feel special, helped her forget how her dreams of marrying John Marc were over, how John Marc and Viola had hurt her. He was the man she'd thought about from time to time since, and had kicked herself over not remembering his name.

He was her sister's pen pal?

She was starting to feel sick.

It didn't matter to Graham that he'd flirted with both sisters. He simply made a choice between them, exchanging letters with Sherry, dismissing Sharon as if they'd never met.

What kind of man did such a thing? Worse, what kind of sister was she for feeling even the smallest bit jealous?

CHAPTER 2

GRAHAM WASN'T EXACTLY SURE WHY HE'D DECIDED TO come greet the Pioneer Trails bus after all. Maybe it was because he was so eager to see Sherilyn. Maybe he was simply tired of his buddies, Matthew and Toby, asking questions. He'd been fairly secretive about his pen pal, never even agreeing to tell them what she looked like.

Or maybe it was because he was too nervous to be completely alone when he and Sherilyn were first reunited.

Whatever the reason, he was now thoroughly confused. Sherilyn looked nothing like he remembered. The Sherilyn he'd recalled had light-brown hair, green eyes, and lovely, high cheekbones. She had a reserved air about her, almost tentative. She made him feel as though she needed a friend, and that friend should be him.

But this Sherilyn was the girl he only now remembered talking to a few times at the wedding. She was redheaded, freckle-faced, rather petite, and bold—not his usual type at all. Definitely not the picture he'd had in his mind all this time, flattered that she'd obtained his address and initiated their letter writing.

How had his memory been so wrong?

Now, after exchanging a few minutes of awkward conversation—a smile plastered on his face, desperately trying to covering up his dismay when she'd said, "Hi, Graham! It's me, Sherilyn!" and listening to her regret that he hadn't received her last letter—he was wishing he had *anywhere* else to go. He needed a few minutes to wrap his mind around the fact that he'd been writing to this near stranger.

"Oh! Now that the crowd has started to thin out, I see our sisters," Sherilyn said to Graham as she moved a step closer to him. Almost as if they were a couple.

He scanned the area. "Where are they?"

"There. The woman with the rose-colored dress is my sister, Sharon, and the woman in the violet-colored dress and wearing glasses is Carla's sister, Vera. Vera is Sharon's best friend."

He scanned the area, then froze as he realized that, while he might not have remembered this woman beside him very well, he definitely remembered the woman in the rose-colored dress.

He almost sighed in relief. Maybe he wasn't going crazy after all.

"I see them too," Carla called out. Seconds later, she groaned. "Uh-oh. They're standing near all our suitcases and bags. Sherry, we better go help them."

Turning to Graham and his friend Toby, Sherilyn said, "Would you guys like to come over and say hello, or just wait to meet the girls when we get to the inn?"

"We'll go over so we can help you with the bags," Toby said. "There's *nee* way we're going to let you carry everything on your own."

"That's so sweet of you."

"That's because we are sweet," Toby teased.

Still staring at the woman in the rose-colored dress, Graham murmured, "*Jah*. We'll go help you." As they started to move through the remaining crowd, he swallowed hard. "Hey, uh, Sherilyn, I'm sorry, but what are their names again?"

"My sister is Sharon. Her friend is Vera."

"Your sister is Sharon and you're Sherilyn. Your names are mighty similar. And Carla just called you Sherry too."

"They are similar, and I remember you commenting on that in one of your letters. And Sherry is a nickname you can call me if you like. Sharon and I were named after our parents' two favorite sisters. Sharon is our father's oldest sister, and Sherilyn is our mother's oldest sister." She sighed, revealing she'd told this story more than once. "Both my parents wanted to honor their sisters. After they named Sharon, *Mamm* teased my father, saying since he got his way for the first baby, she was going to get her way for the second . . . if they had a girl."

Graham couldn't help but chuckle. "And they did."

Smiling back at him, Sherilyn nodded. "Indeed, they did. So that's how I got my name. To be honest, I don't think they considered how our similar names might sometimes be a problem, especially when *Mamm* got mad at us. She'd trip over both our names!"

"I can see how that could happen. Especially, say, if one didn't know either of you well."

Maybe it was because of the tone of his voice, but Sherilyn began to look a little confused. "Um, anyway, that's my sister and Vera. Vera is engaged."

"Is Sharon betrothed too?"

"Oh, *nee*." Looking at him curiously, she said, "Why do you ask?"

"*Nee* reason," he said quickly. "I'm, uh, just trying to get to know everyone a little bit better." He knew that made him sound like an idiot, but at the moment he didn't care. Especially because he now realized he'd been writing to the wrong sister.

How could that have happened? How could he have been so stupid? At the wedding, he hadn't even realized these two were sisters. They were such different ages too. At least four or five years separated them!

"Come on, I'll go introduce you."

"Danke." Following Sherry, Graham knew he had about ten seconds to get his composure and his tongue under control. He needed to not embarrass Sherilyn—Sherry—her sister, or himself.

He had a feeling it was going to be a bit difficult.

The fact of the matter was that Sharon Kramer was even prettier than he remembered. She was truly beautiful. And that pale-pink dress she was wearing set off her pale, porcelainlike skin. Her brown hair was neatly confined under her *kapp*, and as he got closer he noticed the color of her eyes leaned more toward hazel than the true green of her sister's.

But it was the way she carried herself that held his attention and made his pulse beat a little faster. When they met at the wedding, his first impression had been that she needed a protector. But perhaps he'd been mistaken. She looked icily composed and calm. Reflective.

"Whoa," Toby murmured, low enough that Sherry couldn't hear. "Ain't she something?"

Yes. Yes, she was. Torn between continued dismay about what was happening and being strangely possessive over this woman, Graham was feeling more and more awkward. And sweaty.

Then there they were, all standing together.

"Sharon, this is Graham Holland," Sherry said. "Graham, please meet my sister, Sharon."

He held out his hand and gently clasped Sharon's hand in his own. "We've met," he said, searching her face. "Do you remember?"

She smiled, though that warmth didn't spread to her eyes. "I do, now that you mention it. We talked at the good-bye breakfast the morning after the wedding."

Sherry raised her eyebrows, obviously surprised. "You never told me you knew Graham."

"I didn't." Looking a little apologetic, and not as calm, Sharon sputtered, "I mean, we met, but we didn't really talk. Much. We didn't really know each other. I mean, not like you and Graham obviously knew each other before we headed home. We only shared one brief conversation."

Sherry's expression cleared. "Oh." Turning to Graham, she said, "Isn't that something? We only had a couple of short conversations, and that was in groups. Yet it meant enough for you to write me back . . . and send me those lavender seeds."

He hoped she would never find out he sent those seeds because he thought she smelled like fresh, fragrant lavender.

Well, her sister had.

"That is something," he agreed, his mouth going dry.

After Graham managed to introduce Toby to Sharon and Vera, and after Vera—to Graham's further embarrassment—reminded him he had met her at the wedding, too, Toby reached for one of the suitcases. "Are you girls ready to leave this parking lot? It's time to go, I think."

Looking around in surprise, Graham realized most everyone else had left. He took hold of the nearest suitcase. "I'll take this one."

Sherilyn frowned. "That one's Sharon's."

As if it was burning hot, he quickly released the handle. "Is that a problem?"

Sharon shook her head. "Of course not. Sherry, I'll simply take yours."

Suddenly looking embarrassed, Sherilyn mumbled, "*Nee*, I'm being silly. I can take my own. Let's just go."

That was how they all ended up in the formation they did, each one carrying at least one bag or suitcase. Toby was walking next to Vera, Sherry was following—whispering to Carla by her side—and he and Sharon were taking up the rear.

Graham was so tongue-tied he had no earthly idea what to say, so he decided to just keep quiet.

Sharon must have felt the same way, because she seemed content to stroll at his side, glancing at the shop windows and various front yards they passed, never saying a word. After they'd walked two blocks without speaking, Graham gathered himself and cleared his throat. "So, Sharon, are you exhausted from the journey here?"

"I wouldn't say I'm exhausted, but I am certainly tired. I'm not quite the traveler my sister is, I'm afraid," she said in an apologetic tone. "I guess I'm more of a homebody."

"I am, too, though I suppose it's by circumstance instead of choice. Farmers are tied to the land."

She turned to him, fresh awareness shining bright in her eyes. "I had forgotten you said you farmed. Tell me about it."

"About what? Planting corn?" He smiled, giving her an out. After all, who really wanted to hear about a farmer's life?

"*Jah*, I want to hear about planting corn. And plowing fields and whatever else farmers do."

"You're serious?"

She shrugged. "I am. Tell me all about it, Graham. I really am interested."

He doubted that, but he figured conversation about plowing and ears of corn was better than anything else he could think of. So he started talking about crop rotation and rainfall and worms and mud.

Sharon gazed ahead as they walked, but whenever he glanced at her, he could tell she was listening as though he was telling her something of value.

And just like that, he knew. Sharon was exactly the woman he'd remembered. And she truly was more than just a pretty face. She was special.

But of course, now if he told everyone the truth it would only set off a real mess of emotions. No, it was better to keep his secret to himself and hope neither sister ever discovered his mistake.

But then, while he was keeping that secret, maybe he could find a way to extricate himself from Sherry's grip and get Sharon Kramer to give him the time of day.

That was all. *Just that.*

He sighed. This vacation—the one he'd been counting the days toward—suddenly felt like the worst idea ever.

CHAPTER 3

✺

THE REUNION HAD BEEN AWKWARD, AND SHE'D KNOWN exactly why.

Sharon couldn't think of a more accurate word to describe how she felt when Sherry introduced her to Graham. From the moment she'd met his gaze, she'd been flustered—though she was thankful that even Vera hadn't seemed to be able to tell. Even though she'd been sure she blushed like a girl far younger than twenty-five, she had done her best to pretend she wasn't shocked to see this was the man her sister had been writing to for six months.

And she had done her best to pretend to her sister and their friends that she could totally see the two of them together.

But she couldn't. She decided then and there that she'd never tell Vera anything more about this if she didn't have to, even if she was her best friend. It was too embarrassing.

It didn't mean she was right about Graham, however. She'd been wrong about men and relationships before, especially when it came to herself. And not just with John Marc, either. No, she seemed to make a habit of misjudging men's interests, imagining there was spark in places there wasn't.

Now here they all were in the living room of the inn, just a couple of hours after arriving and getting settled in their rooms. Sharon was beginning to wish she was anywhere else.

Not a great way to start a two-week vacation.

Holding a heart-shaped cookie liberally frosted with light-pink frosting, Sharon debated whether to simply set it down on a plate and hope no one noticed she hadn't eaten it, or to find a place to throw it away without anyone seeing her do it.

She couldn't eat a thing.

She was the only one, though. It seemed that every afternoon, Mrs. Beverly Wagler served tea, cake, and cookies to her guests. Today she had fresh-baked brownies too. From what everyone had been telling her, and from what she observed, half her neighborhood stopped by as well. The Sugarcreek crowd, who had already been there two days, told the new arrivals the gathering wasn't to be missed.

Realizing she was going to have to find a way to eat this treat so she wouldn't seem rude, Sharon continued to nibble. It was a perfect sugar cookie. Firm but not hard, sweet and tinged with the faint essence of both vanilla and lemon. This proprietor definitely had a way around the kitchen.

"I trust your room is all right?" the innkeeper asked as she came to stand beside Sharon.

"Oh, yes!"

Beverly visibly relaxed. "Thank you for understanding. I don't know how the reservations got so mixed up, but I've felt awful about it. I know it must be awkward with your sister and friends in the triple upstairs while you're in the single room down here, on your own."

"Please don't worry about it. I like being on the first floor. As you might have noticed already, I'm a little on the quiet side. If I was up in the attic room, I'd be up all night with three women who really like to talk. Now, at least, I can be assured I'll get some rest."

"I've had more than one group of girls here over the years. You may have a point. Plus, it's not as if I'll mind if you go up and down the stairs as often you like, at all hours of the night too."

Sharon liked that image of her sneaking back to her room after a long night of laughing in the attic room upstairs.

"Is the cookie okay?"

"Yes. I'm, uh, just not as hungry as I thought I was."

Beverly pointed to a trash can. "If you don't want it, you can throw it out, dear. I promise I won't be offended."

"Thank you. I don't want to do that, though. It's really good. I work in a bakery, so I know cookies like this are to be treasured."

Beverly's cheeks turned pink. "That's so sweet of you to say. If you work in a bakery, I'm guessing you like to bake too?"

"I do. Very much."

"Maybe we can sit down one day and discuss recipes."

"I'd like that a lot."

Beverly smiled at her again before walking to the next guest.

"Your sister mentioned you work as a baker," Graham said as he drew up beside her, a thick, chocolate-chunk brownie in his hand.

"Yep. I've worked there for eight years now, since I was seventeen. I started washing dishes in the kitchen, then began helping all the ladies with the baking. Now I'm one of the lead bakers. I really enjoy it."

"My aunt works in a bakery in Sugarcreek. She says it's hard work."

"It is. Hot and a lot of heavy lifting too. But I love creating something people can enjoy immediately."

"That must be nice. Nothing happens like that in farming."

"*Jah*, but you also help create something other people enjoy."

He chuckled. "I never thought of corn like that."

"You should."

"I will, then. Anyway, your job sounds interesting. In her letters, Sherilyn told me about her nursery school job. I have to say I don't know how she does it. Watching all those *kinner* sounds chaotic and crazy. She must have the patience of a saint."

"She is patient. Well, with *kinner.*"

Graham's gaze settled on her again, this time almost a bit uncomfortably long.

Sharon might have been imagining things, but she was beginning to get the feeling he wanted to talk to her about something but was trying to figure out the best way to do it.

She decided to put him out of his misery. "Did you want to talk about something special?"

"What? *Nee.*" He looked away.

"Oh." She was disappointed. He was obviously lying. But then he looked at her again, this time a little sheepishly.

"Sharon, I'm sorry. Something has been on my mind, but *nee* matter how I try, I can't think of an un-awkward way to say it."

"Un-awkward, hmm? Well, now you have to tell me. You've got my curiosity piqued."

"All right. Do you . . . do you ever wonder why some things happen the way they do?"

"You're still being awfully vague there, Graham."

"I guess I can't help but wonder why it was Sherilyn and me who started writing to each other."

It was as if he'd read her mind. Her secret, most selfish thoughts. And that stung. Both because he was asking and because there wasn't anything she could say without hurting her little sister's feelings. "Does it matter?" she asked lightly.

"*Nee.* I mean, I guess it doesn't. I was just thinking about how strange it is the way things worked out."

"I can only imagine you encouraged Sherry to keep writing to you. Didn't you?" She was sure she was red-faced by now, but she had to know.

He opened his mouth, looked around in frustration, then signaled her to come with him. She hesitantly followed him through the groups of people and out the front door. Luckily, the rest of their friends had been in deep conversation or sorting through travel brochures. They hadn't seemed to notice them leaving.

When they were standing on the wide covered porch, Sharon said, "This is nice out here."

He leaned against the railing. "I'm sorry I brought any of this up."

"You didn't. I asked what was on your mind, remember?"

He looked relieved. "This is true. Anyway, you were right. It doesn't really matter how things worked out. The Lord is in charge, after all."

She was all for believing in the Lord guiding her life, but she couldn't help but think Graham was making a bit of a stretch. "The Lord?"

"*Jah.* I mean, it could have so easily been maybe Carla and Matthew writing. Or if you'd met him, Toby and you." He swallowed. "Even you and me. But instead it was Sherry and me."

Now that she understood where he was coming from, Sharon relaxed. "I see what you mean now. But you have to know Sherry.

She's a super letter writer. She writes to everyone. And, well, at the wedding, I wasn't myself. And I still wasn't myself for a while afterward. I wouldn't have written to anyone."

"Why not?"

"When we met, it was just two months after I broke up with my boyfriend. I was pretty upset about what I found out afterward. He and my friend had been flirting behind my back."

"Are you doing better now?"

"I think so. It took a while, but I realized even if John Marc hadn't cheated on me, we wouldn't have made a *gut* match. We're too different."

"I'm sorry he treated you so poorly."

"*Danke*. It was hard. I won't lie. Actually, it put me in a bit of a tailspin." She tried to smile to take the sting out of her words. "Now that we're here, I do remember meeting you and some others from Sugarcreek. Normally, I would have wanted to get to know you all better."

"But . . ."

"But because of what happened with my boyfriend and friend, I wasn't sure if I could trust you." Hearing her words, she winced. Not only because what she said was the raw truth, but because she no longer felt Graham had behaved so badly. After all, he made her feel special that day, and she'd needed that.

"I'm sorry. That sounds bad," Sharon said.

"It doesn't. It sounds like you're a cautious woman."

"I've become one. I especially don't trust men too much anymore. At least ones who don't tell the truth."

"I bet you don't," he said after a pause.

To her surprise, Graham now looked even more agitated. "Um, did I say something wrong?"

"Not at all." He'd said that quickly, but his voice had an edge to it.

He seemed to be avoiding her eyes. "Sure?"

"Of course." Taking off his hat, he ran a hand through his hair. "Well . . . I'm sorry, but the truth is, I am concerned about something. It ain't important, though. It's especially not anything you need to worry about."

Taking a stab at what he might be talking about, she said, "If you have any questions about Sherry, feel free to ask them."

He blinked. And looked even more uncomfortable. *"Danke."*

"I'm happy to help. I bet it's a bit difficult for the two of you to learn to communicate face-to-face now. I think it's easier to be more open and honest in a letter, don't you? People can take all the time they need to find just the right words."

"I never really thought about that. You're right. Getting to spend so much time writing those letters felt like a gift. Now I'm doing my best to figure out how to have the same kind of conversations. It *is* difficult."

"Maybe you don't need to worry so much, Graham. I mean, you're doing just fine now."

He swallowed so hard she could see his Adam's apple move. "Honestly, I don't know if I am or not."

"I'm sure everything will work out like it's supposed to." For a second, she was tempted to rest her hand on his arm. To assure him everything was going to work out the way the Lord intended.

But that sounded condescending and would probably reveal that she cared a little bit more for him than she should. Ruthlessly, she pushed her discomfort away. "Just remember that my sister has a soft heart," she said quietly. "She might come off as a little brash, but that's because she wears her heart on her sleeve."

"I'm sure she does," he agreed as the front door opened and the focal point of their conversation popped out.

Sherry looked from Sharon to Graham curiously. "Hey. I've been wandering around looking for each of you. I didn't think you'd be out here together."

Sharon felt guilty even though she knew she'd done nothing to feel bad about. "Graham and I were catching up. The living room was noisy. We were having a difficult time carrying on a conversation."

Sherry smiled at Sharon's hand, which still held three-quarters of a frosted sugar cookie. "At least you took a snack out here with ya."

"I guess so. I, um, had forgotten this was in my hand."

After looking at her quizzically, Sherry turned to Graham and said, "Would you like to go for a walk? I know it's awfully warm, but we could stay in the shade of the trees lining the street."

"Uh, sure. That sounds *gut*. Are you ready to go now?"

The joy that transformed Sherry's features was a sight to behold. "I am."

"Then I am too."

Sharon made sure she kept a happy, carefree smile on her face as the couple walked down the steps.

No matter what, neither of them could ever find out a big part of her wished she was the girl walking by Graham's side.

CHAPTER 4

THIS SITUATION HAD TO BE ONE OF THE MOST AWKWARD of his life.

Graham approached Sharon and then invited her to talk outside with the purpose of getting to know her better—and to admit he hadn't realized he'd been writing to Sherry and not her this whole time.

He'd been certain complete honesty was the right thing. After all, they were about to spend fourteen days together. That was far too long to maintain a lie. So, though he'd been nervous, he'd also been determined to tell her the truth. He would have tried to get her to understand . . . if Sherry hadn't joined them with such an excited, expectant look on her face.

How could he embarrass Sherry by revealing he hadn't meant to be writing to her all these months? That would be cruel. Besides, Sharon had obviously and firmly latched onto the role of the caring older sister, and there was probably no real way she would ever accept that he wanted to date her and not Sherry. There was never going to be a right time to confess his mix-up.

As he and Sherry walked along the street in front of the inn, Graham forced himself to concentrate on the girl beside him and respond to the comment she'd just made. "*Jah*. I mean, it does seem like a nice time to go for a walk."

"I'm relieved to hear you say that. I have a bad habit of being a bit too forward. I think it comes from organizing small *kinner*," she said, joking. "I start wanting to organize everybody around me."

"It's not too forward. It's refreshing."

Sherry smiled. "Carla and Toby and I were making plans. We thought it would be fun to go to Siesta Key on Monday, the day after tomorrow. What do you think?"

There was no mistaking the look of excitement and longing she wore. "I think that sounds like fun. Do you think you girls will be up for a day at the beach so soon after your long trip? It's taken us two days just to catch up on our sleep."

"Carla and I thought we could sleep all day tomorrow. That's the plan, anyway."

"I'll be sure to be quiet if I'm anywhere near the attic," he teased.

Her eyes twinkled. "That will be appreciated. Anyway, we figure by Monday we'll be more than ready to see the ocean. I can't wait to see it."

"You have a point there. You should probably be going to the beach at every opportunity."

"So, um . . . do you want to join us?" Her question sounded awkward and tentative.

It shouldn't have sounded either way.

Fact was, he was definitely not opposed to going to the beach. His buddies had come to Florida for a vacation, not just for his suddenly drama-filled life. That said, he was also opposed to leading Sherry on. His letters had been bad enough, but now he really didn't want to make her think he regarded her as other than a younger sister.

Although . . . maybe he wasn't even sure about that? Her letters had meant something to him. He'd loved them. He'd looked forward to receiving them. Didn't that mean he owed it to Sherry to take the time to get to know her better? He decided to get some more information.

"Who else wants to go? Or is it just the three of you?"

"I haven't talked to Sharon about it yet, but I bet she'll go. And if she goes, then Vera will too."

Here was his answer. "If Vera and Sharon go, I'll go as well. You'll need more men with you."

Sherry looked taken aback for a second before nodding agreeably. "Yeah. Okay. That makes sense."

"What time do you want to leave?"

"Carla wants to be sure she gets some more sleep. Maybe around nine thirty? Is that time *gut* for you? It's late, but maybe not too late for vacation."

"It's a date then," he quipped, then wished he'd said just about anything else when he saw Sherry's look of pure happiness.

How in the world was he going to get himself out of this mess? And if and when he did, how was he ever going to get Sharon to give him the time of day?

He really was too old for this.

❧

It was almost nine o'clock on the day of their trip to the beach, and Sharon was the first to arrive for breakfast. Secretly pleased by this, she took another fortifying sip from her coffee cup and eagerly unwrapped her muffin.

The muffin had an orange marmalade glaze and swirls of

cream cheese running through its center. Saying it was delicious was an understatement.

"Oh, good. I see you've already found the muffins," Beverly said when she entered the dining room. "I hope you're enjoying yours?"

"I think this is one of the best I've ever eaten. Do you share your recipes?"

"Of course. I'll write it out for you before you head back to Ohio."

"*Danke.* But I hate for you to go to any trouble. I'm happy to do the copying myself. I have a feeling I'll be asking you for several recipes. You really are gifted."

"That's very sweet of you to say." Pleasure lit her green eyes. "My husband, Eric, keeps telling me I should put together a cookbook for guests to purchase. I haven't wanted to tackle that project yet, but it might save me time in the long run."

"I bet it will. I can't imagine you aren't asked for recipes at least once a week."

"I am." Her cheeks flushed. "Now I just need to figure out how to get started on it."

"I could help you, if you'd like," Sharon offered. If she worked on the cookbook, she wouldn't have as much time to watch Graham court Sherry. It felt like a perfect solution.

"What? Of course you can't! You're on vacation."

"This would be a fun project for me." Sharon held up a hand. "But I don't want to overstep my bounds. If you don't want any help, I understand. It's just that I really love to bake and would enjoy helping you."

"I . . . well, thank you. I might take you up on that," she said, just as a handsome man in a wrinkled pair of shorts, a dark-blue T-shirt, and bare feet wandered in.

Right in front of Sharon, he pressed a kiss to Beverly's temple. "You sound like you're hatching a plan."

"I am. At least, I think I am." Turning to Sharon, Beverly said, "Sharon, please meet my husband, Eric. Eric, this is Sharon Kramer. She wants to help me work on that cookbook with my recipes while she's here."

Interest lit his eyes. "Really? That's terrific. I've been telling my wife I'll take care of getting everything typed, printed, and bound into books, but I can't do anything without those recipes. This is really kind of you."

"Not so much. Besides, if I help, I'll get to see all the recipes myself," she said, making a joke.

Beverly chuckled. "I like how you think. You just let me know when you want to get started, and we'll come up with a time."

"I will," Sharon promised as the room began to fill with her friends and other guests. "We're going to Siesta Key today, but while we're there, we're also going to make some tentative plans for the rest of our vacation. I'll touch base with you tonight."

"That sounds perfect." Smiling broadly, Beverly added, "I better go get more coffee going."

"I'll help bring out more platters of muffins and that hash brown casserole too," her husband said.

As they darted into the kitchen, the white door swinging in their wake, Sherry arrived at Sharon's side. "Sorry we're late. I'm afraid we stayed up talking last night."

"I wasn't in any hurry. Actually, I was having a *gut* conversation with Beverly and Eric about cookbooks."

Sherry wrinkled her nose. "Only you would be talking about baking when we're heading to the beach."

"I know. I can't seem to help myself, though."

Sherry patted her on the arm. "You know I'm kidding! Now, I need coffee and something to eat."

Sharon took a seat as her sister, joining the other late arrivals at the sideboard, began filling her plate.

"Anyone sitting here?" Graham asked.

"Not yet," she said with a shy smile.

"Great." He set a glass plate piled high with fruit on the table. "I'll be right back."

When he returned with even more food, Sharon couldn't help but be impressed with the amount he planned to consume. "Do you eat like this every morning?"

"I wish, but *nee*. Usually I make myself a big bowl of oatmeal or cook a couple of eggs," he said after he paused for a moment to say a quick, silent prayer of thanks. "But I do eat a lot of food. That's what happens when you work in the fields all day long."

"I bet. You didn't say the other day. Have you harvested your corn yet?"

"*Nee*, it needs another three weeks, which is what made this the perfect time for me to get away. It's going to be a grueling few days when I get home."

"But you have a lot of help, don't you?"

"Sure. My two brothers, Robert and Caleb, plus my father, an uncle, and a cousin. We also hire some temporary workers for two of the three days."

"I'm impressed."

He shrugged. "It's a pretty big farm. We plant over three acres of corn alone. A *gut* crop makes our year."

"*Jah*, I suppose it does." She sipped her coffee and smiled as he dug into his egg-and-sausage casserole with obvious gusto.

He paused in midbite. "Am I being rude?"

"Not at all. I've been here for a while."

"An early riser, hmm?"

"Not especially, but I guess I was today compared to everyone else," she said as Graham's friends Matthew and Toby joined them.

After the two men prayed and they all marveled at the array of breakfast food, Graham said, "Did I overhear you talking to Mrs. Wagler about working on a cookbook?"

She was embarrassed now. "You did. I know I'm on vacation, but I guess I can't help but lean toward all things food and baking."

"You shouldn't apologize for finding something that sparks your interest. It's kind of you to want to help her too."

"The project will do me *gut*. I am looking forward to going to the beach today, but I have *nee* desire to spend every day there."

Matthew held out an arm. "Me neither, Sharon. I'm so pale I'm going to have to slather on sunscreen every ten minutes."

She laughed. "I'm sure you're exaggerating, but I bet you can't be too careful."

"Matthew works third shift at the brickyard in Sugarcreek," Graham told her, explaining why his friend had no tan at all.

"So if you ever need someone to hang out with while everyone else is out in the sun, I'm your man," Matthew said with a grin.

"I'll keep that in mind."

"Now I, on the other hand, already have a *gut* base tan," Toby said, holding out a lightly tanned forearm.

"He works construction," Graham explained.

"That means if you ever need something built, I'm the guy to talk to," he said, winking at her.

His flirty comment was so fun, she giggled. "Careful, Toby, I may just take you up on that."

"I promise, you calling on me wouldn't be a hardship."

She giggled again, liking how lighthearted he was. As she picked up her cup, she glanced Graham's way and was startled to see he was frowning at Toby as though he'd just done something wrong.

Toby must have felt the tension, because he looked at Graham, raised his eyebrows, then smirked. "You got a problem, Graham?"

After a pause, Graham shook his head. *"Nee."*

"Gut."

As Matthew coughed, Graham's expression hardened. Luckily Vera stood up at one end of the table and diffused the burst of tension that had just risen.

Holding up a printed pamphlet, she said, "I've got the schedule of the SCAT, the Sarasota County Area Transit system, and a bus for Siesta Key leaves in fifteen minutes. Can we make it?"

"I can," Sharon said. She stood up and walked to her girlfriend's side. She needed some distance between her and Graham before she began imagining there was something romantic between them.

That would be a huge mistake.

CHAPTER 5

◦◦◦

THOUGH THE SUN WAS SHINING AND SHE WAS EXCITED to be going to the beach, Sherry felt a little uneasy. She was beginning to feel as though something wasn't quite right between her and Graham. Oh, he'd been friendly. He'd also acted pleased to see her again when she arrived on Saturday. But something in his letters to her was missing now.

At first, she thought he was simply a little shy. Then she thought he was one of those rare people who communicated far better in letters than in person. Finally, she began to wonder if maybe his letters hadn't been all that warm or special after all. Maybe they'd simply been . . . letters. Friendly, to be sure, but not filled with hope for a future relationship as she'd imagined.

It was really too bad that she hadn't brought the letters with her. Then she could compare them to the man she was coming to know.

If she ever really got to know Graham, that is, since right now he seemed to be avoiding her.

As the SCAT bus made another stop, Sherry watched Graham and Sharon—and fretted. They were sitting together in front while she was sitting in the last row.

"If you sigh again, people around us are going to think you

41

have some kind of lung ailment," Carla whispered. She was sitting next to Sherry, by the window. "What's wrong with you?"

"Nothing. I'm fine."

"Sherry, please, don't play this game. I know something is bugging you. Tell me. You know I won't give up until you tell me what has you so upset."

Knowing Carla wasn't joking—she would nag until Sherry finally told her what was on her mind—Sherry looked down the aisle. After making sure Toby, Matthew, and Vera weren't in hearing distance, she whispered, "I don't think Graham likes me anymore."

Carla's eyebrows rose. "What makes you say that?"

"A lot of things."

"Such as?"

"First of all, look who he's sitting next to. It's Sharon, not me."

Carla shrugged. "Don't go making a problem where there ain't one. You can see how crowded this bus is. We all had to take seats wherever we could find them."

Shaking her head impatiently, Sherry said, "It's more than that. Graham hardly looks at me. And when I mention something he wrote in one of his letters, he gets this weird expression on his face. It's strange. Almost like he's embarrassed that we wrote to each other for months."

"I'm sure he's not embarrassed. After all, if it hadn't been for you two writing to each other, none of us would be here now."

"Oh, I know that. But he's different, Carla." As she noticed Graham cocking his head, evidently to be sure he heard something Sharon said, frustration and jealousy churned in her stomach. "He's distancing himself. I know it."

"I haven't noticed him doing that."

"I have. And wouldn't I notice it more than you?"

"Not necessarily. We just got here," she said in her matter-of-fact way.

Continuing to stare at Graham and her sister, Sherry mumbled, "This is just terrible. I really . . . I *thought* I knew him." To her embarrassment, she heard her voice tremble. "I had such high hopes too."

Carla pursed her lips as the bus stopped again. Two English teenagers got off, and an older couple climbed aboard and took their seats. When the bus pulled forward, she said, "Sherry, I don't want to hurt your feelings, but I think you've put too much hope in those letters. *Jah*, you've been writing to each other for months. *Jah*, you probably also shared some things. But that doesn't mean you had a relationship. Be honest, now. You don't actually know Graham."

Sherry wanted to argue with her. She wished she could pull out one of those letters and prove to Carla that she hadn't been wrong to expect that she and Graham would be a couple when they reunited in Pinecraft.

But of course, she didn't have the letters with her. She wouldn't embarrass either of them by sharing their private correspondence anyway.

As the bus sped along the long causeway that led to Siesta Key, Sherry began to wonder if she had, in fact, put way too much emphasis on mere letters. Sure, they'd been lovely. The novelty of having a handsome pen pal was exciting too. But they weren't the same as having a real conversation with someone face-to-face—or, in Graham's case, avoiding that conversation.

Unable to help herself, she sighed again.

Carla groaned. "Sherry, you are driving me crazy."

"I'm sorry my pain is causing you to be uncomfortable."

"Your moping around is going to spoil a perfectly nice vacation," she said loud enough for the man sitting across the aisle to look at them in alarm.

"Hush, Carla."

"I'll hush if you promise to stop acting like this meeting in Pinecraft was supposed to result in a marriage proposal. Stop putting so much pressure on yourself and on Graham too. Why don't you just try to relax and enjoy our vacation? It's not going to be the end of the world if you and Graham don't get together. Or if you meet someone else you like better."

As the words sank in, Sherry was finally able to look away from Graham and Sharon. "Do you think that's possible?"

"Of course it is. We're only twenty! Let's just have fun. I mean, even if we go home with only tans and some *gut* memories, that's going to be more than enough."

"*Jah.* You're right." She felt self-conscious now that she was admitting to herself that she had actually dreamed about Graham and their practically running into each other's arms in the bus parking lot. She chuckled softly. "*Danke.* You gave me some perfect advice."

"You're not mad at me for bursting your bubble?"

"Not at all. You are exactly right. Here we are, under the beautiful Florida sun, and I don't have to work for two weeks. I need to definitely start looking on the positive side of things."

"*Gut* job," Carla said as the bus pulled into the middle of a large parking lot next to the beach. "And just in time, too, because we've arrived."

"*Danke* again, Carla."

"*Nee* problem," she replied. "That's what friends are for."

"Indeed."

As everyone got to their feet, Sherry gazed out at the beautiful white sand and turquoise water that was so famous.

Now, this place, at least, wasn't destined for disappointment. She was fairly sure Siesta Key was going to surpass her greatest expectations.

CHAPTER 6

GRAHAM'S FIRST IMPRESSION OF SIESTA KEY WAS THAT it was beautiful—right on the expansive Gulf of Mexico and no doubt one of the most stunning places on God's earth. The beach was wide and uncluttered and went on for miles. A person could walk for a solid hour without having to turn around. The fine sand looked almost pure white and felt like sugar slipping between his fingers and toes.

And the water! It was clear as glass, greenish-blue, and felt just two shades cooler than bath water. Boats and ships and other watercraft bobbed in the distance.

The only structures in sight were a snack shack and evenly spaced lifeguard shacks. All were built out of wood and painted primary colors. Their bright red, blue, and yellow forms dotted the landscape and made him smile. Feeling fanciful, Graham decided those buildings illustrated how absolutely picture-worthy and charming the small island was. Graham felt the builders had done a very fine job.

When they first arrived, Sherry, Carla, and Matthew had led the way. Even though none of them had been to the area before, they had definite ideas about where to set up camp. He, on the other hand, couldn't imagine any spot he wouldn't want to be.

He, Sharon, Vera, and Toby followed the trio and stood to one side while they debated. Graham was amused at how Sharon seemed more than happy to let her little sister take the lead. That was so different from the dynamics with his brothers at home. There was a definite pecking order there. His older brother, Robert, wanted to lead Graham and their younger brother, Caleb, all the time and no matter how old they got.

Once the perfect spot had been selected, Graham followed the rest of the group and laid his towel on the outskirts of their claim. He never liked to be confined and wanted to have room to spread out. Plus, he knew he would want to get up and walk around a lot, especially since it was so hot. He had no desire to disrupt everyone else's relaxation, stepping around them or getting sand in their food or drinks.

He couldn't help but notice Sharon picked the same sort of spot on the opposite side of their group. He wondered if she did that because she, too, wanted room to move around.

But now, from the way she seemed to be trying to look everywhere but at him, he suspected her reasoning had to do with creating distance she didn't have on the bus.

Their talk had been a little stilted, as though she wished she were sitting with someone else. That surprised him after their conversation on the porch Saturday night and this morning at breakfast. He thought she'd warmed up to him a bit.

Or maybe she, too, was aware of the strange connection that was happening between them? A connection she thought her sister wouldn't like? He hadn't been thrilled when Toby flirted with her earlier, but he didn't think she . . .

He didn't know what to think. And he didn't know what to do. He'd written to the wrong sister and hadn't even been brave enough to come right out and tell either of them. Instead, he was mooning over Sharon and avoiding Sherry.

He was fairly sure this wasn't going to end well, and it would be all his fault.

Just as he decided to let the Lord take care of his problems and exhaled, he saw Sherry pull off her dress to reveal a one-piece bathing suit.

Realizing his face was probably turning a deep red, he jumped to his feet.

"What are you doing?" Toby asked, brushing the sand he'd kicked up off his left arm.

"I'm going for a walk."

"Already? We just got here."

"Yeah, well, I like walking."

Turning away, he resolutely kept his gaze straight ahead as he raced away. He had no desire to encourage any further connection to Sherry, and he couldn't get away fast enough.

After a couple of minutes, Toby caught up to him.

"Something wrong?" Graham asked.

"Nah. All of a sudden I just decided I felt like walking too."

Graham doubted that. Toby worked construction in Millersburg. The guy was active all day, every day. All he'd been talking about from the time they'd planned this trip was how great it would be to sit around and do nothing.

But if he knew anything about Toby, it was that he'd share what was on his mind when he felt the time was right. After they passed another lifeguard shack, Graham said, "The sand and surf feel great on bare feet. Ain't so?"

"*Jah.*"

Another couple of minutes of silence passed before Toby said, "Hey, Graham? I need to ask you something."

"Sure. What is it?"

After Toby looked at the waves for a couple of beats, he turned back to Graham. "Well, I need to know this. Which one of the Kramer sisters do you like?"

He was so caught off guard, Graham stopped and stared. He and Toby had been best friends from the time they were seven or eight years old. They'd discussed all kinds of things and had even gotten each other through their *rumspringa* when both of them had done some pretty foolish things.

But they'd never discussed women. At least, not like this. He'd never told Toby much about his correspondence with Sherry, or even Sherry herself. Good thing, since it turned out Sherry wasn't Sharon.

This made him uncomfortable, though he knew it was mainly because he didn't know how to confess what a mess he'd made with both women.

Feeling as though he needed to be walking to continue the conversation, he moved on. "Why are you asking?"

"Because you're making me pretty confused." Pulling up his sunglasses, revealing serious eyes, Toby added, "Maybe you could take a stab at clearing the air."

Ruthlessly, Graham picked up his pace. "I'm not dating either woman. You know that."

"I do know that."

"Then what's the problem?"

"Well, Sherry acts as though your letter writing has been a little more significant than you led me to believe. And when her bus arrived, she seemed like she could be expecting a relationship with you." He paused, then raised one eyebrow. "But on the other hand, it seems to me that you like Sharon as well. A lot. Do you?"

Did he? A lot? He didn't know.

And that was terrible. It was also embarrassing. No. Beyond embarrassing. The last thing he wanted was to be seen as a man who played with women's hearts.

In a poor effort to evade the question, he blurted, "For the last time, I ain't with either woman." Hopefully Toby would get the hint and drop the subject.

Unfortunately, he didn't. Sounding progressively irritated, Toby said, "You know why I'm asking. Don't act like you don't know."

Graham glanced at his best friend again, forcing himself to wrap his mind around the fact that Toby was feeling tentative about a girl. Most likely about Sharon.

The fact was, if Sharon was a woman who was much sought after, Toby was very likely her male counterpart. Blessed with dark-brown eyes, matching hair, and a perpetual tan, he stood out among many of the fair-skinned, fair-haired Amish men. Added to his list of attributes were his quiet, almost old-fashioned demeanor and his size. The man was easily two hundred and fifty pounds and over six feet tall. Yet because he worked construction, specializing in roofs and trusses, he had a grace to him that belied his size. Women all over Holmes County flirted with him. More than a few had let it be known they would love to be courted by him.

In addition, Graham didn't know one person who wasn't fond of the guy. Toby was loyal and friendly. He didn't deserve Graham's attitude.

"You're right," he said at last. "Sherry is the one I've been writing to, but—"

"Wait. Why don't you sound very glad about that?"

"Probably because I, uh, hadn't realized some things about her when we started corresponding."

Toby raised his eyebrows. "What did you discover?"

Graham wished he could blurt out his case of mistaken identity, but he was sure there was no way to admit such a thing without being unkind to both girls. "Um, first off, I hadn't realized how young she is."

"How old is she?"

"Twenty. I heard her tell someone she's twenty."

"Why is that a concern for you? Twenty ain't too young at all. She's more than old enough to be courting."

"That is true. But that doesn't mean I didn't think she was older. I thought she was twenty-two or twenty-three."

Toby scoffed. "You make that sound like a huge difference. It ain't."

Graham sighed. "You're right. It ain't."

"What else is the problem?"

Graham knew he needed to be more forthcoming. Looking off into the distance, he said, "Sherry's sister has been a surprise to me. I find Sharon easy to talk to. And, well, I don't think it's happenstance that she's here too. I'm wondering if maybe the Lord meant for me to meet Sharon through Sherry. So, um, that's why I've been talking to her as well."

Toby's expression turned chilly. "I find that excuse hard to believe."

Graham did as well. But that didn't mean he could back down. "You shouldn't find it hard to believe at all. After all, it's true. It's not an excuse."

"Graham, have you heard what you're saying to me?"

51

He had and he was embarrassed about it. But what was he supposed to do? Hating this situation he'd put himself in, he blurted again. "Toby, I haven't been trying to court two women at the same time. It's all just turned out that way."

"But you are. And if I'm noticing, everyone else is too."

"I feel certain everything will be resolved soon. Don't forget, it's only been a couple of days."

"I'm not forgetting that I've seen both women studying you with questions in their eyes. It ain't right."

Graham felt trapped. "You mean it ain't right for you. Don't you think you're sounding an awful lot like a moony teenage boy? I mean, who notices how much time other people spend together? Maybe the problem lies with you, Toby."

His best friend flinched. But instead of backing off, he raised his hands in frustration. "Comments like that are what I'm talking about. You never talk like this. Something with these women has hit a nerve." Before Graham could dispute that, he added, "Don't start lying again, either. I saw that look you sent my way at breakfast. There was something in your expression when you looked at Sharon and me. It sure wasn't that she meant nothing to you."

"I didn't—"

"Oh, *jah*, you did. You practically sent me a death glare when I offered to spend time with her."

Everything Toby was saying was right. But because he still wasn't sure what to do, Graham decided to stay on the offensive. "Instead of asking me twenty questions and chiding me for not being completely honest, why don't you share what's on your mind? Who are *you* after? Do you want to spend time with Sharon or Sherry?"

Toby laughed. "With Sharon, of course. Her sister is a fire-cracker. She'd wear me out in two minutes. Plus, those freckles and red hair? Not my type."

"Sherry is cute in her own way," he spit out automatically. Now, why did he feel the need to defend the girl he didn't want to date?

Seeing a fence signaling the boundary of a private resort, they turned around and headed back. Graham was surprised how far they'd walked. He couldn't see any of their group in the distance.

Not in any hurry to return, he slowed his pace. Toby matched it exactly, looking more than a little relieved as he wiped a sweat-soaked brow.

"So is that my answer, then? You like Sherry and you're all right if I spend time with Sharon?"

He cared. He cared a lot. But he didn't see how he was ever going to make his wants a reality. He was one of three brothers, but he'd heard sisters had an even stronger bond when it came to love and romance. Never would he want to hurt Sherry because he longed for her older sister.

It would be best to simply stay out of both women's lives.

Plus, Toby was a good man. He was hardworking and kind. And a little on the shy side, he'd be perfect for a quiet woman like Sharon. A kind person who would treat her well.

With all that in mind, was there really any doubt about what his answer should be? "If you want to spend time with Sharon, I think you should. I won't be mad, and I'll even support you in any way I can."

Toby exhaled. "Boy, you had me going there for a bit. *Danke.*"

His buddy sounded so relieved, Graham almost smiled. "Sharon really means that much to you?"

"I don't know if she does or not. I do know she's intrigued me in a way few other women have."

"Ah."

"Graham, the reason I came to talk to you is that our friendship is what means so much. I don't want to step on any toes."

"You won't."

"*Gut.*" Looking a far sight happier, Toby said, "I'm so glad everything is out in the open now. It's better that way, *jah*?"

"For sure and for certain." Well, it would if everything actually *was* out in the open. Realizing they were almost back to the rest of the group, Graham asked, "Is there anything else you want to discuss, Toby?"

"Of course not. We're at the beach to relax, not discuss every problem in our lives." Looking satisfied, he added, "I'm going to go buy myself a bottle of water and then sit on my towel for the rest of the morning and afternoon."

"Me, too, though I'll probably cool off in the water too. It's hot out here."

"Yeah, well, people say July is a hot month."

Toby and his gift for understatement. Graham grinned in spite of himself. "*Danke* for talking to me. And *gut* luck with Sharon." Realizing luck didn't have much to do with it, he said, "I mean, I hope you and Sharon will find yourselves to be happy together."

"*Danke.* I don't know if I'm what she's looking for, but I have to try, you know? Girls like her are few and far between," he said before veering over to the snack shack.

Unfortunately, Graham knew far too well what his buddy meant. Girls like Sharon were mighty special.

But friends like Toby were too.

CHAPTER 7

ALTHOUGH A LOT OF AMISH GIRLS WORE BATHING SUITS, Sharon wasn't quite ready for that. Oh, she'd bought one, of course. She and Sherry had gone into Millersburg and tried on swimsuits almost a month ago.

At first they'd been afraid of what their mother would say about making such a purchase. Sherry, being Sherry, hadn't wanted to tell *Mamm*. She said their mother would never need to know what they'd done. But Sharon hadn't felt okay with that. She'd hesitantly told their mother they intended to wear swimsuits at the beach in Siesta Key. Modest ones, of course.

To her surprise, *Mamm* had just laughed. "You act as if I've never been young, child. Wear one if you must. I'm sure it will be a great deal more comfortable than sitting on the beach in a dress."

They'd taken their mother's comments to heart and had quite a grand time picking out suits to try on.

Checking herself in the dressing room mirror had been a whole other story, however. She frowned when she stared at herself from every angle. Her skin had looked as pale as a newborn babe's, and her hips and thighs had seemed far bigger than the mannequins' in the store.

When Sherry knocked on her door and showed Sharon her

choice, she mentioned the same concerns about herself. But they'd done it. They'd each bought a modest one-piece suit. Modest for the Englishers, that is.

But this morning, even though she knew it covered her up sufficiently, Sharon felt her swimsuit was far too revealing. So she'd worn her lightest and baggiest dress over it, in case she chickened out. Then when Sherry revealed hers—practically the moment she'd sat down on her beach towel—Sharon had known she couldn't do it. Not yet.

Sharon knew her sister's look of triumph had been directed at her. Sherry was pleased she was pushing herself a bit and wanted Sharon to do the same. But although she was hot, Sharon was still too self-conscious.

Thankfully, her sleeves were loose enough that she'd been able to roll them a few inches above her elbows. When she'd sat down, she'd pulled the skirt of her dress up to reveal her knees. And now that was how she was sitting—modestly and mildly warm, with some of her dress's fabric sticking to the middle of her back. Soon after Sherry's big reveal, Carla and Vera had pulled off their dresses and were sunbathing in swimsuits too. Matthew was beside them, putting an awful lot of sunscreen on himself.

Sharon sighed and stretched out her legs, grateful Vera would never push her to do anything she didn't want to do. But boy, she wished she'd been braver! Now if she pulled off her dress it would look awkward. She was going to have to deal with her big reveal the next time they went to Siesta Key. And, she realized with a bit of embarrassment, she should also remember looks aren't that important. She mustn't be too prideful.

"You want a cold bottle of water?" Toby asked as he shook out his towel and sat down next to her.

He had shorts on, and his calves and knees were already starting to darken. Realizing how silly it was to stare at his legs, she diverted her eyes.

But what caught her eye next was the pleasant, kind way he was looking at her. Like he wanted to be her friend.

Forcing herself to examine the bottle he was holding out, she noticed it had droplets of condensation all over it. "*Danke.* Few things have ever looked so *gut.*"

"Oh, I can think of a few," he said with a smile.

"Such as?"

"Why this beach, for one. The ocean for another."

He was absolutely right. She needed to stop worrying what everyone was thinking about her and simply enjoy herself. "I think I walked into that, didn't I? Here I am, sitting on one of the most beautiful beaches in the world, and I haven't even taken the time to properly give thanks for it."

"I'm sure the Lord knows you're pleased with His work, Sharon."

She smiled at him. "Indeed, I'm sure He does."

He unscrewed his bottle cap and promptly swallowed a good half of the bottle's contents. "Boy, was I thirsty."

She laughed. Toby was so open and vibrant! Almost like a puppy. She found him easy to be around and easy to talk to. "You and Graham went on a long walk."

"We went farther than I intended. I hadn't planned on walking with him that long."

Liking how he simply said whatever was on his mind, she added, "I thought maybe you were going to go for a swim, but instead it looked like you were racewalking."

"What you saw was correct." He grimaced. "We were racewalking. Practically running."

If they did it all the time, that meant he liked it, right? But he was acting as if he didn't care for it one bit. "Do you and Graham do that a lot?"

"*Nee.*" After he finished the rest of his water, he put the cap back on the bottle and tossed it into a nearby canvas tote bag. "We had some things to talk about. Graham . . . well, Graham likes to walk and talk at a brisk pace. I reckon it has something to do with all those acres he walks when he inspects his corn."

"But not you?"

"*Nee.* I'm in construction. I spend most of my days running around whatever building I'm working on. I like to sit down when I can. I'm lazy that way."

Sharon firmly pushed down that little burst of appreciation whenever she heard Graham's name. He was her sister's beau. What she needed to do was concentrate on Toby. He was handsome and kind. She could probably learn to like him a lot if she just gave him a chance!

She smiled at him more brightly. "I'm lazy that way too. I work in a bakery, so I like to rest when I can."

"My aunt worked at a bakery in Walnut Creek. She took care to tell me it was much more work than handing out donuts!"

"It is. Absolutely. I've been giving thanks all day for the fact that I'm not pulling heavy trays in and out of ovens. Some nights when I get home, I have to lie down on the floor to relieve the cramps in my back."

Toby stared at her in concern. Then he said softly, "Those commercial ovens can be dangerous, especially for a slight girl like you."

She'd never thought of herself as slight, but she did like the way he said the word. Like being slight was a good thing.

"I'm stronger than I look. Though I have had my share of little accidents while I learned the best way to pull out heavy sheet pans."

"Is this a work injury?"

"Is what a work injury?"

Carefully, as if he feared he was going to bruise her, he looped his thumb and fingers around her wrist and turned her arm.

And sure enough, there was a burn mark on her forearm. Eyeing the dark-red patch that was only about a half inch in length, she said, "I've had that for so long, I'd almost forgotten about it."

His hand remained where it was. Then, ever so slowly, he ran one finger along the mark. She shivered involuntarily.

His brows pulled together. "Does it hurt?"

"*Nee*. Not at all." No, she surely wasn't hurting from his touch. But she was reacting to him in a way that caught her off guard.

With his fingers still on her arm, he murmured, "How did you get it?"

She was becoming flustered.

Nervously, she pulled her arm away, then took another sip from her water bottle. She tried to think of an interesting way to tell what had happened to her. That would be kind of difficult, though, for it was actually a boring story. "I'd love to tell you it was when I was doing something out of the ordinary, but it was just a simple mistake. I was paying more attention to making sure my thumb didn't damage the side of a cake than I was taking care not to touch my arm on the hot rack. Like I said, things like that happen more often than one might expect."

"It happened years ago?"

"*Jah*. Probably five years," she said. Then she winced as she realized how breathless she sounded.

He shifted. She was sure he was going to move away, but he didn't. "That had to hurt."

"It did," she squeaked. "But it served me well. I remembered that experience and minded those racks far better than I had before."

"Put that way, I can see how it might be a blessing."

"*Jah.*" At the moment, that was what that burn felt like. A blessing. Looking at him, she said, "I bet you have a scar or two that has served as a learning experience."

"I do." Gripping the bottom of his shirt with both hands, he pulled it off over his head and tossed it to one side. That wide expanse of smooth skin and defined muscle was shocking.

And, if she admitted it, intriguing too. Toby Miller was a handsome man. Fearing she was staring at him a bit too long, she took another fortifying sip of water.

Of course, he misinterpreted her discomfort. Stretching to one side, he kind of twisted his torso to get a better look. "Oh, it ain't that bad, is it?"

His body? No, it was not.

Of course, her discomfort increased tenfold when she realized he was pointing to a thick, jagged scar on his side. It had to be a quarter-inch wide and at least three inches long.

How mortifying that she'd been so intrigued by his chest that she hadn't even noticed what he'd been trying to show her! "Actually, that scar is bad. Really bad. What happened there?"

Straightening again, he looked her way and grinned. "I had a run-in with the corner of some metal siding. It caught me *gut*, and happened in seconds too. It hurt like the dickens, I tell ya. And it was a real mess."

"My word."

"Yeah. Blood everywhere."

She was starting to feel a little queasy. She was also starting to wonder how they'd ever landed on this subject. "I'm sure you needed stitches?"

"I did. Twenty-six."

She gulped, imagining the sight of that. "That's a lot."

"Sure was. That wound was real deep." He grunted. "Then, just when I thought it was healed, I got impatient and did more than I should have." He paused dramatically. "Next thing I knew, I'd torn the stitches and had an infection. Off I went to the hospital again."

Her queasiness was reaching a dangerous level. "Well. Um, I'm glad you're all right now. Real glad."

"Me too. However, my accident had some *gut* consequences. I learned my lesson about taking the time to care for myself, and it's made for a *gut* story."

"Oh, you."

"It's true."

"I'm sorry you have such a bad scar."

"My *mamm* was so mad at me. She said it would have healed far quicker if only I had been a lot more patient. She was tempted to whip my behind for being so pigheaded and stupid."

Sharon giggled. "Maybe you were simply impatient. Ain't so?"

Toby pulled up his knees and wrapped his arms around them. "I used to be impatient. That is true. But now I'm beginning to think I have all the time in the world for some things." He looked into her eyes when he said that.

She smiled weakly as his full meaning hit her hard.

How strange and unexpected life was! Here she'd assumed her biggest romance concern was going to be watching her sister receive Graham's attention while she watched from a distance and pretended not to be affected. Instead, she was entertaining a possible flirtation of her own. To her surprise, it hadn't been uncomfortable, either.

"Toby, I, uh, I think you have a *gut* point. Patience is a virtue. It's definitely a blessing when one is able to appreciate the value of waiting for the perfect time."

He smiled at her, then glanced just beyond her and grinned broadly before lying down on his towel and closing his eyes.

Unable to help herself, she turned to see what he'd seen.

That's when she saw Graham was looking steadily at her. Intently. Not looking too pleased at all about what he'd just witnessed. Just as he had at breakfast that morning.

Figuring that was something to think about, she stretched out on her towel and pulled the hem of her dress up an inch or so above her knees. She closed her eyes then too. Glad to have an excuse to spend some time with her thoughts.

Her mighty mixed-up, jumbled thoughts.

CHAPTER 8

"It's mighty kind of you to come with me to the Der Dutchman, Graham," Sherry said as they walked along Beneva Road two days later.

"It wasn't out of pure kindness. I wanted to walk with you."

Sherry was so surprised, she almost gaped at him. But then she pulled herself together and told him she'd like a walk. She was looking forward to chatting with him too. She still wasn't sure how Graham felt about her, but she was bound and determined to follow Carla's advice and simply enjoy herself.

After their day at Siesta Key, the heat taking more out of them than they thought it would, the seven of them decided they needed more rest. Graham, Matthew, and Toby had slept in on Tuesday, before ordering pizza for lunch and then proceeding to do nothing more than lounge around the inn's outdoor courtyard for the remainder of the afternoon. The four girls had gone to Yoder's to enjoy a leisurely lunch, followed by wandering in and out of stores. Then the four of them had spent the majority of the evening in the girls' attic room playing cards.

This morning, however, Sherry had wakened ready to explore more of Sarasota. She and Carla borrowed two of the inn's red bikes and rode up and down the streets in Pinecraft. After lunch, Sharon made plans to talk about cookbooks with Beverly.

Since Carla and Vera wanted to sit outside and read, Sherry walked to the front porch where all the guys were. She discovered that, despite all the wonderful baked goods Beverly would provide for tea in just a couple of hours, they'd been trying to convince each other to walk to Der Dutchman and bring back two of their special pies. Sherry volunteered to go, and, surprising her, Graham offered to go along.

Now as they walked down the street together, every so often stepping to the side so mothers with their strollers could get by, Sherry found herself relaxing with him. He'd been teasing her about the way she'd been chatting with every child who crossed their path.

"This is fun, Graham. I'm glad you and the boys were in the mood for pie."

"You came upon us at the right time, for sure and for certain," he said with a smile. "None of us wanted to be seen walking by ourselves with two pies in our hands."

She laughed. "It would be quite a sight, but not necessarily a bad one. And, of course, coconut cream pie is always a *gut* idea."

"To be honest, I didn't really think we needed pie. But Matthew has a terrible sweet tooth. Sometimes it's easier just to give him what he wants."

"I've done things like that with my girlfriends." She smiled at Graham again. Unbidden, hope filled her once more. Maybe she and Graham were meant to be together after all.

As they crossed another intersection, he said, "What do you girls go out to grab? I'm thinking it's probably not pie."

"You're right. It ain't. Sharon is our family's baker, you know.

She's always bringing something home from the bakery that didn't sell or experimenting with a new recipe. We never run out of treats," she said as she pushed the crosswalk button at the intersection. "Sometimes we do go out, to run errands or something, but it's rarely for food. I like activity. I, um, don't do well with just sitting around."

"I'm beginning to get that idea." He smiled at her again, remembering how often he saw her get up to wade into the waves at Siesta Key.

Another minute later, when the light turned, they crossed the street, then walked the rest of the way in easy silence.

As they walked, Graham found himself wondering more about Sherry and even more about his reaction to her. Although he still thought Sharon was special, he'd begun to realize he felt more at ease around Sherry than he did around her sister.

Had he fallen in love with Sherry's letters and simply associated those feelings with a pretty girl, with Sharon? Or had it been the other way around? Had he become so fascinated by his one brief conversation with Sharon that he'd transferred all those feelings to the letter writer?

Surely there was no such thing as love at first sight, was there? Yes, he'd had a strong reaction to Sharon when he met her, but he had become more than interested in Sherry through her letters.

Whatever the case, he was glad his agreement with Toby had prompted him to get to know Sherry better.

When they got to the bakery counter at the restaurant, Sherry pulled out the money she'd collected and asked for the pies. Then they stepped to the side to wait.

Knowing he needed to figure out how he truly felt about Sherry, he thought he better keep their conversation flowing. "Tell me more about your job."

"Well, as you know, I work at a little nursery school as an assistant. I help the teachers with the two- and three-year-olds."

He winced. "That sounds difficult."

"It takes a lot of patience. I'll give you that!"

"But you enjoy it?"

"Very much so."

"Why is that?" he asked after he collected the bag from the hostess and they started their way back home. "Why do you enjoy it? Is it because you like teaching *kinner* or because you want *kinner* of your own one day?"

"Hmm. I never took the time to think about it that way. I guess my best answer would be both," she said with a smile. "I do enjoy *kinner*. I like how free they are. I like how they're unburdened by rules and expectations." She shrugged as they stopped at the light again. "Being with them makes me happy and want to be less worried about such things too." Rather sheepishly, she added, "I hope one day to be blessed with *kinner* like that."

"That's a great answer."

"What? Were you judging me?"

"*Nee*. I just . . . well, you gave me a lot to think about."

Looking up at him, her petite frame so slight but her very being so spunky, something new flickered in her eyes. "Don't take this the wrong way, but I'm starting to think I'm finally seeing the man I've been writing to for the last six months."

"Why would you say that?"

She shrugged again, then admitted, "I don't know how to say this without making either of us look bad. But, uh, looking back at when we first saw each other in the parking lot, I kind of get the feeling you were disappointed when you saw me again."

"I wasn't." This was terrible. He was lying to her.

Looking far more mature than her years, she said, "It's okay if you were. I mean, I know I seem confident, but I also know I'm not much to look at when I'm standing next to my sister."

This was becoming worse and more uncomfortable by the second. "Don't say things like that, Sherry. It's not true. I never thought that, either."

"Maybe not you, but I'm sure a lot of people can't help but compare the two of us. And it's fairly easy to see who'd come out on top."

"I don't think so."

"My sister Sharon is the beauty. She's also cool and reserved."

He hated that she was putting herself down. "Please, stop saying things like that. You're attractive too. And it's pretty obvious you have much to be proud of."

Her expression softened. *"Danke."* When they turned right on Magnolia, she continued. "Graham, please don't misinterpret what I said. I wasn't fishing for compliments. It's just that . . . What I'm trying to say is you shouldn't feel bad if you find me lacking next to Sharon."

"Did your parents do this?" he asked angrily. "Did they make you feel like you weren't as *gut* as your older sister?"

"Nee." With a sigh, she pressed her hands to her cheeks. "I'm just being silly. Please, may we drop this now?"

"We don't have to." Actually, he liked seeing this new, less confident side of Sherry. While he hated for her to have insecurities, her weaknesses made her seem more approachable.

"Well, I'd sure like to." Grimacing, she said, "And while we're at it, maybe we could forget that I brought it up in the first place? That's a fault of mine. I say what's on my mind, then live to regret it."

Just before they turned to walk up the front steps to the inn, Graham stopped. "Sherry, don't apologize anymore for who you are. There's nothing wrong with you and a whole lot that's great. You have qualities Sharon doesn't have. I'm sure she's a little envious of some of your attributes too."

"Maybe so."

"Listen, I'm one of three boys. We all farm together too. I have a lot of experience trying to keep up with my older brother. My younger brother, Caleb, has said he often tries to keep up with me. It's the way of siblings, I think."

She blinked. "I never thought about it that way." As they started walking up the steps, she looked up at him. "You know what, Graham? I'm starting to think maybe all my experience with preschoolers is going to pay off."

"How so?"

"Over and over again, I try to teach them about the value of patience. But maybe I've learned a bit about patience too." She looked down at her feet. "On the way to Pinecraft, I was sure something good was going to happen right away. But now I realize there's not much value in trying to force anything to happen. Maybe it's best when we have to do a little bit of waiting and praying."

Her words couldn't have been more true. They resonated with him . . . though, unfortunately, they also made him feel more confused than ever. He smiled weakly as he held open the door.

Matthew was lounging on one of the easy chairs in the living room. "Do we finally have our pie?"

Graham laughed. "We do, and *nee* thanks to you. Go round up everyone and tell them to meet us in the dining room."

CHAPTER 9

✑

"HEY, GRAHAM?" TOBY ASKED LATE THAT NIGHT WHEN THEY were settled in their beds.

"Hmm?"

"What did you really think was going to happen with Sherry when we booked our bus tickets?"

"You know, I thought I'd see the girl I'd been writing to for months again and fall in love. Instead, I got myself in a real mess."

"Do you still feel like you're in a mess now?"

After his walk with Sherry? He wasn't sure. "*Nee*. One minute I don't want to do anything but relax and have a *gut* time. The next I'm half planning the rest of my life."

"I've been kind of doing the same thing. Do you think it's Pinecraft that's making us so crazy?"

"Maybe." Thinking about Sharon's beauty and Sherry's cuteness and bubbly personality, he said, "Maybe it's the girls. Or maybe I've stopped dwelling on the assumptions I made and started concentrating on the needs of other people. Maybe I'm finally growing up."

"Yeah." Toby punched his pillow and flipped on his side. "I didn't come here with any expectations other than I wanted to take a break from construction. But now . . ." He blew out a harsh breath. "Now I can't stop thinking about Sharon."

"You and she have hit it off, then."

"I think so. Well, we talked a bit on the beach. And we spent some time together after supper."

"I've seen you together more than that."

"What about you and Sherry?"

Thinking about their conversation on the streets going back and forth from Der Dutchman, Graham said, "I'm starting to see she's more than I thought she was."

"Huh."

The burden was killing him. "Will you keep a secret?"

"Of course."

"Well, these letters? I thought I was writing to Sharon. Not Sherry."

Instead of looking horrified, Toby looked merely amused. "Really? That's kind of hard to believe. They're really different."

"I know that now. I didn't when I was writing."

"The signature at the bottom of the letter didn't clue you in?"

"It would have, if I hadn't confused their names. I remembered meeting Sharon but not her first name. I only remembered her last name was Kramer. So when Sherry wrote and said she just wanted to say hi because she liked letter writing, and I saw the name Kramer, I thought she was the woman I remembered."

"But she wasn't."

"*Nee.*" Wondering why he'd even decided to tell Toby the truth because now he was feeling stupid, he said, "At first I thought maybe Sharon wrote chatty letters because was a little shy. I thought maybe shy girls liked to express themselves more through the written word or something."

"The amount of information you don't know about the female mind is staggering."

"Like you are any better."

"I have two sisters. I know better." Making a come-closer gesture with his fingers, he said, "So how did you finally figure it out? Did Sherry say something about her red hair or something?"

That would have been great if she had! "*Nee*. I, um . . . well, I didn't actually discover who exactly Sherry was until I got here and we were all standing in the parking lot."

Toby gaped. "*Nee* way."

"It's true."

"What did the girls say when you told them?" He grinned. "I bet you got an earful!"

"They haven't said anything. Because I haven't told them the truth yet."

Toby stilled. "Are you saying Sherry still thinks you knew you were writing to her?"

"*Jah*." He swallowed. "I couldn't figure out what to do. Or how to tell them without hurting anyone's feelings. I mean, either I tell Sherry I liked her letters but had been picturing her sister, or I tell Sharon I didn't remember her name, so she was essentially forgettable."

"Neither option is *gut*."

"I know that." Thinking he might as well confess the whole story, Graham said, "I almost convinced myself it was okay and that I didn't want to seriously court either of them."

Toby slapped his hands on his face. "But now you do?"

Graham shifted uncomfortably. "*Jah*. I think I do."

"Do I even want to know which one you're interested in now? And before you say anything, I hope you recall that I asked you on the beach who you liked."

"I remember."

"Well? Who?"

"At first I thought it was Sharon, but now I think it might be Sherry."

"You think it might be," he repeated. After a pause, he scowled. "You are seriously playing with people's lives here, Graham."

"It's a mess," Graham agreed. "I feel bad about it too. Anytime either of them mentions the letters, I kind of want to throw up. I hate this secret. But you have to know I'm not playing around. I don't want to hurt anyone's feelings, and I just don't know if I should come clean or not."

He'd known Toby most of his life, but never had Toby looked at him with such disdain. "*Nee*, Graham. That's not what you're doing. You're more concerned with your pride than with being honest. And that's not being grown up at all."

"Hey, now. It ain't—"

"It is. You need to tell those sisters the truth tonight, or I will."

"You can't do that. What about promising to keep my secret?"

"That was before I realized your secret is going to ruin my life," he said before turning away.

After some thinking—and praying—Graham realized two things.

First, Toby was completely right. He hadn't been truly thinking about Sharon or Sherry. He hadn't been thinking about Toby either. He'd been thinking only about his own wants. It was time to change that. He just hoped he wasn't going to be on the receiving end of several cold shoulders for the rest of this vacation. If that happened, this trip was indeed going to go down as one of the worst ideas in his whole life.

Second, he now knew which sister truly made his heart beat just a little faster, and he didn't want a lie to stand between them.

CHAPTER 10

❧

SHERRY WAS DOING HER BEST TO STIFLE HER YAWNS ON the back patio. But it was late, she was tired, and Graham had been incredibly vague about why he wanted to talk to both her and Sharon at ten thirty at night.

"What do you think Graham wants to talk to us about?" she asked Sharon for about the fifth time.

"Like I said before, I have *nee* idea. Maybe Graham wants our opinion about something."

Sherry was just going to ask what opinion could be so urgently needed when the back door opened and Graham came out. Just behind him was Toby. What was going on?

"Hey," Graham said as he looked at one of them, then the other. "*Danke* for meeting me."

"We didn't know Toby was coming too," Sharon said. "Is this a party or something?"

"I wish it was," Toby muttered.

Graham glared at him. "Toby came for moral support."

Sharon raised her eyebrows. "You need moral support to talk to us?"

"I didn't come for Graham's moral support. I came in case you two needed me," Toby clarified.

Sherry had had enough. "Graham, come sit down and get this over with," she said impatiently. "I'm tired, and I'm done guessing what's on your mind."

Graham pulled out one of the wrought-iron chairs and abruptly sat down. Far more slowly, Toby joined them too.

After exhaling a deep breath, Graham blurted, "I have to tell you both something that's been weighing on my mind ever since you arrived in Pinecraft."

"What is it?" Sharon's expression was full of concern.

Looking as though he was about to have a tooth pulled, he said, "I . . . well, I, um, I had a problem with the letters I wrote to Sherry." Before Sherry could ask what he was talking about, he rushed on. "Sherry, I didn't realize I was writing to you. I thought I was writing to Sharon."

Stunned, Sherry looked at Toby, who seemed irritated, and at Sharon, who was gaping. Then she burst out laughing. "You're being ridiculous, Graham. I signed my letters Sherilyn Kramer."

"I know you did. But I didn't remember meeting you, not until you got here. I only remembered meeting Sharon."

And just like that, all her amusement fled. "You didn't remember meeting me?"

Graham got to his feet and clenched his hands at his sides. "I remembered meeting Sharon, but I only remembered her last name. I couldn't remember her first name. I assumed it was Sherilyn when I got that first letter signed Sherilyn Kramer."

Sherry was starting to feel sick, like she'd eaten a beetle or something. "So all this time you were writing to me, telling me about your life and how you couldn't wait to see me in Pinecraft, you were really wanting to see my sister."

Graham hesitated. "Kind of."

Sharon tilted her head to one side. "What do you mean by 'kind of?'" Her voice was hard.

"I wanted to see the person who was writing me so many entertaining letters."

"And you thought the author of the letters looked like Sharon, right?" Sherry asked. "What about when I mentioned my red hair and freckles?"

"You never told me that."

"I did in my last letter. I sent it just before I left for our trip."

"I didn't get that letter, remember? I left a couple of days before you did, and it didn't come in time." Sitting back down, he said, "I'm sorry. I don't know what else to say."

"Only that you didn't remember meeting me."

"Don't feel bad, Sherry," Sharon said. "Graham here might have remembered what I looked like, but he didn't even remember my name."

Graham leaned his head back and took another deep breath. When he looked at them again, he said, "I know I sound like a jerk, but I promise it wasn't like that."

"Graham, why didn't you say anything when we arrived?" Sharon asked.

"I didn't know how to tell you," he said after a brief pause. "Then, well, I tried to tell myself it didn't really matter that I got so confused. After all, it was an honest mistake, and it wasn't like I had known either of you well. I thought maybe we could have a *gut* time in Pinecraft and simply be vacation friends."

Sherry knew what he meant, but she wasn't about to let him off the hook. "And by 'vacation friends,' you mean women you weren't serious about. Women with whom you only wanted to have a fling."

Graham's blue eyes widened. "Hold on now. I haven't been flinging with anyone."

"Yet," Sherry said, feeling angrier by the second. Actually, that anger was a good thing. Far better than sinking to the floor in embarrassment.

"See?" Toby interjected. "This is *exactly* why I came along. I knew you girls would need some support."

"For what?" Sharon asked. "Graham just embarrassed both me and my little sister in front of you."

"What he did and said was *nee* reflection on you," Toby said quickly. "You have nothing to be embarrassed about."

"You know what? Let's just stop this conversation before it gets any worse."

"Sharon, I promise that I'm sorry."

Sharon frowned. "Why does that matter right now?"

"Because I want you to believe me. I never meant to hurt anyone."

"Graham, all I need you to do is promise that you'll keep your distance for the rest of this trip."

Graham flinched. "Neither of you will accept my apology?"

Sharon got to her feet. "Why would you expect us to?"

"Because it's the right thing to do."

Sherry hated that he didn't sound more upset with himself. "Graham, I believe you got us confused. I can even understand how that might have happened. But not telling me when I got here? And admitting what you did to Toby before telling either one of us? That was pretty low."

"I didn't mean to upset you both. Toby is right. This is my fault. Not either of yours."

Sharon looked at him with a sad expression. "This might be

a shock, but I didn't remember your name either. So I would have understood that you got us mixed up."

"And now?"

"Now? Now I have *nee* idea what to think. I'm angry. I just need a break."

"I'm going up to my room," Sherry said, standing as well. "Do you want to come with me, Sharon?"

"*Nee*. I'm going to the front porch," she said over her shoulder as she started around the house.

Just as she was about to encourage Sharon to come inside after all, Sherry noticed Toby was following her sister, and she went into the house alone. As she closed the back door behind her, she noticed Graham was sitting with his head resting in his hands. He looked despondent and so very alone. Sherry knew she should be glad he was suffering the consequences of his behavior.

So why did she suddenly feel kind of sorry for him?

CHAPTER 11

❧

"SHARON, WAIT!" TOBY CALLED OUT AS SHE WALKED along the side of the inn. The narrow flagstone pathway led from the patio to the broad front porch.

Sharon was so mad and confused she didn't want to stop. But she did. After all, it certainly wasn't Toby's fault that his friend had made such a mess of things.

"*Danke,*" he said, scanning her face in the dim light. "Are you okay?"

Since it was obvious that she wasn't, she didn't even attempt to hide her sarcasm. "I'm great. *Wunderbaar.*"

Frustration flickered through his expression. "Let me rephrase that. Are you really disappointed?"

She realized then that Toby thought she was mourning the loss of a man she didn't really know, the loss of a relationship she'd only had a taste of—not enough to even know how it could be.

That realization was all she needed to know she'd been reacting to the situation, yes, but not feeling pain in her heart.

The difference was notable and significant.

Exhaling deeply, she took a second to gather her thoughts. Then, as they walked to the porch together, she tried her best to convey how she felt in a way that would allow her and Toby both to come to terms with what had happened.

"I'm disappointed Sherry wrote to a man for six months, cast a whole lot of hopes on a grand reunion that might blossom into a relationship, only to get her heart stomped on," she said. "I'm disappointed to learn that while Graham remembered what I looked like, he still found me somehow forgettable, believing Sherry's personality in those letters was mine. But I forgot his name, too, so that makes me disappointed with myself."

She paused, half waiting for Toby to nod and turn around. Or worse, give her a simple platitude that meant nothing to either of them. But instead he simply stared at her in that surprisingly patient way of his. She realized he was waiting for her to tell him everything. Even if it made them both uncomfortable.

When was the last time someone had given her permission to be so open and honest? She knew that answer.

Years. Maybe never.

She sat down on one of the porch's rocking chairs, and then, looking up into his dark-brown eyes with only moonlight to illuminate them, she took another fortifying breath and decided to be even more honest. "I'm embarrassed too."

"Why?" he asked, his tone gentle.

She was completely at a loss. "Why? Because it's, uh, it's been a while since I've taken a chance like this. You see, I found out my former boyfriend had cheated on me, and it hurt."

"I'm sure it did."

"It hurt enough that I didn't want to put myself at risk again. But Sherry was so excited about all the possibilities with the man who turned out to be Graham, and that made me want to try to trust again."

"There's nothing wrong with that. Although he never admitted it, I could sense Graham's excitement about seeing the author of those letters again, and it made me want to take a chance too."

"Why was it hard? Have you been hurt too?"

"Not like you. I just . . . well, I get uncomfortable around girls. I never know what to say, so I always joke around. Then they don't take me seriously. But Graham's hope for this trip made me a little hopeful too. I didn't expect to fall in love or anything, but I was hoping I could do a little bit better in the relationship department."

"I don't think you have any problems in that area."

"*Nee?* Well, that's *gut* to know."

Sharon found herself smiling at Toby. "I don't know what's going to happen now, but I'm glad we've become friends."

"Me too."

When he sat down in the rocking chair next to hers, she tensed. "Toby, I appreciate you sitting with me and such, but I should warn you I'm not very *gut* company right now."

But instead of backing off, he chuckled. The sound was low and deep in his throat. "Sharon, I neither want nor need you to be *gut* company. I only want you to be yourself."

She ran a hand over her face. "I don't know if what I'm being at the moment is me either. I'm not usually so emotional."

The corners of his lips curved up. "I'm kinda liking this emotional side of you."

Dropping her hand, she stared at him. "Why?"

"Because, until very recently, you kind of intimidated me."

She scanned his face, looking for signs he was teasing her.

But his eyes were clear, his expression earnest.

While she gaped at him, he held out a hand. "Come on. Let's go for a walk."

Not sure where the discussion was leading her or what destination Toby had in mind, Sharon realized she could either refuse or allow herself to be surprised.

Put that way, there was no choice. She linked her fingers with his and let him pull her up. After another moment of awkwardness, she relaxed and picked up her pace to match his long-legged stride. She might not have any idea what was in store for them, but she did know she trusted Toby. That counted for a lot.

Hand in hand, they walked down Bahia Vista, turned the corner on Magnolia, and ended up on the walking path in one of Pinecraft's public parks she'd visited before. It was fairly dark out, though by the light of the streetlamps she could see a few people walking in the distance. But overall, it was quiet and the area was theirs.

"Isn't this something?" Toby asked as they slowed down.

She was confused. "What are you referring to? The park?"

"*Jah.* But I mean something else too." Dropping her hand, he gestured toward the scene around them. "I mean, look at it around here. Just a couple of hours ago, you couldn't have paid me to return here."

Looking around, Sharon didn't notice anything different—just the small pond, the walking path, the grassy area where groups of teenagers played impromptu kickball games. "Why does it seem different to you now?" she asked.

"Before, it was too crowded, too hot. Too many people, too much noise, too much of, well, everything. But now that it's clearer it seems a whole lot nicer to me."

"Because you don't care for crowds."

Toby laughed. "I don't. You're right. But what I'm trying to say—and not very well—is that maybe I needed to give this place some time, to see it for what it is."

"Is that what you're thinking about our experiences here? And about how Graham has been treating everyone?"

"Maybe. Maybe he wasn't wrong and we weren't right. Maybe he was simply fumbling around, trying to figure out who was a *gut* fit for him . . . and, like me and this park, he changed his mind."

Feeling rather impressed with him, Sharon blinked. "Wow, Toby. And here I thought you were all about having fun."

"I am." Grinning, he reached for her hand again and led her to a bench. "But just like I keep saying there's more to you than most realize, I'm thinking maybe there's more to me than you realize." When she seated herself next to him, he stared at her. "Now, of course, the question is what you want to do about it."

A little buzz went through her as his words settled deep inside her. That was the question now, wasn't it?

What did she want to do? Or rather, what was she willing to do?

CHAPTER 12

⁓✺⁓

"I'm blessed to have such *gut* friends," Sherry said to Vera and Carla. "*Danke* for listening to me fret and moan about everything. Sharon seemed to want to be alone, so we haven't even had a chance to talk about this yet."

"Fret away. You have reason."

"You can fret even more if you want to," Carla offered. "I don't mind."

Sherry thought about that, and shook her head. "*Nee* thanks. I'm done feeling sorry for myself."

"*Gut*," Vera said. "Especially since you and Sharon don't have anything to feel bad about. I think this was all just a mix-up. Graham got confused and then was brave enough to confess it."

"And I let myself get carried away by my dreams. I should have realized people don't fall in love through letters."

"And perhaps that *nee* romance is perfect," Vera said. "My Stefan and I have had our fair share of misunderstandings. No relationship is perfect, especially not at the beginning."

"Point taken." Just as Sherry was about to suggest they get ready for bed, they heard someone approach their attic door.

"Sherry, can we talk?" Graham called through the door.

She answered from inside. "It's late."

"I know. But I'm not going to be able to sleep unless we talk. Please, will you give me a couple of minutes?"

Heart pounding, she turned to Vera and Carla. "What should I do?"

"Give him a chance, Sherry," Carla coaxed. "He sounds pretty upset."

"I am upset." Graham raised his voice a little. "Sherry, please?"

She couldn't believe it, but she was starting to waver. Was it because she felt sorry for him . . . or because he was the man she really wanted? *Lord, what should I do?* she asked silently. *I want Graham in my life, but I don't want him for the wrong reason.*

"Come on, Sherry. Please?" Graham pleaded.

She looked at her girlfriends, then back at the door. What to do? What to do?

But then she remembered that familiar verse from the book of Luke. *Forgive others, and you will be forgiven.*

What more did she need to know?

"Go talk with him," Vera said. "He sounds miserable."

Feeling much better, she turned and opened the door.

"*Danke,*" he said.

Sherry almost smiled when she saw he looked as miserable as he sounded. His shirt was rumpled and untucked, and his hair was sticking up in all directions. Obviously, he'd been running his fingers through it. "Oh, Graham."

He blinked, changing some of the desperation she'd spied into relief. "Where can we talk?"

As Vera and Carla giggled, she stepped into the hallway and closed the door firmly behind her. "Not in here. Let's go downstairs. I bet there's no one in the small alcove by the dining room this time of night."

While he led the way down the stairs, she cautioned herself to forgive, yes, but also to stay strong. She was going to listen to him, offer forgiveness, but then politely tell him she'd talk to him tomorrow before finally going to bed.

But when they got to the small room, Graham turned to her and blurted, "Sherry, since I've already made such a mess of things, I'm just going to tell you something straight out."

"I'm listening."

Still staring at her intently, he said, "I really like you. *You*, not your sister. *You*, not the girl I was writing to but didn't really know."

She loved what he was saying. Of course she did! But she was also afraid. "What if you change your mind again?"

"I'm not going to."

Examining his expression, she looked for signs he was keeping his true feelings from her. But everything about him—from the intensity of his gaze to his firm stance—illustrated he was being completely open and honest. "You sound so certain."

"I am, Sherry." He waved one hand in the air. "You see, this was why I had to tell you and Sharon the truth—and not only because Toby made me realize it was the right thing to do. I realized my feelings for you are real, and I wasn't going to change my mind." He paused. "Distance isn't going to make me forget you," he added, his words practically tumbling over each other. "I like you and it was killing me that I had that secret between us."

His words were sweet. Really sweet. But where did that leave them? "What happens next?"

"That's up to you, of course. But I know what I'm thinking." Before she could utter anything, he reached for her hands. "How about this? I like how you know your mind. I like how you want to stay busy and like to do things and not sit around and wait. I like how you like *kinner*, and I like how you like to organize things too."

As she gaped at him, he added, "I also happen to like your freckles. And since I'm laying it all out there . . ."

"*Jah?*"

"I think you look really nice in that bathing suit."

She felt her cheeks heat again. But this time it wasn't from embarrassment. It was from happiness. She thought of playing it cool. Of pretending she wasn't glad to hear what he said. But that wasn't who she was. She studied their linked hands, how they looked together. Thought about how they felt together.

"That was quite a speech, Graham," she said at last.

"Does that mean you don't want to throw something at me anymore?"

"*Nee.* I mean, not at the moment."

"Well, then. Maybe you'll give me a chance? After all, we're going to be here for another week. Maybe we could try simply being together? You know, as Graham and Sherry."

As Graham and Sherry. Just the two of them, with no more confusion or misunderstanding twisting everything into knots. "That is quite the opportunity. I'd hate to waste it."

His eyes lit up and he smiled. Rubbing his thumb over her knuckles, he said, "*Danke*, Sherry. You have made me mighty happy."

Funny, making him happy had made her mighty happy too.

CHAPTER 13

❧

THE SEVEN OF THEM SPENT THEIR LAST EVENING IN Pinecraft Park. Before they left the inn, Beverly helped them pack a picnic basket with sandwiches, salads, chips, and thick chocolate brownies.

After enjoying their leisurely meal, Matthew played a game of basketball with a couple of guys he'd met, and Carla and Vera lay on a quilt and chatted.

Sharon and Toby were near the swings, talking with each other. Each looked more than a little captivated by the other. Sherry was fairly sure her sister was going to be writing a few letters of her own when they got back home. And she smiled whenever she remembered Sharon bravely wearing her swimsuit without her dress the last few times they'd visited the beach.

As for herself? Well, she hadn't wanted to spend a moment away from Graham. When he asked her to take a walk so they could be alone, she'd jumped at the chance. After just a couple of minutes, Graham practically pulled her down one of the residential streets that lined the park.

"This is better," he said.

Sherry laughed. "If you wanted us to be alone, this is the wrong place."

87

Stepping a little closer, he said, "I guess I didn't want to avoid people as much as I wanted to do everything I possibly could just one more time."

"I've felt the same way. It's going to be so hard to leave here tomorrow."

"It is."

Taking a chance, she added, "It's going to be harder to leave you."

"I've been thinking the same thing about you." After taking a couple more steps, he said, "Sherry, I don't want to lose you again."

She knew what he meant. They'd spent too many days at the beginning of this vacation walking on eggshells around each other, trying to figure out what was real and what they thought the other thought. "You won't. We'll write letters."

"We can do that." Graham paused. "I mean, if that's what you want."

"What choice do we have?" Just then, a dark thought filled her. "You don't want to stop writing to each other, do you?"

He halted abruptly. "After everything we've been through? Absolutely not. Of course not! But I also want to see you every day. I want to court you like my brothers courted their girls, coming to your *haus* every evening and sitting with you on your front porch."

His words made her feel kind of mushy inside. Happy too. Actually, everything he was saying was reassuring. She wasn't alone in this relationship. He wanted the same things she did. "But if we can't do that, then what?"

"What would you think if I visited you in about two weeks and talked with your father?"

Her breath hitched, but she was still afraid to hope. "About . . ."

"About courting you. About one day marrying you, Sherry." Linking his fingers with hers, he said, "Is that clear enough?"

What could she say? After everything they'd been through, all the misunderstandings and all the failed hopes and dreams, they were on the same page in the end.

"*Jah,*" she said. "That is clear enough. Even for me."

His blue eyes looked her over, then little by little sparkled in the fading evening light. Then he leaned closer and lightly brushed his lips against hers. It was a sweet kiss. Perfect, because it hinted of a future together. When he shifted and wrapped an arm around her shoulders, she leaned into him.

Everything had been worked out, and nothing more needed to be said.

EPILOGUE

Dear Sherry,

It was so good to see you last weekend. I enjoyed spending time with your family. Has your father spoken with you yet? I asked him for your hand, but before giving me an answer, he wanted to talk with you. Please tell me you won't torture me for too long, Sherry. A man can take only so much.

Graham

Dear Graham,

My father spoke with me not ten minutes after you left. We talked about love and partnerships and the Lord and commitment. I told him all about sparks and laughter and happiness. That's when he said he had better give us his blessing . . . and fast!

So there you are, Graham. We have my parents' blessing so we can be officially engaged.

Set the date, and don't make me wait too long.

Now I am yours,
Sherry

Dear Sherry,

Is one month too long?

I remain yours,
Graham

Dear Sharon,

We're all coming to Adams County on the fifth of next month for Sherry and Graham's engagement party. I can't wait to see you! I hope you've already scheduled lots of time off. If you haven't, do so now.

I think we're going to have a lot to talk about.

Toby

Dear Toby,

I wish you hadn't had to take that early ride home yesterday! When I was trying not to cry as I told you good-bye, I felt as though I had just hugged you hello.

Didn't Sherry and Graham look happy? And they are so excited too! My mother is having quite the time of it, putting together a wedding in only six months.

I'm looking forward to seeing you in Sugarcreek next month. I can't wait to stay with your mother and sisters . . . that is, if they promise to be kind to me.

Sharon

Dear Sharon,

My family all loved you. But you knew they would, didn't you? You were a perfect houseguest, a perfect friend, and they all say you're perfect for me. Actually, the girls now think I'm a far sight smarter than they'd ever given me credit for. Your appearance in my life has raised their view of me.

In case you didn't realize it, I'm teasing you. It doesn't matter what they think, as long as we can be together.

I'll see you in a month when I stay at your house for a change. I have a feeling we can expect good things in our future.

Toby

Dear Toby,

I'm still feeling tingly about your proposal. It was the most romantic proposal ever, and right on the heels of Sherry and Graham's wedding too.

My mother looks like she's going to pull all her hair out, but I told her a four-month engagement is going to be just fine. I certainly don't want to wait any longer—especially since we're planning to go back to Pinecraft for our honeymoon. Maybe one of us should write to Beverly and let her know. She might want to prepare herself for that reunion!

Love, Sharon

A NOTE FROM THE AUTHOR

Dear Reader,

Thank you for returning to Pinecraft, Florida, with me! When I heard that this collection was going to be all about summer vacations or experiences, I knew that I had to set my story at the Orange Blossom Inn in Pinecraft. This made-up place was the focal point of four books I wrote two years ago for Avon Inspire. While writing this series, I fell in love with not only the innkeeper Beverly Overholt, but also the city of Sarasota, Florida, and the surrounding areas. I've since returned four times!

I really enjoyed writing about some characters who were on vacation. There is something about vacations that makes me smile. I love the freedom that I feel. I love how anything seems possible. And yes, I even love that feeling of dread that comes with knowing that I eventually have to go back home. Because of that, I try to treasure every minute. Maybe you have felt the same way?

If you're reading this book while on vacation, I sincerely hope you are having a great time! If, instead, you are simply enjoying a nice reading vacation from a busy day, thank you for spending it with me. I love hanging out with friends . . . even through the pages of one of my books.

Wishing you many blessings and lots of sunny days ahead,
Shelley Shepard Gray

DISCUSSION QUESTIONS

1. I had so much fun writing about reunions and revisiting Sarasota for this novella. What vacation spot are you anxious to visit again? What made it special?
2. Who in your life has been an unexpected 'surprise'? Who in your life made a positive first impression?
3. What did you think about Sharon and Sherry's relationship?
4. I thought the following verse from Luke fit this story perfectly: "Do not judge others, and you will not be judged. Do not condemn others, or it will all come back against you. Forgive others, and you will be forgiven." How does this verse apply to a person or a situation in your life?
5. When I found the Amish proverb, "Things turn out the best for those who make the best of the way things turn out," I knew it would work well with this story. Do you find this proverb to be true? Why or why not?

ACKNOWLEDGMENTS

Isn't it funny how God picks the right time for everything? I've wanted to be part of an Amish novella collection for quite a while. When it finally happened, the folks at Harper-Collins Christian Fiction placed me with some of the best writers in the genre! Thank you to authors Amy Clipston, Kelly Irvin, and Kathleen Fuller for joining me on this journey. I'm so excited to share a cover with y'all!

Thank you also goes out to the editorial staff at HCCP, most especially Karli Jackson and Jean Bloom. Both made *A Reunion in Pinecraft* something to be proud of.

I also can't help but acknowledge my original editor for the Pinecraft Series, Chelsey Emmelhainz. Because of Chelsey, I was able to write the Amish Brides of Pinecraft series, which this novella is loosely connected to.

Finally, I would never know so many details about Pinecraft without the kindness and patience of my Amish friend. She and her husband took me and my husband all around Pinecraft during our first visit. She's a gem, for sure and for certain.

ABOUT THE AUTHOR

❦

 SHELLEY GRAY IS THE AUTHOR OF THE Heart of a Hero series. Her Amish novel (written as Shelley Shepard Gray), *The Protector,* recently made the New York Times best-seller list. A native of Texas, she earned her bachelor's and master's degrees in Colorado and taught school for ten years. She and her husband have two children and live in Southern Ohio.

❦

Visit her website at www.shelleyshepardgray.com
Facebook: ShelleyShepardGray
Twitter: @ShelleySGray

SUMMER STORMS

AMY CLIPSTON

With love and appreciation for the
members of my Bakery Bunch

CHAPTER 1

HAPPINESS BUBBLED UP FROM INSIDE ARIANA SMUCKER as she leaned back on her palms and gazed up toward the sky. The aroma of sunscreen filled her nostrils, and the hot summer sun kissed her cheeks. Then she smoothed the skirt of her red bathing suit over her thighs before smiling over at her best friend, who was sitting beside her. "This day is absolutely perfect. Don't you agree?"

"*Ya.*" Mariella Ebersol kicked her legs in the water, and the floating dock they were sitting on shifted. She pushed her long, blonde braid behind her shoulder, and her deep-brown eyes sparkled in the bright sunlight. "I can't believe you'll be married in five months." She moved her slim fingers over the skirt on her black bathing suit.

"*Ya,* November is coming quickly." Ariana's heart fluttered and a grin overtook her lips as she looked toward the shoreline. Her fiancé, Jesse Zook, sat on the beach with her brother, close enough that she could see their faces as they talked. They were surrounded by members of their youth group as well as other visitors to Maryland's Cascade Lake.

Resting her hands on the warm wooden dock, Ariana kept

her gaze focused on Jesse. He pushed his hand through his thick sandy-blond hair and nodded. With his cobalt-blue eyes and strong jawline, Jesse was the most handsome man she'd ever known, and she couldn't wait for their wedding.

She looked over at her brother, Tobias, and her smile faded as she took in his deep frown and dark expression. Tension gripped Ariana's shoulders and her thoughts spun with anxiety. It was rare that their youth group could take a day off from work at their homes, jobs, and farms to visit a lake. Why would Tobias be troubled on a beautiful day like today?

A group of teenagers swam near the dock, and a girl squealed as a boy splashed her, pulling Ariana from her concern.

"You look worried." Mariella leaned over toward Ariana. *"Was iss letz?"*

Ariana turned toward her. "I was just watching Tobias talking with Jesse. Tobias looks so *bedauerlich*. I was hoping today would cheer him up."

"Cheer him up?" Mariella tilted her head. "What do you mean?"

Ariana blew out a sigh as she recalled the past week. It seemed as if her brother and father had argued nonstop. She'd hoped a day away from their farm would brighten Tobias's mood, but the scowl on his face as he spoke to Jesse indicated he'd brought his trouble with him to the lake.

"Tobias has been arguing with *mei dat* again."

"Oh." Mariella seemed to hesitate, as if awaiting more details, but Ariana couldn't bring herself to share everything she witnessed daily between her brother and father. "They still aren't getting along?"

"No." Ariana fingered her thick braid as she continued to watch Tobias interact with Jesse. "I'm worried it might be getting worse."

"*Ach*, no." Mariella crossed her arms over her middle. "Do you think you can do anything to help?"

Ariana swallowed a snort. "No. They're both so stubborn. They never seem to listen to each other. I think that's part of their problem."

Mariella gave a little laugh. "That sounds possible."

Jesse and Tobias suddenly stood up from the shoreline and started up the hill that led to the picnic area. They were walking slowly, still talking.

"Is it lunchtime?" Ariana asked.

"It might be. Why?"

Ariana pointed toward the shore. "I think Jesse and Tobias are going to lunch without us." She frowned. Why hadn't Jesse remembered to invite her and Mariella to join them?

Mariella clicked her tongue. "That's awfully thoughtless."

"*Ya*, it is." Ariana turned toward Mariella and raised her eyebrows. "Are you hungry?"

Mariella shrugged. "Sure."

"We'd better go before they eat without us." Ariana stood up on the floating dock, held out her hand, and lifted Mariella to her feet.

She dove into the cool lake water and swam toward the shoreline with Mariella beside her. Ariana relished the feel of the cool water sluicing over her body. When she reached the shallow area, she waded to the beach, where she found her beach towel and pink bandana waiting for her.

She pushed the bandana over her hair and draped the dry towel over her shoulders before trotting up the hill after Jesse and Tobias.

"Jesse!" she called. "Wait for me!"

He stopped and turned, his eyebrows raised. Tobias looked at her, but went on.

"Did you forget I was in the water?" She pointed back toward the lake.

"Whoops." He shook his head as a smile turned up his lips.

She rested her hand on her hip. "I thought I asked you to let me know when you and Tobias were going to have lunch."

"I'm sorry." He ran his hand over his clean-shaven chin. "I forgot."

"You forgot?" She took a deep breath as irritation nipped at her.

"*Ya*, I did. I was caught up in my conversation with Tobias, and I completely forgot you wanted me to call you for lunch." His lips formed a thin line as he walked back down the hill toward her. "I'm sorry."

"It's all right." She shrugged, even though his oversight did send a pang of disappointment through her.

At just under six feet, Jesse stood over her by several inches. She silently admired how the summer sun had already begun to tan his handsome face and naturally highlight his hair to a golden blond. Like the rest of the young men in their youth group, he was clad in swim trunks.

She hugged the towel to her body as her gaze moved to his broad shoulders, and her eyes widened. "Your shoulders are turning pink. You should put on more lotion before you burn."

"I'll be fine." He gestured toward their group of friends as they walked past them toward the picnic area. "We should go before the tables fill up."

He held out his hand and she laced her fingers with his, enjoying the feel of his skin against hers.

As they began the trek up the hill, she glanced around for Mariella. "Where did Mariella go?"

Jesse pointed in front of them. "She's almost up the hill."

Ariana followed his gaze to where Mariella trudged, hugging her blue beach towel around her body. Tobias walked a few feet in front of her.

She looked up at Jesse again. "You and Tobias seemed to be in a deep conversation."

Jesse nodded. "Tobias needed someone to listen."

"Oh?" Holding fast to his hand, she pulled him back, slowing their pace. "What did he need to talk about?"

Jesse blew a breath out through his nose. "I guess he's been arguing with your *dat* a lot lately."

Ariana nodded as worry coursed through her once again. "What did he say?"

"He was venting." Jesse shrugged. "He'll be fine. It's nothing to worry about."

"Okay." She hoped he was right.

"Let's have lunch, and then I'll try to talk to him again later."

"Sounds *gut*." Ariana let Jesse lead her to a picnic table. She sat down on the end beside Mariella as Jesse sat down across from her and beside Tobias. When she closed her eyes in silent prayer, she thanked God not only for their food, but for this beautiful day.

❧

In late afternoon, Ariana lifted a bottle of root beer to take a drink. She was sitting on a glider on the far end of Mariella's back porch with members of her youth group surrounding her. They were all enjoying Mariella's father's cold homemade drink and sharing stories. Ariana searched the sea of familiar faces for Jesse and Tobias, but neither was on the porch.

As one of the young men began telling a story about a hunting trip he took last year, Ariana descended the porch steps and walked toward the pasture. She found Jesse leaning against the fence as he spoke to two of his friends, and she gripped her bottle tighter as she walked toward him.

"Jesse?" she called, but he continued talking as if he hadn't heard her. "Jesse?"

"Jesse." Ivan tapped his arm. "Ariana is calling you."

"Oh." Jesse turned toward her. "Sorry. I didn't hear you."

Ariana pressed her lips together as frustration tightened her shoulders. "Could I please speak to you for a moment?"

"*Ya*, of course." Jesse followed her to the far end of the fence. "What do you need?"

"I thought you were going to join me." She gestured toward the porch. "You said you'd have a bottle of root beer with me, and I even saved you a seat on the glider."

"Oh right." Realization dawned in his blue eyes. "I'm sorry. Ivan, Henry, and I haven't seen one another much since they got so busy working in their *dat*'s store. We were getting caught up. I forgot I promised to sit with you."

"I understand." Ariana nodded despite her disappointment.

"I'll come up there now." He took her hand in his and gently tugged her toward the porch. "Let's go. I'll grab you another root beer from the cooler."

"Wait." She stopped him, and they looked at each other. "I wanted to ask you if you've seen Tobias."

Jesse nodded. "I saw him sitting with Mariella on the porch, but then I saw him walk alone toward the barn a while ago. I meant to follow him, but then I ran into Henry and Ivan, and I lost track of time."

A niggling of worry started at the base of Ariana's neck. Tobias had seemed off all day.

"I was hoping today would help him." She looked out over the pasture. The sky was clogged with gray clouds, and thunder rumbled in the distance.

"Would you like me to find him?"

"*Ya*, please."

"All right. We have to get going soon anyway. I think a storm is coming. Also, I promised *mei dat* I'd be home in time to help feed the animals." His expression seemed tentative. "You're still riding with me to get home, right?"

"*Ya*, I'd like to."

"*Gut*." He gave her hand a gentle squeeze. "I'll go find Tobias. You go back to the porch and enjoy the rest of your time with our *freinden*. Okay?"

"Okay." Her earlier worry dissipated as Jesse smiled at her. Before their trek from Cascade Lake back to Gordonville, Pennsylvania, he'd changed into dark trousers and a deep-blue shirt that accentuated his eyes. Ariana admired him as he headed toward the large barn. Her stomach took flight on the wings of a hundred butterflies at the notion of driving home with him this afternoon. Stealing a quick kiss would be the perfect ending to this special day spent with friends.

CHAPTER 2

❦

Dread bogged Jesse's steps as his boots crunched on the rock path leading to Mariella's father's barn. Tobias's glum mood and initial silence, followed by his venting, had bothered Jesse all day. Despite his efforts to cheer up Tobias before lunch, his best friend had never changed. Maybe he could find a way to cheer up Tobias now, before they headed home for the evening.

The scent of rain wafted over Jesse as he glanced over his shoulder. Ariana sat down on the porch glider and then leaned over to talk to one of their friends. The ties from her prayer covering flittered around her shoulders as she nodded.

Before they climbed into the van to head back to Gordonville, she'd changed into a green dress and pulled her hair up under a prayer *kapp*. She was attractive no matter what she wore, but he already longed for another sight of her long, thick braid and the wisps of dark hair falling around her face when she was swimming in the lake. Since he wasn't permitted to take a photo of her, let alone own a camera, he did his best to commit how she'd looked to memory.

Turning, Jesse hurried into the barn. The aroma of animals mixed with moist earth invaded his nostrils as he walked past the stalls, looking for Tobias. When he reached the back of the barn, he slipped out through the side door and headed around to the back. He stopped short when he found Tobias leaning against the barn wall, holding a translucent glass bottle with a clear liquid sloshing around in it. Was that alcohol? No, it couldn't be. Could it?

Jesse blinked. "What are you doing?"

"Relaxing." Tobias held up the bottle, which was already half empty. "Would you like some?"

"What is that?"

"Vodka." Tobias took a long drink and then cleared his throat as he swiped a hand across his mouth. "It's the *gut* stuff. Have some." He held the bottle out to him.

"No." Jesse approached him, his thoughts spinning with a combination of anger and confusion. "Have you lost your mind?"

"Nope." Tobias took another long draw.

"Give me that before you get sick." Jesse reached for the bottle, but Tobias snatched it away from his grasp. He tucked the bottle behind his back and glared at Jesse. "You said you didn't want any, but don't spoil my fun."

"Spoil your fun?" Jesse gritted his teeth, amazed Tobias had found a way to sneak a bottle out here. "Do you realize how much trouble you'll be in if Mariella's *dat* catches you back here drinking? He's the bishop!"

Tobias snorted. "Please. I'm not hurting anyone. I'm just doing what I have to do to unwind. I don't get much chance to relax, so I need to enjoy it while I can."

Jesse rubbed his temples and flattened his lips together. In the eighteen years he'd known Tobias, ever since they were six years old, he'd never seen him behave so irresponsibly. The man standing in front of him was someone he didn't recognize. What would Ariana say if she found Tobias drinking alcohol? Worse, how would their father react?

Tobias's expression darkened. "Don't look at me like that."

Jesse took a deep breath in a vain attempt to curb the anger and frustration gripping him. "Is this about your *dat*? I'm trying to understand why you're behaving this way. But I can't—"

"Of course you can't understand me. Your life is perfect."

"Perfect?" Jesse shook his head. "No one's life is perfect."

"*Ya*, I suppose that's true." Tobias studied Jesse, a sardonic smirk spreading across his lips. "It must get tiresome for you to have to hear your *dat* compliment you for your hard work and skill all the time. Honestly, Jesse, how do you put up with all that love and appreciation, day in and day out?"

Jesse balled his hands at his sides and fought to keep calm despite his best friend's biting words. *Be patient. It's the alcohol talking, not Tobias.* "You didn't say today at the lake, but did you have an especially bad argument with your *dat* yesterday or this morning?"

Tobias snorted again and then rested the bottle against his thigh. "Would it make any difference if I had?"

"It would explain why you're acting this way." Jesse leaned against the barn wall beside him. "I know you're upset with your *dat* right now, but you're doing the best you can. Don't let it get to you. Things will get better."

Tobias narrowed his eyes. "I came out here to be alone. I don't need your platitudes and empty words."

A muscle ticked in Jesse's jaw as his patience wore thin. He had to get the bottle away from Tobias and then get him into his buggy before he was too drunk to walk, let alone guide the horse home. He couldn't possibly tell Ariana that Tobias had been drinking. She'd be furious, and the last thing Jesse wanted to do was ruin this special day. She'd been looking forward to it for nearly a month.

Jesse leveled his eyes at Tobias. "It's time for you to knock it off. You've wallowed in enough self-pity. Get it together."

"I told you. This is how I unwind." Tobias lifted his chin.

"This is how you unwind," Jesse said the words as their meaning clicked into place in his mind. "Are you saying you drink often?"

Tobias averted his eyes, staring at his shoes.

"Give me that." Jesse grabbed the bottle from Tobias's hand and started spilling the contents onto the ground.

"Stop it!" Tobias fought him, pushing Jesse out of the way before reclaiming the bottle.

With a murderous glare, Tobias replaced the top on the bottle. "You act all high and mighty, but you have no idea what it's like to argue with your *dat* every day. When you get home this evening, your *dat* will welcome you with open arms and ask you how your day was. *Mei dat* will tell me I spend too much time with *mei freinden*, I don't work hard enough, I'm not a *gut* example for *mei schweschder*, and the list goes on and on." His face twisted. "You and your *bruders* are everything your parents ever wanted, but I ruin everything I touch."

Jesse held up his hands as sympathy replaced his anger. "I'm sorry your *dat* makes you feel that way, but this isn't how you deal with your problems. I tried to tell you this afternoon at the lake. You need to talk to your *dat* and work things out."

Tobias gave a bark of laughter. "Sure. It's that easy with Marvin Smucker. You've met him, right?"

Jesse sighed and scrubbed a hand down his face. There was no talking to Tobias today. Thunder rumbled in the distance and a light mist of cool rain trickled down Jesse's arms. It was time to change his goal. Instead of convincing Tobias to stop drinking, he needed to focus on getting him home.

"It's getting late. The best thing you can do is get home before you're too drunk to help with chores." He held out his hand. "Give me the bottle."

Tobias hesitated.

Jesse studied Tobias as his frustration returned. "What are you going to tell your *schweschder* when she sees a bottle of vodka in your hand?"

Tobias blew out a sigh and picked up an empty paper bag from the ground. "Let me put it in my buggy, and then we'll hitch up the horses."

"And what if your *dat* finds it?"

Tobias huffed and then handed the bottle to Jesse, who emptied it.

"I'll take care of it." Jesse took the bag and shoved the bottle into it. He'd toss it into the back of his buggy and dispose of it before he got home. Then he turned his glare back to Tobias. "What are you going to do about your breath? It's a myth that vodka produces no smell."

Tobias smirked and pulled a pack of chewing gum from his pocket. "I got it covered."

Jesse gripped the paper bag as he studied his best friend. Lately he'd noticed Tobias chewing gum frequently. Did he have a drinking problem? Thunder clapped above them and the rain became heavier. "We need to get going."

Tobias took a step and then stumbled before righting himself. He turned toward Jesse and held up his hand. "I'm fine."

"Maybe Arie should take you home."

"I'm fine," he repeated with a growl. "Let's go."

Jesse's shoulders tensed as he followed Tobias to their waiting buggies. He tossed the paper bag into the back of his buggy, and Tobias started helping him hitch up their horses. Worry surged through him. He had to get Tobias home safely. Sleep would do him some good. Jesse could tell Ariana and her parents that Tobias wasn't feeling well. Maybe Jesse could blame it on too much sun, and Marvin would be too distracted to notice the truth.

Jesse stole glances at Tobias, who only stumbled once more. Thank goodness he wasn't completely drunk. Now he had to figure out how to get him home.

Ariana joined them just as they finished hitching the buggies to the horses. With her beach bag slung over her arm, she held a beach towel over her head to shield her prayer covering from the rain. "The rain is a nice break from the heat."

"*Ya*, it is." Jesse tried to smile, but his lips refused to comply.

She tilted her head to the side. "Is everything all right?"

"*Ya.*" *No.* He pointed toward Tobias, who was leaning against his buggy. "I was thinking you might want to take Tobias home since he's not feeling well."

"He's not feeling well?" Ariana's eyes widened as she rushed over to her brother. "I was worried about you when you disappeared from the porch. *Was iss letz?*"

Tobias shot Jesse a glare before addressing his sister. "I'm fine. You can ride with Jesse." He hoisted himself into his buggy.

Jesse rubbed the back of his neck as a feeling of foreboding overtook him. He'd wanted to find a way to convince Tobias not to drive his own buggy, but Tobias's stubborn streak had won out again. He forced a pleasant expression when Ariana turned toward him.

"Ready to go?" she asked.

"*Ya.*" Jesse turned toward the porch and called to Mariella, who was standing on the porch and still talking to a few friends. He waved and thanked her before climbing into the buggy.

"It was a *gut* day," Ariana said.

He looked into her eyes and some of his worry eased. "*Ya,* it was." He guided the horse down the long driveway toward the road, and Tobias followed.

"I'm so glad our parents agreed to allow us to spend the day with our *freinden.*"

"I am too." Out of the corner of his eye, Jesse saw the reflection of Tobias's horse speeding up in his side mirror. "What is he doing?" he mumbled.

"*Was iss letz?*" Ariana turned, craning her neck to look out the back of the buggy. "Why is Tobias going so fast?"

"I'm not sure." Jesse sat up straighter and looked past Ariana as Tobias's buggy came into view beside his. "What are you doing?" he called. He peered into the mirror, checking for cars. "I thought you were going to follow me."

"Let's race!" Tobias yelled with a wicked grin.

"Are you *narrisch*?" Ariana exclaimed.

As Tobias's horse took off running, Jesse prodded his horse in an attempt to catch up to Tobias. He had to stop him before he got hurt.

"Jesse!" Ariana yelled, squeezing his bicep. "Slow down!"

Slow down? Jesse kept his focus trained on the buggy in front of him. He had to concentrate on what he was doing, not try to explain it. Even if Ariana didn't know her brother had been drinking, wasn't it obvious he couldn't let Tobias race ahead like this?

"Jesse, please!" Her voice broke.

Rain pelted the buggy's windshield as the two horses galloped down the two-lane road, Tobias's seemingly at near breakneck speed. Ariana held on to Jesse's arm, her fingers like a vise digging into his skin.

As they approached a sharp turn, Ariana's voice resembled a sob. "Please slow down. Please!"

Afraid now that he, too, was indeed going far too fast for the road conditions, Jesse slowed down, gripping the reins. Fear coursed through him as he kept his eyes on Tobias's buggy.

He's going to crash if he doesn't slow down!

Tobias's horse took the turn too fast and the buggy wobbled. And then as if in slow motion, the buggy teetered just before the driver's side slammed down onto the road. The horse reared and then struggled to drag the buggy around the corner.

Jesse's blood ran cold as the buggy scraped its way down the road with the rain pounding from the darkened sky.

This has to be a dream. No, it's a nightmare.

Like that stormy night when he and Tobias were only sixteen.

CHAPTER 3

❧

"TOBIAS!" ARIANA SHRIEKED, HER VOICE SLAMMING JESSE BACK to the present. "Tobias!"

Jesse had no choice. He snapped the reins, signaling for his horse, Rusty, to speed up again. When he caught up with Tobias's horse, he shoved the reins toward Ariana.

"What are you doing?" Her voice pitched even higher.

"Take them!" Glancing at Ariana just long enough to see her eyes widen, Jesse handed the reins to her and then leapt from the buggy, slipping and sliding on the wet pavement as he rushed toward the wreckage.

"Lester," he called to the horse, his voice trembling as adrenaline raced through him. "Whoa, *bu*. Whoa. Calm down, *bu*." He took the halter in his hands to slow him down. Leaning forward, he grabbed the cheek straps and looked Lester in the eyes. The horse was so terrified that Jesse could see the whites of his eyes.

"It's all right, Les," Jesse cooed in a soft, soothing voice. "Just calm down." He breathed in deeply through his nose to calm his surging heartbeat and catch his breath. "You're fine, *bu*."

The horse's eyes returned to normal, and Jesse blew out a sigh of relief that seemed to bubble up from his toes. He quickly unhitched the straps and led Lester to where Ariana had come to a stop. He tied him to the back of his buggy, then raced to Tobias's buggy.

Ariana climbed out. "Tobias?" she yelled, her voice sounding wobbly. "Tobias! Are you hurt?"

A muffled gasp escaped from inside the battered buggy, and Jesse's heart pounded against his rib cage as he climbed in through the back.

"Tobias!" Jesse hollered. "Are you all right?"

"*Ya.*" Tobias groaned and then snorted. "That didn't turn out the way I planned."

"Give me your hand." Jesse held his out to him. "Let me get you out."

Tobias took his hand and Jesse pulled him out through the back of the buggy.

"*Ach*, no!" Ariana touched her brother's arm as she examined his bloodied face. "You're bleeding." She pulled a tissue from the pocket of her dress and began to mop up the blood on his face.

"It's nothing." Tobias swatted at her hand and chomped his gum. "The windshield busted, but I'm fine." He rubbed his right arm. "Just a little sore. I landed hard on my arm."

Turning, Jesse studied the buggy to survey the damage. The windshield was indeed smashed, the roof had caved in, and the frame was bent. He needed help flipping it back onto its wheels, but it wouldn't ride correctly. How was he going to get this buggy home?

Suddenly aware that his hat was gone, Jesse pushed his hair back from his face as the steady rain soaked through his shirt. He looked at his buggy, wondering if his hat had flown off before or after he'd jumped out of it.

"Are you two *narrisch*?" Ariana's brow furrowed as she turned her glower from Tobias to Jesse. "Why were you racing on a rainy night? Do you realize how dangerous that is?"

Jesse held his hand up to her in defense. "I was only—"

"I can't believe how immature you both are," she snapped, interrupting Jesse as she divided a glare between the two of them once again. "You two were acting like you were sixteen again instead of twenty-four."

Tobias gave a bark of laughter before cupping his hand over his mouth. He swayed slightly on his feet and then righted himself as a smirk overtook his lips.

Jesse's shoulders tensed as resentment crawled up his spine. Had Tobias's drunken haze completely clouded his judgment? He turned to Ariana, but her eyes remained focused on Tobias. Couldn't she tell her brother was drunk? Didn't she realize Jesse was only trying to stop him?

"You think this is funny, Tobias?" Rain trailed down her face and dripped onto her dress. "You could have been badly injured or even killed." Her voice faltered, and she cleared her throat. "This could have been much worse. Lester was obviously spooked, and he could have run in front of a car or a truck."

Her lips trembled, and Jesse's chest constricted. He longed to pull her into his arms and comfort her, to make sure she understood he was only trying to save her brother. As if on cue, a bright bolt of lightning skittered across the sky, followed by a loud crack of thunder that caused Ariana to jump with a start before hugging her arms to her chest. Now was not the time. He had to take charge of the situation and get everyone home safely before the storm worsened.

"Arie," Jesse said, "go sit in my buggy. You're soaked." He reached for her arm, and she took a step back, away from his reach. He gaped at her with surprise. In the three years they'd been dating, she'd never rebuffed him.

Jesse shoved away his concern and nodded toward his buggy. "You should go home so your parents don't worry. Lester is tied to the back of my buggy, so you can guide him. Tobias and I will stay to take care of his buggy."

She glowered at him for a moment before stalking over to his buggy and climbing back into the driver's side.

Jesse checked to make sure Lester's reins were secured and then leaned through Ariana's window as rain continued to soak through the back of his shirt. She was still frowning. Sending her home alone might not be the best idea.

"Are you comfortable riding home alone?"

Her brow creased even more. "I know how to guide a horse."

Jesse winced at her biting words, but pushed on. "Tell your parents Tobias will be home soon. I'll figure out how to get the buggy home as quickly as I can." He tapped the door. "Be safe, all right?" He opened his mouth to remind her he loved her, but before he could speak, she turned, snapped the reins, and started on the trek to her house.

As Jesse watched the buggy's taillights move down the road, cold surged through his veins. But the cold wasn't from the pouring rain soaking his skin. It was from the frosty expression Ariana gave him before she left. She always told him she loved him before they parted ways. But this time she seemed as if she couldn't wait to leave him by the side of the road.

Worry drenched him far more than the rain.

"Don't cry, Jesse," Tobias drawled sardonically as he smacked Jesse's shoulder. "You'll see *mei schweschder* again soon." He swayed and then pointed to the buggy. "So, genius, how are we going to get that home now that you've sent Ariana on her way in the only functioning buggy we have?"

"That's what I'm trying to figure out," Jesse spat back and then eyed him with disgust. "How much did you drink? Did you finish off another bottle before I got there?"

Tobias's eyes narrowed. "Only one, but I don't know how much I drank since you decided to pour out the rest. Do you have any idea how expensive that vodka was?"

Jesse rubbed the back of his head as frustration overtook him once again. Could this night get any worse?

Lightning flashed, followed immediately by a loud rumble of thunder.

Jesse looked toward the road as ideas swirled through his mind. He could jog to his older brother Nathaniel's house and use his phone to call his driver and ask him to come with his pickup truck. But how would they lift the buggy into the bed of the pickup truck without a tractor? Nathaniel's farm was also nearly four miles away, and getting there would mean a grueling run in the pouring rain.

Tobias sank down onto the wet grass and crossed his long legs before pulling his pack of gum from his trouser pocket. After shoving another piece of gum into his mouth, he held the pack up, offering Jesse a piece. Jesse shook his head and gritted his teeth while resisting the urge to smack the pack of gum out of Tobias's hand. Tobias shrugged and slipped the pack into his pocket.

Headlights flashed in Jesse's eyes as a pickup truck motored toward them. It came to a stop beside them, and the driver's window lowered. Jesse held his breath, hoping the people in the vehicle would offer help instead of gawking at the soaked and stranded Amish men with the broken buggy.

"Do you two need help?" a man asked before recognition flashed in his eyes. "Is that you, Jesse Zook?"

"*Ya*." Jesse approached the truck, recognizing the driver as one of his father's customers. "Hi, Brian." He gestured toward the buggy. "My friend Tobias had an accident. His sister took the horse home, but we need help transporting the buggy. Any chance you know someone with a flatbed tow truck?"

A man sitting beside Brian leaned forward. "I have one. We'll go get it and be right back."

"Oh, thank you. I can pay you," Jesse offered.

"That's not necessary," the other man said. "We'll go get it right now. I just live up the road. I'm Todd." He reached across Brian, and Jesse shook his hand.

"Thank you so much." Jesse pushed his wet hair back from his forehead. "I appreciate it."

Brian nodded and then hesitated. "You two are soaked to the bone. Do you want to ride back to the house with us?" He pointed toward the bed of his truck. "There's no room in the cab, but you can sit back there."

"No, thanks." Jesse shook his head. "We'll be fine."

"I'll bring you a few towels," Todd offered.

"Sounds good." Jesse thanked them again, backed away from the pickup truck, and swiveled toward Tobias as their rescuers left. "Brian Walker and his friend are coming back with a flatbed."

Tobias chomped his gum. "That's *gut*." He rested his chin on a bent knee as more thunder rumbled above them.

Renewed fury burned through Jesse as Tobias sat quietly waiting for the tow truck. "Why am I the only one worried about getting your buggy home?"

Tobias shrugged. "You've got it under control. Everything will be fine."

Something inside Jesse snapped, and his temper flared. "Have you considered what your *dat* is going to say?" He gestured toward the buggy. "Don't you think your situation at home is going to be worse when he finds you drunk with a smashed buggy?"

"Don't stand there and judge me."

"Who said anything about judging you?" Jesse crossed his arms over the front of his soaked shirt and shivered as the rain continued to drip through his hair and onto his clothes. "I'm still trying to understand you. We have some time to kill, so why don't you explain how you think getting drunk at a youth gathering and then trying to get yourself home was an intelligent plan?"

"Fine." Tobias stood and took a step, swayed slightly, and then righted himself. "Let me try again. You have no idea what it's like to be me. You only know what it's like to be Jesse Zook, the perfect *sohn*."

"I'm not perfect, nor is my home life. I've let *mei dat* down plenty of times, but you don't see me getting drunk and racing buggies as a way of dealing with it. What if Arie had been in that buggy with you?" Jesse's voice rose as his body shuddered with renewed consternation. "How would you have felt if she'd been hurt?"

Tobias glared at him and then slowly shook his head before jamming his finger into Jesse's chest. "Your life is so easy. You have everything you've ever wanted, and you've never had to work for any of it. You've had everything handed to you without any effort."

"That's not true." Jesse slapped Tobias's hand away.

"*Ya*, it's true. You've known for years that you were going to marry *mei schweschder*. You didn't even have to chase after Ariana since she's always been in love with you. She's had a crush on you since she was eight. All you had to do was smile at her and pay attention to her, and you had her loyalty and her heart." He began ticking things off on his fingers. "You have a *haus* of your own, and you're only twenty-four. You have a successful business. Both of them were given to you by your *dat*. You have no idea what it's like to actually work for something."

"I work hard every day." Jesse's body tightened with growing animosity. He took a deep breath in an effort to calm himself. *Tobias doesn't mean it. His emotions are blurred from the alcohol.* "Training horses is hard work."

Tobias sneered. "And you have no idea what it's like to feel like a stranger in your own family's home."

"What are you talking about? Your parents and Arie love you. Your thoughts are hazy because of the alcohol. You have no idea what you're saying."

"Actually, I know exactly what I'm saying." Tobias's expression darkened and his eyes glistened. "All I do is mess up, and *mei dat* criticizes me nonstop."

"Have you told him how you feel?"

"*Ya*, but he doesn't understand me."

"What do you mean?"

"He thinks I should be *froh* to inherit the farm and run it, but that's not what I want." Tobias looked down at the ground and kicked a stone. "I want to work with my hands. I want to build things. Maybe even make furniture like *mei onkel* Titus, but *mei dat* won't listen to me."

"You'd rather be a carpenter?" Jesse was stunned, and then memories filled his mind. He recalled how, when they were children, Tobias used to frequently ask Marvin to take him to visit his uncle Titus's furniture store. He also remembered a time when Marvin yelled at Tobias for spending too much time in the small workshop at the back of their barn where Tobias built birdhouses. His uncle would sell them for Tobias in his store.

It never occurred to Jesse that Tobias longed to become a carpenter. "Have you ever considered suggesting that you sell the farm when your *dat* is ready to retire? Maybe then you can go to work for your *onkel*."

Tobias kicked another stone. "*Ya*, I actually did suggest that once, and he said no. He insisted the farm has to stay in the family, and since I'm the only *sohn*, I have to take it over. He told me to face the fact that I'm a dairy farmer, and I always will be." Glancing up, he gritted his teeth and pointed at his chest. "What about what *I* want? Why can't *I* decide what future I have? What if I want a life like yours, doing a job I love with the opportunity to build a *haus* of my own?"

Suddenly, empathy shoved away Jesse's fury. "You're just upset, Tobias. But everything will be okay. You can have the same things I have. You can have a future. Maybe you'll meet the right *maedel* and get married soon after Arie and I do."

Tobias snorted as a wry smirk overtook his lips. "You think I should get married? And just where would *mei fraa* and I live? In my bedroom?" His expression hardened. "How could I have a family while living under *mei dat*'s thumb?"

"You're a great guy and have a lot to offer. You should try to—"

"Don't patronize me," Tobias snarled. "You know as well as I do that I don't have anything to offer any *maedel* in this community. It's time for you to wake up and see just how easy you have it. Most of us don't have the privilege you're used to."

"Privilege?" Jesse's back stiffened with defiance and offense.

"That's a joke, right? Look, you're very drunk. You should stop talking and shut your mouth before you say something you'll regret."

"Why would I regret the truth?" His voice was barely audible over the rumble of thunder.

Jesse flinched as if Tobias had struck him. Tobias had been his best friend since they were in first grade, and Jesse had thought of him as a brother. Tobias had never shown any signs of considering Jesse privileged and lazy before. Had the alcohol inspired Tobias to speak the truth after their nearly lifelong friendship? The realization sent a pang of confusion and disappointment through him.

Jesse leaned against the buggy as Tobias sat back down on the ground with his back toward him. Jesse tried to ignore the hurt washing over him. Tobias was drunk, and any chance of reconciling their differences would have to wait until he'd sobered up.

The rattle of a diesel engine drew Jesse's attention to the road. He stood up straight and prepared himself for the struggle of loading the damaged buggy onto the flatbed.

In his heart, however, he feared the real struggle had just begun.

Ariana halted Jesse's buggy in front of the back porch. As his horse came to a stop, a *tink-tink-tink* sounded from somewhere in the back of the buggy. Leaning over the seat, her fingers brushed against a paper bag. She lifted it, opened it, and found a cool glass bottle. She read the label.

"Vodka?" *Where did this come from?* Her eyes widened. Suddenly, everything came into sharper focus—her brother and Jesse racing in the rain and Jesse blatantly ignoring her pleas to slow down.

Jesse and Tobias had been *drunk*.

Shock cemented her to the bench seat in the buggy. She'd never seen Tobias or Jesse drink alcohol. Sure, when they were teenagers they got into their fair share of scrapes—even a couple of serious ones. But that had been years ago. They were men now, and she thought they'd put that reckless behavior behind them. Jesse worked hard on his father's horse breeding and training farm and kept his promises to her. How could they both be so irresponsible? And worse, how could Jesse, the love of her life, put her in danger by drinking and then driving a buggy to take her home?

Perhaps Jesse Zook wasn't the mature, solid Christian man she'd believed he was. Maybe he was a fraud. He had forgotten about her twice today—at the lake and then again at Mariella's house. Did she really know him as well as she had believed she did? The notion stabbed at her heart.

Her hands trembled as she dropped the bottle into the back of the buggy. She yearned to ask Jesse to explain himself, but obviously she had to wait until he and Tobias brought the damaged buggy home.

For now, she had to push aside her confusion and anger and face her parents. She was already late, and soon her parents would become worried about the delay.

She quickly stowed Lester along with Jesse's horse and buggy in the barn, grateful summer temperatures had been warm enough to keep the horses from getting cold in the rain. Tobias and Jesse would groom them for the night later.

She hurried through the rain toward the back steps of the

two-story whitewashed farmhouse she'd lived in her entire life. When she reached the back door, she stopped, sniffed, and swiped her hand over her eyes, hoping to conceal both her raging emotions and the evidence that she'd cried during the ride home.

But she couldn't wipe from her mind the image of Tobias's buggy flipping onto its side. The thought of the smashed buggy sent a shudder through her and stole her breath for a moment. The terror of holding on to Jesse and begging him to slow down overtook her, and her legs wobbled.

Why would Jesse and Tobias risk their lives for alcohol? Why would Jesse risk hers?

Thunder crashed, and Ariana gripped the knob on the closed back door. She peered through the window into the mudroom, and through the open doorway to the kitchen she saw her father sitting in his usual spot at the head of the table. Her mother brought a platter of food over to him. Taking a deep breath, she prayed her eyes weren't puffy. She had to try to act as if everything was okay. If her father knew about the racing, he would be furious. She couldn't bear to witness another argument between *Dat* and Tobias.

Ariana pulled the door open, and as she stepped into the mudroom, the aroma of baked chicken wafted over her.

She kicked off her soggy shoes and pulled at her dress where it was stuck to her legs. Then she touched her prayer cover, gasping when she felt it was also soaked. She'd been so worried about Tobias that she hadn't thought to take it off before rushing from Jesse's buggy to check on him. She cringed, imagining the lecture her parents would give her for not only getting wet but for not shielding or removing her prayer covering.

"Ariana?" *Mamm* called from the kitchen. "Tobias? Is that you?"

Ariana forced her lips to curl up in a smile and then stepped into the kitchen. "I'm home. Supper smells *appeditlich*."

Mamm's pleasant expression melted into a frown as she studied Ariana. "Are you wet?"

"*Ya*." Ariana tried to laugh it off, but her laughter warbled. "I got caught in the rain." She started for the stairs. "I'm going to go change. I'll be right down for supper."

"Where's Tobias?" *Mamm* asked as Ariana hurried past her. "Is Jesse staying for supper?"

"They're on their way. They'll be here soon." Ariana reached the stairs and started up, hoping Tobias would walk in before *Mamm* could ask more questions. She couldn't bear the thought of her mother being upset over the accident.

"Wait," *Mamm* said, and Ariana stilled. "I don't understand. Why isn't Tobias with you?"

Ariana swallowed. "They're delayed."

"Delayed?" *Mamm* tilted her head to the side. "What do you mean?"

"They'll be here shortly." Spinning on her foot, she gripped the banister and started up the stairs.

"Ariana Kathryn!" *Dat's* voice boomed, and Ariana froze, gripping the banister with such force that, looking down, she saw her knuckles turn white. "Please answer your *mamm* before you run off."

Ariana slowly turned back toward the kitchen. She cleared her throat, and her mother's deep-brown eyes widened. "Tobias was in an accident, but he's fine."

Mamm blew out a puff of air, rushed over, and grabbed hold of Ariana's arms. "What happened?"

"He's fine," Ariana repeated. "He flipped the buggy, but he's okay. Jesse had me come home in his buggy. I brought Lester home too. Jesse thought he could figure out a way to get Tobias's buggy home."

"Tobias flipped the buggy?" *Dat* pushed the chair back and then stood before crossing the kitchen and coming to a stop in front of Ariana. "How did he flip the buggy?"

"Well, it was raining, and . . . and Tobias was going too fast," Ariana began, her voice small and thin. "I was in Jesse's buggy, and Tobias passed us. Jesse sped up after him, and I kept screaming for him to slow down, but he didn't. I've never been so scared before." The words tumbled out of her mouth as a tear spilled down her cheek.

"And, well, Tobias took a turn and something must have broken on the buggy because the buggy flipped onto its side. Lester kept going, dragging the buggy along until Jesse caught up to him, jumped out of his buggy, and chased him down. It was so horrible and scary. I was so afraid Tobias had been hurt."

"Why were they going too fast?" *Dat's* voice seemed to echo in the kitchen. "Both Tobias and Jesse know better than to push their horses in the rain."

Ariana opened her mouth and then closed it. While she felt obligated to tell her father about the alcohol, she didn't want to get her brother into more trouble than he would already face when *Dat* saw the condition of the buggy. Her bottom lip trembled and tears stung her eyes.

"What aren't you telling me?" *Dat* demanded. "It's obvious you're holding something back. Tell me what it is. Now."

"Marvin, please." *Mamm's* voice was quiet but firm. "Calm down. Can't you tell she's upset?" She rubbed Ariana's arm.

Dat's expression softened as he turned to *Mamm*. "I understand she's upset, but I need to know what happened." He focused on Ariana again, but his gaze was warmer. "Please tell me what happened."

"They were racing," Ariana said, her voice wobbling.

"What?" *Dat* exclaimed. "They were racing in the rain? They know from past experience how dangerous that can be."

"I begged Jesse to slow down, but he wouldn't. He just kept chasing after Tobias." Ariana sniffed as tears poured from her eyes. "I've never seen Jesse so reckless and irresponsible. It was as if he was someone else and not the Jesse I know so well." She gaped when she realized what she'd said. "But Tobias is fine, and Lester is fine," she added quickly. "Only Tobias's buggy was damaged in the crash."

Dat gritted his teeth. "When will that *bu* learn? Last week he left the gate open and four of the cows escaped. It's like his mind isn't focused on the present. His head is always in the clouds." He shoved his hands through his thinning hair. "Now he's done this. No matter how much I instruct him to get his life together, he still disobeys me." Grumbling, he stalked over to the table and sank into his chair. "I'll deal with him when he gets home. Let's eat."

Ariana sniffed, and *Mamm* pulled her into a hug. "I was so scared," she murmured into her mother's shoulder.

"It's all right," *Mamm* whispered. "You're home now and you're safe. Go get changed and we'll eat. I'm just thankful Tobias and Lester are okay." She rubbed Ariana's back. "Everything will be just fine."

"*Danki, Mamm.*" Ariana climbed the stairs to the second floor and stepped into her room. After drying off and pulling on a fresh dress, she stood by her window and looked out past the rain, toward the road.

Ariana hoped Jesse and Tobias would be back soon. Anger

simmered through her veins as the image of the vodka bottle filled her mind. When she had a moment to talk to Jesse alone, she would demand he explain why he would risk her safety for alcohol. Depending upon his answer, she'd determine if he was the man she believed would build a family with her and take care of her for the rest of her life.

CHAPTER 4

◦~∾◦

Jesse's heart pounded as he and Tobias stepped into the Smucker family's kitchen.

"Can you possibly explain why you two were racing in a storm?" Marvin demanded. "Didn't you two learn about the dangers of racing when you were sixteen and you both wound up in the emergency room? I would think your broken arm would have taught you a lesson back then, Jesse."

Driving rain pelted the kitchen windows, filling the heavy silence as Marvin speared Jesse and Tobias with harsh and furious eyes. In his early fifties, Marvin Smucker stood just under six feet and had graying dark hair and a matching beard. While his two children had inherited his dark hair, they had received their mother's dark eyes instead of Marvin's bright hazel.

"Well?" Marvin stood just inches from Jesse and Tobias. "I'm still waiting for an answer." His voice was loud as his cheeks flushed pink with anger. "You scared Rosanna and me and also Jesse's parents when you two raced in a storm all those years ago. Were you trying to scare us again? Or did you just forget how to act like adults?"

Jesse looked across the kitchen to where Ariana stood at the sink holding a pot suspended in the air. She glanced at him. She'd changed into a blue dress, and her hair was covered with a matching blue scarf. When their eyes met, her lips pressed together and a frown clouded her pretty face. Her dark eyes moved to Tobias and remained focused on him. Jesse suddenly had the distinct feeling Ariana was avoiding his gaze. Why would she ignore him? Did she really share her father's belief that he had been acting like a sixteen-year-old?

Jesse folded his arms over his chest and shivered as droplets of water dripped down his face and onto his already drenched shirt. Although he'd dried off with a towel Todd had loaned him during the short drive to Marvin's farm, Jesse had gotten soaked once again when they struggled to unload the buggy and stow it in the barn.

Beside him, Tobias leveled a hard gaze at his father, and a muscle in his jaw twitched as he cradled his right arm in his left. Jesse took in the injuries he hadn't noticed as they were working to move the buggy in the rain. Purple-and-blue bruises stained Tobias's right cheek, and a thin cut sliced from his temple to the bridge of his nose.

"Tobias!" Rosanna rushed over to them as she entered the room. She stifled a sob after she touched his cheek. "*Ach!* You're hurt."

"I'm fine," Tobias grumbled, not taking his glare off his father.

"Ariana!" Rosanna called, examining Tobias's arm. "Get the salve and a couple of towels."

Ariana scurried out of the kitchen.

"You still haven't answered my questions," Marvin boomed. "Why were you racing? What were you thinking?" He shook a finger millimeters from Tobias's nose. "What do you have to say for yourself, Tobias John?"

"Nothing," Tobias snapped, then winced as his mother moved his arm.

"Nothing?" Marvin's bushy eyebrows shot up toward his receding hairline. "Why don't you have anything to say for yourself?"

"Because I don't have to say anything," Tobias seethed. "You'll say it for me."

Jesse gaped, staring at Tobias with wonder. Jesse had never dreamt of speaking to his father in such a disrespectful tone. He braced himself, awaiting Marvin's explosion.

Marvin's chubby face flushed bright crimson, and his jaw worked, but no words passed his lips.

Ariana reappeared with two towels and a container of homemade salve. She handed one towel and the salve to her mother. While Tobias dried himself with his left hand, Rosanna began to spread salve over his wounds, causing Tobias to squeeze his eyes shut and hiss in protest.

"Stop squirming," Rosanna said. "This cut looks bad, and we don't want it to get infected. It's awfully close to your eye."

With her eyes focused on the second towel, Ariana stepped over to Jesse and handed it to him.

"Danki." He hugged the towel to his middle. He studied her face, hoping she'd look up at him, but she kept her eyes focused on his hands. "Arie?" he whispered. "Are you all right?"

Ignoring him, she quickly crossed to the sink, and, with her back to him, began washing dishes. Her coldness stung deep into his soul. He stared at her back, waiting for a sign, any sign, that their relationship was still okay, but she kept working at the sink as if she were alone in the kitchen.

"Tobias," Marvin's voice bellowed. "I'm still waiting on an explanation for your behavior. Do you realize how much worse your accident could have been?"

Tobias responded with a sarcastic snicker. "You should see the buggy."

Jesse blinked as he looked at his best friend. *Does he want to start an argument?*

"What do you mean?" Marvin looked over at Ariana and then back at Tobias. "Your *schweschder* said you could get the buggy home."

"*Ya*, on a flatbed." Tobias moved the towel over his soggy trousers. "The windshield is smashed. The roof and frame are twisted too. It's pretty far gone, right, Jesse? It's almost as bad as that accident we had when we were sixteen."

Jesse nodded with a frown. He longed to sneak out and head to his own house, but he couldn't leave without assurance that he and Ariana were okay, that their relationship was still intact.

Marvin shook his head. "I'm so tired of your irresponsible behavior. I'm also tired of your attitude."

"Well, *Dat*, that's one thing we have in common." Tobias lifted his chin. "I'm tired of your attitude toward me. I'm tired of your constant criticism and your lectures. And I'm tired of you trying to force me to be someone I'm not." He handed the towel to his mother and started toward the stairs. "I'm going to take a shower."

"Get back here!" Marvin started after him. "I'm not done with you."

Tobias spun toward his father, his eyes glittering in the low light. "I'm done with you. I have nothing else to say to you." His voice faltered, and he cleared his throat.

Jesse scanned the kitchen, taking in Rosanna's frown and glistening eyes. At the sink, Ariana's shoulders slumped as she sagged against the sink. The tension was palpable, and Jesse's chest tightened. Jesse and his brothers rarely argued with their father or with each other. If only Jesse could help Tobias and his father work out their differences. But how could he help fix this broken relationship when it seemed nearly beyond repair? Besides, this was a private family matter.

"You may be tired of it, but I'm determined to make a *gut* man out of you," Marvin continued. "How do you expect to get married and raise a family if you can't take care of yourself? You need to learn how to take responsibility for your actions. Racing buggies in the rain won't earn my praise. It's time you started acting like a man instead of an overgrown *kind*."

Tobias's expression hardened. "I'm going to live my life the way I want to, and I don't need your permission."

"Is that so?" Marvin folded his arms over his rotund middle. "As long as you live in *mei haus*, you will follow my rules and ask for my permission."

"You've made that abundantly clear. Maybe it's time that changed."

Marvin stood nose to nose with his son, the two men the same height. "I don't see you moving out anytime soon since you don't have any means to live on your own."

"Please stop arguing," Rosanna cut in, her voice sounding thick. "I've heard enough!"

Marvin spun to face her, and Tobias jogged up the stairs.

Jesse finished drying himself, folded the towel, and set it on a kitchen chair. He turned toward Rosanna as she wiped two stray tears from her chin.

"*Danki* for the towel," he told her before looking at Marvin, who was leaning against another kitchen chair. "The buggy is in the barn. You might be able to salvage some of it."

"I'm going to go check on Tobias," Rosanna muttered as she picked up the wet towel and headed up the stairs.

Jesse pulled Todd's business card from his pocket and placed it on the table. "That's the name of the tow truck driver who brought it home. He can take it to the carriage shop if you'd like." He started toward the door and then turned toward the sink, hoping Ariana would look at him.

"Wait." Marvin walked over to him. "I want a word with you too."

Jesse swallowed and cut his eyes back to Ariana. *Look at me, Arie. Give me a sign that you still love me.* When she didn't turn around, he focused on Marvin. "All right."

"I'm shocked you would take such a dangerous risk, racing with *mei dochder* in your buggy." His expression was grim. "I expected more from you. I thought you'd learned your lesson after the dangerous pranks you and Tobias pulled as teenagers."

"Wait." Jesse held his hands up. "I wasn't—"

"It's apparent to me that you haven't learned anything. You're still the same reckless young man who helped Tobias set the back pasture on fire when you decided to have a bonfire in the middle of the summer during a drought."

Jesse took a deep, shuddering breath as fury flowed through his veins. "That was a long time ago."

"*Ya*, it was a long time ago, but your behavior today has shown me you haven't changed. I've lost all trust in you, and I want you to stay away from *mei dochder*. You're not a *gut* influence for her."

Jesse stilled as Marvin's words filtered through his mind, and out of the corner of his eye, he saw Ariana freeze too.

"What . . . what are you saying?" Jesse asked Marvin slowly.

"What I'm saying is that I can't allow Ariana to marry or even date a man who can't be trusted to keep her safe."

"You're breaking my engagement to Ariana?" Jesse's body went cold with a mixture of frustration, shock, and grief.

"*Ya*, that's right."

The floor seemed to fall out beneath Jesse, and the world spun. *I can't lose her.* "But we-we've set the date," he stammered. "We have plans, and I've already built her a *haus*." He turned toward Ariana, hoping she'd defend Jesse and their future plans.

Ariana looked at Jesse, then Marvin, her brown eyes wide. *"Dat?"* Her voice trembled, and her eyes misted over. "You're forbidding me from marrying Jesse?"

Marvin nodded. "That's right. He's not *gut* for you. He's shown his true colors, and I need to keep you away from him. It's for the best. You'll thank me someday."

Tears streamed down Ariana's face. "I don't think that's your decision."

"*Ya*, it is." Marvin's voice rose, and Ariana cringed. "I'm your *dat*, and it's my job to decide what's best for you." He turned toward Jesse again. "I think it would be best if you left now."

"Please listen to me," Jesse began, holding his hands up again. "I'm sorry for giving you the wrong impression. I was only trying to—"

"You need to leave." Marvin pointed toward the door. "We've had enough stress in this *haus* tonight."

Jesse's body shook and his heart squeezed with anguish as he looked at Ariana. He craved her reassurance. *Tell me you love me.*

Ariana's chest heaved as tears poured down her face. She met his eyes but remained silent.

"Jesse." Marvin's voice began with a hint of warning. "Leave now."

Jesse looked at Ariana one last time and started out.

~⊙~

Ariana swallowed a sob as Jesse disappeared into the mudroom. When the back door slammed shut, her body trembled and fear gripped her. Her future was crumbling right before her eyes. She couldn't lose him! She was upset with him, but she had to believe there was still a chance they could work things out.

She wasn't ready to give up on him yet. They could work through their problems, if only he would confess he'd been drinking—though she wasn't convinced now that he'd actually been as drunk as Tobias no doubt had been. And if he promised never to drink again and explained why he hadn't slowed down when she pleaded for him to . . .

"Jesse!" Ariana screamed, rushing toward the door.

"Ariana! Get back here," *Dat* snapped, following her.

Ariana hurried through the mudroom and pushed open the back door. Her shoes skidded on the porch floor as she slid toward the railing. A cool mist of rain drifted over her as she leaned on the railing.

"Jesse! Wait!" she screamed as he neared the barn. "Please don't go!"

Jesse spun to face her, his handsome face twisted in a scowl. Her heart squeezed, and tears pricked her eyes.

"Arie, you have to believe I would never do anything to

deliberately put you in danger. I was only trying to stop Tobias from racing." He glanced behind her and then took a step back. "I better go. Your *dat* told me to leave."

"Stay!" she begged him. "We'll talk to him and work this out."

"There's nothing to work out," *Dat* growled behind her. "Go back in the *haus* now."

She looked over her shoulder at her father's glare. "But *Dat*, we're engaged, and I—"

"You don't know what's *gut* for you." *Dat* pointed toward the house. "Please go inside now."

Ariana longed to stand up to her father, but she knew better than to go against him. With her shoulders sagging, she turned toward Jesse one last time before rushing into the house with tears spilling down her cheeks. If only she could go back in time and convince Tobias and Jesse not to drink.

Sniffing, she wiped away her tears and returned to the sink. *Mamm* appeared beside her and began drying the dishes in the rack.

"I tried to encourage Tobias to come down and eat something," *Mamm* said. "He refused. If only Tobias and your *dat* could see just how much alike they are. They're both so very stubborn. Their relationship would be so much easier if they could have a civil and calm conversation. They both need to learn to keep their tempers in check."

Ariana nodded while keeping her eyes trained on the frothy water.

Mamm stopped drying the dish in her hand and leaned toward her. "*Was iss letz?*"

Ariana raised her eyes to *Mamm* as a knot of despair swelled in her throat. "*Dat* said I can't see Jesse anymore. The wedding is canceled. He says Jesse isn't *gut* for me because he was reckless today." She cleared her throat. "I'm upset with Jesse, but I didn't want to break things off." More tears spilled down her hot cheeks.

"*Ach, mei liewe.*" *Mamm* pulled her into her arms for a hug. "Everything will be fine. I'll talk to your *dat*." She stepped back and touched Ariana's shoulder. "Don't worry about anything." She nodded toward the stairs. "I'll finish the dishes. Why don't you try to get Tobias to agree to eat something? He seems to listen to you better than anyone else in this *haus*. I'll talk to your *dat*. Don't give up hope."

Ariana agreed and headed upstairs. She found her brother lying on his bed, staring up at the ceiling. She lingered in the doorway for a moment, waiting for him to acknowledge her. When he didn't, she stepped inside the room and stood at the foot of his bed. "Don't you want something to eat?"

He lowered his eyes to her and blinked. "No, *danki*."

"You should eat something. Lunch was hours ago. I'll bring a plate up to you if you'd like."

"*Danki*, but I've lost my appetite after arguing with *Dat*." Tobias sat up and sighed, resting his elbows on his thighs. "I've had it. I can't take it anymore. I think it's time for me to leave."

"Leave?" Ariana's eyes widened and her stomach twisted. "Where will you go?"

"I haven't figured that out yet." He stood, crossed the room, and took a black duffel bag from his closet. "Nothing is ever going to change around here, so I need to find somewhere else to live." He set the opened bag on his bed and began pulling clothes out of his dresser drawers and tossing them in.

"Things could change if you and *Dat* both compromised," she hedged, hoping Tobias wouldn't get upset with her.

"What do you mean?" He stopped packing and studied her.

"What if you tried just a little harder to please *Dat*?" She fingered the wooden post of his footboard. "He gets frustrated when you don't finish your chores on time or when you wander off into the back pasture when you're supposed to be cleaning the dairy barn. If you just did as *Dat* asked, then he wouldn't get so upset." She held her breath and silently prayed he'd consider her suggestions.

Tobias paused, and then his frown deepened. "It won't work. All *Dat* and I do is fight, so it's better if I leave."

"Don't say that. *Mamm* and *Dat* love you. We're a family and we belong together."

Tobias shook his head as he continued to fill his bag.

An image of the vodka bottle filled Ariana's mind. Jesse and Tobias had been behind Mariella's barn together. She had to know the whole truth before it drove her crazy. She took a deep breath. "You've been drinking."

"What?" His eyes flickered with something that looked like worry, and then his frown returned. "Why would you think that?"

She looked over her shoulder toward the doorway and then leaned in closer to Tobias. "I found an empty bottle of vodka in the back of Jesse's buggy," she whispered.

Avoiding her eyes, he returned to packing. "Look, I'm fine. I'm not drunk. I'm just tired of dealing with *Dat*."

"Please stop packing." Alarm coursed through her. She grabbed his arm, holding it still. "You can't go. You have to stay. You're *mei bruder*. I need you here. *Mamm* and *Dat* need you too." She released his arm and sank down onto the bed.

"It's not that simple for me."

"What do you mean?"

"You're the *dochder*. You're engaged, and your life is planned for you. I'm expected to take over the farm someday when *Mamm* and *Dat* move into a *daadihaus*. I don't want to be a dairy farmer, but *Dat* won't listen. He doesn't understand that this is his dream, not mine. How can I live here the rest of my life with *Dat* always chastising me? It will never work."

"You and *Dat* can work things out if you swallow your pride and talk to him. You're both stubborn and set in your ways, but you can compromise if you really try to talk to him without losing your temper. Swallow your pride and listen to *Dat* without immediately jumping to conclusions." She folded her hands together, pleading with him. "Please think about it. Work things out with him for *Mamm* and me."

"You've had to listen to *Dat* and me argue nearly your whole life, and *Mamm* has had to listen to us too." His eyes misted over. "If I leave, things will be easier on both of you." He turned toward the dresser for the remainder of his belongings.

She sniffed. "I've already lost Jesse. I can't lose you too."

"What do you mean?" He turned toward her.

"*Dat* told Jesse to stay away from me. Our wedding is off." She swiped at her eyes. "He said Jesse was too reckless today, and he can't trust him with me."

Moving the bag, Tobias sank down onto the bed beside her. "That's my fault. If I hadn't wrecked the buggy this never would have happened." He sighed. "Things will get better for you. *Dat* will forgive Jesse."

"You think so?"

"Definitely. Jesse has his life together. He and his *dat* run a successful business. Just give *Dat* time to calm down, and your wedding will go on as planned."

"I hope you're right."

"You know I am. You and Jesse are meant to be together."

"Just like you're meant to be here. If we do get married, I want you to be here to witness it." Ariana's lip trembled as she looked up at him. "Promise me you won't make any decisions until tomorrow. Just sleep on it tonight and then decide in the morning."

He nodded. "Fine."

"*Danki.*" She stood and crossed the room. Stopping in the doorway, she looked at him again. "I can still get you a plate."

"I'm not hungry, but *danki.*"

As Ariana made her way downstairs, she whispered an urgent prayer asking God to help Tobias and *Dat*—and Jesse too—work out their problems. The three most important men in her life needed help she couldn't give them on her own.

CHAPTER 5

"Tobias!" Ariana hurried up the stairs the following morning, her pulse pounding with every step.

"Tobias!" she called again, knocking on his bedroom door. "You overslept. *Dat* is really upset since this is the second time this week. He's waiting for you in the barn. You'd better get downstairs right now before he starts yelling." She leaned her ear against the door and listened for any movement. "Are you in there?"

She knocked once more and then pushed open the door. The room was empty. Tobias's green window shades were closed, and his bed was neatly made. Maybe he was in the bathroom?

She marched down the hallway to the small bathroom they shared and found it also empty. Her stomach pitched as their conversation the night before echoed through her mind. Surely he hadn't left as he'd threatened. He was only angry, and a good night's sleep should have changed his mind and brought his raging emotions into clear focus.

Ariana entered Tobias's room once again and searched for signs he hadn't left in the middle of the night. But when she checked his dresser, his wallet was gone. Her shoulders tensed with worry. She looked in his closet, and the black duffel bag was also gone. When she opened every dresser drawer and found them empty, threatening tears pricked her eyes.

"No, no," she whispered. "Why didn't you wait another day, Tobias?"

Ariana returned to the kitchen, where *Mamm* stood at the stove making home fries. She took a deep breath as *Mamm* looked at her. "Tobias is gone."

"Gone?" *Mamm* tilted her head. "What do you mean?"

"Last night he told me he was going to leave home. I asked him to sleep on it, but all his clothes are gone. His duffel bag and wallet are gone too."

"Leave? I don't understand."

"He said he was tired of arguing with *Dat*." Ariana explained more as *Mamm* gaped, her dark eyes glistening with tears. "He did it. He left."

"Who left?" *Dat's* voice startled Ariana.

"Tobias did." *Mamm's* voice was thin and reedy. "He told Ariana last night he was going to leave home. That was after you told him he had no way to live on his own."

Dat looked to Ariana as if she held all the answers. "That doesn't make sense. Where would he even go?"

Ariana repeated her conversation with Tobias as *Dat* stared at her. "I tried to convince him to stay, but I guess he snuck out while we were asleep."

Dat's face reddened. "This is all Jesse's fault. He's a bad influence. Maybe he even encouraged Tobias to leave home. And if he hadn't been racing with Tobias this never would've happened. Tobias wouldn't have crashed the buggy, and he'd be out in the barn helping me with the cows. You'd better stay away from Jesse. I mean it, Ariana. He's irresponsible and nothing but trouble."

Ariana blinked as more tears filled her eyes. She recalled what Jesse said before he left last night, that he had only been trying to stop Tobias from going so fast. But why hadn't Jesse done a better job before they left Mariella's house? Jesse could have prevented all this. Not only didn't he keep Tobias from drinking, but most likely he polished off that bottle of vodka she'd found in his buggy himself.

As *Dat* marched outside, Ariana pushed back her shoulders. She had to be strong. She had to find a way to go on without Jesse and Tobias, but it seemed an impossible task.

Then again, maybe *Dat* was right. Maybe she *was* better off without Jesse. But if that was true, why did the thought of losing him rock her to her very core?

⟲⟳

Jesse tied his horse to the fence outside the Smuckers' dairy barn and started up the rock pathway toward the structure's large doors. He'd finished all his chores at home and then rushed over to see Marvin, hoping to convince him to revoke his cancelation of his and Ariana's engagement. He also hoped to explain to Marvin that he wasn't responsible for Tobias's accident.

He reached the barn doors and swallowed a yawn. He'd spent all night thinking of Ariana and trying to come up with a plan to win back Marvin's favor. He couldn't let Ariana go. She was the love of his life, and he couldn't wait to marry her. There had to be a way to make Marvin see he'd do everything in his power to protect Ariana and that he'd never deliberately risk her safety.

When he realized he and Ariana were truly going too fast for the road conditions yesterday, at the risk—and reality—of not being able to stop Tobias from crashing, he'd slowed down. Only when Tobias's buggy turned over had he sped up again, desperate to stop Lester before Tobias could be hurt anymore than he already was.

After taking a deep breath, he stepped into the barn, and the scent of animals drifted over him.

"Marvin?" He scanned the large dairy barn, searching for Marvin. "Are you in here?"

Marvin emerged from the back corner, a glower twisting his face as he approached Jesse. "What are you doing here after I told you to stay away?"

Jesse held up his hands in an attempt to calm the older man. "I just want to talk. You were upset last night and I—"

"And I'm even more upset today." He lifted his hat and pushed his hand through his sweaty, dark hair. "Where's Tobias?"

"What?" Jesse asked, dumbfounded by the question.

"Is he staying with you?"

"No, he's not with me. He's not here?"

"No, he was gone when we got up this morning. All his belongings too. I want to know where he went." Marvin's voice was harsh. "Rosanna spent the morning calling all the relatives and *freinden* we thought he may have reached out to, but no one has seen him or heard from him. I'm sure you know something."

"I don't know anything at all. I'm just as surprised as you are." Jesse recalled his last conversation with Tobias. "He was upset yesterday. I tried to talk to him, but he was too distraught to listen to me." *And he was also too drunk.*

Jesse opened his mouth to tell Marvin his son had been drinking, but the anger he saw on Marvin's face prevented him from sharing the truth. Learning Tobias was drunk would push Marvin over the edge, and right now Jesse needed him to calm down. He needed Marvin's forgiveness and blessing, not his fury. Besides, telling him about the alcohol now ran the risk of sounding like a lie meant to move the blame from him to Tobias.

"Look, I'm sorry about what happened yesterday." Jesse fought to keep his voice calm despite his galloping pulse. "I know I made some bad decisions when I was younger, but I would never deliberately do anything that would hurt Arie or put her in jeopardy. I came here to ask for your forgiveness for going too fast yesterday, even though—"

"I forgive you, but the wedding is still off. You're not to see my Ariana anymore."

"What?" Marvin's word punched Jesse in the gut. Why was he being so unreasonable? "If you forgive me, then why can't we move past this?"

"I am moving past it. I have work to do. I'm sure you have chores to do at your farm too. So you should get home." Marvin turned and started walking away.

"Marvin!" Jesse called after him, his voice shaky. "You've known me nearly my whole life, and you know how much Ariana means to me. Why are you treating me like this?"

Marvin spun, lancing him with a hard glare. "If it weren't for you, *mei sohn* would be here, and his buggy wouldn't be in shambles."

Jesse blew out a tremulous rush of air as Marvin disappeared into the back of the large barn. Anguish and despair swamped him. His world was crumbing around him. In less than twenty-four hours, he'd lost his fiancée and his best friend. How had this happened? And, more importantly, how could he fix it?

"Jesse?"

Craning his neck to look over his shoulder, Jesse's body relaxed when he took in the sight of Ariana staring at him. Despite her deep frown, she looked radiant clad in a rose-colored dress with her hair covered by a matching scarf.

"Hi." A weight lifted off his shoulders as he drank in the sight of her gorgeous face. "I didn't hear you walk into the barn."

"What are you doing here?"

When her frown didn't soften, his shoulders stiffened with apprehension. "I came to try to talk to your *dat* and to hopefully see you. I couldn't sleep after the way things were left last night. I worried about you and our relationship all night long."

"You should go." She fingered her black apron and her eyes glistened.

"Was iss letz?" He closed the distance between them and reached for her hand, but she backed away before he could touch her.

"Tobias is gone." Her voice was watery. "He left sometime last night, and he didn't leave us a note. We have no idea where he is."

"I know." Jesse sighed. "Your *dat* told me."

"Do you know where he is?"

"No, I don't. Your *dat* asked me the same thing. How could I possibly know where he is?"

"He told me last night he was thinking of leaving, and I begged him to sleep on it. I told him not to make any decisions before morning, but he left anyway." She studied him. "If he was already thinking about leaving before he got home last night, then he could have told you where he was going. You also talked with him for quite a while at the lake yesterday." She lifted her chin, defiance on her face. "You're his best *freind*. Why wouldn't he tell you he was leaving? I would tell Mariella if I were thinking of making a big decision like that. Why didn't you stop him?"

"He didn't say anything to me about leaving. He only talked about how your *dat* treats him." Jesse pinched the bridge of his nose, trying in vain to calm his frayed nerves. "If I had known Tobias was thinking about leaving, I would've tried to talk him out of it."

He studied her eyes. "Where is this hostility coming from? You know me. You know how much I care about you and your family."

She shook her head. "Actually, I don't think I know you at all."

"What does that mean?"

She looked past him as if checking to see if Marvin was there and then lowered her voice. "I found the vodka bottle in the back of your buggy. You were drinking yesterday. The Jesse I knew would never drink. You're not the person I thought you were."

"Wait a minute." He held his hands up. "That wasn't my bottle. I was just disposing of it."

She crossed her arms over her apron. "Do you think I'm that naïve?"

"I'm telling you the truth. It wasn't mine. It was Tobias's." He explained his conversation with Tobias when he found him behind the barn. "I had to wrestle the bottle away from him. I poured the remaining vodka out and then told Tobias I would dispose of the bottle for him. I was going to throw it out before I got home."

"I don't believe you. I don't think you would have risked my safety if you hadn't been drinking."

"Why would I lie to you? I told you. I was only trying to stop

Tobias. *Ya*, I was driving fast, and I know you were scared. But as soon as I realized we could be in danger, I slowed down."

"It doesn't matter. *Mei dat* has forbidden me from seeing you." She pointed toward the barn door. "You should go before he catches us talking."

Confusion and hurt flooded him. "Don't you still love me?"

She stared down at the toe of her black shoe.

"We can work this out." He placed his finger under her chin and angled her face so she was forced to look him in the eye. "I won't give up until you believe me and your *dat* allows us to get married."

"I can't see you anymore." Her voice broke.

"It will be okay," he said, his heart breaking as a tear trickled down her chin. "I promise you I'll make this right."

"You can't." She wiped the tear away and then took a step back, away from his touch. "It's over between us."

"Why are you giving up so easily? I know you'll soon realize I'm telling the truth, and I just told you I'll talk to your *dat*."

"If you truly cared about me," she began, tears flowing down her cheeks, "then you never would have been drinking, and you would have stopped *mei bruder* from leaving my family."

Turning, she ran out of the barn. He rushed after her, calling her name, but she kept going until she was inside the house.

Jesse stood beside his buggy and swiped his hand down his face. Somehow he'd managed to make the situation worse. Now he was at a loss as to how to repair his relationship with Ariana and restore their engagement.

As he stared at her house, guilt and regret coiled through him. He should have stopped Tobias from driving last night, but how could he have prevented him from climbing into his buggy?

Perhaps if he'd told Ariana her brother was drunk then, she could have convinced Tobias to let her guide the horse home, and none of this would have happened.

But he still didn't understand why Marvin was so determined to blame him for everything that had happened.

Squinting, he looked up at the blue summer sky. He needed guidance. He needed help getting Ariana back and convincing her father he was worthy of her hand.

As he climbed into his buggy, Jesse sent a silent prayer up to God, begging Him for guidance.

∿

"You broke up with Jesse and Tobias is gone?" Mariella's eyes widened as she sat on the bench beside Ariana at church.

"*Ya,*" Ariana whispered in response. Despite crying herself to sleep last night, she managed to tell Mariella the entire story without shedding a tear. She left out the part about the empty vodka bottle since she still had a difficult time accepting that Jesse had been drinking and then lied to her.

"*Ach, mei liewe.* Are you all right?"

Ariana shrugged, hoping to give the appearance everything was okay, even though she felt as if her heart had been trampled by a team of horses. "I'll be all right eventually." No, she'd never be all right without Jesse and Tobias in her life.

"Where is Tobias now?"

"We don't know." Ariana moved closer and lowered her voice. "I keep hoping he'll contact us to at least let us know he's okay. *Mei mamm* is distraught. She can't handle not knowing where he is. We've called all our relatives, and no one has heard from him."

"I'm so sorry." Mariella sniffed, and her brown eyes sparkled in the low light of the Fisher family's barn where the church service was being held today. "I hope he contacts your family soon." She looked over toward the unmarried men and her eyes widened. "Jesse is staring at you."

"Don't look at him," Ariana warned through gritted teeth as her cheeks heated. "I've been trying to ignore him."

Mariella raised an eyebrow. "You've loved him your whole life. How can you ignore him?"

"I don't know." Ariana sighed. "You're right. It will take some time for me to mend my broken heart."

Against her better judgment, Ariana sneaked a glance toward the section where Jesse sat, and her eyes locked with his. Her breath paused, and her pulse thrummed as he studied her. His handsome face contorted with a frown, and she longed to rush over and hug him. But she couldn't. Not only would the behavior be inappropriate, but her father had made it clear she was to steer clear of him. Also, she was still angry with him for drinking and then putting her at risk during their trek home on Friday. Tobias was to blame too, but . . .

As much as her heart ached for Jesse, she had to somehow put him out of her mind. She was better off without him. He was too irresponsible.

But how could she forget Jesse when she loved him so much?

Jesse leaned his shoulder against the corner of the Fishers' barn. He'd tried in vain not to stare at Ariana during the three-hour service, but his gaze gravitated to her as if pulled by an invisible magnet. She'd looked at him only once and then kept her eyes focused on the hymnal or on her lap, staring at her emerald-green dress. He yearned to talk to her and find out how she could turn off her feelings for him after all their years as friends, then dating.

Last night he'd stayed awake for the second night in a row, racking his mind for an idea of how to get her alone to talk to her. During the service he decided standing outside the barn and watching for her to walk by with a serving tray during the noon meal seemed to be the best solution. Now he just had to patiently wait for her to appear.

When Ariana and Mariella headed from the barn toward the Fishers' house, his stomach clenched. This was his chance.

"Arie!" he called. She stilled for a brief moment before continuing toward the house. "Ariana Kathryn Smucker!"

Ariana stopped and turned toward him. When her eyes focused on him, she hesitated. Mariella gave him a tentative nod. Then she took Ariana's tray from her and whispered something before nudging Ariana forward. Ariana paused and then looked toward the barn before hurrying toward him.

"*Danki*, Mariella," he whispered as his shoulders relaxed slightly.

"What do you want, Jesse?" Ariana hissed as she motioned for him to follow her around to the back of the barn. "I've told you I can't see you. If *mei dat* sees us together, he will explode."

"I know, but I can't stand the silence between us. It's killing me."

Ariana clasped her hands together, and something in her eyes softened. Was he getting through to her? His pulse leapt with hope.

"I shouldn't be talking to you."

"How are you?" he asked, ignoring her warning. He stood so close to her that he could smell the familiar aroma of her favorite vanilla lotion. He bit back the urge to caress her soft cheek.

"It's been horrible. I tiptoed downstairs last night to get a glass of water, and I heard *mei mamm* crying in her bedroom. She misses Tobias so much, and we haven't heard from him. *Mei dat* has been quiet and I can tell he's *bedauerlich*. Tobias told me it would make things better for *Mamm* and me if he left, but he's only made everything worse." She paused and sniffed. "And I miss him too."

"Do you miss me?" Jesse held his breath with anticipation. *Please say yes!*

"I have to go."

Before he could stop her, Ariana rushed back around the side of the barn and hurried toward the Fishers' back door. Jesse kicked a rock and leaned against the side of the barn as disappointment and affliction crawled up his back and stung his eyes.

"Jesse?"

Nathaniel, his older brother, approached him. At twenty-nine, Nathaniel stood slightly taller than Jesse at six feet even. He had light-brown hair, a matching beard, and the same blue eyes Jesse had inherited from their mother.

Nathaniel raised an eyebrow. "Why are you hiding out here?"

"I was trying to talk to Arie."

"Trying to talk to her?" Nathaniel leaned his back against the barn wall and folded his arms over his wide chest. "Are you two arguing?"

"I wish it were that simple. We've broken up. Marvin won't let me see her."

"What?" His brother stood up straight, his eyes wide. "What happened?"

Jesse summarized what had happened between him and Ariana during the past forty-eight hours, leaving out the part about Tobias's drunkenness. Nathaniel listened with interest, his eyes remaining wide.

"I don't know how to get her back," Jesse said after sharing the story. "I can't figure out how to convince Marvin I'm not a bad influence for her either."

Nathaniel shrugged. "That's easy."

"Easy?" Jesse ground out the question. "Now is not the time for jokes."

"I'm not joking." Nathaniel leaned forward, jamming a finger in Jesse's chest. "If you really want to marry her, then you need to find a way to prove to Ariana and Marvin that you will do *anything* to get her back. Show them how much you love her and how committed you are to her."

Jesse blinked as his older brother's words soaked through him.

Nathaniel patted Jesse's shoulder. "Come on. Let's go have a piece of pie."

As Nathaniel started toward the barn door, Jesse looked up at the sky, again asking God for the help he so desperately needed. *Show me, God. Show me how to prove my love for Ariana.*

CHAPTER 6

❧

"How many times do I have to tell you to stay away?" Marvin growled as Jesse entered the stable Monday afternoon.

"I'm not leaving," Jesse countered, standing a little taller as a surge of confidence flowed through him. "I'm here to help with chores."

"I don't need your help."

"*Ya*, you do. Tobias isn't here, so I'll take his place." Jesse pulled on his work gloves, grabbed a pitchfork from the corner of the stable, and started toward the horse stalls.

"Don't you have chores to do at your *dat*'s farm?" Marvin followed him.

"I finished all my chores this morning. Caleb is helping this afternoon," Jesse said, referring to his nineteen-year-old brother. "Caleb said he was *froh* to do a little extra so I could help you." He rolled the sleeves on his short-sleeved tan shirt up to his shoulders. "When I'm done with the stalls, you can tell me what else you need done."

Marvin eyed him as red stained his cheeks. Just like the night he argued with Tobias, his jaw worked, but no words escaped his mouth.

Jesse clamped his own mouth shut to discourage the grin threatening his lips. In all the years he'd known the Smucker family, this was only the second time he'd ever seen Marvin speechless.

"Fine! But only for today," Marvin finally blurted before stalking toward the stable door.

Sweat beaded on Jesse's forehead and trickled between his shoulder blades as he worked. It was another brutally hot June day, but he could take the heat. As he continued to muck the first stall, his thoughts spun. After his strained conversation with Ariana yesterday, Jesse had spent the remainder of the afternoon thinking about the Smucker family and all they were facing after Tobias's departure.

Jesse's chest had squeezed as he recalled the worry and sadness in Ariana's eyes while she talked about how Tobias's disappearance was tearing her parents apart. He loved Ariana, but he also cared deeply for her family. Jesse longed to console both Ariana and her parents. He yearned to find a way to help them.

And then an idea hit him like a bolt of lightning streaking across the night sky. Marvin depended heavily on Tobias since Tobias was his only son, and he needed help with chores now that Tobias was gone. This morning, Jesse briefly explained to his parents that Tobias had left and that he would like to make time to help Marvin. Naturally, his parents were supportive, and Caleb agreed to do extra chores to allow Jesse the time away from the horse farm. He was grateful for his family's understanding and support of the Smucker family.

Tobias's alcohol-induced words had echoed through his mind last night and came to him once again while he worked in the stable.

"Your life is so easy. You have everything you've ever wanted, and

you've never had to work for any of it. You've had everything handed to you without any effort . . . You've known for years that you were going to marry mei schweschder. *You didn't even have to chase after Ariana since she's always been in love with you. She's had a crush on you since she was eight. All you had to do was smile at her and pay attention to her and you had her loyalty and her heart."*

Jesse was going to prove Tobias wrong, and he was ready to work hard to show Ariana how much she meant to him. He prayed it would work, because his life was empty without her. He was determined to convince Marvin how much his family meant to him. Jesse wouldn't give up easily on winning back both Marvin's favor and Ariana's heart.

"Dat!" Ariana called as she stepped into the stable. "I made fresh lemonade. Would you like some?"

Her shoes crunched on the hay as she approached the first stall. *Dat* had been in a bad mood all morning, complaining about all the chores he had to do and grumbling about how thoughtless and irresponsible Tobias had been to leave.

When *Dat* announced he was going to the stable to muck the stalls, Ariana tried to think of a way to brighten his mood. Since he always liked her homemade lemonade, she whipped up a batch and then carried a glass out to the stable with the hope of seeing her father smile. It would be the first time since Tobias left them.

"Dat?" She balanced the sweating glass of lemonade and ice in her hand. When she rounded the corner to face the first stall, she blew out a sharp breath. Jesse was there, grinning at her.

"Jesse? Wha-what are you doing here?" she stammered.

His grin widened. "Did you bring that for me?"

Jesse yanked off his work gloves and stuffed them into his pockets before swiping the back of his hand over his glistening brow. Then he lifted his straw hat and raked his fingers through his hair before setting the hat back onto his head. Ariana took in his tall, muscular frame as he leaned the pitchfork against the stall wall, and her words were trapped in her throat. He somehow seemed more handsome than usual. His face was tanned after their day spent at the lake, and his eyes somehow seemed a deeper shade of blue. The sleeves of his shirt were rolled up, revealing his muscular biceps.

When he lifted his eyebrows in question, she realized he was awaiting her response. What had he asked her? *Oh, right. The lemonade.*

"Oh, this?" She cleared her throat as her cheeks flamed. "I was looking for *mei dat*. I thought he might like some lemonade."

"He's not here, but I'll be *froh* to take it off your hands. It's hot in here, and lemonade sounds refreshing."

When she hesitated, the corners of his mouth tipped up. She held out the glass to him, and when he took it, their fingers brushed, sending sparks of electricity skittering up her arm. She sucked in a breath, and her eyes widened as she looked up at him. *Did Jesse feel that too?*

He seemed unaffected as he took a long draw of lemonade and then wiped the back of his hand over his mouth. "You make the best lemonade."

"*Danki*," she said as he took another long draw from the glass. "You didn't answer my question. Why are you here?"

"I'm helping with chores."

"Why?"

"Because your *dat* needs the help." He shrugged and took another long drink, polishing off the last of the lemonade.

"Does he know you're here?" She held out her hand, and he returned the empty glass.

Jesse gave her a breathtaking smile, and her knees wobbled at the sight of it. "*Ya*, of course he knows. He was just as shocked as you were to see me, but I convinced him he needed my help since Tobias is gone."

"Oh." She blinked as his words filtered through her mind. Jesse was here to assist *Dat* because her brother was gone. Jesse wanted to help her family. Something warm unfurled in her chest. Despite what had happened, Jesse was still the thoughtful, kind man she'd always adored. Maybe he hadn't lied about the vodka bottle?

But if he hadn't been drinking, then why was the bottle stowed in his buggy? Was it really there so he could get rid of it for Tobias?

She suddenly recalled her father's warning to stay away from Jesse. *Dat*'s mood might darken even more if he found her talking to Jesse. Panic seized her as she peered over her shoulder toward the stable door, in search of her father.

"Arie . . ." Jesse began, his voice sounding thin.

His voice pulled her attention back to him. She stared up at his attractive face, twisted with a deep frown.

"I need to talk to you," he continued. "You've been my best *freind* since we were teenagers. I can't just walk away from you and pretend like I don't feel something for you." The pain in his eyes nearly broke her in two.

She longed to forgive him, but she still had questions. "If you feel something for me, then why did you drink the alcohol?"

"I didn't drink it." His brow furrowed. "Did you see me stumble? Did I slur my words?"

"No."

"Would I have been able to leap from the buggy and stop Lester if I had been drunk?"

She sighed, the fight draining out of her. "No, you wouldn't have."

"I didn't touch a drop of that vodka. I wrestled the bottle from Tobias and poured the rest of it out. It was only in my buggy so I could throw it away. I didn't tell you because I believed I was protecting Tobias, but that was a bad decision. I should have told you the truth, and I'm sorry. I was just so worried about getting you and Tobias home safely."

She let his words marinate in her mind, then asked, "If you worried about getting us home safely, then why didn't you stop Tobias from driving?"

Jesse leaned back against the stall, bending one knee and resting his boot on the wall. "I didn't know how to stop him."

"Why didn't you try?" She took a step closer to him.

"I did try, but Tobias didn't seem like he was really drunk, and when he got into his buggy, what could I do? Then when he started racing, I yelled at him to stop, and I tried to catch up to him, but he wouldn't slow down."

Her eyes widened as the details of Friday afternoon clicked into place in her mind. "Tobias was acting strangely. I saw him stumble, and everything was funny to him. He was drunk, but you weren't."

"Exactly." He stood up straight. "He was slurring his words, and he was chewing gum."

"What does gum have to do with it?"

"He chewed gum to cover the smell of the alcohol on his breath."

She cupped her hand to her mouth. How could she have been so blind? Hot tears prickled at her eyelids. "And he's been chewing gum frequently lately. Does that mean he's been drinking a lot?"

"It might." Jesse took the glass out of her hand, set it on the ground, and placed his hands on her arms. "Please hear me. I never meant to put you in jeopardy. I would never, ever deliberately do anything that would hurt you. You know that, right?"

"*Ya*," she whispered, her voice trembling as tears escaped her eyes and trickled down her hot cheeks. "I'm sorry for not believing you."

"It's okay. It was a stressful situation. *Ich liebe dich.*" His eyes seemed to search hers. "Do you still love me?"

"Of course I do." She choked out the words and then cleared her throat. "But *mei dat* has made it clear he wants me to stay away from you. As much as it hurts me to do that, you know I can't go against his rules." She stepped out of his grasp and picked up the glass. "I need to go before *mei dat* finds us together." She backed away. "*Danki* for helping him."

Before he could respond, she rushed off toward the house, her heart beating wildly.

"I've told you repeatedly I don't need your help, so why do you keep coming back here every afternoon?"

Jesse set down the hammer he was using to repair the back porch steps. Then he tented his hand over his eyes as he looked up at Marvin, who gazed down at him with his arms crossed over his portly middle.

"You don't need my help, huh?" He wiped his forearm over his sweaty forehead and then stood. "Let's see. On Monday I mucked the stalls and then cleaned the milkers. Tuesday I helped you harvest the hay by running the baler and then helping you store the bales in the loft. Wednesday I cleaned out the dairy barn before mucking the stalls again, and yesterday I repaired the fencing around the chicken coop."

Jesse pointed down at the steps. "Today I'm going to finish repairing the porch and then fix the pasture fence before mucking the stalls again." He rested his hands on his hips. "So, don't you actually *need* my help?"

Marvin shook his head. "You're wasting your time if you think all your hard work is going to change my mind about your relationship with Ariana. You're still not going to marry her."

Marvin's words hit Jesse like a smack across the face, knocking away his smile and replacing it with a frown. Jesse squared his shoulders and lifted his chin. Despite Marvin's cutting words, Jesse wasn't ready to give up. He would paint the house with a toothbrush if that was what it took to prove he would be loyal to the Smucker family and cherish Ariana for the rest of his life.

"I'm going to finish repairing these steps and then move on to the fence," Jesse said, fighting to keep his tone even. "Let me know if you need anything else."

Marvin gave a harrumph and stalked off toward the dairy barn.

Jesse blew out a gust of air he hadn't realized he'd been holding, then squatted down to return to the task of repairing the porch. His mind whirled as he hammered new slats of wood onto the steps.

For five days, he'd rushed through his morning chores at his father's horse farm and then hurried over to Marvin's to work there. Each day, Marvin asked Jesse to go home and then walked off, and then Jesse completed as many chores as possible before suppertime. Every night he fell asleep as soon as his head hit his pillow. He'd never been more tired or sore as he'd been this week.

Tobias's comments about Jesse never having to work for anything in his privileged life haunted him. As much as Jesse loathed Tobias's words, he had also found truth in them. For the first time in his life, Jesse poured his heart and soul into every task he undertook, into all the chores he completed at Marvin's farm. He refused to take anything for granted.

Jesse finished fixing the last step and then looked up at the back door, willing Ariana to walk outside and talk to him. He yearned to hear her voice and see her gorgeous smile. Although he'd had the opportunity to see her from afar while he worked on her farm, he hadn't spoken to her since Monday when they'd talked in the stable. He longed to get their wedding plans back on track, but first he had to concentrate on proving to Marvin he was worthy of Ariana's hand in marriage.

Jesse cleaned up the mess and disposed of the rotten wooden planks, then gathered his supplies to repair the pasture fence. He began replacing the rotten boards at the far end of the fence and worked his way toward the front of the pasture, facing the house.

As Jesse came around a corner, he spotted Ariana in her mother's garden, pulling weeds before dropping them into a bucket. He stilled for a moment, taking in her adorable face as she stuck out her tongue and struggled with one that seemed particularly troublesome. He gripped the hammer in his hand, fighting against the urge to rush over and help her rip up the irksome thing. The emotional distance between them sent a pang through his chest, but he couldn't risk violating Marvin's rules. If Marvin caught Jesse and Ariana together, it might make the situation even worse, and he couldn't chance that happening.

With his teeth clenched in frustration, Jesse turned away from Ariana and continued his work.

❧

Ariana dropped a long, thick weed into the bucket and then wiped her hands on her black apron. Brushing her hands across her temples, she looked up as the hot sun beat down on her prayer covering and shoulders, warming them both.

She'd been working in her mother's garden for nearly thirty minutes, and soreness radiated down her neck to her back and arms. She stood and rolled her neck and shoulders in an attempt to loosen her stiff muscles.

When she caught movement in the corner of her eye, she turned toward the pasture. Her stomach flip-flopped when she saw Jesse working on the fence. He'd come back for the fifth day in a row to help her father with chores.

She'd seen him working from afar since their talk in the stable on Monday, and he continued to command her thoughts. Yesterday she watched him fix the fencing around the chicken coop while she hung out the laundry. She'd longed to talk to him, but she didn't want to upset her father.

And now as she took in the breadth of his back and arms, watching him hammer a new slat into the pasture fence, she felt an invisible attraction pulling her to him. She couldn't bear to go another day without speaking to him.

Ariana's heart skipped a beat as she looked toward the house and then toward the barn in search of her father. She held her breath, for a moment doubting her decision to approach Jesse. Then, throwing caution to the wind, she ran her sweating palms down her apron before hurrying down the rock path to the fence.

"Jesse." She walked up behind him.

He craned his neck and looked at her before setting the hammer on the ground and facing her. "Hi."

"I saw you working on the porch steps earlier, but you were gone when I finished cleaning the *haus*. I thought you'd gone home." She glanced over her shoulder toward the dairy barn to check for her father once again, and then looked back at Jesse. "Why are you still here?"

He wiped his face with his shirtsleeve. "There's still plenty to do."

"Don't you have chores to do at your *haus*?"

"*Ya*, but I've been doing most of my work there in the morning so I can come here in the afternoons." He rested his arm on the fence post. "Caleb has been picking up the slack for me so I can help your *dat*."

"You must be tired." She took a step toward him while searching his eyes.

"I am, but that's okay. I want to help your *dat*. He can't run this entire farm by himself." He rubbed his chin as he seemed to be carefully considering his next words. "I've also realized I've made a lot of mistakes in our relationship, and I'd like to make it up to you."

Mistakes? Her stomach plummeted. "What do you mean?"

"I've taken you for granted, and I want to make it right."

She shook her head. "You haven't taken me for granted."

"*Ya*, I have," he insisted. "Your *bruder* said some hard things to me last week, but I've realized he made a few valid points. He said I've never had to work for anything, and that everything comes easily to me. He implied I'm spoiled, and he's right. I was able to build a *haus* when I was only twenty-three. You've always had feelings for me, and I never had to work to prove I was worthy of your affection."

He gestured toward the fence. "Now I'm trying to prove how much I care about you and your family." He clenched his jaw. "I'll do anything necessary to show you and your *dat* I intend to take care of you for the rest of my life." He took her hands in his. "I promise I'll always do my best to not take you for granted."

Her chest constricted. "I still don't think it's true that you've taken me for granted."

"*Ya*, I have. Remember when I forgot to tell you it was time to go to lunch at the lake? And then when I didn't join you on the porch at Mariella's, even though I'd promised? I'm so sorry." His voice quavered.

"I told you that was okay." She sniffed.

"No, it wasn't okay." He shook his head. "You're precious to me, and I can't bear the thought of losing you."

Reaching up, she cupped her hand to his cheek. "I promise you won't lose me." Standing on her tiptoes, she brushed her lips across his cheek, and he sighed as his shoulders relaxed.

Ariana cut her gaze toward the barn, where her father stood

talking to his driver. She took a step back. "I have to go. We'll talk again soon."

As she rushed back to the garden, she couldn't help but think it wouldn't be much longer before her father realized how genuine and good Jesse truly was.

CHAPTER 7

DISCOURAGEMENT AND ANXIETY SETTLED OVER JESSE as he moved a paintbrush up and down the slats of Marvin's pasture fence. The early morning July sun beat down on his straw hat, and his shoulders, back, and neck ached after spending the past two afternoons painting the fence.

He'd arrived early this morning to finish the last section so he could concentrate on other chores this afternoon. He'd hoped his hard work during the past three weeks would have gained him at least a pleasant greeting from Marvin, but again this morning he'd growled a half greeting. It seemed no matter how hard Jesse worked, he still hadn't earned an ounce of forgiveness or respect. But he wouldn't capitulate and go home.

As he worked, his mind spun with thoughts of Ariana. They'd stolen glances and a quick conversation here and there, but he longed for more time with her. He'd managed to speak to her alone at the youth gathering Sunday night, but the time had flown by too quickly and their privacy was limited. He hoped to see her again today.

As he moved his brush across the slats, his thoughts turned to Tobias. No one had heard from him. Ariana shared that she and her mother were consumed with worry about him.

He was painting the last slat in the fence when he heard boots crunch on the ground behind him.

"Did Caleb take over all your chores again today?"

Jesse craned his neck, glancing over his shoulder at Marvin. "*Ya*, he did, and I also worked late last night."

"And then you got up early this morning and came here to work some more," Marvin finished his thought.

"That's right." Jesse set the paintbrush on top of the can and spun toward him. "I think I'm finally done." He made a sweeping gesture toward the wooden fence, the fresh white paint gleaming in the bright sunlight.

Marvin studied the fence and then gave him a stiff nod.

Jesse's shoulders sagged. That was as close to a thank you as he would get, but he would accept it. Any acknowledgment was better than none.

"I don't think that fence has been painted in twenty years." Marvin's words sounded almost wistful as his expression flashed what seemed like melancholy. "I'm going in for lunch."

"Is it lunchtime already?" Jesse wiped his forearm across his sweaty brow.

"*Ya*." Marvin stared at him for a moment, and to Jesse's complete surprise, the old man's scowl softened. "Are you hungry?"

Jesse blinked. Was Marvin inviting him to eat lunch with him? Hope bloomed inside his chest. Perhaps he was making headway with Marvin after all.

"Well, are you?" Marvin asked.

Jesse shook himself from his shock. "*Ya*, I am, actually."

"Come inside. Rosanna and Ariana are making lunch." And with that, Marvin turned and started toward the back porch.

After rinsing out the paintbrush and stowing the paint can

in the barn, Jesse went in the back door of the house and stepped into the kitchen. Rosanna was placing a bowl of potato salad and a bowl of macaroni salad on the table. Jesse scanned the kitchen for Ariana, and disappointment filled him when he didn't see her.

"Ariana went to check the mail. She'll be right back," Rosanna said as if reading his thoughts. Her lips tipped up as she nodded toward the sink. "You can wash up."

"Danki." Jesse scrubbed his hands and arms before sitting down at the table, which had been set for four. He looked over at Rosanna as she set down a platter of lunch meat beside a basket of rolls. Had it been her idea to invite Jesse in for lunch? Or maybe Ariana's?

The front door clicked shut and Ariana entered the kitchen carrying a stack of mail. She looked beautiful in her light-blue dress. When she met his gaze, her cheeks stained pink and a tentative smile curled her lips. He returned the gesture as his heart squeezed. Oh, how he'd missed her.

"Looks like we received quite a bit of mail today," Rosanna commented as Ariana crossed to the table and set the stack down.

"Ya, we did." Ariana held up a white envelope. "This one is addressed to the Smucker family. It doesn't have a return address, but it's postmarked from a town in Florida."

"Open it," Rosanna instructed, coming to stand beside her.

Ariana opened the envelope and unfolded a piece of lined notebook paper with handwriting on it. She inhaled a sharp breath, and then held it out to her mother. "It's from Tobias."

Jesse's stomach clenched as Ariana's parents echoed her gasp.

"Read it." Marvin's voice sounded shaky. "Please."

"Ya, please read it," Rosanna said, wiping her eyes. "I don't think I can."

Ariana cleared her throat and began to read.

Dear Mamm, Dat, and Ariana,

I'm sorry for the way I left. I'm certain you're going crazy with worry, and I want you to know I'm safe.

I'm in Florida. I decided to visit Mamm's bruder Earl. I remember Mamm once saying she had a younger bruder who left the community. I found his contact information in an old address book in the kitchen and decided to take a chance that he would let me stay with him. I found out Onkel Earl and I have a lot in common.

You're probably wondering why I decided to leave the community, and you have a right to know the whole truth. First, I left because I thought it would make life easier for Ariana and Mamm. They've had to listen to Dat and me argue for years now, and I know it tore them up inside to hear it. I'm sorry for all the heartache I've caused. I didn't mean to be such a burden.

The night before I left, Ariana told me I should try harder and compromise with Dat. I've had three weeks to think about Ariana's advice, and I've come to the conclusion that she was right. For years I've been blaming Dat for our problems, but I realized it wasn't only Dat's fault. The truth is I've been part of the problem. I haven't been carrying my load as far as chores and responsibilities go. I'm truly sorry. I've been too selfish and self-centered to realize how much pain my behavior has caused all of you. I hope you can find it in your hearts to forgive me.

I also believe Ariana was right when she said that both Dat and I are stubborn. While I haven't been carrying my load, Dat also hasn't respected my feelings.

I understand the farm has been in our family for generations, but it's not my dream to be a farmer. I want to be a carpenter and create things with my hands. I've tried to enjoy being a dairy farmer, but I don't. Instead, I resent it. I'm not sure how we can come to a compromise on this issue when he won't listen and respect my dreams for my future.

Dat, Ich liebe dich, but I can't live with you right now. I will come back someday, but right now it's best that I just stay away for a while and work out all my issues.

I've also finally admitted to myself that I need help. I've been drinking alcohol in secret for a few months now. I was using it as a way to deal with my problems, and as Jesse wisely told me the night of the accident, it's not the way to deal with things. I've accepted that I have a problem. Onkel Earl told me he had a problem with alcohol, too, and he recommended a facility that can help me. I'm going there soon. In fact, by the time you receive this letter, I will probably be admitted into the center.

Dat, please don't blame Jesse for the accident. It wasn't his fault. I had gotten drunk that night after our trip to the lake, and it was my idea to race. Jesse never meant to put Ariana in danger. Don't punish Ariana and Jesse for my mistakes. Jesse is a great man, and he will take gut care of Ariana. He tried to stop me from drinking, and he also tried to stop me from guiding my horse home. I was too stubborn and drunk to listen to him. I'm sorry for wrecking the buggy. I will send you money to repair it when I have a job. Please forgive me for my dangerous and immature actions.

When you see Jesse, please tell him I'm sorry. I was cruel and hateful to him that night. I'm sure he'll recall what I said to him. I said those terrible things because I was envious of the relationship he has with his family. He didn't deserve my wrath. He's been my best freind since we were kinner, and I hope he finds it in his heart to forgive me too.

I will contact you again soon.

Sincerely,
Tobias

Tears sprinkled down Ariana's face as she sank into the chair across from Jesse. She grabbed a few napkins and mopped up her cheeks. Then she looked at her father, her eyes shimmering in the bright sunlight pouring in through the kitchen windows.

Marvin turned his gaze to Jesse. "Is that true?" His voice quavered. "Was Tobias drunk that night?"

Jesse nodded. "*Ya*, it's true."

"Why didn't you tell me?" Marvin leaned forward in his chair, his eyes seeming more curious than accusatory.

"I tried to tell you the night of the accident, but you wouldn't listen." Jesse shook his head. "After you forbade me from seeing Ariana, I didn't know how to tell you. I was worried you'd think I was lying about Tobias to push the blame for the accident onto him."

Marvin pursed his lips and stared down at the tablecloth. The room fell silent for several moments with only the sound of birds singing outside the windows. Rosanna sniffed and wiped her eyes, and Ariana rubbed her mother's arm.

"I didn't want Tobias to leave," Marvin said. "He kept telling me he wanted to be a carpenter, but I needed him to take over the farm for me. I was wrong not to respect his opinion, but I thought he would eventually agree to help me. This farm has been in our family for three generations, and I didn't want to even think about selling. I just wanted Tobias to take responsibility, for his life and for his inheritance.

"I was wrong. I should have considered his point of view. I never meant to drive him away." Marvin looked at Jesse. "I'm sorry for misjudging you and blaming you for Tobias's actions. I was wrong to take my frustrations out on you. You've never been anything but responsible. I hope you can forgive me."

Jesse nodded. "Of course I forgive you."

"And *danki* for all your help during these past few weeks," Marvin said. "I couldn't have run this farm without you."

"*Gern gschehne,*" Jesse said. "I'm *froh* I could help, and I'll keep helping you for as long as you'll allow me to. I'll do anything I can to help your family."

Marvin cleared his throat and quickly swiped his hand across his glistening eyes. Then he motioned toward the food in the center of the table. "Let's eat. We can talk about this more later."

Jesse stole a glance at Ariana, and when she smiled at him, warmth flooded his chest. They were going to be okay, and it seemed as if Tobias was going to be okay too.

Jesse followed Marvin into the barn after lunch. "I have a question for you."

"*Ya?*" Marvin swiveled toward him, his bushy eyebrows careening toward his hairline.

Jesse cupped his hand to the back of his neck and took a deep breath, gathering all his courage. "You asked for my forgiveness, which you already have. Does that mean I'm permitted to date Ariana again?"

"*Ya.*"

"Does that also mean I can marry her in the fall?" His voice sounded small and foreign to him. Where had his courage gone?

"*Ya,* of course it does." Marvin patted Jesse's shoulder. "Rosanna and I would be thrilled to have you as a member of our family."

"*Danki.*" Jesse's grin was wide.

Now he just had to ask Ariana if she would still marry him. His chest tightened as ideas filtered through his mind for how he could ask her.

❧

That evening Ariana laced her fingers in Jesse's as she walked beside him toward the pasture behind the house he'd built for her. "Where are you taking me?"

"You'll see." He shifted the cooler in his hands and bottles rattled inside.

"Do you have homemade root beer in that cooler?"

"Maybe," he said, teasing her with a grin.

Her heart fluttered. "It's a *schee* night."

"*Ya,* it is."

She gazed toward the small pond at the far end of the pasture and gaped when she spotted a bench under a beautiful oak tree. "Did you install a bench?"

"I put it out there earlier today. Do you like it?"

"I love it." She squeezed his hand as they approached the

bench and then sat down beside him. He opened the cooler, revealing four bottles of homemade root beer.

He lifted one bottle, opened it, and handed it to her.

"Danki." She took a long drink and then ran her fingers over the cool condensation. "This is perfect." She looked up at him and happiness buzzed through her. Not only had they finally heard from Tobias, but her father had given her permission to see Jesse again. She thought she might burst from all the excitement coursing through her veins.

Jesse opened a bottle for himself and then closed the cooler. "What are you thinking?"

"I was just thinking about how *froh* I am." She placed her bottle on the bench beside her. *"Mei mamm* is relieved to know Tobias is okay, and I am too."

"Ya, I feel like a weight has been lifted from my shoulders." Something unreadable flickered in his eyes as he set his bottle on the bench too. "I put this bench out here because I thought you and I could sit out here together and talk on warm evenings."

His tone and expression were so serious that worry nipped at her.

"That sounds perfect. I've always loved this pond."

"Gut." He looked down at his lap for a moment, as if gathering his thoughts. "I brought you out here tonight so we could talk alone. I've been doing a lot of thinking, and I realized I haven't been a very *gut* boyfriend, and I wasn't a *gut* fiancé when we were engaged."

She opened her mouth to protest, but he held up a hand to stop her.

"Please, let me finish. A *gut* fiancé would put you first in his life, but I haven't done that. I've been too busy working for *mei dat* and worrying about my own life. I've never had to fight for you, but that's going to change." He tapped the seat of the bench. "This bench is just a small token to show you how I will always put you first from now on. I'll always make time for you, and I'll work on being the best man I can be for you. If you agree to marry me, I promise our marriage will always be my top priority."

He took her hands in his. "I've already asked your *dat*'s permission and he's said yes, so now I need to ask you." He took a deep breath. "Arie, will you marry me?"

She sniffed as tears filled her eyes. "Of course I will."

"Oh, *danki*." He blew out a deep breath.

"Did you think I'd say no?"

He shrugged and gave her a shy grin. "I was afraid I'd messed up so badly you'd be afraid to trust me again, and that you'd find someone else who would treat you better than I have."

"You're talking *narrisch*." She touched his arm. "I was afraid I was going to lose you when *mei dat* said I couldn't see you. I can't imagine my life without you."

"I feel the same way." He draped his arm on the back of the bench behind her. "I suppose we should start discussing our wedding plans again."

"*Ya.*" She rested her head on his shoulder. "I need to start sewing dresses for Mariella and me."

"You do." He rubbed her shoulder. "We should try to convince Tobias to come to the wedding."

Ariana sat up straight. "*Ya*, we should. If we don't hear from him soon, I can write a letter to *mei onkel* Earl and ask him how I can contact Tobias."

"That's a *wunderbaar* idea." He touched her cheek. "I was so worried I wasn't going to be able to marry you. *Ich liebe dich,* and I promise I will always take care of you."

"I love you too. I can't wait to be your *fraa.*"

He leaned down and his lips brushed hers, sending electric pulses singing through her veins. She closed her eyes, savoring the feel of his lips against hers.

Jesse traced her cheek with the tip of his finger. "I will cherish you forever."

Ariana silently thanked God for softening her father's heart toward Jesse, and she prayed that someday Tobias would come back to their family. But as Jesse leaned in for another kiss, all other thoughts retreated as she looked forward to a future with the man she'd love for nearly her entire life.

DISCUSSION QUESTIONS

1. Ariana is devastated when her father forbids her from marrying Jesse. Have you ever found yourself in a similar situation? If so, how did it turn out? Which Bible verses helped you through this difficult time? Share this with the group.

2. Jesse pours himself into working on Marvin's farm as a way to prove to Marvin that he is worthy of marrying Ariana. What do you think caused him to grow as a character throughout the story?

3. Read Hebrews 11:1 (print out the verse). What does this verse mean to you? Share this with the group.

4. Which character can you identify with the most? Which character seemed to carry the most emotional stake in the story? Was it Ariana, Jesse, Tobias, or someone else?

5. At the beginning of the story, Marvin blames Jesse for the buggy accident. His feelings toward Jesse change by the end of the story. What do you think causes this transformation?

6. When Tobias leaves home, he finds solace with his uncle Earl. Have you ever helped someone in need? If so, how did you feel after you helped that person? Share this with the group.

7. What did you know about the Amish before reading this book? What did you learn?

ACKNOWLEDGMENTS

As always, I'm thankful for my loving family.

I'm grateful for my special Amish friend who patiently answers my endless stream of questions. You're a blessing in my life.

To my agent, Natasha Kern—I can't thank you enough for your guidance, advice, and friendship. You are a tremendous blessing in my life.

Thank you to my amazing editor, Becky Monds, for your friendship and guidance. Thank you also to editor Jean Bloom, who always helps polish my stories and connect the dots between my books. I'm grateful to each and every person at HarperCollins Christian Publishing who helped make this book a reality.

Thank you most of all to God—for giving me the inspiration and the words to glorify You. I'm grateful and humbled You've chosen this path for me.

ABOUT THE AUTHOR

 AMY CLIPSTON IS THE AWARD-WINNING and bestselling author of the Kauffman Amish Bakery series. Her novels have hit multiple best-seller lists including CBD, CBA, and ECPA. Amy holds a degree in communications from Virginia Wesleyan College and works full-time for the City of Charlotte. Amy lives in North Carolina with her husband, two sons, and three spoiled rotten cats.

Visit her online at amyclipston.com
Facebook: AmyClipstonBooks
Twitter: @AmyClipston

LAKESIDE LOVE

KATHLEEN FULLER

To my husband, James. I love you.

CHAPTER 1

"ESTHER, IT'S ALMOST TIME FOR THE NEXT TOUR."

"Be right there." Esther Coblentz sighed. She loved guiding the groups of Yankees who signed up to tour her family's house and farm, and usually she was the one waiting on them instead of the other way around. But right now she was busy watching Judah King. She had a perfect view of him from the front porch as he helped her father and brother, Reuben, plow the large field her father had purchased last month, adding to their existing farm. Since it was already July, they were working hard to get in some late crops.

"Esther, did you hear me? They're already gathered in the living room."

She barely glanced at her younger sister. "I'll be there in a minute."

"I hope so. I don't want to have to do the tour."

She heard Sarah leave, presumably to go back to the house. Esther knew she couldn't stand here watching for much longer, but she didn't want to leave. Not yet. She wanted one last look at Judah. He really was perfect, with hair the color of black licorice, a sloped nose a little upturned at the end, and a mouth she really shouldn't notice as much as she did.

But it was his dark eyes—soft, kind, and warm—that had caught and kept her attention four years ago when he and his family moved to their district and her father hired him as a farmhand.

Pulling her gaze away, she went inside through the small gift shop. Her father, ever the entrepreneur, had decided five years ago to add on to the house, move the family into the new addition, build the small gift shop, and conduct tours. His business instincts had been spot-on. Not only did the family run a successful farm, but their tourist business also thrived.

Esther smiled at her mother, Fanny. She was ringing up a customer who was purchasing a few of Sarah's homemade jellies and jams. Esther didn't sell anything in the gift shop. She wasn't a gifted seamstress like *Mamm* or a great cook like Sarah. She was . . . average. Average looks, average skills, average everything. Most of the time she was okay with that. Except when she saw Judah. Then she was reminded that average wasn't good enough, not compared to Sarah.

Sarah was the beautiful one. The talented one. The one Judah was in love with.

Esther's smile dimmed. She couldn't think about Judah and Sarah right now. She had a tour to give, and she always made sure to do her best when it came to the Yankee visitors, including speaking only English for them, which her family did with all Yankees.

She entered the living room and smiled at a group of six Yankees standing near the front door. The five women looked to be in their midsixties, and a school-aged boy looked about nine or ten—and very out of place.

"Hello everyone," she said. "My name's Esther. If you're

ready, I'll take you on the tour. We'll start with the house, then go out to the barn where you can meet our animals. From there you'll see our fields. All this makes up a real working farm. Please let me know if you have questions anytime during the tour."

The women and boy followed Esther as she moved about the living room. Pointing to the woodstove, she said, "Amish families usually have this going during the other seasons, but it's not needed in the summer, of course." Then she showed the group the gas-powered lamp, explaining how a typical Amish family spends their evenings in each season.

As she observed the group, she realized four of the women were friends and the boy and the fifth woman were together.

"Where's the TV?" the boy asked, searching the room.

"The Amish don't watch TV," the woman nearest to him said.

"So no Xbox?" he said in disbelief. "What about an iPad?"

"Jefferson," the woman with him said. She adjusted her wire-rimmed glasses. "The Amish don't use any electronics at all."

"Actually, that's not true," Esther interjected. "We use some electronics, as long as they're associated with our businesses."

"I see," she said. "I had no idea."

The boy muttered something under his breath, stuck his hands in the pockets of his tan shorts, which seemed a size too big for his slight frame, and shuffled his feet against the spotless wood floor. Esther gave him a small smile. He didn't return it, but she didn't mind. This wasn't exactly the type of tour that would interest a boy his age, and it was clear he'd been dragged along by the woman, who was probably his grandmother.

Esther showed them the rest of the house—three bedrooms in pristine condition, one bathroom, the mudroom—decorated with Amish hats, boots, aprons, and a *kapp* for effect—and finally the kitchen, which was the room that always brought the most questions.

"Can I have one of these?" Jefferson looked at the bowl of peppermint candies in the middle of the table.

"Of course," Esther said, pushing the bowl toward him.

Jefferson reached in and grabbed a handful. Esther waited for the woman with him to say something, but all the adults were busy looking at the "adorable" touches *Daed* had insisted on when *Mamm* decorated the kitchen. "A percolator!" one of them said. "I haven't seen one of these in years."

"And a gas lamp in the corner," another woman said. "Oh, Denise, look at this." She pointed to a cast iron popcorn popper, several gold bracelets jangling on her thin wrist. "Isn't this wonderful? I would love to have one of these."

"I want something to drink." Jefferson plopped down on one of the chairs and shoved a piece of the peppermint candy in his mouth. "It's hot in here."

"I'll get you something in the gift shop." The woman with him looked at Esther apologetically. "His mother didn't sign him up for day camp this week."

"Dad was supposed to do it, Grandma."

Ah, she *was* his grandmother.

"Regardless, there was a snafu. So Jefferson is spending some quality time with me. I thought visiting an Amish home would be very educational."

"More like very boring."

"Don't be rude." She smiled at Esther again, but the smile was strained at the corners of her thin lips. "This is all fascinating. I don't see a refrigerator here. How do you keep your food cold?"

"In the winter we put our food in a wooden pantry my father

built. In the summer we use coolers. There's also an ice machine a few houses down."

"You don't worry about the food spoiling?"

She shook her head. "We eat it fast enough, especially my brother and my father." And Judah, who spent a lot of time here, probably more to see Sarah than to help their father. She pushed the thought away. "We also make sure not to buy more than we need."

Another woman nodded her head. Her eyeglasses were on a thin decorative chain that hung around her neck. "That's a wonderful way to live."

Esther thought so too. She'd met a lot of Yankees in her life, especially since she started doing the tours. While some aspects of non-Amish life appealed to her, none of them rivaled her faith, family, and community. Still, that didn't mean she couldn't sympathize with Jefferson. "Let's head out to the barn," she said, looking at the boy. "I think you'll find something to interest you there."

As Esther expected, he perked up when he had the chance to see the animals. As he patted Peanut, their pet miniature pony who loved attention, Esther stood back at the edge of the barn while the women walked through it. None of them were as enthusiastic as Jefferson about the cow, two sheep, one old draft horse, and a pen of cute bunnies. Two of them wrinkled their noses, but Jefferson's grandmother apparently decided to be adventurous. She awkwardly patted the gentle cow on top of its head.

"Small group today?"

At Judah's question, Esther's confidence evaporated. "*Ya,*" she replied, but she didn't look at him. She kept her gaze glued on Jefferson, who had turned his attention to the bunnies. Still, she couldn't resist taking a glance at Judah.

He leaned against the barn wall, his handsome face reddened by the heat and farm work. His pants and shirt were dusty, and he smelled like a man who'd spent most of the day in the field. But none of that put her off. Judah King was also a hard worker, which she appreciated. His intention might be to get closer to Sarah, but he was a great help to *Daed* and Reuben.

"Seen Sarah lately?" he asked. He'd straightened, put his hands on his trim waist, and caught her eye. "I looked for her in the gift shop, but she wasn't there. *Yer mamm* said she hadn't seen her either."

"*Nee*. I haven't seen her." She bit her bottom lip.

"Grandma, can I take one of the bunnies home?" Jefferson said, his head popping up over the rabbits' pen.

"No."

"Please?"

"Your parents don't have room for pets. Besides, your father is allergic to animal dander." Grandma walked over to the pen. "Why don't you say hello to the draft horse?"

"I want to be with the bunnies." Jefferson gripped one under his chin.

"I think an intervention is in order." Judah winked at Esther before moving toward the boy. "Don't hold the bunny so tightly," he said as he climbed into the pen. He picked up another bunny and held it gently in his hands. "Like this, see? You don't want to hurt them."

Jefferson loosened his grip and cradled the bunny like Judah showed him.

All Esther could do was sigh. Or rather swoon. There was something wonderful about seeing a cute, delicate creature in Judah's large hand, safe and secure.

"Now," Judah said, putting the bunny down, "let's go see Maisy. She looks lonely, and she likes company." He led Jefferson out of the pen and over to the draft horse, who didn't look the least bit lonely and only tolerated visitors. Esther smiled.

"Your young man is very good with kids," one of the ladies said to her as she moved to stand beside Esther.

"Oh, he's not—" She clamped her lips. What harm would it be in letting them think she and Judah were together? It wasn't as if they could be confused for siblings. Esther was blond and fair with average blue eyes, a sharp contrast to Judah's dark hair and eyes and tan skin.

"I think we're finished here," Grandma said, wrinkling her nose at Maisy's whinny. "I've seen enough animals, thank you." She smiled, her upturned lips wrinkling deeply at the corners as she turned to Esther. "If I don't get Jefferson out of here, he'll be asking to take home the cow and the horse."

The other women laughed and Esther regained her senses. They'd spent longer in the barn than normal, thanks to her gazing at and daydreaming about Judah. "We'll go outside and I'll show you our garden and fields."

"That sounds boring," Jefferson said, not moving from Maisy's side.

"Remember, I told you I'd get you something to drink in the gift shop when we were finished with the tour," his grandmother reminded him. "And if you're extra good, I might get you a treat."

"Coming!" Jefferson gave the horse one more pat on the nose and jogged to the rest of the group.

Again, Esther wanted a last look at Judah, who was now talking in a low voice to Maisy, gently stroking her nose. Esther had never been jealous of an animal before. *Always a first time.* She watched Judah for another brief moment, then started to follow the group.

"Esther?" Judah called out.

She turned, putting on what she hoped was her prettiest smile. "*Ya*, Judah?"

"If you see Sarah, tell her I'm looking for her."

Her smile dimmed. Of course Sarah was uppermost in his mind. When hadn't she been? "I will," she said, hiding her disappointment. And she would keep her promise. She always did, even though a little bit of her heart shattered every time she was confronted with the reality that Judah was in love with Sarah, not her.

She left to join the tour group, wondering if she would ever get over Judah King.

━━━━━◆◇◆━━━━━

Judah gave Maisy one more pat on the nose and the rest of the animals a bit more feed for a special treat, then left the barn and headed for the new field. Enoch and Reuben had taken their break in the family's kitchen, and Judah had used the respite to try to find Sarah. As usual, she wasn't around when he had a break. If he didn't know better, he'd think she planned it that way.

But Sarah wouldn't do something underhanded like that. She was beautiful, sweet, charming . . . perfect. Problem was, he wasn't the only one in their district who thought so. Sarah Coblentz had more men interested in her than should be decent. But again, that wasn't her fault.

How could they not be attracted to her? Judah had fallen head over heels the first day he'd seen her four years ago. And one day he would win her. He was determined to. If persistence meant anything, Judah was ahead of the other guys by miles. It was a bonus that he liked working at Coblentz Farms. Enoch paid well, and he'd rather be farming than working construction, which was what he did in the fall and winter months until it was time for spring planting.

He walked out of the barn into the hot but fresh outdoor air and glanced at the house. Should he check there for Sarah again? He decided not to. Esther would give Sarah his message. Good old dependable Esther. She always kept her word.

He glanced over at Esther as she talked to the group of older ladies and Jefferson. The young boy was kneeling in front of a row of sunflowers and tugging at the stems. Judah was about to intervene when Esther smoothly walked toward the kid, still explaining about the different vegetables and flowers the Coblentzes planted every year, and put her hand on Jefferson's shoulder. Just a light touch, but enough to get the boy's attention. He straightened, and she kept her hand on his shoulder until she had guided him to his grandmother.

Judah was impressed. Esther was not only dependable, but great with children. He'd noticed that after church services. She never hesitated to kick off her shoes and play with the kids, whether it was volleyball, baseball, or horseshoes. Esther definitely liked to have fun.

"Judah!"

His ears perked up at the sound of Sarah's voice. She stopped in front of him, and he was nearly struck dumb by her beauty. Flawless skin, crystal-blue eyes that were so pale they seemed to constantly sparkle, full lips that were perpetually rosy and begging to be kissed.

"Esther said you wanted to see me?" Sarah said.

Danki, Esther.

"I thought after supper today we could go get some ice cream at the Parlor." The Parlor was a small ice cream and sundry shop that catered to both Yankees and the Amish.

"Oh, Judah. That's so nice of you. But I already have plans."

Plans? With whom?

"Maybe we can go some other time. You could invite Esther, though. She loves the Parlor's ice cream." With that Sarah turned around and left. Although he was disappointed she'd turned him down, he couldn't help but notice that even her walk was perfect.

Hmm. Maybe he should ask Esther to go with him to the Parlor. But what would they talk about? Esther was a quiet and shy woman, emphasis on the quiet. Then again, she might know what Sarah was doing tonight. *Or if she's seeing someone.* It made his head pound to think about it, but if Sarah was seeing someone else, he needed to size up his competition.

Decision made, he went back to the new field. Enoch planned to plant lettuce, beets, spinach, peas, and kale in the freshly plowed ground. They would be harvesting well into October, but Judah didn't mind helping out until then. It meant more time to get closer to Sarah. This wasn't the first time he'd asked her out, and it wasn't the first time she'd said no. But she'd said yes plenty of times too. She was unpredictable. Almost playing hard to get . . . but in the end Judah would get her, and she would be worth it.

Esther kept her head down as she nibbled on a tiny taste of butter pecan ice cream, one of the Parlor's signature flavors. She glanced up at Judah, who was attacking with gusto a double scoop of

Triple Fudge Delight in a waffle cone. They were seated at one of the small, round tables that had room for only two. Around them, customers—both Yankee and Amish—were milling near the counter, trying to decide what frozen treat to order.

She'd been stunned when Judah asked her to go with him to get ice cream tonight. Stunned and confused. He'd never asked her out before, and she wasn't foolish enough to think they were on a date. She could *wish* they were on a date, but she knew better.

Judah licked a spot of chocolate from the corner of his mouth. "*Gut* ice cream, *ya*?"

She looked up and froze. Ice cream was the last thought on her mind right now. "Um . . ." Where were her words? No wonder Judah wasn't interested in her. She was practically mute.

He leaned back in the chair, his mouth lifting in a half grin. "*Nee* need to be shy around me, Esther." He winked and took another bite of his cone.

If only that was more than a friendly wink. Judah was open-hearted and, yes, friendly—two more reasons for her to be attracted to him. But she was . . .

Sigh. She was silent. Nervous. And she didn't stand a chance with Judah.

"So . . ." He pushed back his chair and put his ankle over his knee. "What's Sarah up to tonight?"

Esther shrugged, returning her gaze to her ice cream.

"She didn't tell you about her plans?"

She looked up again and saw the tension underneath his calm exterior. That made her want to ease his mind. "I think she went over to Celia's. She's a Yankee *freind* Sarah has known for years."

"Oh." He seemed to mull that over in his mind. "Okay." His shoulders relaxed as he polished off his cone.

Esther's ice cream was melting. Forgetting about taking tiny bites, she licked around the top edge of the cone. She started to say something else, but when she looked at Judah, he was staring at her. At her nose in particular.

"You've got . . ." He grabbed a napkin from the holder on the table, then leaned forward and wiped the tip of her nose. "Ice cream," he said, balling up the napkin and putting it on the table.

Her face reddened. She couldn't even lick an ice cream cone without making a mess. "Sorry," she said, tempted to throw away the cone.

He shrugged. "It was kind of . . . cute."

She froze for the second time, barely feeling the cold drips of ice cream over her fingers. Cute? He thought she was cute?

"You going to finish that?" He tilted his head toward her cone. When she shook her head he took the cone from her. "Hate to waste *gut* ice cream."

Normally she did too, but right now she was still trying to wrap her mind around the fact that Judah had not only said she was cute, but he was also eating her ice cream. Maybe there was more to tonight than him quizzing her about Sarah. Maybe he was attracted to her and somehow she'd missed the signals. Missing signals wouldn't surprise her—she wasn't exactly experienced when it came to dating and flirting. Maybe this really was a date—

"Do you know if Sarah's free tomorrow?" He took another lick of her ice cream. "I've got *mei* open buggy all cleaned up and thought she'd like to *geh* for a ride."

Esther's heart sank. She'd love to go for a ride with Judah in his open buggy. "You'll . . . you'll have to ask her."

He grinned. "I will." He polished off the rest of the cone. "You ready to *geh*? I've got stuff to do tonight."

She picked up the napkin and threw it away. She'd eaten approximately three bites of her ice cream. The evening was turning into a big disappointment.

As she climbed into Judah's buggy, her foot slipped. "Hey," he said, catching her elbow. "Watch *yer* step." And although she didn't need his assistance, he held on to her as she got into the buggy.

"*Danki* for *yer* help, Judah," she told him when he got in and took the reins.

"*Nee* problem. Did I ever tell you about the time I slipped and fell facedown in the mud? Almost chipped a tooth on a rock." He smiled and tapped on one of his front teeth. "If I had, I would have deserved it. I was mouthing off at *Mamm* after church."

"I can't imagine you doing that," Esther said, folding her hands in her lap.

"It was before we moved here. I was about ten, and she wouldn't let me *geh* over to a *freind's haus*." He chuckled. "I can't even remember which *freind* that was now. But at the time I thought *Mamm* was the meanest woman in the world."

Esther laughed. "I tried running away when I was about that age."

"I find that hard to believe." He guided the horse onto the street and headed for Esther's house.

"*Ya*, I did. I think I was nine, and I informed *mei* parents I was moving into the barn."

"Wait . . . You ran away to the *barn*?"

"You know how far the barn is from our *haus*. At least five hundred yards."

Judah started laughing. "I thought you were going to tell me you packed *yer* bags and took off down the street."

"Oh, I packed a bag. It was a small paper one that had held apples."

"The ones with the handles?"

She nodded. "It fit exactly one dress, one pair of socks, and *mei* toothbrush." Grinning, she added, "Just the essentials."

"Of course." He tapped the reins lightly as a car sped by. "What was *yer* parents' reaction?"

"*Daed* told me to clean the barn while I was out there."

Another laugh from Judah. "That sounds like him."

"*Mamm* actually packed me a lunch. She was pretty supportive, considering I was running away."

After a pause Judah asked, "What were you upset about?"

"I didn't want to share a room with Sarah anymore." She was tempted to add that Sarah had been almost unbearably messy as a child, but that wouldn't be fair to her sister. She was almost as tidy as Esther was now. And her messiness wasn't the real reason. "I wanted *mei* own space," was all she would admit.

"How long did you live in the barn?"

"Two nights, with some food deliveries from *Mamm*. After that she said I had to *geh* back in the *haus*. I was glad to. It was all right sleeping in the barn for a little while, but I missed *mei* bed. I even missed Sarah." She glanced at Judah. "A little."

She expected him to say something about Sarah now that she'd given him the opening. But he didn't. He stared straight ahead for a few moments. They were nearly to her house when he turned to her. "I always thought you and Sarah were close."

"We are. But we had our fights and scrapes growing up. We're both so . . . different."

"*Ya*," he said, his warm eyes drifting over her face. "You two sure are." He continued to look at her, letting the horse take the lead. Which made her wonder—could he possibly see something in her he liked, even though she was so different from Sarah?

Judah's horse knew the way to her house as if it were his own. Then Judah turned away, taking control of the reins again. When he pulled up in front of her house, she started to get out of the buggy.

"Thanks for going with me," he said.

She glanced over her shoulder and almost smiled. At least he appreciated her company. And she had to admit, it was fun talking about their childhoods. She hadn't felt nervous or anxious at all. It had been nice. Natural. Normal.

"Tell Sarah I'll see her tomorrow."

Friendly. So much for him seeing her as someone other than Sarah's sister. Biting the inside of her cheek, Esther nodded. As he drove away, she fought the jealousy growing inside her. She loved her sister, and she didn't want to be jealous of her. But when it came to Judah, she couldn't help it.

She also knew she couldn't keep pining after him this way. It was only a matter of time before Sarah decided to settle down, and when she did, Esther knew it would be with Judah. How could she choose anyone else? Not a single man in the district could compare to him. Soon Sarah would realize that, and then what would Esther do? Continually covet? She couldn't live like that either.

Turning, Esther headed toward the house, rubbing her temples. Something had to give, and soon.

CHAPTER 2

❧

THE NEXT MORNING IT WAS BLISTERING HOT, EVEN WELL before noon. Esther carried out a jug of cold water and cups to her *daed*, Reuben, and Judah. She handed Judah his cup and then poured water into it for him. He drained it quickly, pushed his hat back, and smiled at her. "*Danki*, Esther. That hit the spot."

And just like that, she was smitten again, as if he hadn't made it 100 percent clear last night that he was completely enamored with Sarah. Would she ever learn?

"Could I have a little more?" he asked, holding out his cup.

She nodded, mute once again. After she filled his cup, he took off his hat and poured a little of the water over the back of his neck and the rest over his head. All she could do was stare.

Judah handed her his cup, then picked up his hoe and went back to work. Esther walked over to Reuben, who was working farther downfield. She poured a cup of water and handed it to him.

"Had to give water to *yer* boyfriend first?" Reuben said, smirking before downing the water.

"He's not *mei* boyfriend," she hissed.

"You wish he was." He took the jug from Esther and filled the cup again. "Try not being so obvious about it."

She sighed. No sense in arguing with Reuben, since he would continue to tease her until she was fed up. "It's pointless anyway," she muttered.

"You and Judah?" Reuben took another long drink. "I wouldn't be so sure about that."

That made her snap to attention. Did her brother know something she didn't? "What?"

He shrugged. "I hate to admit it, but we men sometimes have blinders on. We don't see that the best thing is right in front of our eyes." He smiled. "Don't lose hope, Essie."

Grimacing, she took his empty cup and walked away. He was the only one who called her that. Most of the time he said it to bug her. Her frown faded as she realized Reuben was trying to encourage her. She glanced over her shoulder at Judah, who seemed to be concentrating on his work. Reuben's words gave her a bit of hope . . . which was suddenly dashed when she heard Sarah call out Judah's name.

"Judah!" Sarah strode toward him, all confidence and beauty and grace.

Not wanting to see the two of them together, Esther walked over to her father. He was crouched on the ground, sifting the plowed dirt through his fingers—his ritual before planting seed every year. When she asked him why he did it, he merely said, "Tradition," then went back to work. "I brought you some water, *Daed.*"

He rose from the ground, a little more slowly than in years past. He was only in his late forties, as was *Mamm,* but both of them had threads of silver in their hair and a few crinkles around their eyes. "You're a blessing, Esther. Hottest *daag* we've had all summer."

She started to hand him a cup, then changed her mind and gave him the jug. He drank almost all of it in one gulp. Wiping the water from his mouth, he said, "We might need some more."

"I'll *geh* back and fill the jug. We don't have any tours set up for today."

Daed frowned. "Maybe we should stop taking reservations and open the place to the public. I've been trying to convince *yer mamm* of that, but she wants to guard our privacy. Can't really blame her for that." He looked over at Judah and Sarah. "Wonder what they're talking about."

Despite herself, she glanced their way. Sarah was talking animatedly, the way she did when she was excited or angry. She didn't seem upset, and from the smile spreading across Judah's face, she must be excited about something. That extinguished the last shred of hope Reuben had instilled. Esther looked away when Sarah touched Judah's shoulder. "I'll get you some more water, *Daed.*" She took the empty jug from him, and he was already kneeling back down and touching the dirt again. *Tradition.*

As she walked toward the house, Sarah joined her. "Isn't it exciting?"

"What?" Esther said, not slowing her steps or caring what was so exciting between her and Judah.

"Rhett Davidson will be here sometime tonight."

Esther nodded. She had forgotten about the college student who was staying with them for a month.

Sarah clasped her hands together. "I asked Judah if he would show Rhett around Middlefield. I'd ask Reuben, but you know how he can be."

"Unpredictable." Which was true. As the youngest of the three, he was an excellent and committed farmer, but that didn't extend to any other part of his life. While he still dressed Amish and lived and worked with the family, he had yet to join the church. Esther often wondered if he would. He was twenty, and both she and Sarah had joined by that age.

Mamm and *Daed* didn't seem concerned, but Esther was. She wanted her brother to be a full part of the community, not chasing outside interests. Not that he'd given any indication he was. He just held back from joining the church for some unknown reason.

"I told Judah I'd go with them." Sarah sighed. "I can't wait to meet him. With a name like Rhett, he has to be handsome, right?"

"He's a Yankee, Sarah. Handsome or not, it shouldn't matter to us."

"You're always so serious. There's *nix* wrong with a little appreciation of God's creation."

Esther fought not to roll her eyes. There was plenty wrong with it, and when it came to Judah, it was something she struggled with. But Sarah didn't need to know that. "When does he arrive again?"

"Tonight. *Mamm* said he had to finish up a summer class and then he'd drive right over from Ohio State. Maybe he'll take me for a ride in his car."

"Sarah, are you listening to *yerself*? Why would you want to ride around in a car?"

"Because it's *different*. Don't you get tired of the same thing all the time? Get up. Do chores. Work. Go to bed. Do it all over again."

"That's not all we do. There's visiting with *familye* and *freinden*, church services, weddings, barn raisings, frolics, singings—"

"And that's all fun, but there's a lot of drudgery in between."

Esther stopped, concerned. She faced Sarah. "Are you saying you want to leave the church?" she whispered.

"Good heavens, *nee*." Sarah looked shocked. "All I'm saying is . . ." She tapped her finger against her chin. Even in the sweltering heat, while sweat ran down Esther's back, Sarah's cheeks were a lovely shade of pale pink, and there wasn't a single indication that she was the least bit hot. "I want to experience life to the fullest." She tapped Esther on the nose. "You should try it sometime." Then she practically skipped toward the house.

Esther's shoulders slumped. Didn't Sarah realize Esther wished she could be lighthearted and spontaneous? After all, that's what Judah liked. The one time she'd tried to emulate her sister, it had gone badly. Her cheeks heated at the memory, which made her perspire even more.

She'd approached Judah one day in May. He wouldn't start working with *Daed* and Reuben for the season until the next day, but traditionally the three men got together the evening before to plan how they would divvy up the farm responsibilities. He usually ate supper with them all season before going home to his parents' house, where he still lived with his younger brother and three sisters. She knew he would eat with them this night as well.

She'd practiced walking gracefully for an entire week, imitating Sarah's tinkling laugh and the way she looked at Judah with her chin dipped down and her eyes wide and sparkling. Although Esther thought she looked ridiculous in the mirror, she still worked at it, perfected it, until she thought she was as close to Sarah as she could possibly get.

"Hi, Judah," she'd said when he arrived that night for supper. She'd opened the door and touched her chin to her chest, then batted her eyelids several times.

"Uh, hi, Esther." He frowned. "Something wrong with *yer* eyes?"

"Nee." She stopped batting them, which was good, because it was giving her a headache. She leaned against the doorframe, one hand sliding up the doorjamb and straight into a splinter. "Ow!" she said, jerking her hand away.

"Let me take a look." He backed her up until they were all the way in the living room, then shut the door behind him. He took her hand and ran his rough fingers over the large and obvious splinter. "Do you have some tweezers?" he asked.

A little blood oozed from the place where the splinter was lodged. *"Mamm* does in the top drawer of the little table over there."

He got the tweezers, cradled her hand in his large palm, and paused. "This might sting a bit."

"It's okay—ow!"

Judah yanked out the splinter, then dropped her hand. "You should wash that and put some peroxide on it. Next time, don't slide *yer* hand across wood like that. Even if it's stained it could still end up splintery over time."

She nodded, a little awestruck at his concern and the gentle attention her hand received.

"Is Sarah around?" he'd asked, not skipping a beat. As if she'd heard him talking about her, Sarah appeared, and Esther was immediately forgotten.

Esther shook her head, bringing herself back to the present. Sarah, Sarah, Sarah. For as long as she could remember, and despite being the older sister, Esther had always been in Sarah's shadow, and always would be. Despite that, Esther would never change herself. Trying to be someone else—especially her sister—had been a monumental mistake. She'd never tried to mimic Sarah again.

She went back into the house, pushing Judah out of her mind and thinking about Sarah's reaction to Rhett's coming. Her sister had always had a fleeting attention span, and Esther wasn't all that surprised that Sarah was excited about their impending company. But Sarah seemed a little too excited. And what about Judah? How could she consider showing interest in Rhett while Judah was here? How could Sarah even think about hurting him that way?

Esther paused in the kitchen doorway, wondering if she should talk to Sarah about it. Or maybe mention something to *Mamm*. Then again, maybe she was overreacting. Besides, Sarah wouldn't have to do much to gain Rhett's attention. If anything, Esther would probably have to keep her eye on *him*, not her sister. She blew out a breath. July was going to be an interesting month, to say the least.

CHAPTER 3

Later that night, after supper was finished and the dishes were done, Esther went outside and sat on the porch steps in front of their addition's front door. The wide porch faced the original house and its front door, too, and the family still used it as long as there wasn't a tourist group scheduled.

Barefoot, she curled her toes over the edge of the top step. It was still hot, stifling so, but a bit cooler out here than in the house. She folded her hands and rested her wrists on her knees, leaning forward, listening to the sounds of the approaching night as she watched the sun move toward the horizon. Her father had built this house in such a way that the sunset was easily seen from the porch, which was what her mother had always wanted.

Over the years, she and her family had spent many evenings here, waiting for the sunset, she and her siblings playing on the porch or in the yard, *Mamm* and *Daed* sitting in the hickory rockers and watching them. When—*if*—she had her own house, she wanted it to face the sunset just like this one. When—if, again— she had a husband and children, she wanted to spend their evenings together, enjoying God's masterpieces in the sky.

But all that was faint hope right now. At the rate she was going, Reuben would get married before she did—and he had stated many times he had no interest in finding a wife anytime soon, if ever.

A car pulled into the driveway as Sarah opened the door behind her. "It's him," she said almost breathlessly. She touched Esther on the shoulder. "Rhett is here."

The small silver car stopped in the middle of the driveway. The engine turned off, the trunk popped open, and Esther found she was almost holding her breath in anticipation, thanks to Sarah's contagious enthusiasm. Telling herself she was acting foolish, she stood and smoothed out her skirt, then went to greet their guest properly.

Only when he got out of the car did she stop short. Sarah, as usual, had been right. Rhett Davidson was a stunningly hand-some man. For a Yankee, anyway. He grinned, showing straight white teeth that seemed a little too bright in contrast with his tanned face. He was wearing sunglasses, and when he removed them his hazel, almost gold-colored eyes were revealed. He was broad-shouldered, and as he rounded the car and walked toward her, she could see he was well built, as if he worked on a farm himself—or worked out in a gym. Considering he was a college student, she assumed the latter.

"Hi," he said, extending his hand toward her. "I'm Rhett. Are you . . . Sarah?"

Esther almost laughed out loud at that. She'd never been taken for her sister before. "No, I'm Esther." She took his hand, and her gym theory was confirmed. He had a firm handshake, but, unlike Judah, his palms and fingers were soft. She pulled out of his grip.

"*I'm* Sarah." Her sister brushed past her and held out her hand. Esther watched as Sarah effortlessly smiled, sparkled, and gleamed so much in front of this man Esther thought he'd have to put his sunglasses back on. "Welcome to Coblentz Farms."

He shook Sarah's hand, but let it go immediately. "I'm glad to be here. Really glad. I'm looking forward to learning about daily life among the Amish."

"You'll learn a lot while you're here, I'm sure. Why don't you come inside? I just made some fresh lemonade."

"That sounds great." He gestured to his car. "Is it okay if I park here?"

"Of course," Sarah said. "My father has a permanent parking spot for you out back, since you said you didn't want to drive at all while you're here. But you can park there later."

"Okay, I'll get my bag and meet you inside."

Esther watched this exchange with slight amusement and a bit of annoyance. Each time she tried not to be envious of Sarah's way with people—especially men—she was drawn back into the green whirlpool. It had happened a couple of times today with Judah already. Tonight she knew exactly what she would add to her nightly prayers.

"I have a better idea." Sarah turned to her. "Why don't *you* get Rhett's bag, Esther?"

Lifting an annoyed eyebrow at her sister, Esther started for the car. But Rhett moved in front of her. "I can get it." He smiled, and for some reason she felt a little spark in her chest.

Rhett opened the trunk of his car, pulled out a suitcase, then shut the trunk lid and pressed a button on his keychain. The car beeped. "Show me the way," he said, looking at Esther and still grinning as though he was ready for the time of his life.

But Esther remained discombobulated. "You two go ahead," she said, putting her hands over her abdomen. Then when she

215

realized what she'd done, she thrust them behind her back. "I'll be inside in a little bit."

Sarah nodded, giving Esther her secret *thank you* smile. But Sarah didn't need to thank her . . . at least Esther didn't think so. Bother. Esther couldn't remember the last time she was this off-kilter.

After they'd gone inside, she sat down on the bottom porch step, ignoring the sunset in front of her. Surely she wasn't attracted to a Yankee man, one with short hair and soft hands. She liked Judah. She had for so long she didn't know what it was like to be interested in someone else. Which she wasn't. This was just a momentary reaction to a handsome man. Nothing else.

"Esther?" A snapping sound. "Esther, are you in there?"

Blinking, she looked up to see Judah snapping his fingers in front of her, beautiful soft shades of lavender, peach, pink, and coral streaking the sky behind him.

Her hand went to her belly again. No, she didn't feel a spark in her chest or a fleeting feeling of butterflies at the sight of him. She felt a full onslaught, a frisson flowing through her that expelled whatever minute attraction she'd experienced when she saw Rhett. Which relieved her. And irritated. How was she supposed to forget about a future with Judah if her body and heart wouldn't cooperate?

Judah moved to sit next to her. He'd taken a shower upstairs before supper, which he always did after a hot day's work. He was at home here and even kept extra clothes in the bottom drawer of Reuben's dresser. He smelled like soap and sunshine and farm-land, and something particular to Judah that made her want to lean her head against his shoulder and breathe deeply. No, this wasn't helping.

"I'm assuming that's Rhett's car?" Judah asked, dipping his head toward the automobile.

"*Ya.* He just got here."

"I'm not so sure about this." He rubbed his chin, which had a sprinkling of five o'clock shadow over it. "I know I don't have a say, being I'm not *familye*—"

"You're like *familye*," she said, interrupting him, something she never did. Great. Now she'd compared him to her brother. Although that might be the trick to putting him out of her mind and putting herself out of her misery.

"Who knows, maybe someday I will be," he said quietly.

His words caused her stomach to flip, and not with attraction. More like indigestion. If only he were talking about their future instead of his and Sarah's. She couldn't respond, so she just stared at the sunset in front of her, willing the colors and shadows and gradients to soothe her.

"I was surprised *yer mamm* agreed to host him for a month," Judah continued. "Enoch I understand. He's a shrewd business-man, and this could drum up some publicity for the farm. Hope-fully *gut* publicity."

"Are you worried something will happen?" Esther asked, pulling her gaze from the sunset.

"*Nee.* Well, maybe a little bit. People think they can give up electricity and wear suspenders and they're Amish. They don't know anything about our faith, about why we live the way we do."

"He wants to learn, though."

Judah paused. "Or maybe he just thinks he does. Oh well," he said, shrugging. "It's only for a month." He looked at Esther. "Hold still," he said, then reached over and brushed his finger against the top of her cheek.

She hoped it was because of an eyelash. She'd heard Sarah talk about the time Christopher Mullet had taken her for a ride in his open buggy and reached over to brush an eyelash off her cheek. "It was so romantic," Sarah had gushed. "He made a wish and blew the eyelash off his finger."

Judah wiped his hand on his pants and got up from the porch. "Guess I better get home. Sarah around? Thought I might ask her about that buggy ride."

This time Esther couldn't hide her sigh. "She's inside with Rhett." She pointed to the front door with her thumb, keeping her gaze on the ground.

"Huh."

At that Esther looked up. Judah had his hands on his waist—a pose she would never get tired of—and he was frowning. Something dark flashed in his eyes, an emotion she was familiar with. Jealousy. She rose and moved to him. Without thinking, she put her hand on his arm, wanting to reassure him, knowing how jealousy could eat up a person faster than a child could catch a firefly. "I'm sure they're just talking. And she'll need to show him where he's sleeping tonight."

A muscle jerked in his jaw. "Huh," he said again, the word now sounding like he was shoving it through a cheese grater.

"Why don't we go inside? I'll introduce you to Rhett. You can get to know him a little before you take him on a tour around Middlefield."

But Judah didn't move. "I'll meet him tomorrow." He glanced down at Esther's hand on his arm.

She quickly moved away. "Are you sure?"

"*Ya*. See you tomorrow."

She watched as he went around the house to the barn where

his horse and buggy were kept. She waited on the porch until he left, then watched him as he turned out of the driveway and made his way down the road.

⚬⚬⚬

Judah rubbed the back of his neck as he drove home. In his other hand he held the reins loosely, as he always did when he went to and from Coblentz Farms. He and his horse had traversed this distance so many times over the past four years. And he'd always known what to expect when he dealt with the family: hard work, good food, respect from Enoch and—most of the time—from Reuben, a few treasured moments with Sarah, and if he was lucky, a date.

Now all that was changing. He could feel it deep inside. Starting today, things would be different at the Coblentzes. He wasn't sure what to think about that.

His arm itched and he reached to scratch it, then inexplicably thought about Esther's hand. She'd never touched him before. Sarah did it all the time, mostly on the shoulder, sometimes on the forearm. Those little touches always fed the fire of hope within him.

But Esther's touch was . . . confusing. Warm, reassuring, steady. Then again, that was Esther in a nutshell. When he was around her, he could be himself. He didn't have to try to impress her or think about what to say or try to figure out how to gain her attention. He could just . . . be.

Like last night at the ice cream shop. He was used to her being shy, and he usually tried to loosen her up with a little joke to get her relaxed and talking. When she did, he learned new things about her. He'd had no idea she'd run away from home as a child, even if it was to the barn. Esther never broke rules. He liked that about her. There was something to be said for predictability.

He'd felt a churning in his gut when she told him Sarah and Rhett were inside, and he recognized it for what it was—jealousy. For some reason he sensed Esther understood, not only why he was jealous but how it made him feel. But how would she know that? As far as he knew, she wasn't hung up on anyone. If she was, she'd kept it a tight-lipped secret. Not that it was any of his business. In fact, he'd be happy to see Esther settled and happy. She'd make someone a great wife.

Speaking of a wife . . . the churning returned. He was being ridiculous. He shook his head and straightened out his thoughts. Things were fine between him and Sarah, he was concerned about this Rhett person for nothing, and everything would stay the same at the Coblentzes. He was letting his imagination get the better of him, something he often did to his great annoyance. Tomorrow evening he would take Rhett and Sarah around Middlefield, and not only would Rhett see Sarah was off-limits, but Judah would also have done his duty, which would score points in Sarah's eyes.

He really didn't have time to play tour guide. But for Sarah, he would do anything, even spend a few hours with a Yankee who had no business being here.

Judah was wrong about everything—except for feeling certain their visitor knew nothing about farming.

It was obvious that Rhett had never been on a farm. From the moment the guy stepped on the land, he looked lost. Enoch and Reuben helped him differentiate between the various tools they used, and Judah would give him slight credit for knowing the difference between a shovel and a hoe.

But as far as planting crops, forget it. Judah was finished with his row of beet seed before Rhett was even a third of the way down the next row. He kept stopping and applying sunscreen on his neck and face, which were dripping with sweat before noon. After lunch Enoch gave him an old, battered Amish hat. Judah figured a student of Amish culture would have at least thought to bring a hat.

Things kept going steadily downhill after their planting was done for the day. First, he had to wait on Rhett to finish in the shower, which irked him to no end. Yeah, Rhett was actually living here while Judah had his own home to go to, but still. He always took his showers right after Reuben and Enoch, who spent at the most five minutes each washing off the dirt and sweat of the day. By the time Judah took his shower, the hot water was gone.

But that wasn't the worst of it. When they all sat down for supper, it was clear that Sarah's attention was focused on Rhett. Judah saw the empty chair next to Sarah and tried to sit down beside her. "Rhett's sitting here," she'd said, her voice still filled with its usual sweetness—the same tone he was used to her using with him.

"Huh," he'd said, then went to sit next to Esther, who, as usual, kept her head down and her mouth closed. They bumped elbows once when she passed him potatoes and he was reaching for the jar of bread-and-butter pickles.

"Sorry." Her voice was low, apologetic . . . and for some reason he noticed how pleasant it sounded, which didn't make any sense.

He'd heard Esther talk over the years, though never saying much and in a near whisper most of the time. But this was the first time he thought of her voice as *pleasant*.

"No worries." Without thinking, he smiled at her and opened the jar of pickles. "Would you like one?"

She shook her head, and didn't say anything for the rest of the meal. That was fine, because Sarah talked enough for both of them. She peppered Rhett with questions, laughed at his not-so-funny attempts at humor, and batted her eyes at him. The same way she'd batted her eyes at Judah. *Huh.*

"You're still going to take Rhett on a tour of Middlefield after supper, right, Judah?" Sarah said.

Judah was tempted to say no, but he'd already given his word, and he would never go back on a promise. "Yes." He took a bite of carrot and cabbage salad, chewed and swallowed, then looked at Rhett. "We'll probably just drive around Mespo," he said, referring to the small town they lived in near Middlefield, where their community's district was centered.

"We can take him to the gazebo. And the general store. Plus the statue." Sarah looked at Rhett wearing a smile that would instantly melt frozen butter.

"We?" Enoch said with an arch of his brow.

"I thought I'd go with them." Sarah smiled sweetly at her father. "It's a lovely evening for a ride."

"It certainly is," Fanny said. "Esther, why don't you go with them too?"

Esther's head bobbed up. "What?"

"Like your sister said, it's a beautiful evening, not as hot as yesterday. You should join them."

"I'm sure Esther has other things to do," Sarah said, looking at Esther as if she were noticing her for the first time. Which was kind of rude, Judah realized.

"I do have some reading to catch up on," Esther said. It seemed she didn't want to go on the ride any more than Judah did.

"You can do that anytime," Enoch added. He grabbed a slice of bread and slathered butter on it.

"I suppose you want Reuben to come too." Sarah's voice had lost its sweetness, the corners of her pretty mouth downturned into almost a pout.

"I'll pass," Reuben said, digging into the mashed potatoes.

"I don't have to go." Esther picked at the edge of her plate. "I don't want to be in the way."

"You won't be," Rhett said. "The more the merrier, right?"

"Right." Sarah leaned back in her chair. Yep, she was definitely pouting. Which made her extremely unattractive at the moment. Judah wasn't thrilled that he'd agreed out of a moment of weakness to cart around this Yankee, but he'd do it and he'd keep his feelings to himself. Just like Sarah should have.

Like Esther was doing. Judah glanced at her. She scooped up a small amount of potatoes and took a bite. She had a delicate and deliberate way of eating, separating each food from the others and picking up only small bites.

"Mrs. Coblentz, is there a place in town where I can buy some Amish clothes?" Rhett asked. "I'd really like to immerse myself in the full Amish experience."

Judah gripped his fork. Did this guy really think if he put on Amish clothes he would understand the Amish? Judah didn't have anything against Yankees in general, but since he'd been working summers for Enoch, he'd been privy to the conversations of people who took the house and farm tour. Words like *quaint, peaceful, adorable,* and the worst one in his opinion, *simple,* were bandied about with regularity. He didn't like that his faith and way of life were reduced to a few adjectives.

Being Amish was more complicated than that. It took serious commitment to God and to the community. Wearing the clothes and puttering around a farm was not the Amish "experience."

"No need to buy anything, Rhett," Fanny said. "Reuben probably has some clothes that would fit you."

"Or maybe Judah has some." Sarah turned her attention to Judah for the first time. As usual, her eyes sparkled like jewels. Her long, lush eyelashes were moving up and down just enough that they drew his attention, and she bit her bottom lip, drawing his gaze to her mouth. The jolt that went through him when she looked at him this way was still there, but with less intensity—much less intensity since she had looked at Rhett the exact same way.

"I'm taller than he is." Judah shoved his fork into the last bite of his mashed potatoes.

"He can borrow some of mine," Reuben said, not looking up from his plate. "I don't mind."

And with that, Sarah angled her body toward Rhett.

Dismissed. Judah wiped his mouth on his napkin and shot up from the chair. "I'll go get the buggy hitched," he said, heading for the door. Then he remembered his manners, stopped himself, and took a breath as he turned around.

"Delicious supper, Fanny. As always." Pleased he'd brought a smile to her face, he went outside, his own, fake smile disappearing. The food was good. It was the company that left much to be desired.

He took his time getting his horse out of the stall, partly because his quick exit had given him even more time to spare while they waited for Sarah and Esther to help their mother clean up the kitchen. And partly because he needed to get his wits about him. If he wanted to show Rhett the real Amish way, he would have to be more accepting and less irritable. Not to mention less jealous.

Before long, Esther entered the barn. Her face was pinched together and she looked like she was being sent to sit on a bed of nails for an hour. She gave him a strained smile, then turned her back to him, her head down as if she was staring at something fascinating on the barn floor. He patted his horse on the nose and went to her. "You okay, Esther?"

She jumped a little. "Sorry," she said, looking at him as she took a step back.

"For what? I startled you." For some reason he felt the need to soften his voice. She was acting like a skittish colt, which she often did when he was around, with the exception of the buggy ride home from the Parlor. Why, he had no idea. But this time it bothered him a little bit. "Have I done something?"

Her eyes widened in surprise. "*Nee.* Not at all."

Judah exhaled with relief. At least he hadn't put Esther off. "*Gut.* It's just that . . ." He rubbed the back of his neck, not sure why he was bringing the subject up.

"It's just what?" she asked when he didn't finish the sentence.

"You always seem to act a little strange around me." At her dismayed face he added, "Not weird or anything like that. Just . . . different."

Then she lifted her chin. "Maybe because I *am* different."

Her response surprised him, because this time she wasn't referring to the differences between her and Sarah. She was speaking solely for herself. He looked at her for a moment. Really looked at her, not just a casual glance, and despite himself he compared her to Sarah. Willowy, graceful Sarah, who had eyes that could melt the ice around a snowman's heart. Esther was shorter, stockier, and, unfortunately, couldn't be called beautiful. Looks weren't everything, but combined with her shy demeanor, the best descriptor he could apply to her was . . . plain. For some reason, that caused a pinch in his heart.

Her chin drooped a little, and he knew he hadn't hidden his thoughts very well, which was one of his drawbacks. Heart on his sleeve, that was Judah King. It had led to more than his fair share of teasing, especially since he started pursuing Sarah. "You're like a moon-eyed puppy dog around her," his brother Stephen had said last year. "The only thing you haven't done is sit up and beg at her feet."

But he didn't want to think about Sarah right now. He moved toward Esther, wanting to apologize. Yet how could he do that and not hurt her feelings? "Esther, I . . ."

She lifted her chin once more. "I should see what's taking Sarah and Rhett so long." Turning around, she left the barn.

Judah clamped his lips together. Oh, he'd hurt her all right. What he didn't understand was why it bothered him as much as it did.

CHAPTER 4

ESTHER RUSHED TO THE BACK SIDE OF THE BARN, OUT OF
Judah's sight and hopefully hidden from Rhett and Sarah, who
would be coming any minute. Rhett was upstairs with Reuben
trying on some of his clothes, and Sarah had insisted on waiting
for him. She'd decided to have a talk with Sarah later. Her flirting
with the Yankee man was wrong, and she was doing it in front of
Judah. Esther wondered if Sarah even realized her behavior was
unseemly, not to mention hurtful.

But Sarah's behavior wasn't making her throat burn. She
pressed her thumbs to her eyes, as if she could push her tears back
in. It worked somewhat, but a couple escaped. So now she felt
ridiculous on top of hurt.

Unlike when she'd referred to her and Sarah being different last night, tonight she'd seen Judah's true feelings when she
declared she was indeed different, not like anyone else. At the
time she'd been happy with her reply, even a little proud that
she'd stood her ground and didn't let on that his comment about
her acting weird had hit her square in the heart. Then she risked
a look into his eyes, his beautiful eyes with thick black eyelashes
that were long, but not too long for a man, and irises that were an

unusual combination of dark blues and greens, colors that could only be seen up close.

Judah could never hide his feelings because of those eyes. Everything he thought and felt could be seen. She should know; she'd seen his nearly complete adoration of Sarah every time he looked at her sister.

But he hadn't looked at Esther with adoration. No, when he looked at her just now, his eyes had held pity. When she saw that, she could barely hold it together.

Judah pitied her. Why, she wasn't sure. Because she wasn't gorgeous like Sarah? Because she couldn't keep her own feelings for him locked down tight enough that she could behave like a normal human being around him? That she would always be lacking in looks and personality? Knowing the reason wasn't important.

She lifted her head and gazed out at the farm. The cows softly lowed as they grazed in the pasture. The garden was lush and full of delicious vegetables. Flowers, many of which she'd planted, decorated the landscape with their vibrant colors. She had a part in making this farm a success, and she played a key role in her family's tourist business. She had a good life. An important purpose to fulfill. Yet she spent her time yearning for a man who could feel only pity for her.

Wasn't she better than that? Wasn't she worthy of more?

Despite her pain, she smiled. The invisible cord of hope that she and Judah would be together had finally been cut. It was unexpected, and it hurt, not to mention she would probably have a good cry about it later. But for now she felt free. She didn't have to live her life wishing Judah would love her or being jealous of her sister. Esther deserved happiness, and she wouldn't find it in Judah, or any other man.

Peace had been within her reach all along. For once she was ready to grab it—to enjoy life and the blessings God had given her and her family.

She walked around to the front of the barn, making one last swipe at her eyes to make sure there wasn't a trace of tears left. She wouldn't cry over Judah King anymore.

Judah hadn't hitched up his horse yet, probably because he was waiting for Sarah to show up. The thought of him and Sarah together didn't bring the thread of jealousy she was used to, and that brought another smile to her face. She glanced up at the sky. It was a beautiful, warm evening. Perfect for a buggy ride.

Rhett and Sarah approached the barn, and Esther's smile widened as her eyes met Rhett's. He actually looked pretty good in Reuben's clothes. He had on a short-sleeved yellow shirt, suspenders, broadfall pants, and a yellow straw hat that didn't do much to hide his Yankee haircut. He was also wearing white sneakers, which looked odd with the pants, since Amish men usually wore work boots.

He stopped in front of her and grinned. He was always smiling, always cheerful. It was contagious, like Sarah's breezy enthusiasm. "What do you think?" he asked Esther, turning around so she could get a full view.

"You look very Amish."

"I'll take that as a compliment. The suspenders will take some getting used to, though."

"You don't have to wear them, unless Reuben's pants are too big."

"They're actually a little snug." Rhett put his thumb in the waistband, which was a bit tight. "But with all the work I'll be doing, I imagine I'll drop a few pounds."

"Don't be so sure. Our mother is an excellent cook. You might even gain some weight while you're here."

He chuckled. "If tonight's supper was any indication, I think you're right." He moved to stand closer to her. "Maybe after the buggy ride you can give me a tour of the old house."

"You can go over there anytime you'd like," Esther said.

"I'd like the tour, though. I imagine as a guide you include details that make it extra special."

Esther couldn't keep from smiling. He wasn't flirting with her. She was sure of that. There wasn't a single butterfly in sight. He was being sincere, and she appreciated it.

"Where's Judah?" Sarah said, sounding a little annoyed. "I thought the buggy would be hitched by now."

"I'm right here." Judah came outside, leading his horse to the buggy. "I'll be ready in a minute."

Esther looked at him, her smile dimming a bit. His voice sounded gruff, which it never did in Sarah's presence. Even Sarah seemed surprised and turned to Esther, mouthing the words, "What's wrong with him?"

Esther shrugged. Judah's moods didn't interest her anymore. The quick glance she was giving him now was only to make sure he was hitching up the buggy, nothing more.

"You need some help?" Rhett asked, walking toward the buggy.

"I've got it."

Rhett stopped in his tracks, obviously because of Judah's clipped tone. He held out his hands. "Okay. Let me know if I can do anything, though."

After the horse was securely hitched, Esther entered the buggy first, sitting in the back and ignoring Judah. When Rhett climbed in after her, Sarah protested.

"You can sit up front with me and Judah," she said.

"Nah, I'm good." He sat down next to Esther and flashed another grin. "I don't mind sitting in the back."

"But you can see more from up front."

"It will be a little crowded with the three of you, don't you think?" Esther asked.

Sarah's expression darkened. "Not if I'm sitting in the middle."

"Esther's right." Rhett settled against the seat, then glanced at Esther again. "Besides, I've got the best tour guide in town right next to me."

She smiled back at Rhett. There was no underlying message to his words, no false sentiment. Best of all, no *pity*. She settled herself in the seat and prepared for a wonderful ride.

This was the worst ride of Judah's life.

Sarah sat next to him like a statue. There was enough space between them in the front seat of the buggy for his friend Elvin, who was six four, rotund, and took up more room than anyone he knew. But he barely noticed that because of the incessant chatter in the backseat.

Judah had never heard Esther talk so much. Sure, he'd heard her going through her spiel with the tourists she guided, answering their questions with direct precision. But she and Rhett had chatted nonstop, and not just about the scenery in Mespo. At first Esther pointed out things of interest and answered Rhett's questions. But soon they abandoned the tour. Now they were talking about more personal things—Rhett's studies, his university, and their hobbies.

"You took a quilting class?" Esther said, sounding shocked.

"I did. Actually it was the quilting that led to my interest in the Amish, which led me to changing my major from law to cultural studies."

"What made you decide to learn to quilt?"

Judah, his gaze straight on the road, could almost imagine Rhett shrugging.

"It looked interesting. I'm always game to try something new and unusual. I'm thinking about taking a semester off school this fall and spending the time in the Himalayas."

"That's a mountain range in Asia, right?"

"Yes," Rhett said. "Did you learn about that in school?"

"*Nee*. We didn't learn much world geography. But I do love to read."

"Me too. What's the latest book you've read?"

And that launched them into a literary conversation Judah wanted to tune out, but couldn't because he also liked to read. He frowned when he learned he and Rhett had the same taste in fiction—thrillers and mysteries. Esther liked mysteries—another fact Judah didn't know—but didn't care for thrillers, and her favorite genre was historical fiction.

Sarah turned back and faced the front of the buggy, her arms crossed. Judah glanced at her. What was wrong with him? He had the perfect scenario here. Sarah was in the buggy with him, and they might as well be alone since Esther and Rhett were doing a fine job keeping each other company.

Judah knew he should say something to break the tension and bring a smile to Sarah's face. But he didn't want to. He didn't like this side of Sarah, one he'd never seen before. She was broody and pouty. Why? Because she wasn't getting any attention from Rhett? He shook his head. "Huh."

"What did you say?" Sarah asked, speaking to him for the first time since supper.

"*Nix.*" He glanced at her again. "What's *yer* favorite genre?"

"Genre?"

"Book genre. What books do you like to read?"

"I'm not that much of a reader." She glanced over her shoulder at Rhett and Esther again, then blew out a sigh. "Although I used to love the Little House on the Prairie books when I was a girl."

"What do you like to do now?" He realized he didn't really know. The few dates they'd been on, they hadn't talked very much. Well, Sarah had talked a lot, but mostly about her friends or where she wanted him to take her on their date. Judah frowned. Now that he thought about it, he and Sarah hadn't had a single meaningful conversation. He'd been content to just look at her. Unlike his conversations with Esther. It took time to get Esther to talk to him, but when she did, he enjoyed it.

"I like to cook and sew." Sarah turned around again. "I've made several quilts," she said to Rhett.

"Oh?" He leaned forward. "What kind of patterns?"

As Rhett and Sarah started discussing quilt patterns, Judah contemplated jumping out of the buggy. Goldie was an old, reliable horse who could get the three of them back to Coblentz Farms on her own. Meanwhile Judah would bang his head against a tree or go walk through some thornbushes. Either would be preferable to a quilt discussion.

Finally they reached their destination—a small park in Mespo that split the single road into two separate ones. A general store was on the corner, and the park had a gazebo, small pavilion, trees, and some swings on the grassy area. Yankee houses lined each side, and near the road opposite the gazebo was a huge wooden horse and buggy structure. Judah pulled his buggy to the hitching post.

"I'd like to get some pictures," Rhett said as they all climbed out of the buggy.

"Do you want some with you in them?" Sarah asked, her voice sounding a little high and tight and . . . desperate? Where was the composed woman Judah had fallen for? "If so, I—"

"That's a great idea. Esther, do you mind?" He handed Esther the camera and she hesitated a moment. Judah figured she was trying to decide whether using the camera would be a violation of the *Ordnung*. Being in the pictures definitely would. Then she nodded at Rhett, and they walked together to the wooden statue.

"Good grief." Sarah lifted her hands, her pretty face scrunched into a scowl. "I'm going to get something to drink." She spun away from him, flung her purse over her shoulder, and marched to the general store, her hands clenched at her sides, looking about as willowy as a steel beam.

Normally Judah would have jumped at the chance to follow her. This was another prime opportunity to have some alone time with Sarah. They could get a cold pop and sit in the gazebo. It was a clear evening, with only a few puffy clouds in the sky, and a light breeze that provided a nice respite from the warm temperature. Ideal conditions to convince Sarah they belonged together.

Instead he turned and looked at Esther and Rhett. Rhett was standing close to her—too close, Judah thought—while showing her how to use his tiny camera. Then he went and stood by the statue, leaning to the side a bit, knees bent, and showing two thumbs-up. Judah rolled his eyes. Rhett looked ridiculous. But Esther laughed as she snapped his photo.

Her laugh. Wow, she had a lovely laugh. How had he not noticed that before?

Judah stood guard at the buggy while Rhett and Esther continued to take pictures, with Rhett doing most of the picture taking while Esther observed. When Sarah still wasn't back, Judah was a little worried. He had started walking toward the store when he saw her coming out, talking to an Amish man near his age. Judah squinted and realized it was his friend Samuel Keim.

He waited for the irritation and jealousy to rear their ugly heads like they usually did when he saw Sarah with someone else. This time . . . nothing. Now that he knew she was fine, he turned around and searched for Rhett and Esther. When he saw them sitting on the swings, he groaned.

He couldn't wait for this so-called tour to be over.

CHAPTER 5

✺

As she thought about the evening, Esther sat on the edge of her bed and ran a brush through her waist-length locks. She smiled. Not only had she been set free of Judah, but she had made a new friend.

Rhett was smart—really smart. On the surface he seemed a bit air-headed and more than a little quirky—the quilting class proved that—but as she got to know him she realized he was highly intelligent. He loved reading about philosophy, his third favorite kind of book next to mysteries and thrillers. And as they had walked to the swings and sat down, he told her how much he valued the experience the Coblentzes were giving him.

"I just wish my girlfriend was here," he said. "She would enjoy this."

Esther wasn't surprised to discover Rhett had a girlfriend. "Why didn't she come with you?"

"For one, there's no way the two of us would stay together, even if an Amish family would allow it. We wouldn't want to. But she wouldn't have wanted to stay anywhere alone either. Also, she's in nursing school right now, and she wants to graduate early. So she's taking classes all summer."

"How did you two meet?"

"At church, two years ago." He smiled, but this smile was different from the ones he had given her and her family. "I knew she was special the first time I saw her."

"Is she going with you to the Himalayas?"

He shook his head. "No, unfortunately. Which is giving me second thoughts about the idea of that trip. I haven't booked it yet. It's always been a dream of mine to go, and this opportunity came up with some friends of mine who are missionaries. But I don't know if I can be gone from Shelby for that long. I'm missing her already and I've only been here two days."

"Maybe this is a way to see if you can be apart that long."

"That's what I thought." He looked up at Judah and Sarah, who were standing near the buggy. "Guess they're ready to go." Then he looked at Esther. "What's up with those two? Are they together?"

"Judah would like them to be." She was so pleased she could say that out loud. "But Sarah's not interested in settling down."

"I can tell." He gave her a rueful smile. "Is she always so . . ."

"Flirty?"

"That's one way to put it." He pushed against the ground with his toe and the swing moved forward. "I was thinking overwhelming, though."

"She doesn't mean anything by it," Esther said, feeling the need to defend Sarah. "She's just . . . friendly."

He leaned toward her slightly. "You're friendly, Esther. You're easy to talk to, and you're a good listener. She's . . ." He shook his head. "You two seem very different." He stopped the swing and stood up. "I think that's cool."

Esther smiled again at the memory. She and Rhett hadn't talked that much on the ride home. He'd been focused on the scenery, and probably thinking about Shelby too. Judah and Sarah were also quiet. That surprised her. She'd expected Judah to take advantage of his close proximity to Sarah. Then she reminded herself that she wasn't concerned about Judah anymore, and focused on relaxing.

She set her hairbrush on her nightstand just as Sarah burst into her room, then shut the door behind her. When they moved into the addition, she and Sarah no longer had to share a bedroom. "Are you satisfied with *yourself*?" she snapped.

"What?" she asked, bewildered by her sister's anger.

"Monopolizing Rhett's time like that." Sarah crossed her arms over her chest. "You'll probably get in trouble for using a camera."

"It was *yer* idea to take pictures of him," Esther said, rising from the bed.

"You looked silly."

Esther frowned. "I looked silly taking pictures?"

"You looked silly because he's not interested in you."

Frustrated, Esther said, "I know he's not interested in me. I'm not interested in him."

"You sure acted like it tonight."

"Sarah, we were just talking—"

"We were just talking," Sarah mocked, batting her eyelashes almost grotesquely. "He was talking. You were flirting."

"I was not. I don't even know how to flirt."

"Which is why you looked so pathetic."

Her sister's words hurt to the core. It was one thing to think of herself as pathetic, but to hear her sister say it undid every pleasant and confident feeling she'd experienced for the past few hours. "You better leave now." Esther sat down on the bed. "Before we both say something we regret."

Sarah paused. Esther wasn't looking at her, but she could tell

her sister was hesitating to leave. Probably firing up more ammu-
nition to hurl at her. It wasn't enough that she was the sister who
had everything—beauty, grace, popularity, men like Judah falling at her feet. She could also be hateful when she was upset.

When Sarah didn't move, Esther turned to her. To her surprise the anger on her sister's face was gone, replaced by remorse.
But Esther was too hurt to care. "Leave, Sarah."

Sarah paused, biting her bottom lip as her crystal-blue eyes
became glassy. Then she turned, opened the door, and left the
room.

Although it was nearly ninety degrees outside, the chilliness
between the Coblentz sisters was palpable. Judah leaned against
his rake and watched as Sarah and Esther sat at opposite ends of
the bench Enoch had put under a huge oak tree, both of them
shelling peas.

He'd never seen them like this before. Even more puzzling,
when he'd arrived a few hours ago, he hadn't sought out Sarah like
he usually did. But he'd been happy to see Esther right away—
until he saw the pain on her face. The same pain was also on Sarah's
face. Something had happened between them after he left last
night. He had to remind himself it wasn't his business, but that
didn't stem his curiosity.

He went back to raking up the grass and stray hay in front
of the petting barn. It was Saturday, and Judah normally worked
half a day, then went home and spent the rest of the time with
his family until Monday. But today he was here longer than usual,
mostly because Reuben and Enoch had gone to a farm implement

auction, which left Rhett to his own devices. Considering the guy's lack of farm experience, Judah figured he'd stick around and make sure Rhett didn't inadvertently destroy anything. Right now he was cleaning out the stalls in the petting barn, a hot, smelly task Judah was glad to give him and, oddly enough, Rhett seemed happy to take.

Judah paused in his raking and looked at the women again. Sarah got up, took her bowl of shelled peas, and went inside the house. Esther put her bowl next to her, then leaned her head against her hands.

He couldn't stand to see Esther in pain. Although he didn't know what he was going to say to her, he had started for the bench when Rhett came up beside him. Judah smelled the sweat and manure coming off of him, and he hoped that was a result of cleaning out the stalls, not falling into a pile of something he shouldn't have.

"Thought I'd take a little break." Rhett took off his hat and wiped his forehead with the back of his hand. "If that's all right with you."

There was no sarcasm in the man's voice. Judah looked at him. His smile was faded and a bit work-worn, but still there. He'd eagerly accepted the most menial chore Judah could think of. It was becoming difficult to keep disliking him. "Sure. Get some water too. It's easy to get dehydrated if you're not used to the work."

"Or the heat. I'm a wimp. I'll admit it. I use the gym, but it's air-conditioned. So is my apartment." His face was flushed. "I don't know if I'll ever get used to the heat."

"It takes time. Or so I've heard. I don't know anything different, except when I go into a store or restaurant. Gotta admit, the cold air feels good on a hot summer day."

"That it does." He started walking away. "You want anything from the house?"

"No, but thanks for asking." That was another thing about the guy. He was considerate, and not because he was trying to earn points. Everything about him was genuine. Yes, it was hard to dislike Rhett Davidson.

Despite his complaining about the heat, Rhett moved toward the house with quick steps. He paused at the bench, then sat down next to Esther—too close to Esther, Judah noticed. Without thinking, Judah put aside the rake and went to them.

"You sure you're okay?" Judah heard Rhett ask as he approached.

Esther nodded, giving him a strained smile that didn't reach her eyes. Judah had seen that look in her eyes before, right after he'd hurt her yesterday. Was she still upset with him?

"Do you want a drink of water?" Rhett asked.

"No. I'm fine." She searched his face. "You look like you could use one."

"I'm headed inside now. But if you want to talk, I'm here."

Jealousy stabbed at Judah with intensity. Why would Esther want to talk to Rhett? Had they already become so close that she felt comfortable confiding in him?

"I appreciate the offer." A small smile formed on her lips again. And again, it didn't reach her eyes.

Rhett got up and went inside. Just as the screen door banged shut, Judah slid in next to Esther. "What's wrong?" he demanded.

She looked up at him, her brow lifted. *"Nix."*

"You're lying."

"Judah, I'm not lying—"

"Esther, I've known you a long time, and I can tell when you're lying. You're upset with me, aren't you?"

"I . . . I—"

"I'm sorry, okay?" He took off his hat and ran a hand through his damp hair. "I know I hurt you yesterday. I'm not exactly sure how. I guess I shouldn't have called you weird."

"You didn't call me weird. You said I was acting weird. That's a big difference. Unless you meant to call me weird."

There went the lift of that chin, and Judah had to admit it was cute, even more cute than when she'd had that dot of ice cream on her nose at the Parlor. And when did he start thinking of Esther as cute?

"You're not weird, okay?" He sounded agitated. He was agitated, and he had no idea why. That awareness didn't stop him from blurting out his next words. "There, does that make you feel better?"

She shot up from the bench, her eyes sparking with anger. "For *yer* information, Judah King, what I'm feeling has *nix* to do with you." She picked up her bowl and went inside the house.

This time Judah flinched as the screen door banged shut. He'd made a mess of that, all right. But if she wasn't upset with him, what was she upset about? More importantly, why did he care so much?

❦

That Sunday, as Esther sat on a wood bench during their church service held in a barn, she tried to focus on the minister's preaching. Wally Schlabach was hard to listen to, even when Esther's thoughts and feelings weren't in turmoil. He was a fine, kind man, a good minister, but probably the worst preacher on the planet. He stumbled over words, mangled scripture passages, and went off on tangents that even had the bishop scratching his head. Then there was the monotone delivery. But every fourth Sunday, Wally Schlabach delivered the message. Without fail.

This morning Esther desperately wanted something to distract her from what had happened yesterday. Sarah still wasn't speaking to her, and she wasn't all that willing to talk to Sarah. Not until she apologized, at least. Rhett had been his usual kind self, and she appreciated the offer to talk.

But what puzzled her most was Judah's behavior. He'd apologized to her for saying she acted weird, but the apology wasn't necessary. She hadn't even thought about that since it happened. But his apology had not only been sincere, it had been . . . fervent. That was a fancy word, but the only one she could think of to describe what she'd seen in his eyes, heard in his voice. Judah couldn't hide that sincerity, not if he tried. It had reached inside her, pulled out the tiny fragment of that cord of hope that apparently hadn't disappeared completely, and yanked it tight—which had disturbed her even more. The last thing she needed was to have those feelings rekindled.

As Wally droned on, her gaze drifted to the other side of the barn. Sitting next to Reuben, Rhett was easy to spot. He was paying rapt attention to the minister's sermon, as if Wally was the most eloquent speaker he'd ever heard. Reuben, on the other hand, was struggling to stay awake. Although she didn't want to, her gaze strayed to Judah, seated a couple of benches back.

The moment she spotted him he turned and looked at her, as if he'd sensed her watching him. Her cheeks heated and she pulled her gaze away, but not before she saw something she'd never seen in Judah's eyes before, at least not when he'd looked at her.

Interest. He had looked at her with interest.

After the service, Sarah, who had been seated at the end of Esther's bench on the other side of their mother, hurried out of the barn. *Mamm* gave Esther a puzzled look. Esther shrugged. Obviously *Mamm* suspected something was going on with her and Sarah, but Esther didn't want to talk about it. Her feelings still stung from Sarah's verbal assault.

Esther walked outside, pausing for a moment to talk to her friend Julia, who had married last year. She promised to visit Julia during the week, then left the barn and stood in the front yard of Samuel Keim's house. The service was being held at his family's farm, so she was within walking distance of her house, and she didn't want to stay for fellowship this afternoon. She wanted to be alone.

She went to her parents, told them she was walking home, and then started for the road. Rhett stopped her. "You're not staying?"

Shaking her head, she said, "I'm a little tired. I'm going home, and I'll probably take a nap."

"I totally get it. A nap sounds good right now, but I'm staying. Reuben said he'd introduce me to a few of his friends. Everyone's been really nice." He grinned, then said, "Maybe a group of us guys could visit Lake Erie while I'm here. Do you know anything about fishing charters there?"

"*Ya.* Our family reserves one every summer, usually the second week of July. We'll be going this weekend."

"Really?" His eyes grew wide with excitement. "Do you think I could go with you?"

"I'm surprised *Daed* hasn't told you about it. I'm sure he doesn't intend to leave you here by yourself." Esther explained how they always went to Geneva-on-the-Lake. This year they were trying out a new rental area, with nice cottages that had a lovely view of

Lake Erie's shoreline. "We're usually there from Friday to Monday. *Daed* doesn't like to be gone from the farm much longer than that."

Rhett nodded. "Are you sure there's room?"

"Since *Daed* knew you were coming, he probably rented an extra cottage. He hasn't said much about the trip lately, probably because of getting all the extra crops in."

"I'll pay for it," he said quickly. "And whatever it costs for the charter too."

Esther thought for a moment. "I'm sure Reuben will be more than happy to split a cottage rental with you to get that much space to himself. I wouldn't worry about the charter fee—"

"I'm paying my way," Rhett insisted.

"Okay, okay." She chuckled. "You can work it out with *Daed*."

Rhett grinned. "Do you like to fish?"

"I'm not the best at fishing, but I enjoy it. It's peaceful, sitting on a boat or on the shore of a lake or pond."

"I fished a couple of times when I was a kid," he said. "But not on Lake Erie, so I'm looking forward to it." He glanced at Reuben, who was waving him over to a group of his friends. "I'll see you later," he said, then took off.

At supper the next night, *Daed* said, "I'm glad Rhett brought up our vacation today. We've been so busy with that new field I've been forgetting to mention that all those cottages were already booked for this weekend. With buying that property and making plans for it, I waited too long to contact them."

Esther frowned. "What about the weekend after?"

"I didn't check." He took a slice of watermelon from the platter in the middle of the table and placed it on his plate. Usually they ate watermelon outside, but it had started raining a couple of hours ago. "We've always gone the second weekend of July. It's tradition."

She knew better than to argue with him. One glance at her mother told her she was right. Her father would forgo vacation before he'd change the date. She pushed at a watermelon seed with her fork, disappointed. She enjoyed their yearly vacations, and she'd been looking forward to this one.

"So we're going camping instead," *Daed* proclaimed.

"Camping?" Sarah said, looking incredulous. "In a tent?"

Daed held up two fingers. "Two tents. Reuben and Rhett can share one."

Reuben was grinning so widely Esther thought his face had to hurt.

Sarah scowled at him. "What are you so happy about?"

"I don't have to share with you two." He pointed his fork at her, then at Esther. "This will be the best vacation ever."

"*Mamm*, are you okay with this?" Sarah asked.

"Of course. *Yer daed* and I used to *geh* camping before you *kinner* were born. I even found our old sleeping bags, and they're in *gut* shape."

"We'll have to get four more." *Daed* took a bite of his watermelon, then wiped his bearded chin with his napkin. "Plus another tent."

"I called and reserved a fishing charter for Saturday," Rhett added, looking at Esther. "We'll have the boat for the whole day."

"Count me out," Reuben said. He pushed his plate away.

Esther wasn't surprised Reuben wasn't interested in an all-day charter. Her brother could fish for a couple of hours, but he got bored quickly.

"I'll *geh*," Sarah said.

"But you get motion sickness," *Mamm* reminded her.

Reuben nudged Rhett with his elbow. "Last time she was on a boat she barfed over the side. Twice. And that was in a little canoe."

Sarah's lips pressed into a thin line. "That was ten years ago."

"I don't think being on the water all day is a *gut* idea." *Mamm* patted her hand. Her family had been slipping into *Deitsch* with Rhett present from time to time, which Esther noticed he actually seemed to appreciate. "I thought you and I could spend the *daag* at the gift shops instead."

Sarah nodded, her lips still tight.

Esther looked away from her sister and glanced at Judah. He'd been quiet during the conversation, and she expected him to be gazing at Sarah, or at least looking at her with concern since Reuben had just embarrassed her. Instead his attention was on her father. "I've got a tent you can use," he said. "Extra sleeping bags too. Are you camping at the state park?"

"*Ya*," *Daed* said, taking a bite of the watermelon rind as was his habit. A distasteful one, Esther always thought. But he loved watermelon rind. "Already reserved the campsite as soon as I knew we couldn't get cottages. It's probably not one of their best spots, but we're fortunate the park even had one available."

He turned to Rhett. "I won't be able to fish that day with you and Esther either."

"You're going shopping with *Mamm* and Sarah?" Reuben cracked.

"*Nee*." He gave Reuben a pointed look. "I'm meeting with a *freind* from Holmes. Found out a couple of *daags* ago that he'll be in the Geneva area at the same time."

"So it's just me and Esther, then?" Rhett asked.

"And the charter captain," Esther added with a small smile. "Don't forget him."

Sarah pushed away from the table. "The rabbits need feeding."

"I already fed them," Rhett said. But Sarah ignored him and walked out of the kitchen.

Esther half expected Judah to go after her. But he stayed in his seat, his watermelon only partially eaten.

"Sounds like everything is settled," *Daed* said. "The van will be here for us Friday morning bright and early. *Danki* for loaning us the tent and sleeping bags, Judah."

Judah didn't say anything in return. He didn't even nod. His gaze bounced from Esther to Rhett, then back to Esther again. "I'll *geh* fishing with you." His brow lifted, as if he'd surprised himself with the words. "I can meet you on Saturday morning."

"Why don't you just *geh* camping with us?" Reuben asked. "That would be easier. The van is big enough for all of us."

Esther swallowed as Judah slowly nodded, his eyes never leaving hers. Was he asking for permission to fish? Camp? She was caught so off guard by his sudden decision that she had no idea what he was thinking.

Then he turned to *Daed*. "I'd like to, if it's okay with you, Enoch."

"Sure. The more the merrier." He stood. "You're pretty much *familye* as it is, so why not *geh* on a *familye* vacation with us?"

Esther stared at her watermelon, confused. Judah had never expressed an interest in vacationing with them before. Then again, maybe he realized he could spend more time with Sarah if he went. But that didn't explain him wanting to go fishing with her and Rhett, enough that he was willing to go to the trouble to meet them Saturday morning.

When she looked up, Judah was already standing and *Mamm* was clearing the table. Judah gave Esther a short nod, then left, her father, Reuben, and Rhett not far behind.

Esther saw her mother pause as the men left. "What?" she asked, able to tell there was something on *Mamm's* mind.

"*Nix.*" She held the platter of watermelon. A few juicy pieces still remained on the large white plate. "It's just . . ." She shook her head, but Esther didn't miss her slight smile. "It's going to be an interesting vacation this year."

Esther glanced at the empty doorway. She was thinking the same thing.

CHAPTER 6

Judah didn't like fish—catching them or eating them. But the thought of Esther being on a boat in the middle of Lake Erie with Rhett had made his thoughts go berserk. Now he found himself helping Rhett and Reuben set up a tent a few feet from where Esther would be sleeping tonight—again.

He'd offered to help set up the large tent where Esther and Sarah and her parents would sleep, but Enoch asked him to help set up the other tent with Reuben and Rhett. They'd done just that, only to have the tent collapse on one side, and for once a mishap wasn't Rhett's fault. Turned out he had a lot of experience tent camping. No, it was Reuben who hadn't secured the tent stakes properly on his side of the tent.

He glanced at Esther as she helped her father, hammering the last of their tent's stakes more firmly into the ground. He hadn't been able to keep his eyes off her since arriving at the Coblentzes before dawn. He'd even tried to sit next to her in the van Enoch hired to take them and all their gear to Geneva State Park, but she climbed into the backseat next to her mother. Sarah made sure to sit next to Rhett, which left Judah to sit next to Reuben on the bench seat closest to the front of the van.

After the tents were set up, Reuben and Rhett insisted Judah go with them for a long and vigorous hike through the park. By the time they came back, Esther had taken off on one of the two bikes the Coblentzes brought from home. She didn't return until suppertime, and then she was busy helping her mother and Sarah—who still looked more than a little put out about the whole camping thing—make a delicious supper of grilled beef hot dogs, packaged coleslaw, homemade pickles, and potato chips.

He sat at the picnic table as he watched Esther. He noticed little things about her, like the efficiency of her movements as she prepared the meal. She didn't have graceful movements like Sarah, but she wasn't clumsy or clunky. He took note of the smallness of her hands, the daintiness of her wrists. The curve of her neck.

The perfect area on her neck to place a kiss.

"Huh," he said out loud.

"What?" Reuben said from the space next to him.

"*Nix.*" He quickly pulled his gaze away from Esther and focused on Sarah, which he should have been doing to begin with. Wasn't this another prime opportunity to spend time with her? To convince her they belonged together? What he shouldn't be doing was thinking about Esther's neck. Or about kissing it. Where had that thought come from, anyway?

As he watched Sarah, he waited for that familiar jolt of attraction he always experienced when she was near. She'd even glanced at him, giving him a tiny smile that should have made his heart do cartwheels. Instead . . . he felt nothing.

"Here you *geh*," Esther said, handing him a full plate.

Jolt. He stared at her, then at the plate blankly, then back at her.

"Judah." She sounded impatient. "Here's *yer* food."

"Right. Sorry." He took the plate from her, said a quick silent prayer, and tried to focus on eating and not on the shot of attraction he'd just felt for Esther. This didn't make any sense. Sarah was the woman for him. The one he was attracted to. The one he loved. Esther was . . . Esther. A friend. Nothing special.

She sat down at the end of the table near Rhett and closed her eyes. Judah couldn't stop watching her. Her lashes rested against her soft cheeks, which were rosy from the summer heat.

Jolt. This one was stronger. Deeper. More confusing than anything he'd felt before. "I'm going to take a walk," he said, standing up and ignoring his full plate.

"We just hiked ten miles," Rhett said.

"You haven't even touched *yer* food," Reuben added around a mouthful of coleslaw.

But Judah disregarded both of them. He needed to get away from Esther, to figure out what was going on. He'd been in love with Sarah for four years. Yet for the past few days he hadn't given her a second thought.

What's going on, Lord? You'll have to tell me, because I have no idea.

The next morning Esther walked onto the wood dock of the Geneva Marina, carrying her tackle box and fishing pole. She tried to focus on enjoying the upcoming charter and not on Judah, but it was difficult. He was acting strange. Very strange. He hadn't returned from his walk last night by the time she turned in, which was pretty early, even before everyone else had gone to bed. She was tired, not just from bike riding and camping, but also from the strain between her and Sarah all week. They were being civil to each other, which was at least something. But being at odds with Sarah put a damper on everything.

She knew they should talk, but she couldn't bring herself to start the conversation. Sarah had hurt her, not the other way around. It was her sister's job to fix things between them, and so far she hadn't. Between that and Judah's bizarre behavior, Esther was having trouble enjoying herself.

Pulling herself out of those thoughts, she focused on fishing. Rhett said they could purchase worms at the dock, and that's where he and Judah were now. But she wanted to try a few special lures she'd never used. The seagulls soared above them, the waves from the lake lapping against the rocky edges, the sun high and hot in the summer sky. A perfect day for fishing.

As she approached the boat Rhett told her was the one he chartered, she realized Rhett and Judah were right behind her. They carried the cooler Esther packed earlier. After a few minutes, the captain greeted them.

"Another small group was going to come with us, but they canceled at the last minute. So it's just the four of us."

"Sounds great!" Rhett said.

Esther didn't have to look at him to know he was grinning.

They listened as the captain explained the process and procedure.

"Make sure you don't fall over," the leathery-skinned man said with intense seriousness. "And don't take any unnecessary chances."

Feeling like she was back in the schoolhouse, Esther nodded.

They climbed on board, and before long they shoved off. Esther stood close to the edge of the boat, her face feeling the wind that glided across the lake while her body rocked with the boat's movement. Now, this was freedom. She closed her eyes and finally allowed herself to relax.

"Sunscreen?"

She looked at the tube of sunscreen in Rhett's hand. "Thank you," she said. "I'd forgotten about it." She put some in her hand and placed a few dots on her face before rubbing it in. Then she applied the rest to the back of her neck.

"You missed a spot." Rhett reached around and rubbed his fingers on her neck. "There, got it."

She smiled as he took the sunscreen and went to the other side of the boat. Her smile disappeared when she saw Judah looking at her with a mix of confusion, then at Rhett with a look of . . . No, that couldn't be right. Jealousy? Esther blinked as Judah looked away.

She had to have imagined it. Judah would be jealous of Rhett with Sarah, not of Rhett with her. Not that there was anything to be jealous of when it came to either of them. Rhett had shown her a picture of Shelby the other day. She was a stunning dark-haired woman with almond-shaped eyes and a vibrant smile that nearly rivaled Rhett's. He must have told her he didn't plan to use his cell phone, because they'd been sending letters or postcards all week. Esther was pretty sure Rhett wouldn't go on that Himalayan trip after all.

They fished for the rest of the morning, catching mostly perch. They stopped midday and ate their packed lunch beneath the shade of the boat's awning. Rhett, who Esther realized could talk to anyone about anything, was in deep conversation with the captain about the strangest charter trips he'd had.

For some reason Judah had isolated himself and was sitting

on the opposite end of the shaded area. He'd been by himself all morning, too, and, she heard him tell Rhett when he asked, had caught only one fish. A small one that had to be thrown back.

Esther finished her apple, put it in a paper bag, and folded down the top. She'd throw all their trash away when they got back to the dock. She set the bag aside, then went to the stern. She peered into the lake water, fascinated by the bubbles and foam floating on the surface. Trying to get a better view, she stood on tiptoe and tried to spy any fish that might be swimming close to the surface.

Realizing she was too short, she looked around for something to stand on and saw the cooler. She tested her weight on it, then stepped up. The bar of the boat rail pressed against her knees as she leaned forward. Then she saw it—a huge perch. It swam back and forth in front of the boat as if daring her to reach down and try to catch it. She knew it was foolish to try, but she reached out anyway.

"Esther!"

Judah's bellow startled her and she whirled around. The cooler tilted. She grabbed for the boat rail, missed, then tipped right over into the water.

CHAPTER 7

‿❧‿

"Esther!" Judah yelled as she went overboard. He ran toward the railing and saw her flailing about in the water. Without thinking—or taking off his hat or boots—he dove in after her.

"What in the—"

The captain's angry voice rang in Judah's ears, along with his expletive. He had dived a little bit past Esther, so he turned around and swam back to her, the water seeping into his boots and making him feel as though he had anchors tied around his ankles.

"Judah, what are you doing?" Esther said.

He put his arm around her waist . . . and realized she was fine. She wasn't fighting for breath or stability. She was bobbing in the waves, looking completely comfortable . . . and completely water-logged. Her *kapp* sagged on her head and water dripped down her cheeks. He tightened his arm around her waist and drew her close, nearly losing himself in the mix of excitement and confusion he saw in her eyes. His gaze dropped to her mouth—

"Are you two okay?" Rhett yelled.

No. He definitely wasn't okay. Right at that moment, holding

Esther close—his face only inches from hers—thinking about kissing her breathless . . . He was better than okay. He was fantastic.

She put her hand on his shoulder. "Judah . . ."

Yep. He'd kiss her right now, right in front of the bellowing captain, who was threatening to throw them a rope. Right in front of Rhett, who Judah was sure was grinning from ear to ear since that seemed to be his only expression. He didn't care who was watching.

Then, just like that, Esther wriggled away from him and swam back to the boat, as if he were a poisonous water snake.

He followed her, grabbing his hat along the way. He was a pretty good swimmer, and they weren't that far from the boat, but with his boots dragging him down, it was an effort to reach the ladder. He hauled himself up behind her and sat down on the boat's seat. Unable to bring himself to look at Esther, he focused on yanking off his boots and pouring out the water.

"Here."

Judah couldn't keep from looking up as Rhett put a towel around Esther's shoulders. For once Rhett wasn't smiling. He was sitting next to her, and they were talking in hushed tones. Jealousy twisted inside Judah, not for the first time since they'd boarded this boat. Any clarity he might have gained from his long walk last night disappeared the moment he saw the two of them together this morning at breakfast. Esther and Rhett seemed way too cozy for comfort, especially when he was putting sunscreen on her neck when they got here. Her pretty neck. Which made him want to throw Rhett overboard and finish putting the sunscreen on her himself.

He yanked off a sock and wrung it out over the side of the boat. When he turned around, the captain held out a towel to him, but didn't say anything. He didn't have to. The dark scowl on his face spoke volumes.

"I'm ready to go back to the campsite." Esther's voice sounded small. She even looked small, her shoulders slumped as if the towel around her weighed fifty pounds, her *kapp* pressed against her head, water dripping from the hem of her dress.

Rhett nodded and went to speak to the captain, who immediately started the boat engine. They headed for the marina.

Judah shook off his hat, set it down next to his waterlogged boots and damp socks, and stared at his bare feet. Rhett seemed annoyed, the captain was still angry, and worst of all, Esther was upset. With him. He didn't get it. She was the one who fell overboard. All he did was jump in to save her.

She didn't need saving. She didn't need me.

That truth slammed into him. Esther didn't need him. But why did he want her to? Wondering why he cared so much about what Esther did or thought or needed had plagued him the last few days, and he still didn't have any answers.

The ride to the marina seemed interminable. Finally the captain pulled the boat into the dock, begrudgingly offering to let them bring the towels back tomorrow. Rhett conversed with him while Esther made her way off the boat. Judah saw that she'd forgotten her pole and tackle box. He grabbed his boots, socks, and hat, snatched up her things, and leapt over the side of the boat, hoping Rhett would grab the cooler. His bare feet landed on the scorching hot dock, but he barely felt the heat as he went after her. He hadn't realized how fast she was walking, but finally he caught up to her.

"Esther," he said, sounding a little breathless, and he wasn't sure it was from the exercise.

She didn't answer him, keeping her chin down, the towel around her shoulders, and quickening her steps.

"You forgot *yer* pole and tackle box." Judah walked alongside her. When she didn't acknowledge him, he moved to stand in front of her, making her stop. "Esther, talk to me."

"About what?" Her voice sounded strained and high pitched.

"The fact that you embarrassed me back there?"

"Embarrassed? How?"

"I know how to swim." She tilted her chin, and he recognized the gesture as defiance and a reach for confidence.

"I know."

"You didn't have to *geh* in after me and . . . and . . ."

His eyebrow lifted. "And what?"

"And manhandle me!"

And then Judah did exactly the wrong thing. He laughed. "Manhandle you? I was helping you."

"You were . . ." She looked upset and confused. "I don't know what you were doing. I didn't need help. I didn't need rescuing." She tried to move past him, but he stepped in front of her again.

"Esther, we need to talk about this. But not here." He looked around. They'd caught the attention of the few people around them, and although he and Esther were arguing in Deitsch, they were making a spectacle. Why she thought this was less embarrassing than him swimming after her was beyond him. "When we get to the campground, we'll *geh* for a walk—"

"I'm not going anywhere with you."

The snap in her voice cut him, as did the faint quivering of her chin.

She pushed past him and walked away, heading for the bait shop.

The heat from the dock burned through the bottoms of his feet, and he high-stepped it to the grassy area near the parking lot. Although his socks were still damp, he shoved them on, then walked to the bait shop. Judah saw Esther leaving, looking as if she'd quickly tidied up a little in the shop's bathroom. Presumably she was heading back to the campsite. He started after her, only to have Rhett stop him.

"I wouldn't follow her if I were you," Rhett said.

Judah spun around. "Mind your own business."

"I usually do." Rhett set down the cooler and his gear, then pushed back his Amish hat. He hadn't worn a stitch of Yankee clothing since his second day here.

But Judah wasn't in the mood to give him any credit. "You should stay your course, then." Judah started to turn when Rhett interrupted him again.

"You're pretty dense for a smart guy."

Judah walked toward him, stopping when they were inches away from each other. Judah was a couple of inches taller than Rhett, and he took a bit of satisfaction in that since right now he felt as though he was otherwise at a disadvantage. "Don't think I haven't noticed you've had your eye on Esther ever since you arrived at the farm."

"Whoa." Rhett held up his hands and stepped back. "You think I have a thing for Esther?"

"Why is that so hard to believe? Any man would be lucky to have her."

"And you want that man to be you."

Judah froze.

Rhett shook his head, and a bit of his typical smile returned. "First off, I've got a girlfriend. A serious girlfriend. I'll probably ask her to marry me when I get home, I've missed her that much. Second, why are you mad at me? You're the one who's made a mess of things."

"What?" Judah said in a strangled voice.

"You're interested in Esther, right?"

Judah paused. Was he interested in her? He thought about how his feelings for her had changed. How he'd noticed things about her he'd never noticed before. Her sweet kindness. Her pretty smile. The way she took care of everyone, and even how much she was affected by her falling out with Sarah. He still didn't know what all that was about.

Most of all, he recalled the words he'd just said to Rhett. Remembered how he felt holding Esther in the water, the warmth of her hand when it touched his shoulder. How he had wanted to kiss her with a strength and intensity he'd never felt before . . . not even with Sarah.

"See, that's the problem right there," Rhett said, interrupting Judah's confused train of thought. "You can't even answer a simple question when it comes to Esther. Until you get your head on straight, you need to leave her alone . . . before you break her heart."

CHAPTER 8

AFTER SHE RETURNED HOME FROM VACATION ON MONDAY, Esther went through the motions of life. She led the tours, smiled at the tourists at the appropriate times, answered their questions, and helped *Mamm* with meals and chores. She made it through the daytime hours. Nighttime was a different story.

The last two nights at the lake had been bad enough, but for the two nights they'd been back, she'd tossed and turned, tried to pray, tried counting sheep, tried deep breathing. But all she could do was see Judah's face, the way he'd looked at her when he'd held her in the water. If she didn't know any better, she'd think he'd wanted to kiss her. And that's where the anger started. Not at him, but with herself. Not only was she a fool, but she was a love-struck fool for once again believing she stood a chance with Judah.

That feeling wouldn't go away, even though she hadn't seen him since he'd abruptly left the campground after the fishing trip. She'd taken her time walking back from the marina, slowly drying out as she took the long way around the park, not wanting to face Judah. When she finally arrived at the site, Rhett was worried. "I was about to try to find you," he'd said. "But Enoch convinced me you were fine."

"She knows how to take care of herself." *Daed* didn't even look up from the fish he was cleaning.

Esther looked around the campsite, expecting to see Judah close by. But she soon learned he'd used the bait shop phone to call for a driver and had gone back home. "Decided he wasn't cut out for this camping thing." *Daed*'s words were cryptic, and he didn't look at her when he spoke.

Esther should have been relieved, and a part of her was. At least she didn't have to spend the rest of her vacation feeling awkward around him. She had enough of that with Sarah.

But another part of her was disappointed. He hadn't gone after her. Hadn't stayed so they could talk, like he'd insisted they needed to do at the marina. Either whatever she thought she saw in his eyes wasn't real or he'd changed his mind—again.

Judah had not only left the campsite, but also hadn't returned to work on the farm yesterday. And her father hadn't said anything about why he was absent. To top it all off, she and Sarah still weren't on good terms. Even Rhett seemed subdued. Esther felt some guilt about that—he hadn't bargained for all this family drama.

By Wednesday evening, she couldn't take the tension anymore. After a mostly silent supper, she went for a walk. Ohio got its fair share of humid weather in the summer, and the evening air was thick and steamy. Perspiration appeared on her skin by the time she made it to the end of their driveway. She turned onto the road in front of their house as the sun was close to dipping below the horizon. But she didn't stop to admire the colors she loved. She couldn't go on like this, her heart in turmoil, confusion churning in her stomach.

Why was Judah staying away? Was it because of her? He

hadn't even been by to see Sarah, not that her sister was concerned. She'd gone out last night with Levi Erb, another one of her admirers. Sarah was living her life, despite being at odds with Esther and Judah being a no-show.

Esther was the exact opposite. She missed Sarah and hated that they couldn't work things out. She'd finally tried to talk to her sister about their fight before they left the lake, only to give up when Sarah barely responded.

Esther's thoughts returned to Judah. More than once recently, she'd felt she was free of him. Yet when she wasn't fretting about Sarah, she was missing him. She glanced up at the sky. *Lord, why am I so confused?* No, she wasn't only confused. She was hurting, and she didn't know how to stop.

She was about to cross the road to turn around and head home when she heard the *clip-clop* of a horse and buggy behind her. She stepped to the side to let the buggy by. When it slowed down beside her, she glanced at the driver and almost tripped over her feet. Judah.

"Hi, Esther," he said.

He wasn't smiling, not exactly. In fact, he looked a little nervous, but also calm. She had no idea how he managed that.

"Do you need a ride home?" he asked.

That was Judah. Polite. Friendly. And acting like he hadn't disappeared for days without a trace. Which annoyed her, come to think of it. She'd take that over her troubled heart right now. "I'm fine," she said, walking a little faster, planning to turn around toward home as soon as he left.

"It's getting dark."

She hurried her steps, and the horse immediately matched them.

"Esther, I'd really like to give you a ride."

His words stopped her. He pulled on the horse's reins as she turned to him. "Sarah's not home," she said. Although if he wanted to see Sarah, why had he passed their driveway coming here?

He frowned, his black eyebrows flattening in confusion. "Sarah? What does she have to do with me giving you a ride home?"

She sighed. He could be so dense sometimes. Maybe he'd come after her to make some sort of apology or something, but of course he'd want to see Sarah after being away from her for a few days. And now that he knew she wasn't home, she was sure he'd want Esther to give her a message.

"Sarah and I still aren't talking. If you want to get a message to her, you'll have to do it *yerself*." She started walking again, crossing her arms over her chest and feeling sweat trickling between her shoulder blades. How feminine. She grimaced and unfolded her arms.

Before she'd gone more than a few feet, he was right beside her again. "I don't want to talk to Sarah, Esther. I want to talk to you."

"I'm busy." She sounded like a child, but she couldn't help it. She was tired. Tired of being disappointed, of not being able to let Judah go because she couldn't stop seeing—and wishing for—something that wasn't there. Of knowing that he'd rather chase after Sarah, who didn't care about him, than be with her. She swallowed the sudden lump in her throat.

Esther heard the buggy pull to a stop. She stepped in front of the horse to cross the road—and didn't stop until Judah stood in front of her. She had to halt, or slam into his chest, and she wasn't about to do that. "Judah, please. Just leave me alone."

"I can't."

Shocked at the tender urgency in his voice, she looked up at him.

"I want to talk to you . . . I need to . . ." His brow furrowed ever so slightly, and his eyes darkened in a way that made her toes automatically curl in her sneakers. Her palms grew damp, and not because of the sultry air.

She'd never known Judah to be at a loss for words. She couldn't break her gaze from his or steady her pulse. Or even think clearly. She gasped as he cradled her face in his hands.

"Words later," he whispered, then gently kissed her.

And it was everything she'd ever dreamed of and more. For a moment she melted into the kiss, unable to believe this was actually happening. She regained her senses and pulled away. "Why did you do that?" she asked, then put her fingers to her still-tingling mouth.

"I had to."

"You *had* to?" His words cut through her shock and surprised delight. "You *had* to?" she repeated.

"*Ya.* I mean, *nee.* I mean . . ." He wasn't wearing his hat, and he threaded his fingers through his hair. Then he grabbed her hand, as if he could tell she was about to bolt again. "You're not going anywhere," he said. "Not until we talk."

~∾∽

Judah was handling this badly. He'd spent the past few days alone and in prayer, seeking God for clarity. Enoch gave him the time off when Judah asked for it before he even left the campsite on Saturday, and Judah had taken advantage of the time. He'd gone on long walks, ridden his brother's horse, sat in the woods, and even tried to go fishing in his neighbor's pond. Fishing had been a mistake, since that reminded him of Esther—of wanting to kiss Esther, to be specific—and he didn't want his thoughts more muddied than they already were.

A little over an hour ago he'd realized what he needed to do. He wasted no time seeking out Esther. Enoch had told him she'd gone for a walk. When he caught up to her, any residual doubts about his feelings disappeared. It was as if everything had fallen into place the moment he saw her.

He'd planned to take her home, letting Goldie lead at the slow, leisurely pace the old mare usually enjoyed. He'd imagined they'd talk, he'd declare his feelings for her, and she might give him a chance to make up for last week. If he was lucky, she'd let him take her to the Parlor again or for an evening ride in his open buggy. She'd get to know him. To find out he was sincere about his feelings for her. And maybe, just maybe, she would start to like him too.

Instead he'd kissed her, which he only regretted because of timing. Kissing her soft lips was more than he could have imagined. But he'd overstepped a line, a huge one. Now he'd have a lot of backtracking to do for her to give him a chance.

She wasn't looking at him now, and her hand laid in his like a limp fish. He did let go of her hand, though ready to grab it again if she tried to disappear.

"Leave me alone, Judah."

"Esther, please listen to me. I know I shouldn't have kissed you."

Her chest heaved as she let out a long-suffering sigh. "Don't worry, I won't bring it up again." She looked at him, her beautiful eyes dull and lifeless. "Sarah will never know."

"I don't care if you tell Sarah."

Her brow lifted, shock in her eyes. Her beautiful blue eyes. "You don't?"

"Sarah's not the one I'm interested in."

She tilted her gaze at him and frowned. "Did you hit *yer* head while you were away?"

He laughed. "*Nee.* I'm perfectly levelheaded."

Esther crossed her arms, her expression dubious. "You just kissed me in the middle of the street. That's not levelheaded."

Behind him he heard Goldie whinny, and he was grateful not only for her patience, but for the fact that the Coblentzes lived on a low-traffic road. "I'm levelheaded, except when it comes to you."

She took a step back. "Stop making fun of me."

"I'm not," he said, bewildered she would even think that. "I would never make fun of you."

Her eyes widened, then narrowed as her lower lip trembled. She whispered, "Did Reuben say something?"

"About what?"

"About . . ." She turned away.

He shook his head. "Esther, I promise, *nee* one told me anything." He froze. "Wait . . . Do you have feelings for me?"

She let out a huff and glared at him. "You are the thickest man I've ever met in *mei* life!"

He felt pretty stupid as realization dawned. Rhett must have seen more between him and Esther than he thought. Why else would he have cautioned him about breaking Esther's heart that day at the lake? "I . . . didn't know."

"Because you're in love with Sarah." She wiped her cheek, and he couldn't tell if she was wiping away perspiration or tears. "It's always been Sarah for you."

He couldn't deny her words. But he could convince her they weren't true anymore. "Until now. I'm in love with you, Esther."

"And I'm supposed to believe that." She crossed her arms again. "I'm *nee* one's second choice. And I won't be used so you can get closer to *mei schweschder*. If you want her, you'll have to get her *yerself*."

Now Esther was freely crying, each tear burning a mark on his heart. The last thing he wanted was to hurt her, and here he was doing exactly that. He started to say something. Words, though, wouldn't be enough. Despite the heat and the very real possibility that she would reject him, he took her in his arms. "I'm sorry," he whispered fiercely in her ear. "I've been stupid and a *dummkopf* and definitely dense. I didn't know . . . I didn't see."

"Because you could only see Sarah."

She didn't embrace him, but she didn't pull away from him either. He took that as a good sign and held her tighter. "Now I see only you." When he felt her stiffen, he released his hold enough so he could look down into her face. How had he not seen her all this time? How had he missed the beautiful woman who had been right in front of him all these years? Who had been shy and sweet. Always giving him a smile. Always locking her own feelings away to help him gain Sarah's attention.

At that moment it was as if the last cloud lifted, and he was finally seeing—and feeling—everything clearly. "I'm going to prove it to you." He could barely speak past the sudden constriction of his throat. "If it takes every single *daag* of the rest of *mei* life, I'm going to prove how much I love you."

"Love?" She gazed up at him, her eyes wet with tears. "You . . . love me?" She spoke as if he hadn't said he was in love with her only moments ago.

"I do." He'd never been so certain of anything in his life. What he felt for Esther ran deeper than anything he'd ever *thought* he felt for Sarah. With Sarah he'd been able to walk away and not feel like his heart had been torn out. If he walked away from Esther right now . . . His chest squeezed. He couldn't even entertain the possibility. "I know it seems sudden—"

"*Ya*, very sudden. *Unbelievably* sudden."

She wasn't going to make this easy, and she shouldn't. He'd been willing to work for Sarah, and he'd only been infatuated with her. But he loved Esther, and he would *fight* for her. He finally understood what love was, and he wasn't going to let it—or her—go. "Did I mention I was a *dummkopf*?"

She softened a bit in his arms. "You're not a *dummkopf*. You're one of the smartest men I know. It's why I—"

He tilted up her chin with his forefinger. "You what?"

"It's why I love you." Somehow she managed to fold her arms across her chest again in the small space between them. "There, I said it."

"I said it first." He grinned.

The sparkle in her eyes warmed him more deeply than the summer sun ever could. "We're kind of going about this backward, aren't we? Usually people date before falling in love."

"I've never been usual," she said in a straight tone.

A statement of fact, one he'd known all along but had never fully appreciated until now. He was eager to catch up on everything he'd missed about this woman, everything he had left to discover. "I know." He found himself leaning toward her, ready to kiss the tip of her cute nose.

"I need to know something," she said, her voice wavering.

"Are you . . ." She averted her gaze, retreating into silence as she'd done so many times around him.

This time, he wasn't going to let her. He brushed his thumb across her cheek. "You can talk to me," he said. "You can ask me anything. I want you to know that."

"*Am* I *yer* second choice? Are you saying all this because you've given up on Sarah?"

He kissed her again, answering her the only way he knew how. When they parted, he said, "Would I kiss you like that if I was still hung up on Sarah?"

"*Nee*," she said, sounding as breathless as he felt.

"Then you believe me?" She nodded, and he pulled back, dropping his arms and putting his hands in his pockets not only for his benefit but for hers. He was more than ready to follow up that kiss with another one. "I do want us to date, you know. I was thinking a trip to the Parlor would be a *gut* place to start."

"Now?" she asked.

"I'm having a sudden craving for ice cream."

She laughed, her smile warming him through. "Funny, so am I."

CHAPTER 9

Inside her living room, Esther shut the front door behind her and leaned against it. She wanted to squeal with delight, but it was late and everyone was asleep.

Judah loved her. He really loved her. At first she couldn't believe it. But over a double scoop of rocky road he'd explained how he'd spent time in prayer, trying to understand his feelings and getting things straight with God.

She admired that. In a way he had stayed away from the farm because of her, but there was a higher purpose involved. That he would seek God's will above his own, that he had to make sure of his heart before talking to her was the final proof he was being genuine. When he'd dropped her off a few minutes ago, he asked her out on a second date, and a third ... and now they were booked up for the next two months.

The gas lamp hissed to life and she jumped. Sarah appeared in the yellow lamplight, sitting in the rocking chair opposite the couch. Esther pressed her hand to her chest. "Sarah, you startled me."

Sarah didn't say anything, her full lips pressed into a thin line. "Where were you?"

"Out." She wasn't going to let Sarah dampen her evening. "I'm going to bed."

"Not before you tell me where you've been."

"None of *yer* business." Her tone was sharper than she intended, but the sharpness behind the words was real. Taking a deep breath, she started for the staircase.

"I was worried about you."

Esther froze. Then she turned. Sarah's face had softened, and Esther could see the sheen of tears in her eyes. "You were?"

"You've been gone for hours." Sarah sniffed. "I wanted to *geh* looking for you, but *Daed* said you'd be okay."

"Did he tell you I was with Judah?"

Sarah shook her head. "*Nee*. Wait . . . You were with Judah?"

Esther nodded, still keeping up her guard.

"Oh." Sarah tilted her head and looked at her. "You do seem . . . different. *Yer* cheeks are flushed, for one thing."

"It's the middle of summer, Sarah."

Sarah chuckled, although there was a bit of melancholy to it. "He finally figured it out."

"What?"

She lifted her head. "Judah never wanted me. At least not for anything but a trophy."

"I don't understand."

"He's like all the other guys. They think they like me. Or love me." She rolled her eyes. "Then we spend time together and it fizzles. All they can do is stare at me, and I have to force the conversation along."

"Must be awful being so beautiful," Esther said dryly.

"You wouldn't understand."

"Because I'm ugly?"

"For heaven's sake, *nee*. You're not ugly, Esther. You're *schee*. You always have been. I don't get why you would think you weren't."

Because I've spent my entire life comparing myself to you.

"You're so easy to get to know. Everyone likes you. Look at Rhett. He took right to you from the moment he arrived."

"He has a girlfriend."

"I know. I knew that before he got here. *Mamm* showed me the letters he wrote, telling her and *Daed* about himself and why he wanted to stay with us. Right away he mentioned Shelby."

"Then why were you flirting with him?"

"I don't know." She shrugged and slumped in the chair. "I have *nee* idea how to be myself around men. Around anyone, for that matter."

Esther was surprised to hear this. Her sister had always been the confident one, the one who got all the attention. "Why not?"

She didn't say anything for a long moment. Then she said, "They may not like the real me."

Esther sat down on the edge of the couch. "Sarah, that's not true."

"Isn't it? Aren't I just a shell?" Tears flowed down her cheeks. "Something to be looked at?"

"Sarah." She had no idea Sarah struggled with self-esteem. "But you're always so sure of *yerself*."

"I'm *gut* at pretending." She leaned forward in the chair. "I'm so sorry I hurt you. I didn't mean to. But when Rhett ignored me in favor of you . . ."

"You felt rejected."

"I felt hollow. Empty. If I couldn't gain his attention with *mei* looks and flirting, then what else is there?"

"Plenty. Listen to me, Sarah. You are more than a *schee* face.

You're fun and a great cook and so wonderful with the animals. Those bunnies adore you."

"They're bunnies, Esther. They adore the snacks I give them."

"And you're the only one who spends extra time with them. You're also amazing with customers. You're *gut* at sewing. Rhett definitely was interested when you brought up quilting patterns."

"True, he was." She laughed. "He's a bit odd, isn't he?"

"But the *gut* kind of odd."

"Definitely." Sarah got up and sat down next to Esther. "*Danki* for understanding."

"I love you, Sarah." She embraced her sister, remembering all the times she'd been envious of her. All the comparisons she'd made. Above everything else there was still sisterly love. And now maybe a friendship was blossoming. But she had to make sure about one thing. She released Sarah. "Are you okay with me and Judah dating?"

"Of course. Like I said, he finally realized you two are perfect for each other."

"But I thought you liked him."

"I do, as a *freind*. Actually more like a *bruder*, so if you two get married, he'll fit right in with the *familye*."

"Then why didn't you tell him how you really felt? Why didn't you tell me?"

"Judah had to figure out his feelings himself. At least when he was after me, he was still around you."

"So you led him on for *mei* sake?"

"*Ya.* You were never going to say anything to him, and it wasn't *mei* place to reveal *yer* feelings. Although you did a terrible job of hiding them. Even *Daed* knows how smitten you are." She smiled. "You're still smitten, right?"

Esther smiled. "Definitely."

Sarah glanced down at her lap. "I have to admit that I liked the attention too. Not just from Judah, but from everyone else." She looked at Esther. "I know it's not right, but I can't help it."

"*Nee.* You can't. Not alone, anyway." She grasped Sarah's hand. "But with God's help, you will."

⤸⌇⤳

The next day Judah arrived at the Coblentzes eager to see Esther, but he needed to talk to Rhett first. When he entered the barn, he found him cleaning out the stables. It was a job best done early in the morning, before the heat of the day made the stench almost unbearable. As usual, Rhett was shoveling the dirty hay and manure with enthusiasm. He looked up as Judah approached. "Hey, dude," he said, holding a pitchfork filled with dung. "You back to work?"

"Yep."

"Good. We could use the extra pair of hands." He turned and went to the back of the barn, where a large door was open. He tossed the dung into a pile, then faced Judah again. "Everything okay?"

More than okay, but he had to settle one more thing. "You were right," he said to Rhett. "About me needing to get my head on straight."

"And did you?"

"*Ya.* Although it took me a while."

"That happens." He grinned. "Esther looked happy this morning. I'm assuming you had something to do with it?"

Judah was pleased to hear that tidbit of news. "Maybe."

Rhett's grin grew. "Glad to hear it." He gestured to the stall.

"I better finish up here. Enoch said the summer lettuce is ready for harvest."

"Have you got another minute?"

"Sure."

"I owe you an apology. Actually more than one. I wasn't nice to you when you first got here. That was wrong of me. I'll also admit to some jealousy."

"About what?"

"You and Esther."

Rhett scoffed. "I explained that. Esther's a great girl. But that's it. She's only had eyes for you, dude."

He believed that now. "Still, I was angry and I took it out on you."

"Hey, don't worry about it." He extended his hand. "We're all about forgiveness, right?"

Judah had misjudged this man. He'd assumed Rhett was here to play at being Amish, but he'd been wrong. Rhett had taken every advantage of the experience. He'd even picked up some Deitsch. He worked hard every day on the farm and never complained. He'd been attentive during church, and had made friends with other people in the congregation. They realized his sincerity. Rhett was genuine, and in his blindness and resentment, Judah had missed that.

I've missed a lot of things, Lord. But mei *eyes are open now.*

He shook Rhett's hand. Then he got another pitchfork off the wall of the barn.

"You don't have to help," Rhett said. "I know this is grunt work, and I don't mind doing it."

"I know you don't." He entered one of the stalls. "I don't mind doing it either."

CHAPTER 10

∿

One Year Later

ESTHER WAVED THE WEDDING PROGRAM IN FRONT OF her flushed face. It was hot today, even for the end of July. But despite the heat, the bride and groom looked stunning. She glanced at Judah. Sitting next to her, his cheeks were red from the heat too. She waved the program in front of him in an attempt to cool him off. He responded by grabbing her hand—and not letting it go.

"Do you, Rhett Thomas Davidson, take Shelby Marie Monroe to be your wife?"

Esther stifled a swoony sigh. After Rhett had returned home last summer, he'd kept in touch with the family, sending a few extra letters to Judah. They had become good friends before Rhett left. Rhett had decided not to go to the Himalayas, instead finishing his senior year on time. Shelby had graduated from nursing school too.

"I already have my dream," he'd written, right before announcing that Shelby had said yes to his marriage proposal. The couple had visited Middlefield several times and decided to have their wedding outdoors at the Mespo gazebo.

After the ceremony, the guests mingled and congratulated the bride and groom. This was the first time she'd ever been to a Yankee wedding, and while there were differences in traditions, the feeling of love and happiness surrounding the couple was the same. When their turn came, Esther gave Shelby a hug, then to her surprise was drawn into Rhett's big embrace.

"Hey," Judah said. "Stay away from my wife. You've got your own now."

Rhett kissed her on the cheek in front of everybody, which was a very non-Amish thing to do but very much in line with his personality.

As they left the happy couple, Judah pointed toward Sarah and Samuel Keim. They were sitting on the swings even though several long tables were set up, covered with white tablecloths and vases of summer flowers. "I wonder what that's about," he said.

"I don't know." Esther shrugged, despite knowing exactly what Sarah and Samuel were about. Samuel wasn't Sarah's type, or at least Esther hadn't thought so until Sarah admitted her interest in him. He was short and stocky, with wire-rimmed glasses that never seemed to fit straight on the bridge of his nose. But he was so nice, and Sarah adored him.

"He listens to me," she'd told Esther one night after he brought her home from a ride in his open buggy. "Really listens to me. He asks me about *mei* dreams, about what I'm interested in. He sees the real me."

"Huh," Judah said. "They almost look like a couple."

Esther smiled at her husband. They had married in the spring, to no one's surprise, and now lived in the house where Esther used to give tours. With the addition of the new farmland, *Daed* had decided to close down the tourist business. "It's time to have more privacy," he said, which made *Mamm* happy.

Sarah had a job working in a fabric store in Middlefield, and while Reuben was still contemplating joining the church, at least he was talking about it a little more openly.

"Want to go for a walk?" Judah asked.

"But what about the reception?"

"We'll be back in time for the food."

"I wasn't thinking about that."

"You should be, since you're eating for two."

Her hand went to her abdomen. They hadn't told anyone about the pregnancy. It was a special secret to keep between themselves until she started showing.

They walked down the grassy area, then crossed the street. Esther thought they were going to turn around and walk back toward the general store, but Judah took her hand and led her into a small wooded patch near a row of houses.

He put his arms around her waist and drew her close. "There's something about weddings," he said, looking down at her.

"The romance?"

"What, you think I'm a sappy man?"

She leaned forward and whispered, "I know you are. But it's our little secret."

He kissed her, and as with every kiss, he confirmed his love for her. A year ago she'd been hopelessly in love with him. Now she was filled with hope for their future.

"I guess we should go back," he said, pulling away from her but still within kissing distance. "Before someone sees us."

"I wouldn't mind."

"*Yer* parents would."

That worked like a bucket of cold water. They headed back to the reception, where the guests were seating themselves at the tables. Another table was filled with potluck items, similar to an Amish wedding reception.

"They look happy," Esther said, looking at Rhett and Shelby as they sat next to each other on one side of the center table.

"Are you happy?" Judah asked.

She looked up at him, seeing the love in his eyes. "*Ya,*" she said, linking her pinky finger with his. "I couldn't be happier. There's one thing I'd like to do, though."

"Name it," he said.

"I'd like to go back to the lake. Just the two of us. Before the *boppli* comes."

He looked down at her, one black brow lifting. "You want to *geh* fishing? In a boat?"

"*Ya.*"

He laughed. "Okay, but you have to promise me one thing."

"What?"

"Don't fall in." Then he leaned over and whispered, "But *I* promise I'll kiss you if you do."

She grinned and whispered back, "I'm holding you to it."

DISCUSSION QUESTIONS

1. Jealousy is one of the themes explored in *Lakeside Love*. How do you deal with jealousy? How has God helped you?
2. If you were Esther's friend, what advice would you give her about her feelings for Judah?
3. Rhett had a great opportunity to immerse himself in Amish culture. Would you do the same if given the chance? What would you hope to learn?
4. *Lakeside Love* is inspired by the story of Leah and Rachel in the Bible. What are the similarities of *Lakeside Love* to that Biblical story?
5. Why do you think Judah had a difficult time understanding his feelings for Esther? Has there ever been a time when you didn't see something clearly, only to have God show you what you were missing?
6. Esther struggled with being plain, while Sarah struggled with being beautiful. Discuss a time when God showed you that He sees our hearts and not our outward appearance.

ACKNOWLEDGMENTS

WRITING IS NEVER A SOLO ENDEAVOR, AND AS ALWAYS there are people I want to thank. A big thank-you to my editors Becky Monds and Jean Bloom. We've worked on many books together, and I know this sounds redundant, but I appreciate everything you do, your expertise, and your encouragement. For the friends in my life who get me through my life: Eddie Columbia, Tera Moore, Laura Spangler, and Kelly Long—thank you for walking this journey with me. I love you all.

Special thanks to you, dear reader: I always end my acknowledgments with you. I'm so grateful to every single person who reads my stories. You are all special to me, and I'm honored to call so many of you my friends. Happy reading, many blessings, and thank you for joining me on another visit to Amish country.

ABOUT THE AUTHOR

 KATHLEEN FULLER IS THE AUTHOR OF several bestselling novels, including *A Man of His Word* and *Treasuring Emma,* as well as a middle-grade Amish series, the Mysteries of Middlefield.

Visit her online at www.kathleenfuller.com
Twitter: @TheKatJam
Facebook: Kathleen Fuller.

ONE SWEET KISS

KELLY IRVIN

*To my son Nicholas, who grew up when
I wasn't looking. Love always.*

Trust in the LORD *with all your heart,*
And lean not on your own understanding;
In all your ways acknowledge Him,
And He shall direct your paths.

PROVERBS 3:5–6 (NKJV)

Blessed is the man who trusts in the LORD,
And whose hope is the LORD.
For he shall be like a tree planted by the waters,
Which spreads out its roots by the river,
And will not fear when heat comes;
But its leaf will be green,
And will not be anxious in the year of drought,
Nor will cease from yielding fruit.

JEREMIAH 17:7–8 (NKJV)

FEATURED BEE COUNTY
AMISH FAMILIES

MORDECAI AND ABIGAIL KING

Caleb

Hazel

Esther

Samuel

Jacob

ABRAM AND THERESA KING

DEBORAH AND PHINEAS KING

Timothy

Melinda

TOBIAS AND REBEKAH BYLER

Matthew

LEILA AND JESSE GLICK

Grace

Emmanuel

Featured Bee County Amish Families

Leroy and Naomi Glick

Adam

Jesse

Joseph

Simon

Sally

Mary

Elizabeth

Aaron and Jolene Shrock

Ethan

Seth

Amanda

Molly

William

Will and Isabella (Shrock) Glick

Jason

Katherine

Levi and Susan (King) Byler

David

Martha

Milo

Rueben

Micah

Ida

Nyla

Liam

Henry

CHAPTER 1

THE LAST NOTE DIED AWAY. SMILING TO HERSELF, MARTHA Byler opened her eyes. She always closed them during the German rendition of "How Great Thou Art," enjoying the sound of her friends' voices lifted in praise. Still, her eyelids grew heavy. The temptation to drift off to sleep during the singings mounted as the stifling south Texas heat in Bishop Jeremiah's front room warmed her cheeks. On Sundays, she paid the price for rising early to prepare breakfast for her family before church, helping with the meal after the service, and then spending the afternoon playing volleyball and tag with the little ones. She was worn out by the time the singings started. She wiggled on the hard pine stool. Surely, the ache of her bony behind would keep her awake. Still, she wouldn't miss this special time for anything. The sweet songs of praise filled a spot in her heart like nothing else could.

"Jacob's staring at you." Vesta Hostetler elbowed Martha in the ribs. Her loud whisper carried to the other girls crowded on a bench. They giggled. Vesta leaned closer. "When will you let him off the hook? He's sorry. You know he is."

Martha hazarded a quick glance at Jacob King, lounging between his friends who were busy whispering and horsing around instead of singing. Sure enough, he studied her with that same

293

hurt, puppy-dog look he'd been giving her since that last Saturday night when he'd failed to show up at her farm as promised. With his unruly black hair peeking out from his straw hat, blue-green eyes made more blue than green by the blue of his shirt, dimpled cheeks, and rueful expression, he reminded her of a scholar called to the front of the room after misbehaving in school.

She didn't need to take care of another child. She had six of those at home—six younger brothers and sisters who looked to her every day as an example of what to do next in a home that had lacked a mother for nearly ten years. "He's just sorry I'm mad." She fixed her gaze on the hymnal with its yellowed pages and crumbling spine. "Not that he can't be trusted to do what he says he'll do."

"But he *is* easy on the eyes." Vesta took the pitcher of water from her sister Rachel and helped herself to a drink before passing it to Martha. "And a hard worker. It's not like we have a bunch of choices in this little *Gmay*."

The sweet, lukewarm water soothed Martha's throat, parched from the heat and from singing for nearly two hours—first the slower German songs and then the old English hymns. She took another sip and passed the pitcher. She wasn't looking for choices. Her family needed her. It was obvious Jacob did not. "I don't have time for courting right now."

"With your *daed* remarried, you don't have to take care of everything yourself anymore." The start of another song didn't keep Vesta from pestering her. Her friend made a habit of reminding Martha of these things. "You're not the *mudder* anymore."

Inhaling the scent of boy sweat mingled with the aroma of baking cookies, Martha pretended to be engrossed in the song. Susan was a sweet woman who made *Daed* happy. The baby made them happy too. She was happy for them. She really was. So why did tears make her throat tight and her eyes burn? She bowed her head and focused on the words of the next song, "Amazing Grace."

It ended far too soon. She took a quick swipe at her face and stood as Rachel carried in a tray loaded with snickerdoodles, gingersnaps, and chocolate chip cookies. The Hostetlers could be counted on for the best after-singing snacks. The boys jostled for the door while the girls milled around in clusters, chattering. The noise level rose in direct proportion to the number of teenage girls in the room.

Martha laid the hymnal in the stack on the spindly end table by Jeremiah's desk and slipped through the crowd. She had a long walk ahead of her. At least the sun had set, taking with it the worst of the June heat. Still, the dank, humid air stuck to her skin as she trudged down the porch steps and headed toward the dirt road that led from the Hostetlers' farm to hers.

"You'll not forgive me then?"

Jacob's deep, sandpaper-rough voice sent a prickle of goose bumps careening up her arms. Why did he have that effect on her when she knew good and well he couldn't be trusted? She halted and turned. "A person is required to forgive."

He clomped down the steps, his work boots heavy on the wood, and kept walking until he stood within arm's length. Too close, in her way of thinking. "Then let me give you a ride home, and I'll convince you of all the reasons you shouldn't hold my transgressions against me."

His white teeth glinted in the light of a full moon that hung heavy overhead. Martha listened to the distant croak of bull frogs and the rustle of a lackadaisical breeze in the leaves of a nearby live oak tree. Tiredness won. Not the way he looked—tall, broad through the shoulders, and tanned from working with his father's beehives. "I would like a ride."

The smile transformed his face. Martha breathed. Looks meant nothing. She wasn't so shallow as to be taken in by a handsome face.

"I'll get the buggy."

"I'm capable of walking with you to get it."

She whirled, stumbled over a rock so rude as to settle in her path, and pitched forward, arms pinwheeling in an effort to catch herself.

Jacob's mammoth hand gripped her arm above the elbow. His fingers were warm and strong. His breath touched her cheek. A soft chuckle floated in the air around her. The danger of face-planting in the dirt passed, yet her balance still wavered with the realization that he was touching her. She looked up at his face, so close she could see a tiny scar on the bridge of his nose. His full lips were a hairsbreadth away from hers. He smelled of clothes soap and peppermint. His smile widened as if he divined her thoughts. "Are you sure? I could carry you, if need be. You don't likely weigh more than a kitten."

"It's not nice to make fun." Her voice didn't quiver, just the right nonchalant tone. "It's rude and I'm not a kitten."

"I'm always nice."

"Not always."

He ducked his head. "Milo and Samuel got the car stuck in the mud. I had to help them move it. We couldn't leave it out where someone would see it."

She tugged free of his grip. "I don't want to know about the car."

The fact that he and some of their friends had pooled their money to buy an old beat-up car and kept it hidden away behind an abandoned barn was none of her business. Two years of *rumspringa* and it was time to grow up. A man who still played at boys' games didn't interest her.

So why did her heart careen into that silly *rat-a-tat-tat* every time Jacob wandered into her line of sight at church? Or *Gmay* picnics? Or singings and volleyball games?

"Do you always do the right thing?" He strode in front of her and then turned so he was walking backward as if he needed to see her face-to-face to talk. His ability to maintain his balance seemed like a slap in the face at the moment. "Name one fun thing you've done during your *rumspringa*."

"I play with the *kinner*. We have fun all the time."

"I'm talking about things you wouldn't normally do." He spun around one short step before backing into his buggy and held out his hand as if to help her up. "This is your chance to be someone else for a little bit."

"I like who I am just fine." She ignored his hand and hoisted herself into the buggy. "I'm starting baptism classes this summer so I can join in the fall."

If she found the answers she sought in those classes. Surely Mordecai King, Jacob's father, would tell her how she could trust *Gott*, even when He let her mother die. Jacob didn't need to know of her uncertainty. No one did. Good Plain girls and boys didn't question matters of faith.

"Me too." He climbed into the buggy and sat. Again, closer than necessary. "That'll be fun."

If committing to memory in German the eighteen articles of the Dordrecht Confession could be described as fun. That Jacob thought so gave Martha hope for him. "Mordecai will make it interesting."

Jacob shrugged. "If we can keep *mei daed* from going off on a wild goose chase with his stories, we might get through all eighteen articles before we're ready for the *dawdy haus*."

The way he said "we" sent a white-hot flare leaping across Martha's face. The *dawdy haus* was for couples who grew old together. Did he see the two of them married, their children grown, grandchildren racing about the yard? It made for a nice picture.

One she couldn't count on. God had taught her not to rely on love when He let her mother die a scant two weeks after little Liam's birth. Hard as he tried, her father could not hide the pain that etched lines around his mouth and eyes in those dark days that followed. He said all the right things—her days were done, we're only passing through this world, God has a plan—yet the pain blossomed every time he thought she wasn't looking.

She studied the stars and tried to think of something—anything—to say that didn't lead to a place she refused to go. They rode along in silence for a piece. The *clip-clop* of hooves and the creak of buggy wheels on the sun-hardened dirt kept time with her thoughts. Jacob turned the buggy onto her farm road. A few more minutes and the ride would end. For reasons she couldn't fathom, Martha didn't want that. Not yet. The memory of Jacob's hand on her arm floated through her mind, sweet and warm. *Stop it!*

"If you've decided to get baptized, you'll need to get rid of that car—"

Her words were drowned in the shrill blast of a horn. Startled, she pivoted. An enormous, shiny tomato-red pickup truck loomed.

Dwayne Chapman stuck his head out and waved. "Hey, King! I've been looking all over for you." The words had a strange slur to them. The truck swerved closer to the buggy. He laughed and pulled away again. "I need a backup man for an alligator that has my name on it. You in?"

Jacob slowed the buggy. "Whoa, whoa."

They halted in the middle of the road. Dwayne spun the truck around so it blocked the way to Martha's farm. Dwayne might be nineteen and married with two children, but he still acted like a kid most of the time.

"Have you been drinking again?" Jacob wrapped the reins around his hand, the look on his face one Martha didn't recognize. Humor mixed with concern filled his voice. "Rory will have your hide, if she finds out. Not to mention the highway patrol and the Bee County sheriff."

"I'm fine. I'm fine." Dwayne twisted his Texas Rangers cap around so the bill faced the back of his head. "My posse bailed on me. Bunch of babies who think they have to go to bed early on Sunday night 'cause they got to work on Monday. Me, I can go twenty-four seven. Know what I mean? So I'm looking for another strong back to help me bag me a gator."

"This isn't alligator hunting season." Jacob's gaze met Martha's and skittered away. "It's not something you do in the dark, anyway. You'll fall in and drown—or get eaten."

"I could do it blindfolded, dude. I never caught one during the season. I still have my license and everything. They owe me one."

Dwayne probably thought everyone owed him one. Martha didn't know much about him. Her family had moved to Bee County after Leila Lantz, now Leila Glick, had started working at a day care in town with Dwayne's wife Rory. Leila eventually married Jesse Glick and they both left the *Gmay*. It was a sad story that some blamed on Dwayne and Rory. Martha knew better. People had to take responsibility for their own actions. That included Jacob. If he decided to go with Dwayne, she was done with him.

The thought twisted like a rototiller blade in the vicinity of her heart. Better she should spend her life alone than yoked to a man who couldn't grow up. She'd always have her brothers and sisters—until they grew up and married.

Jacob's snort startled her from her reverie. "I don't think it works that way." He shook his head, his dark curls bouncing under his hat. "Go on home. Sleep it off."

"Don't be a wuss, dude." The words became an almost unintelligible slur. "Thought I could count on my Amish man, man. But be that way, I'll do it myself. Got my raw meat, got my fire power. Got my cane poles in the back."

He held up a Styrofoam package that contained a huge slab of meat that looked like a boneless shoulder roast. The kind Martha passed in the grocery store because it was too expensive for their table. His thumb jabbed toward the back of the truck where a rifle hung from a gun rack.

She knew little to nothing about laws in Texas, but she did know mixing alcohol and guns was a dangerous combination. "You'll fall in the river and drown, or the alligator will eat you." She shouldn't have to explain the obvious. "Or you'll shoot yourself. Then what will your babies do without a daddy?"

"I bagged a gator two years ago. I know what I'm doing."

"Not by yourself, you didn't. Your dad and Nolan and your cousins were in on it." Jacob hunched his shoulders. "I may have to get this."

The last part was directed at Martha.

"You're going alligator hunting?" She knew it. She'd always known it. "With a drunk *Englischer*?"

"That's the thing." Jacob's voice took on a pleading tone. "I can't let him drive like this. It's not safe. He has *kinner*."

True, but it wasn't safe for a Plain man with no license to drive either. Out of the frying pan, into the fire. "He probably has a phone. Call the sheriff to come get him. A night in jail would straighten him out."

It might be harsh, but her father always said people had to reap the consequences of their actions. They learned the lesson that way. No one could learn it for them.

"Hey, y'all, I'm right here. I can hear you. I'm not going to jail." Dwayne turned the key in the ignition. The truck's engine rumbled. "I thought I could trust y'all. Guess I'll have to have fun on my own."

Jacob held up his hand as if to hush the man. His pleading gaze stayed on Martha. "I'll drop you off and leave the buggy there behind your barn until I can get him home. His father-in-law will bring me back."

He wanted to use her home to hide his *rumspringa* fun? "You really want to hunt alligator right now? You'll never grow up, will you?"

"That's not it. He's a friend." Jacob's voice rose in protest. "You could come with us. You've never been gator hunting. There's a *rumspringa* experience for you. Besides, it's early."

It was late. They'd been doing this two-steps-forward, two-steps-back thing for two years. Every time she thought they might finally make it to that sweet place where she could see the road to a future together, something like this happened. The time he chose to joyride with his friends. The keg party in Mac Moreno's back pasture. Playing pool at the tavern in town. Sure, he invited her, begged her to go. But she couldn't do it. Not knowing the consequences of underage drinking or driving without a license. Her father had suffered enough. The children needed her. She had to think of them, not herself or her desire to have her own children one day. Her desire to have a husband and a life of her own would wait. Had to wait.

She didn't need a special friend. She needed to do the pile of laundry that threatened to take over the laundry room. She needed to sew new pants for Liam. The boy was growing like weeds along a south Texas road. Sunrise would come all too soon, and she needed sleep. "I can't. I have too much to do tomorrow. You go. Do what you need to do. I can get myself home."

"Just wait. Just wait one minute." Jacob hopped from the buggy and strode around to the truck. "Keys."

"What?" Dwayne's head disappeared from the window like a turtle's whipping back into its shell. "I ain't giving up the keys to a guy in suspenders and a straw hat. You ain't got a license, dude."

"And you can't drive drunk." Jacob sounded like Mordecai when he got after the children who decided to chase each other around the yard instead of collect eggs from the chicken coop. "You might run into a car and hurt someone."

"Your concern for me getting hurt really touches my heart. You're sweet on me, aren't 'cha?"

Jacob slipped his long arm into the truck. The engine died. He extracted a silver key chain shaped like a beer bottle with half a dozen keys dangling from it.

"Hey!" Dwayne swiped at the keys to no avail. He opened the

door. Jacob took several steps back, keys behind his back. Dwayne growled like a dog defending his supper. "You can't do that."

Fear swept through Martha, making her stomach feel queasy. Would Jacob be all right? Would he get hurt? Anxiety ate at her. "He's right. You can't drive that truck." She tried to keep her voice cool. He didn't need to know how much she cared. He didn't have the same feelings or he wouldn't keep leaving her for others. "Either you'll have an accident or you'll end up in jail for hunting out of season, or worse yet, driving drunk yourself. Mordecai wouldn't like that."

"I don't drink. Not anymore. Besides, I'm more worried about how you'll take it." Jacob made his way back around the buggy and climbed in, closer to her than she would've liked. He tossed the keys up and down in his palm, his gaze on them as if they held the answer to a riddle only he could see. "I'm not worried about driving his truck. It's no different from a car."

He hadn't denied the hunting part. He'd rather hunt than spend time sitting on the front porch with her. It didn't matter. It couldn't be allowed to matter. "You told me you were getting rid of the car."

"I am. I want to, but it belongs to the others too. And we have to find someone who wants it."

"You should give it away, if it's standing between you and baptism—"

"Don't be comparing my ride to that heap of rust you sneak around in." Apparently it took words a while to worm their way into an alcohol-soaked brain. Dwayne sounded truly offended. "Besides this beauty is a standard. You ain't got no idea how to drive a standard."

Martha had no idea what *standard* meant, but Dwayne made

it sound complicated. "Is he right? Do you know how to drive this standard thing?"

"You remember Jesse's friend Colton—the one from his youth group? He taught Jesse to drive so Jesse asked him to give me a few lessons." Jacob sounded proud of himself. "Jesse learned to drive a standard, so I figured I could too."

"You've been hanging around with Colton? Have you been to his youth group?" Her heart, already full of holes, stopped beating. The *Gmay* had lost Jesse and Leila to this group nearly three years ago. Leila's mother still mourned the life she would not have as a mother and grandmother to Leila and Jesse's growing brood, as did Jesse's mother and father. They mourned the life their children didn't have with their Plain families. "Are you thinking of joining Jesse's church?"

"*Nee. Nee.*" He shook his head so hard his hat flopped. "I never went to the meetings on Wednesday nights. And we don't party. They're not like that. Colton is married and so is Jesse. We eat at the pancake house together sometimes. Go fishing now and then. But they're busy."

Not too busy to give Jacob driving lessons. He could have pancakes with his family at home. The danger of being sucked into another life was too great. Look at Leila and Jesse. Their families saw the babies once in a blue moon. Jesse almost never came around. It was too hard on his mother and father. They couldn't bear it.

Jacob's expression, the way he stared at her with those mesmerizing blue-green eyes that reminded her of the Gulf of Mexico on a sunny day, made her want to believe him. Her heart said she could. Her head said don't be an idiot. She couldn't bear the thought of spending time with Jacob, only to have him choose another path. She wasn't like Leila. She would never leave her brothers and sisters to follow him. They'd suffered enough loss already.

It wasn't about her. It was about her brothers and sisters. They all loved their new stepmother, but Susan couldn't take the place of a sister who'd raised them from little bitty.

That was that. It couldn't matter what she needed. They needed her. Jacob didn't. Martha climbed out of the buggy and marched past the pickup truck.

"Don't go away mad, Amish girl!" Dwayne hollered. "Dude, I didn't mean to get you in trouble with the girlfriend."

Martha closed her eyes and reopened them, just in time to see a rut in the road and swerve right. "I'm not his girlfriend."

"Martha! It's not that big of a deal."

"Have fun." She waved her hand in the air without looking back. "Be safe."

He might decide to join an English church. Or he might get eaten by an alligator.

Served him right.

CHAPTER 2

❧

THE *CLIP-CLOP* OF THE HORSE'S HOOVES AND CREAK OF
the wooden buggy wheels followed Martha, telling her Jacob followed along like a shadow or a faithful puppy she couldn't shake.
She didn't look back at the dirt road. *Keep going. Keep going. Keep
going.*

"Come on! It's silly for you to walk. Get back in the buggy."

Martha walked faster. Sweat trickled down her cheeks. Mos-
quitos buzzed around her face. She slapped them away. Her feet
and back ached. Finally, the porch was yards away, then right in
front of her. The sound of the buggy faded away. He wouldn't come
closer. If her father or her brother David were around, they'd want
to know why she was walking instead of riding in the buggy. Courting might be private, but some questions begged to be answered.

At the screen door, she dared to look back. Jacob sat in the
buggy by the corral fence, watching her, his face forlorn. She
loved that face.

How did that thought get in her head? She loved his face like
she loved Liam's face. God would strike her dead for lying to herself. Gott, *have mercy. I don't want to love him. I don't even want to
like him.*

Sighing, she waved. He raised one hand and waved back, a swift smile bringing out his dimples.

She loved that smile. How could she love that smile, knowing what she knew about him? He couldn't be trusted with her heart. The children could. They needed her.

She slipped inside and shut the door with a gentle nudge, not wanting to wake her family. A light flickered on the wall that led to the kitchen. No one should be up at this hour.

A baby's wail cut the still night air. *Ach.* Someone wasn't happy. Poor Susan. Martha slipped off her shoes and padded barefoot into the kitchen. Susan sat at the pine table, little Henry in her lap. The one-year-old's cheeks were red, his brown curls tousled and wet with sweat. Susan, with her long, brown hair loose down her back and her wrinkled nightgown, didn't look much better.

"Teething?" Martha whispered. "Poor *bopli* looks miserable. So do you."

Susan shook her head, her smile bright. "One day he won't need me anymore. I waited many years for these nights. I don't begrudge him one minute."

Susan always had a positive view on life. Martha loved that about her stepmother. The former schoolteacher had a deep well of wisdom she freely shared. Did it come from growing up with Mordecai King, her brother who was a beekeeper and deacon, or did she give it to him? Women never received the credit for these things. Martha grabbed a peanut butter cookie from the pan on the counter and squeezed into a chair.

"You looked peeved about something." Susan shifted Henry to her other arm. The boy whimpered and snuggled closer. "Didn't you have fun at the singing?"

"It was fine." Martha broke the cookie in half, then began

crumbling one side with her thumb and forefinger. "How did you know for sure you wanted to marry *Daed*?"

"Does this have to do with Jacob?"

Martha hopped up and poured a glass of water. She drank half of it before facing Susan again. "I like taking care of the *kinner*. They need me."

"I can take care of the *kinner*. We've had this talk before. It's time to think about starting your own family."

Susan had been a part of their lives for two years. Martha had been the mother for ten years, ever since *Daed* deposited a tiny, restless, two-week-old Liam in her arms and asked her—no, begged her with pain and tears in his eyes—to make him stop crying. "They are my family."

"Wait too long and there won't be anyone around to ask you." Susan rocked. Henry's eyes closed. "I know from experience."

"You didn't marry until later and it turned out fine."

"Because I thought my *bruders* and *schweschder* couldn't do without me." Susan patted her damp, round face with a tattered dish towel. "Sound familiar?"

"There was someone before *Daed*?"

"By the time I realized my *bruders* and *schweschder* were going to go live their lives without me, it was too late." Susan's gaze meandered somewhere in the distance over Martha's shoulder. "Andrew married another. They have half a dozen *kinner* now up in Missouri."

"But it was *Gott*'s plan because you were meant to wait for *Daed*. You were meant to be together."

"I wouldn't dare to assume I know what *Gott*'s plan is." Susan frowned and shook her head. "The young think they know so much. You are a smart girl, but *Gott* knows all. Trust in Him, and He will make your path straight."

Straight to Jacob? The path between them zigged and zagged. There was nothing straight about it.

"I have to go to bed." Martha brushed cookie crumbs from the table and stood. "I hope Henry sleeps through the rest of the night, for both your sakes. We have so much laundry to do tomorrow."

"If he doesn't sleep now, he'll nap tomorrow. It'll make doing laundry easier." Susan tucked the toddler's long night-shirt around his chunky legs. He sighed a sweet, content sound. "Either way, we'll be fine. See you in the morning."

Exhaustion weighing her down, Martha began the trek up the stairs. A shriek broke the silence. Startled, she paused, head cocked, listening. A quieter whimper. Liam. She bolted up the stairs and raced down the hallway to the bedroom the boys shared. Liam sat up in his narrow bunk, hands to his face. Rueben lay on his stomach, arms flung out, not moving in the double bed he shared with Milo, who was likely still roaming the countryside with his buddies. Or maybe he had a special friend by now. She had no idea.

"What's the matter, little one?" she whispered as she crept closer. Rueben had hard work to do. He needed his sleep. David was also missing from the other twin bed shoved against the far wall. Still gallivanting about on his endless *rumspringa*. "What happened?"

"Bad dream." Liam sniffed and leaned into her hug. "The snakes were everywhere."

Bad dream indeed —for Martha. "You like snakes."

"Not huge ones crawling all over the house." His small chin

trembled and his voice quivered. "They should stay outside where they belong."

"I agree. Scooch over." She squeezed in and leaned her head against his flat pillow. "Should I tell you a story?"

"The one about the dog who walks all the way from Ohio to Texas to find his little boy after getting left behind when they move." He snuggled against her. "I like that one."

"Me too." She collected her thoughts. Every time she told the story, it came out differently, but Liam never complained. "Once upon a time there was a black-and-white spotted puppy named—"

"Me too."

Rueben's deep voice, husky with sleep, floated from across the room. "Don't leave out any of the good parts this time."

She smiled in the dark and started again.

CHAPTER 3

DOING THE RIGHT THING SHOULD FEEL BETTER THAN IT did. Jacob lengthened his stride and walked faster. He could see Dwayne's truck still parked half on the road and half off. At least he hadn't decided to take off after spoiling Jacob's plan for this evening. He'd had every intention of making amends with Martha and along came Dwayne Chapman. Father of two, master of nothing. Not to be mean about it. The man had problems. But he couldn't be allowed to race around on the farm-to-market roads in Bee County just because he lacked the good sense and will power to stop partying with his friends.

Rory must be beside herself. The sooner Jacob got her husband home the better. Before Nolan Beale, grandfather to those two little ones, noticed his son-in-law was at it again. Ignoring the urge to whip his hat from his head and slam it into the weeds, Jacob turned his weary bones to the task at hand.

It took ten minutes to walk to the truck—way too much time to contemplate his situation. He'd celebrated his twentieth birthday two weeks earlier, but Martha treated him like one of her little brothers.

He needed to show her he was a man. She needed to learn not to jump to conclusions. She needed to trust in God's plan.

No. This wasn't about Martha. She needed to be able to trust him to stick around. He understood that. They'd both lost their mothers far too soon. He had older brothers and sisters to help him through it. She had been the oldest girl in the Byler family. Taking care of newborn Liam had been her job at the ripe old age of ten. That kind of thing left its mark. He understood more than most. He had been at home sick with the flu when the van-semi collision took his mother's life, but the accident left a fat, ugly scar where his heart should be. Not the best thing in the world to have in common, but at least he understood in a way most couldn't.

Gott, help me do the right thing. He was tempted to say the words aloud, but Plain folks didn't do that much. Jesus had been mute in the face of His accusers and attackers. Not that anyone attacked Jacob. He simply received the when-are-you-going-to-grow-up looks. Swatting away a horsefly the size of his thumb, he two-stepped around a pile of cow patties and nearly hurled face first into a rut that could swallow a buggy. The road would keep him awake if nothing else.

The truck's headlights were off. No hazards flashing. The passenger door hung open.

No Dwayne.

Lord, give me strength.

"Dwayne? Dwayne!"

The distinct sound of someone puking floated on the dank breeze. Swiping at sweat dripping from his forehead under a hat that seemed too tight after a long day, Jacob tromped through the weeds hoping he wouldn't disturb a rattlesnake out for an evening slither. "Dwayne? Are you okay?"

A half grunt, half whine told him the answer was likely no. It came from his left. He swerved and swept a mass of black-eyed

Susans out of his way. Dwayne had propped himself up with one hand against a scraggly mesquite tree that didn't look strong enough to hold his six-foot-plus, one-hundred-eighty-some-pound high school wrestler's frame.

"Are you gonna live?"

Dwayne swiped at gnats and flies that had arrived like uninvited guests to a supper party. He cleared his throat and snorted. "Nothing another brew won't cure. I got a six-pack under the seat." He leaned over and hurled again. This time his swipe removed spit from his chin. "Why don't you go snag it for me? You're welcome to help yourself."

"Give me your phone."

"Uh-uh. You're gonna call Rory and she's gonna yell and throw a hissy fit like she's my mother or something." He staggered away from the tree. His hands went to his knees. Odds were the gnats would get dessert with the main course. He heaved a big breath. "I got chips in there too. Tortilla chips and that bean dip you like. It's a party, dude, come on."

Careful to step around the splash zone, Jacob eyed Dwayne's jeans. One pocket bulged with a wallet, the other had that telltale white ring that spoke of a can of chew. Dwayne had given up smoking in deference to his role as father of two toddlers. Chew wasn't much better in Jacob's estimation, but no one had asked him. He slapped the pocket on Dwayne's blue-and-white striped cotton shirt that bore the logo of the car repair shop where he'd worked since graduating from high school. Rick Santillan, owner of the shop, would be thrilled to know Dwayne had been out drinking in a shirt advertising his business. Sure enough, the phone was in the shirt pocket. Jacob snatched it out.

"Hey, hey, don't be touching me." Dwayne staggered back,

both hands in the air, as if doing a little dance. Puke covered one of his pointy cowboy boots. "We're out in the middle of nowhere all alone, but you ain't my type."

"Shut up. Give me your password, then shut up."

"Don't call Rory. She'll just rag on me about how I said I would quit and I didn't. I ain't giving up my hops and barley. I shouldn't have to."

Jacob didn't answer as he contemplated the phone. He preferred not to lie, but he didn't want to argue with a drunk, however harmless. "What's your code to open the phone?"

"Who ya gonna call?" Dwayne guffawed, head thrown back, then slapped his chest with one hand. "Hear what I just said? 'Who you gonna call'? Ghostbusters. It's an old, stupid movie that my parents watch whenever it comes on the rerun movie channel. I guess you ain't seen it."

The man might as well talk gibberish. "What's your code?"

Dwayne swayed and put a hand on the tree. "You can't call her."

"You know she's worried sick about you. Let me tell her you're all right."

"I don't need another mother. Whatever. Six two ninety-seven."

Jacob flicked through Dwayne's favorites and punched Rory's number. After a few rings, it went to voice mail. Jacob knew better. Rory was walking the floor, muttering to herself, talking herself into calling a lawyer and divorcing her high school sweetheart, the love of her life. She was a Dwayne junkie. Jacob couldn't really see what she saw in the guy. But then she'd been sixteen when they'd produced Trevor, followed by Harper two years later. Those babies were worth fighting for.

Biting his lip, he opened the message program and used his

one-finger typing skills to tap out a text. "Got Dwayne. Will bring him home. Jacob."

He'd barely hit Send when her response arrived. The phone should've melted in his hand. "Don't u dare. I got 2 babies. Don't need another 1. Take home to m & d."

She didn't mean it.

The cymbals told him another text had arrived, hot on the heels of the first one. "Tell h I sd w'r done. Tell h I'm not j this time. Got lawyer n speed dial."

She couldn't afford a lawyer. Nolan Beale, her father, could. But by morning, she would cool off. She always did.

Jacob studied the star-studded sky for a second. Wispy clouds dressed the moon in lace. The breeze held a hint of coolness, finally. Still, he didn't feel like sitting in a truck all night. He had work to do tomorrow. So did Dwayne. He needed to sleep it off, take a shower, and drink a gallon of coffee. Not at Jacob's house. Dwayne had spent the night in Jacob's barn once before, after crashing his truck into Will Glick's buggy. Mordecai was among the most forgiving of men. He took his role as deacon seriously, but he also had a practical streak. He wouldn't want to expose the children a second time to Dwayne's way of living.

"I'm thirsty." Dwayne started toward the road, giving Jacob a wide berth. He plunged to a stop, then swayed. A couple of cusswords followed, delivered at a decibel Jacob could've done without. "Aw, man, this sucks. Nature calls."

Jacob turned his back on the man and started for the truck. "Hurry up. We're going into town."

"Aw, man, you calling Jesse? Don't call Jesse. He'll rip me a new one." More cusswords. "He's gonna bust a vessel in his brain ragging on me."

Pastor Jesse Glick did have a way with words. And he would not be happy that a member of his small congregation had fallen into his old ways. Dwayne and Rory had joined the Beeville church before Jesse had been ordained, and both their babies had been dedicated there. Jacob scrolled through the contacts and punched Jesse's cell phone number.

Voice mail. Again.

He maneuvered around the truck and opened the driver's side door. It felt good to ease onto the seat. He leaned back and contemplated the wheel. This was a Dodge Ram, four-door with an extended cab. Not new, but Dwayne had spent a lot of time gussying it up. Nice paint job, powerful stereo, new seat covers. If he spent as much time and effort on his marriage as he did the truck, he would make Rory the happiest, most blessed woman around.

"Hey, head to the river." Dwayne climbed into the passenger seat. "There's an alligator with our name on it."

It was a black night out. The Frio River was up by Choke Canyon Lake. A long drive, even in a pickup truck. Besides, even if they caught an alligator, it would take several people to reel it in and then it had to be taken to El Campo for processing. And a man had to show a license to do that. "No hunting tonight."

"You know, you're not as much fun as you used to be. Take me to Shawn's house." Dwayne flopped back against the seat and let out a loud burp that smelled of puke and stale beer. He patted his flat stomach. "Man, that felt good. Shawn'll go with me. He knows how to have a good time."

Jacob held his breath, fighting the urge to stick his head out the window. Instead he punched in the number for Jesse's house. He hated to do it, knowing he would likely wake Leila, mother of two little ones. The phone buzzed and buzzed. Finally, Leila's sleepy voice came over the line. "*Jah*—I mean yes? It's Leila." She cleared her throat. "How can I help you?"

"I'm so sorry. I know you're sleeping, but I didn't know who else to call. Jesse isn't answering his cell so I was hoping to reach him at home. Rory said no way—"

"Jacob? Is this Jacob?" Leila's voice rose. Rustling noise told him she sat up. "Is *Mudder* all right? Has something happened to one of the *kinner*? Deborah? Rebekah? Is Hazel all right? Caleb?"

She ran through the names in a rapid-fire succession that left Jacob with no option but to wait until she ran out. When she stopped, her breathing ragged, Jacob jumped in. "Everyone's fine. Healthy. Sleeping, I reckon. Is Jesse there?"

"*Nee*, he's driving back from the valley. He's been there for the last week working with refugee children. I expect he'll be here in a few hours. He's homesick and the *kinner* miss him something awful, so he decided to drive back tonight. If you tried to call him and he didn't answer, he's driving, that's why." Leila always did talk more than three men put together. Even more than Rebekah, who used to monopolize the supper table conversation until she married Tobias, and now she monopolized all his conversations. Better him than Jacob. Pain throbbed in Jacob's right temple. The start of a headache he could ill afford right now. Sweat burned his eyes. He breathed a gusty sigh punctuated by a trumpet snore from Dwayne. He glanced in his direction. The man was sprawled against the seat, his mouth open with drool forming at the corner. Not a pretty picture, but at least *he'd* stopped talking.

"Dwayne's at it again."

"*Ach*, that man. Rory will take a shotgun to him one of these days if Nolan doesn't get to him first." Crackling came over the line and the next few words were lost. "I'm getting up. I'll call Rory, talk her down from whatever ledge she's on."

Leila talked like that now. Like she read articles in magazines and watched morning talk shows on TV. The English called them stay-at-home moms. The Plain simply called them mothers. "I need a place to take him."

"Bring him here. I can sleep in Gracie's bed. We upgraded her to a twin a few months ago. She loves it, but she loves sleeping with her mommy too. Manny—"

"I can't bring him there until Jesse gets home. I'll find a convenience store and get some coffee—for him and me."

Dwayne couldn't stay at Leila's without Jesse there. It wouldn't be right.

"Don't be giving him coffee at this time of night. He needs to sleep it off. Bring him here." Her tone turned crisp. "And don't be silly. Jesse brings immigrants here all the time on their way to court hearings and such. His lawyer friends use us as a halfway point to San Antonio. He'll be here in less than two or three hours—"

"Okay, okay. I'll be there in about twenty minutes."

Leila had a way of wearing a man down. She was a sweet, pretty girl. All the Lantz girls were. They just talked too much. Martha wasn't like that. No point in thinking about her now. She probably wouldn't talk to him again anytime soon.

He jammed the key in the ignition and the truck rumbled to life. The stereo followed. Guitars and drums mixed in a high velocity country tune. Something about sitting on the tailgate of a truck drinking from a red cup.

Dwayne snorted and bolted upright. "What, what? Where are we? Are we at the river?"

"Shut up and go to sleep."

"Man, don't be harsh with me." Dwayne wriggled and shoved his cowboy hat back on his head. The slur had begun to fade from his speech. "I know you think I'm messed up, but walk a mile in my boots, why don't you?"

"I've tried." Jacob swallowed sudden, embarrassing emotion. What had gotten hold of him? A virus, or something worse. "All I see are blessings. A good woman who loves you. Two healthy babies. A father-in-law who gives you shelter. A decent job. What do you have to whine about?"

"You know what my high school friends are doing these days?"

Jacob shrugged. He could only guess. "Going to college?"

"Brent is playing football at A&M. Marshall is in the army, and he's stationed in Germany." Dwayne made it sound like a very special place. "Me, I was born in Beeville and I'll die in Beeville. Rory's the best and I love my kids, but nothing I do is good enough. Ever. Nolan looks down his nose at me every day. Rory's constantly ragging on me to get a better job that pays more. She wants to go to Disney World and Cancun. Meantime, she orders all these expensive baby clothes online. Who knew babies needed so many clothes? And toys and junk. The house is full of it. I'm always stepping on stuff."

He ran down, finally. The man had made his choices, and now he'd like to blame someone else for them. Jacob wanted what Dwayne had, but his path to such riches would be a very different one. Or none at all. "I'm not married, so I don't know much about this stuff, but I do know a man has responsibilities and he doesn't shirk them. Not when he has children depending on him."

"I ain't shirking nothing. Those babies don't want for anything. I work my fingers to the bone to make sure."

"That's good."

Dwayne leaned his head against the window and pulled his hat down over his eyes. "Wake me up when we get there."

Jacob inhaled and blew out the air. He was the last person on earth to give advice about women and marriage. He knew next to nothing about it. If tonight was any indication, he would never get to know more. Ever.

CHAPTER 4

Jacob slammed on the brakes. The truck swerved. The
tires squealed, gears screeching, and the engine died in the
middle of the road. He'd been doing so well with the gear-shifting
stuff. Dwayne snorted and flailed with both arms. "What the—"

"Who is that?" A man sauntered along the farm-to-market
road's shoulder, his dark shape outlined by the headlights. He
didn't look up. "What is he doing walking around in the dark like
that?"

Dwayne muttered and rolled to one side, giving Jacob his
back. Whatever. He peered into the dark, restarted the truck, and
moved on to the shoulder, well out of the path of any random car
that might be traveling the back roads late at night. Cowboy hat
or straw? Straw hat. A Plain man.

He wasn't very tall, shaped like a barrel, shoulders hunched.
Was he old? What would an elderly Plain man be doing out on
the road this time of night? Jacob waited for the man to get closer.
Instead he stopped and made as if to turn around.

"Hey, wait." Jacob turned off the engine, shoved open the door,
and jumped out. "Wait, do you need a ride?"

The man turned. Not old. Simon Glick. He'd been at the

singing earlier. Much earlier. His brother Joseph should have given him a ride home by now.

"What are you doing out here by yourself in the dark?"

Simon peered at him through wire-rimmed glasses that had slid down his nose. He shoved them up with his stubby index finger. "Home. I-I-I can-can find my way home. I'm a man."

Indeed, he and Jacob were the same age, but he always thought of Simon as a little brother. Simon's simple good nature appealed to Jacob. Simon never had a bad word to say about anyone, and he loved to "help out" as he put it. "Where's Joseph?"

"He had to take Vesta home. He said he had to talk to her about something. It's a se-se-se-cret." The stutter and Simon's crestfallen look told Jacob he realized he'd said something he shouldn't have. "Don't tell."

Joseph should have planned ahead better. He should've asked someone else to give Simon a ride. He probably figured no harm could come to a man walking around Bee County alone at night. With a prison down the road, they all knew better. "I won't tell." He wouldn't say anything, except to Joseph himself. "But you should get in. I'll give you a ride."

Simon's forehead wrinkled over his glasses. He looked so much like his father, Bishop Leroy. Leroy hadn't been bishop in a few years, but Jacob still thought of him that way. Simon cocked his head and looked at the truck. "You're driving Dwayne's truck?"

"How do you know it's Dwayne's truck?"

"Seen it around. He drives real fast up and down the dirt roads." Still looking confused, Simon shrugged. "I have to be careful not to get in his way. You drive his truck now?"

Simon hadn't been trusted with his own buggy since he failed to attach the rig properly, which led to a mishap that hurt the horse and destroyed the buggy beyond what the Glicks, well-known for their buggy-making business, could repair. People should be looking out for Simon, not the other way around. "I'm helping him out by driving. He's tired. I have to take him into town, but I can take you home after that."

Simon would likely tell Leroy about Jacob driving the truck, but it couldn't be helped. *Rumspringa* covered a multitude of activities.

"I can help out." Simon's face lit up with a smile reminiscent of his brother Jesse who had the same stocky, barrel-chested body and dark brown eyes. "I like to help."

"I know you do. Why don't you climb in the back seat and we'll get everyone squared away?"

Simon dashed forward as if afraid the offer might be rescinded. Hand on the extended cab's door, he paused, frowning. "Why isn't he going home? Is Ro-Ro-Rory mad?"

He might have the mind of someone closer to Liam Byler's age—about ten—but he still didn't miss much. Jacob opened the driver's door. "*Jah*, she's mad and Dwayne deserves it, but he needs a place to sleep tonight so we're taking him to Jesse and Leila's."

Another big grin. "Jesse is my *bru-bruder*. I like Leila. She has cookies and she shares."

"I know. I like them too."

Once Jacob started driving, he had to concentrate on shifting gears. He didn't try to make conversation, and Simon seemed content to take in the interior of the truck. Likely, he'd never been in one before. The seats had new covers, George Strait seemed to feel blessed that all his exes lived in Texas, and the air smelled like pine trees. A few more shifts of the gears and Jacob managed to stop at the Stop sign and turn onto Highway 59 leading into Beeville. Not bad. He could do this.

"I wan-wan-wanna girl. A girl li-li-like . . . a girl like you got. Li-li-like . . ." Simon's words were so garbled Jacob could barely understand. "I-I-I mean li-li-like Jesse and Leila. Like everyone."

He glanced in the rearview mirror. Simon's face was radish red. His eyes were bright with tears and his lower lip trembled. He wanted a special friend. A girl to take on a buggy ride. Like any man his physical age would. But his mental age? Jacob would never have guessed such a thing.

"I don't really have a girl. Not yet. So I understand."

Simon squirmed. "Can w-w-we both get one?"

The temptation to say he couldn't even get one for himself overwhelmed Jacob. He inhaled the fake pine scent that emanated from the tree air freshener hanging from the mirror. "It's not that easy, but we can try."

"You like Martha."

A statement of fact without the slightest stutter.

"I do."

"My *mudder* says I don't need a special friend."

Naomi most likely wanted to shield her son from the hurt he would feel when girls chose men who would be the heads of the households they needed. The men who could be *manns* and *daeds* in ways Simon could not. "Do you have someone particular in mind?"

Simon nodded so vigorously his straw hat flopped. He grabbed it. "I like Amanda."

Amanda. Aaron and Jolene Shrock's special girl. Simon had picked exactly the right girl for a man like himself. She was sweet and pretty and she would see him as her equal. Which indeed he was. "Amanda is nice."

"She's pretty."

"She is."

"Jacob will help me." Simon clapped his hands together as if applauding. "This is *gut*. Very *gut*."

Jacob wasn't even able to help himself. How could he help Simon? He kept his gaze on the windshield after that.

They pulled into Jesse's driveway at eleven thirty. Simon had his door open before Jacob turned off the ignition. Leila peeked through the screen door. "There you are. Simon! I didn't know you were coming."

She hugged Simon, a gesture he returned with great enthusiasm. She might have given Jacob one as well if he hadn't taken a step back. Her Plain instincts had definitely eroded. She wore a short robe of shiny material over running shorts and an oversize white T-shirt that didn't hide the fact she and Jesse were adding another *bopli* to their brood. Her feet were bare.

"Let me roust Dwayne out of the truck." Jacob turned away. "Did you get ahold of Rory?"

"She says he can take a long hike and rot at the end of that trail. Not in those words, but that was the gist of it."

A lot more words, likely. "She's giving up?"

"She'll cool off. Jesse will talk to Dwayne and I'll talk to Rory. Marriage takes work. You don't just give up on it, and Rory knows it. But this kind of behavior . . ." Leila swept her arm toward the truck. "It has to stop. He can't be a good father and husband like this."

"He has a problem."

"No doubt."

Jacob jerked open the door. Dwayne's package of raw meat tumbled to the ground. He scooped it up and handed it to Leila. "This should still be *gut*."

"*Ach*, I could make four meals out of this—five." She took it as if he'd handed her a gift. "*Nee*, I'll give it to Dwayne tomorrow. He can take it home to Rory. They're on a tight budget too."

The Lantz sisters were ones to think of others before themselves. Jacob turned to Dwayne, still passed out on the seat. "Come on, time to go to bed, buddy."

Dwayne didn't budge. His mouth hung open, spittle dribbling from his lower lip. It took both of the men to wrestle him out of the truck. His legs dragged and his head flopped.

"How much did he drink?" Leila laid the package of meat on the steps and stuck her hands on her hips. "Should I put him in the shower or call 9-1-1?"

"*Nee*. He snored all the way here. He's fine."

They dragged him in the house, through a living room littered with dolls, Lincoln Logs, and toddler picture books. The room smelled of baby wipes, dirty diapers, and something sweet recently baked. Gingersnaps maybe. Jacob heard a crunch under his boot. He'd crushed something.

"Don't worry about it." Leila's tone was airy. "At least you're not barefoot. I do that half a dozen times a day. It's all I can do not to say something I don't want the *kinner* repeating, but there's no point in picking it all up. They just get it right back out."

At the narrow door to the bedroom, Dwayne's head snapped up. His eyes opened. Both arms flailed until he connected with the frame and wouldn't let go. "Where am I? What the—"

"It's me, Leila. You're at Jesse's house."

"What am I doing here?" Dwayne jerked from the men's grasp and hauled himself backward. "I want to talk to my wife. I need to talk to Rory."

"Rory doesn't want to talk to you." Leila shook her finger,

eyes narrowed, frowning. "You blew it again and she has every right to be angry. Right now, what you need to do is sleep it off and let her cool down."

"I need to talk to my baby. I need to tell her I'm sorry."

"Tomorrow." Leila relented and patted his shoulder. "She's asleep now. You should be too."

"Where's my truck? Where are my keys?" He stumbled back and smacked his head on the doorframe. "Ouch. You can't keep me here against my will."

"Is it your will to disappoint your wife over and over again? To disappoint God? To take the chance of driving drunk and leaving your children fatherless?" Jacob heaved a breath. Who was he to judge? He had his own sins to confess when it came to a long, drawn-out *rumspringa*. No wonder Martha kept her distance. "Tomorrow is a work day. Get some sleep, go to work so you don't lose your job, then you can go home and make things right with Rory."

Dwayne's gaze swung from Jacob to Leila to Simon, who'd squeezed himself against the wall, his face scrunched up as if expecting a blow. Dwayne's fists unclenched. He sighed. "Okay." His tone had turned meek. He launched himself onto the narrow bunk bed covered with some sort of pink and purple princess blanket. "Take my boots off, will you? My feet are killing me."

His face was covered with sweat and his shirt was damp under the arms. Jacob held his breath as he tugged off the ostrich skin boots and the rank odor of feet floated around him.

"Thanks, dude." Dwayne rolled over, feet hanging off the edge of the bed, and closed his eyes.

The three of them tromped from the room. Leila smiled up at Jacob. "You did good in there. You could be a teen counselor. Jesse needs help."

"Are you trying to recruit me?" An odd, cold feeling whirled round his neck, raising goose bumps. "I'm starting baptism classes soon."

"I would never do that." Leila's cheeks colored. "Don't go home and tell *Mudder* I tried to steal you away from your Plain faith. She doesn't see the babies often enough as it is."

"I wouldn't do that."

She sighed. "I miss everyone so much. All of you."

She and Jesse had made their choice long ago. "A lot of water under that bridge."

"Can I make you some coffee before you go back? Or some iced tea? I have a travel cup I could put it in." She didn't seem the least fazed that he was driving a truck. "I don't want you falling asleep on the road. Precious cargo and all."

Simon's face turned red again. "I like cookies."

"No *kaffi*. Tea would be nice to cool off." Jacob wiped sweat from his forehead with his sleeve. Iced tea would cool him off and not keep him awake like coffee. "*Daed* has me helping with the apiaries in the morning. And I still have to take Simon home and get my buggy back."

"Simon can stay here. I'll take him home in the morning."

And have to explain how he ended up at her house after the singing. And Jacob's role in it. Simon would be in trouble and so would Jacob. "That won't work."

"I like cookies." Simon looked hopeful. "I smell cookies."

Leila laughed. "You have a good nose." She bustled into the kitchen and returned a few minutes later with tea mugs and two sandwich bags filled with gingersnaps. "For the road."

Simon grinned, grabbed his share of the loot, and fairly skipped out the front door.

Moving more slowly, Jacob paused on the top step. He could ask Leila. She and Jesse worked with a church youth group. Jesse did faith counseling, whatever that was. "Do you think it's possible for men like Simon to be in *lieb* and get married?"

Leila crossed her arms, her eyebrows lifted. She looked so much like her mother Abigail in that moment. "Why, Jacob King, are you considering matchmaking?"

"I don't know." Embarrassment heated his face. He couldn't meet her gaze. "It just makes me feel like he shouldn't be alone because he's different. We say *kinner* like him are special gifts from *Gott*. Don't they deserve the same happiness as the rest of us?"

He couldn't believe he was having this conversation with a woman, who was, for all intents and purposes, English now.

She squeezed his arm. Definitely English. "You are the sweetest thing ever. It would take a special kind of woman to yoke herself to Simon, but he's sweet and kind and hardworking. He looks an awful lot like his brother, and I think Jesse is cute. What more could a woman want?"

Jacob didn't want to think about how cute or not cute Jesse was, but he understood Leila's point. "Like Amanda Shrock. They would sort of fit together."

"The Shrocks came after Jesse and I left." Her skin turned a rosy pink, but she didn't break eye contact. "But if Amanda is half as sweet and nice as Simon, they'd fit together perfectly."

"*Gott* intended for us to be with someone, no matter how smart a person is. I know some really smart people who are dumb."

"You are so much like Mordecai. So wise." Leila rewarded him with another one of those Lantz sister smiles that could knock a man from his boots. "A deep thinker. You'll make some lucky woman a *gut mann*."

He could think of no answer to such a statement. No one had ever said that about him. Mordecai knew something about everything, and mostly people focused on Phineas because they felt sorry for him and his scarred face. Jacob had been left to make his own way after his mother's death more than ten years ago.

Except for Aunt Susan. Her kisses on his forehead and her soft fingers smoothing back his hair when she thought he was sleeping had gotten him through many lonely nights after Mother died.

He cleared his throat, nodded, and climbed into the truck.

From Leila's lips to Martha's ears.

CHAPTER 5

❧

Set. Spike. *Wham!* Martha whooped and landed hard in the tired-looking weeds that served as a volleyball court in Leroy's yard. Grasshoppers flew in all directions, apparently as surprised as Jacob at the ferocity of the hit. The startled look on his face as he ducked and let the ball sail into the second row gave her a sense of satisfaction. She loved a good game of volleyball. It didn't hurt that Jacob had pushed Rueben aside so he could be directly across the net from her. He'd been doggedly returning her volleys for more than an hour, but this time she got him good.

I'm sorry, Gott. *I'm only human.*

Obviously. Or she wouldn't be questioning His plan for her all the time. How could she consider baptism when she couldn't keep the simplest of rules? Trust *Gott.*

"You've been eating your spinach." Breathing hard, Jacob smiled, straightened, and wiped sweat from his flushed face. "I'll get even, you watch."

"I don't like spinach." Martha hunched forward, poised on the balls of her feet, hands together, ready for the next volley. "How's Dwayne?"

"Dwayne's fine." His smile didn't slip. "Rory took him back.

She made him stay at his father's for three days, but she finally gave in."

"Poor babies." She bumped Rueben's serve neatly to Vesta, who grunted and smacked it overhand with more enthusiasm than accuracy. It hit the sagging net and bounced back. "Their daddy prefers alligator hunting to growing up. Like a lot of men I know."

Point for the boys. She tossed the ball over the net to Rueben. The volleys continued back and forth, this time while Deborah, Abigail, and the older folks on the sidelines cheered and clapped. They all loved a good game.

So did Martha, but she liked to win too.

"There was no alligator hunting." Jacob whacked the ball so hard it flew past the second row, hit a mesquite tree, ricocheted, and slammed into the corral fence. "For him or for me."

Game! Martha managed to stop just short of jumping up and down and screaming in victory. It was only a game, after all. Ignoring Vesta's confused looks, she sauntered from the yard to the picnic table where they'd set up plates of cookies, chips, and sandwiches. She poured water in a cup and took a long drink.

"I need your help on something."

She jumped and spilled water on the front of her dress. Jacob took a step back. "Sorry, I didn't mean to scare you."

"I'm not scared of you." Why did she always sound so defensive when she talked to him? He stood close, smelling of soap, sweat, and good cheer. She wiped at her dress, heat spreading across her already warm cheeks. "Help with what?"

He cocked his head toward the cluster of kids clowning around in the yard. Simon chased after Rueben, who had stolen his hat and held it over his head as he ran. Both were hooting and hollering like eight-year-olds. Much like Liam, who tried to keep up on his shorter legs but couldn't. "I want to help Simon ask Amanda to take a walk."

Just when she thought Jacob couldn't surprise her. Grinning despite herself, she swiveled to peek at Aaron and Jolene Shrock's middle daughter, a sweet girl who never stopped smiling but rarely said a word. Amanda sat cross-legged on a gnarly old stump, cuddling a kitten in her lap. She had clapped every time Simon hit the ball during the volleyball game—which wasn't too often, truth be told—and now she giggled at his hat antics. "That's sweet of you."

"You don't have to sound so surprised. I've been known to have a good idea now and then." Jacob grinned that grin that made Martha's breath play hide and seek with her lungs. "Simon told me the other night when . . ." His smooth cheeks turned a deeper red than exertion and sun warranted. "Anyway, he said he'd like to have a special friend too."

She managed a quick breath. Too? As if Jacob had one? Never mind. This wasn't about them. It was about helping two nice people find each other. "What did you have in mind?"

"Ask Amanda to take a walk with you down to the pond. I'll get Simon to head that direction with me. We'll run into each other, so to speak."

"I can do that."

He nodded. "*Gut.*"

"It's a *gut* idea."

"I'm glad you think so." The smile fading, he shifted his gaze to the chips on the table, then back to her face. "We could take our own walk, once we get them situated."

The trepidation in his voice told her he didn't expect a yes, but he longed for it. So did she. If only she could be sure of him.

But nothing could be for sure. Her mother's passing had taught her as much. She studied his face with its blue-green eyes, long nose, and dimples. He knew loss as well. His mother had died in an accident when he was a small boy. Like Rueben. Yet he still sought love. "We could."

"*Jah? Jah!*" He pumped his fist in such an English manner, she took a step back. "*Nee*, don't change your mind. See you down at the pond."

He whirled and strode away as if to stave off the opportunity for her to speak again. Feeling like she had a special mission in life, Martha traipsed over to Amanda's spot, knelt, and petted the tiny, black-and-white kitten. "Your kitty looks comfy."

Amanda smiled. She had a round face, dark-blue almond-shaped eyes, and a smattering of freckles that added to the impression of her as a young child, even though she was the same age as Martha. "She's a sweet baby. She loves me. She doesn't have a *mudder* so I take care of her. *Mudder* lets me."

"You think kitty would like to go for a walk?"

Beaming, Amanda hopped up, her baby clutched close to her chest. "Her name is Patches. She loves to be walked."

"Let's take Patches down by the pond."

Allowing for Amanda's shorter legs, Martha strolled down the dirt path worn by many a couple who decided to sneak away from the frolics held every other Sunday when they didn't have church. The pond came into view. It held so little water it could hardly be called a pond, and it was only the last week of June. They sorely needed rain. A singsong whistle mingled with the croak of frogs and the buzz of flies as big as her pinky. "Jacob?"

"Jacob's here?" Amanda sounded pleased. "He's funny and he always gives me his cookies after church."

Funny and giving. Martha had seen both those qualities in him. So why had she chosen to focus on the negative? For fear. She had never thought of herself as cowardly. She'd been brave when Mother died. Her throat tight, she brushed away a swarm of gnats. "So is Simon."

"I like Simon. He gave me a flower once."

"He did?"

Amanda nodded so hard her *kapp* slid down the back of her head. "*Jah*, a dandelion. We blew on it together."

"That was nice." Martha stopped and fixed the *kapp*, admiring the girl's shiny blond hair. Her own had more frizz than curl. "Simon is sweet."

"He helped me take care of my puppy too. Her name is Star because she has a white spot on her forehead shaped just like a star."

A heart for caring for babies. Was it enough for Amanda to mother puppies and kittens? It seemed sad she might never be a mother. "You have lots to do."

"I'm a *gut mudder* to my *boplin*."

"*Gut* for you."

Jacob stood on the banks with Simon. They tossed rocks in the murky, scum-covered water. "*Gut* job." Jacob slapped Simon on the back. "You have a *gut* arm."

Simon hooted. "I have a *gut* arm."

Jacob turned. "Look who's here."

Simon remained intent on perfecting his rock-throwing technique. Jacob tapped his arm. "We have visitors. Amanda is here."

His face crinkled in a smile, Simon turned. "Amanda is here."

Martha took no offense that he didn't seem to notice her standing next to the object of his affection. She was busy looking at Jacob. He started forward. "I have to tell Martha a secret. You two talk and then you can walk back up to the house together. Simon, you know the way, right?"

Simon nodded his head up and down, but his gaze stayed on Amanda, who held out Patches. "Want to hold my baby?"

"*Jah.*"

They'd already forgotten about Jacob and Martha. She glanced at Jacob. He was watching the couple, his expression delighted. He had a gift for finding joy in life. For someone who'd had a rough row to hoe in his early years, he had no bitterness, no hard edges. His joy wasn't a sign of immaturity, just the opposite. For her to find that same joy would be a blessing. She moved closer. "What's your secret?"

He took her hand in his.

Her first inclination was to faint, but that would be silly. She tightened her grip and prayed her legs would remember how to walk.

If I die now, Gott, *I would die happy.* Jacob squeezed Martha's hand and led her up the path. The skimpy tree cover consisted of a mix of live oak and mesquite. Not much privacy. Still, he knew of a spot where a fallen tree trunk just off the path could serve as a place to sit for a few minutes. The tall weeds, nopals, and black-eyed Susans would give them cover. There. He pointed to the trunk, suddenly overcome with a timidity he'd never felt before in his life. "Let's sit for a minute."

Martha didn't let go of his hand. She led Jacob to the trunk and sat. He did the same. She didn't say anything. His mind, normally so full of junk he couldn't decide what to think on first, shut down and went out of business. The silence stretched.

"You said—"

"I thought—"

He breathed. "You first."

"You said you wanted to tell me a secret."

"It's not much of a secret." He rubbed a spot of mustard on his pants. "I am in *lieb* with you."

The pause lasted longer than summer in south Texas. "Are you sure?"

Not the answer he'd hoped for. He didn't feel unsure at all. He met her gaze head-on. "A man says he loves you and your first response is to question if he's sure. Are you so unlovable?" To his consternation her eyes filled with tears. "Don't cry."

"I'm not crying. I never cry." She dabbed at her face with her apron. "My *mudder* died when I was ten."

He knew the awfulness of not understanding, of trying to wrap his mind around never seeing *Mudder* again. One morning, she came in and touched his feverish cheek with her cool, soft fingers and told him *Daed* would stay with him while the rest of the family went on a long-planned, much-longed-for trip to the beach in Corpus Christi. He'd been mad at her. He wanted to go, but she said sick little boys needed to rest. There would be other trips to the beach. She'd kissed his forehead and hugged him even though he tried to wiggle from her grasp. Her scent of vanilla and soap lingered long after she left the room.

Aunt Susan had been the one to tell him *Mudder* would never come back. His father spent days with Phineas in the hospital, and Jacob had been sure he, too, would never return. But he had. They both had. "I was eight."

"I know."

"She left and you think everyone who loves you will leave? Everyone will disappoint you? It's not so." The indecision in her face told him he'd careened into the heart of her fear. "You use caring for the *kinner* as an excuse for not taking a chance. Don't do that."

"It's not an excuse. They do need me. But it's true, you can't know."

"No. That's why it's called faith." Never had an argument been more important. "Believing in the unknowable."

"You drive a car. You hunt for alligators."

"For now. Those are things I do for fun. I want to know what life feels like out there. We're only passing through. We don't know how long we have. I want to touch and feel it all. That's part of what *rumspringa* is about." He would settle down, eventually. There was no rush. Life as a Plain man with responsibilities stretched before him. So, for now, he wanted this season of diving into odd, strange, exciting experiences. "It's also about finding that person you want to be yoked to for the rest of your life."

She stood as if to walk away, then sat once again. "I don't know who you are. How can I know how I feel about you?"

"I'm a Plain man who loves a Plain woman and wants to get to know her better. That doesn't mean I'll take her away from her family. They'll always be her family."

She sighed, not looking at all convinced. "That's *gut* to know."

When he most needed words, nothing seemed to come. "Is there any chance you might take a chance on me?"

"When you grow up, it's possible."

Pictures flashed in his mind. The rust-and-green Olds. His friend Milo with a pool stick, his rump in the air as he leaned over the pool table. A red cup full of beer. A season, only a season. "I *am* grown up."

"Not if you're still hanging around boys like Dwayne Chapman."

That again. "Dwayne isn't a bad person. He gets turned sideways sometimes and needs help."

"Is that what you call it when you go to those parties with him in the fields with the beer kegs?"

He hadn't done that in a long time, but the fact that she didn't trust him stung far worse than any bee sting, and he'd had plenty of those over the years. "It's not right to sit in judgment because I chose to help out a friend who doesn't seem to be able to grow up. He needed help getting home. I helped. That's all. You know that. Your self-righteousness is just a cover for your fear."

"I'm not afraid."

"Then why don't you let me get closer? We're stuck. We can't go forward because you're afraid."

"We can't go forward because you won't grow up. I don't need any more *kinner*."

"I don't need taking care of." He drove cars. He helped friends in need. Like Dwayne. Like Simon. He didn't do it to earn her good graces, but surely she could see that he tried hard to be a decent person, a person worthy of her love. "I'm a man, and I'll do what I think is right. A woman who plans to be a good *fraa* would know how to accept that."

"Are you saying I won't be a good *fraa*?"

"I'm saying you have to trust your *mann* to make good decisions and know when to bow to his wishes."

She stared up at him, her blue eyes dark with anger and something else. Hurt. He'd hurt her feelings. "So I wouldn't measure up to your standards for a good *fraa*?"

"I'm sorry."

"I'm not." She sniffed and crossed her arms. "It's better we know these things now, than later. You find me lacking. So be it."

"Not lacking at all. You find me lacking." He'd made her feel bad about herself. This had not gone well at all. His fault. All his fault. He cupped her face in his hands and leaned down, wanting to wipe the hurt from her face.

She stared up at him, her breathing ragged, eyes wide. Her lips parted.

"Mandy? Simon? Mandy!"

A woman's high voice mixed with the lower bass of a man's. Tromping sounds followed. Will and Isabella Glick broke through the high grass and weeds to the tiny clearing. Will halted. His wife nearly ran into him. "You two?"

CHAPTER 6

❧

Disaster averted. A kiss from Jacob would surely lead to disaster. He wanted a woman who knew how to acquiesce to his will. Martha couldn't, not if he wasn't willing to leave behind his teenage ways and English friends. She had to be able to trust him.

Feeling as if she'd been thrown from a runaway buggy, Martha scrambled from the downed tree trunk, hoping her legs would hold her. She moved away from Jacob, but it was too late. From the sly looks on their faces, Will and Isabella knew exactly what was going on. Which was more than Martha could say. He infuriated her, yet she'd wanted that kiss. She still wanted it. "We were talking."

Her voice sounded peculiar. Like she'd just come up for air after swimming underwater.

"*Jah*, about old times." Jacob stood more slowly. He didn't sound at all flustered. "And how important our *mudders* were to us."

"We're looking for my *schweschder*." Isabella fanned her damp, red face with one hand. "She's not supposed to leave the yard, and she's likely to follow a dog or a cat to who knows where. One time she ended up at the Archers on Tynan Road."

"And my *Onkel* Leroy asked me to look for Simon." Will

341

jumped in when his *fraa* ran out of breath. "He wandered off about an hour ago. It's not like him to leave a frolic without saying anything. He's not allowed to take a buggy, so he has to be on foot. You haven't seen him, have you?"

Martha forced herself to make eye contact with Jacob. He raised his eyebrows and offered a rueful smile. Time to own up. It might have been his idea, but she had embraced it with all her heart. "We helped them get together. They're down by the pond."

"Get together?" Isabella's voice rose a full octave. She shook her head. "My little sister with Simon? Why would you do that? You know how special they are. They don't know about . . ."

She floundered.

"These things," Will offered, his expression equally horrified. "Simon and Amanda are like *kinner*. It would be like getting Liam together with one of the little girls."

"Simon asked for my help." Jacob spread out his hands, shoulders hunched. "He says he likes Amanda. Those aren't the words of a boy. Liam would rather eat spiders than touch a girl."

"Mandy says she likes Simon too," Martha added. "She says he helps her take care of her *boplin*."

"Her *boplin* are puppies and kittens." Isabella crossed her arms. "She's not capable of being a *mudder*."

Jacob interceded again. "We're not talking about *mann-fraa* things here. Only simple fun. They have feelings too."

Why couldn't he be as wise about his own life? Martha swallowed her disappointment in him, a bitter drink. "We weren't thinking that far ahead, only of them having fun together for now. Like others their age. They're included in all the other activities, except this. Do you think they don't notice everyone else pairing off, getting married, having *kinner*?"

"The two of you weren't thinking at all. They are special gifts from *Gott,* given to our care. They think like *kinner* so they don't know what they're missing." Will whirled toward the path. "We need to find them and get them home."

"What are y'all doing here?"

Simon and Amanda traipsed into the now very crowded clearing. They held hands and looked as pleased as two children sneaking a pecan pie from the windowsill after a pie-baking frolic. "We heard people arguing." Simon turned his face to the sun, eyes squinted. "It's too nice a day for arguing."

He didn't stutter. Not once.

"We were talking, not arguing." Will shot Jacob and Martha an accusing look. "See what you've done? Now we have to explain why they can't do this."

"Do what?" Amanda looked puzzled. "Who did what?"

"It's nothing, *schweschder.*" Isabella put an arm around her sister and glared at Martha. "Any ideas on how we do that without making them feel bad?"

Martha shook her head. Now everyone would feel bad. What did people say about the path paved with good intentions?

CHAPTER 7

THE SMELL OF STINK BAIT IN THE AFTERNOON COULD only mean one thing. Fish fry for supper. Jacob grinned at *Daed*, who washed his knife under a nearby spigot in the fish-cleaning area. *Daed* grinned back. It was a good thing they'd staked their camping area with tents a few days before the Fourth of July holiday. A steady stream of campers had inundated Choke Canyon State Park since their arrival. The lake was a popular place all summer long, but the holiday meant a four-day weekend for a lot of folks. It seemed half the Lone Star state had decided to pack up campers and join them.

Jacob rubbed his face on his sleeve, trying to stave off the sweat tickling his cheeks. The haul today included five nice-size channel catfish, three largemouth bass—one a big flopper caught by Caleb who was so excited he fell in the water—and two small crappie courtesy of Liam and Hazel, their youngest fishers. Jacob cut off the head and tail of the last catfish and hurled them in the trash bin.

"Might as well get it off your chest." *Daed* laid a skinned crappie in the ice chest. The snap of the lid sent a long-legged white egret scurrying away. "If it keeps eating at you, you'll be nothing but bone by the time we head home."

Brushing away the flies that buzzed around his ears, Jacob let his gaze travel to the picnic pavilion across an expanse of brown straw that passed as grass in south Texas's withering heat. Martha stood at the Coleman stove, showing Amanda how to control the flames under two dozen greasy hot dogs. The two also sat together at church earlier in the week. Amanda trotted after Martha, helping serve food afterward. She stood next to her when they played volleyball. The two were joined at the hips now. Beyond the pavilion, children played a wild game of tag designed to dry clothes wet from playing in the lake's swimming area. A cluster of women sat at the picnic table husking corn. The aroma of hot dogs floated and mingled with the odor of bait and fish guts. Jacob loved summer. Why spoil all this by talking about his problems?

"Gazing from afar ain't gonna get you much." *Daed* climbed onto a nearby picnic table and propped himself up with both hands behind him. "What's holding you back, *suh*?"

That *Daed* knew of his feelings didn't surprise Jacob. It was a well-known fact in this little *Gmay* that Mordecai King knew everything. His ability to pull facts from seemingly thin air still amazed the children but not Jacob. No one made a big deal about it, least of all Mordecai, and if anyone brought it up, Mordecai would be the first to deny it. His knowledge was dwarfed by his humility. Having a father like that served to make Jacob acutely aware of his own shortcomings. "She thinks I need to grow up. She says she has enough *kinner* to take care of."

"I can see her point." Mordecai leaned forward and put his elbows on his knees, his wrinkled hands clasped in front of him. The silver in his beard threatened to overtake the black, but his blue-green eyes were as sharp as ever. "Gallivanting around the countryside in a noisy, gas-guzzling, fume-belching Olds doesn't beget an image of a grown Plain man."

Mordecai did, indeed, know everything. Shame beat a fiery path from the back of Jacob's neck across his cheeks and down his chin. "We—I plan to get rid of it before baptism classes start." He wouldn't give away his partners in fun—or sin, depending on whom he asked—it wouldn't be right. "Leastways, we've talked about it."

"Not much time left, I reckon." Mordecai jerked his head toward Martha. "Not like the men around here have a plethora of young women from which to choose. Elijah's been talking to her after church."

"A pletho-what?"

Mordecai's vocabulary matched his voracious appetite for reading. Jacob's brother Phineas was the same way. Jacob preferred sports—another way his oldest brother was closer to his father. Not that either Mordecai or Phin ever intentionally made him or the other *kinner* feel left out.

"A lot."

"Right. I know." While Martha had been avoiding him that day after the volleyball game, she'd taken pains to let him see her chatting with Elijah Hostetler as she served potato salad or baked beans after church. "She's mad."

"Should she be?"

"I thought women were supposed to follow the man's lead."

"If the man is wise and fair, *jah*. Even if she doesn't agree. On the other hand, a man who does or says wrong—he should want a *gut* woman to point it out. She will and she should, and then she should bite her tongue and bide her time while he figures it out."

Jacob tried to imagine Martha biting her tongue. She might not be a big talker, but she surely had an opinion about things. She,

Vesta, and Amanda laughed as Simon walked by. He stopped and said something. The girls' giggles could be heard all the way across the open field. Simon ambled away, his baggy pants sagging at the waist despite his suspenders. The three put their heads together as if they were whispering. At least he and Martha agreed on that one thing. Amanda and Simon deserved to be happy too. "What do you think about *kinner* who are special gifts? I mean when they grow up and aren't *kinner* anymore. Should they have special friends?"

Mordecai's forehead wrinkled. He smoothed his unruly beard, his lips pulled down in a thoughtful frown. Before he could answer, Dwayne Chapman strode into the fish-cleaning area, a pole slung over one shoulder and an ice chest in the other hand. "Hey, pardner. Long time no see."

"You look better than you did the last time I saw you." Jacob slapped the last bass into the ice chest and closed it. "We're done if you want this spot."

Dwayne cast a glance at Mordecai, who tipped his hat and stood.

"Everyone deserves to have a special friend. *Gott* put someone on this earth for everyone. Read Genesis 2:18–24." Mordecai strode past Dwayne, his words floating behind him. "I'll let you whippersnappers visit. But that doesn't mean you get away with changing the subject. Talk to her."

Leave it to the deacon to know exactly which Scripture applied to a situation. Will was the minister. Maybe Jacob could talk to him again about Simon and Amanda. Or to Leroy. Simon was his son after all. Jacob wanted to talk to Martha too. He eyed the herd of women in the pavilion. The chances of catching her alone didn't seem as good as they had when Mordecai informed the family they would be taking a vacation to the lake.

"What's he talking about?" Dwayne laid the fishing pole on the table and dumped the ice chest on the ground. "Never mind. I wanted to talk to you anyway. You know they have some of the biggest alligators in the state here. They only allowed hunting here like four years ago or something so the gators are like thirty years old. A guy caught an eight-hundred-pound one here a couple years ago. Rory already cooked the pot roast, so I had to buy more meat—"

"Stop with the gator hunting." Jacob tore his gaze from the girls. "They're not in season. This place is packed. Aren't Rory and your babies here? Do you want them to see you breaking the law?"

"Rory, the rug rats, Nolan, Leila, and Jesse—everybody is here. It's a family fling, dude. But it's a big lake. They won't see anything." Dwayne propped open the lid to his ice chest and pulled out a largemouth bass that must've weighed four or five pounds. Its frantic flop caused Dwayne to lose his grip. The fish flipped and landed on the cement, its mouth gaping, eyes wide. He cussed and grabbed the wily fish. "I got fireworks for tonight. Afterward, I'll sneak away and we can do the deed. It'll be cool. Shawn is here somewhere. So is Kyle."

That Leila and Jesse had come with the Beale-Chapman clan didn't surprise Jacob. Leila and Rory had been friends since the early days. Leila and Jesse couldn't be with their real family, so their church family became much more special. It would be good for Abigail to see her daughter and grandkids, even if it was from afar.

Jacob forced himself to focus on Dwayne and his crazy plans.

"Fireworks aren't allowed in state parks. Alligators can't be hunted in July. And I have other plans." An overly optimistic statement, but he would ask Martha to take a walk by the shore once they got the fire going and the children gathered round for s'mores, fry pies, and Mordecai's endless repertoire of funny stories. Amanda loved s'mores and stories. Maybe she'd leave Martha's side when she saw the chocolate and roasted marshmallows. "Plans that don't include you."

"All your folks will be asleep by then."

"Not likely."

Fireworks that made noise might be out of the question—not that it mattered on their skinny budget these days—but the children had their sparklers, worms, and other small treats that wouldn't bother the park's permanent wildlife residents. The older folks would sit in their lawn chairs and enjoy the stars and the evening breeze while the children wore themselves out. Vacation meant staying up later than they normally would. And no chores in the morning. Jacob stuck the knives in a canvas bag he slung over one shoulder. He picked up his ice chest. When he looked up, Martha walked past, arm in arm with Amanda.

The look on her face said it all.

"Hey, we're not here together," he called after her. "He came looking for me. Ask Mordecai."

Martha kept walking.

Jacob kicked at a rock, sending it spinning away.

He turned to Dwayne. "You know anyone who wants to buy a '95 Olds Cutlass Ciera with a hundred-twenty-five-thousand miles on it?"

Dwayne's expression turned shrewd. "That old rust bucket of yours? I just might know someone. Kyle wrecked his truck and his folks won't buy him another one. How much do you want?"

Dwayne didn't know it, but he was about to make up for the trouble he'd caused Jacob.

CHAPTER 8

Sometimes helping others was the best way to shake off a funk. One of *Daed*'s favorite sayings. *Daed* had married Susan in his effort to find happiness. Martha didn't see that option in her future. Jacob had come all the way to Choke Canyon Lake to look for trouble with Dwayne Chapman once again. Tigers couldn't change their stripes, it seemed. She forced herself to smile at Amanda, who sat next to her mother eating a brownie the size of a small cake. She had frosting on her upper lip, a smattering of new freckles, and the start of a sunburn. She looked so content. Jolene, who snapped green beans with an efficiency born of much experience, paused long enough to pat her daughter's knee. "Slow down there, *dochder*, you'll choke."

Amanda grinned, revealing teeth smeared with chocolate. "I like brownie." The words were muffled by a mouthful of food. "It *gut*."

"Don't talk with your mouth full." Jolene went back to her beans, the *pop-pop* like music to Martha's ears. "Take a load off, Martha."

"I should check on the *kinner*. They were getting in the water again."

"Isabella and Will are down there with their two. They won't let them out of their sight."

Relieved, Martha sank into the battered lawn chair. Its frayed, faded nylon seat gave way under even her slight weight. She gazed out at the water, crystal clear in the sun. It might be low, allowing tree branches to stick up along the edges, but it was still beautiful. The pond grass, rushes, and cattails lined it like a green, growing frame that rippled in the breeze. The smell of water, mud, and rotting plants soothed her soul. "It's so peaceful here. I could stay for weeks."

She could camp out, embrace the quiet with no bickering siblings, boisterous boy jokes, or discussions about who should wash and who should dry. She could learn to fish. Fishing made her *daed* content. It might work for her too.

"I know. It's something about the sound of the water and the rustling of the leaves in the trees." Jolene sighed, a contented sound. "A body needs to work hard, but it needs rest too."

Amanda coughed, inhaled, coughed again, harder.

"I told you to slow down." Jolene slapped her daughter's back with two quick whacks. "Go get a drink of water, little piglet. I'll finish your brownie."

"*Nee!*" Amanda coughed again. "Love brownie."

"Get a drink of water. I'll guard it for you. I won't eat it, I promise."

Amanda bestowed a smile on her mother and trotted away.

"She's so funny." Martha settled back. "She never has a bad word to say about anyone, and she's always smiling."

"She is a *gut* girl." A pensive expression stole over Jolene's face. Her gaze followed Amanda's meandering progress toward the picnic pavilion. "I know *Gott* has a plan for her, but sometimes

I can't help but wonder what the future will bring for my sweet *bopli*."

"You mean when you're gone?" The other Shrock children would care for Amanda. It was expected, but no one would mind anyway. "She's such a sweetheart, they'll argue over who gets her."

"I know. I thank *Gott* for that and for her." Jolene's hands slowed, then rested over the pan of beans. "But that doesn't mean I don't imagine how different her life would be if she could . . . do the things other girls do when they grow up."

The perfect opening. Martha chose her words carefully. "Has she ever mentioned Simon to you?"

"Only every other word." Jolene held out the pan to Martha. "Your turn. I must be getting old. The joints in my fingers hurt. Anyway, Mandy chatters on endlessly about Simon did this and Simon did that."

Martha took the pan and settled it on her lap. "She likes Simon."

"He's a nice boy."

"He's a man and he likes Amanda too."

"You mean likes, *likes*?"

Her cheeks suddenly warm, Martha grabbed a bean, snapped it, and dropped the pieces in the pan. *Snap-snap.* "Special likes."

Jolene held her hand to her forehead and squinted as if she wanted to see the future. "I always think of her as a little girl."

"A little girl's mind in a grown-up body."

"I don't know what to think. I pray for her to be happy." Jolene let her hand drop. "A little bit of happiness isn't too much to ask, is it?"

"Isabella told me I shouldn't encourage her. She was very upset with me."

"She didn't mention it. My oldest *dochder* is very protective of her *schweschder*. And of me too. With Aaron's bad heart and trying to make ends meet, she often tries to carry the load by her lonesome. It's a bad habit."

"So what would you think? Not of them getting married or anything. Just passing the time together."

Amanda traipsed across the grass toward them, arms swinging, face lifted to the sun, and a big splotch of water soaking the front of her apron. Jolene shook her head and smiled. "I think my *dochder* will be happy no matter what, but I don't begrudge her the experience every girl wants."

Martha agreed. Who could look at that shining face and stand in the way? She might spend her life alone, but that didn't mean others should do the same. Something good might still come from her time spent with Jacob King.

Even if he never grew up.

CHAPTER 9

MARTHA SETTLED THE BASKET OF CHOCOLATE BARS, marshmallows, and graham crackers next to the fire pit and reviewed the contents. Vesta and Amanda had carried over everything needed for the fry pies too. Chocolate. Maybe chocolate would help her forget Jacob for a few minutes. Followed by a hot peach fry pie.

The lawn chairs were strategically placed for conversation and storytelling. Fluffy pink-and-purple clouds huffed and disappeared with the setting sun when the children started their games. Their shrieks of joy as they played olly olly oxen free made her smile despite herself. Life would go on. Chocolate would definitely help. She unwrapped a Hershey's bar and popped a chunk in her mouth. Two little ones squatted side by side, their chubby cheeks dimpled from wide grins, watching as their mother lighted the lumps that turned into writhing "worms" with the heat from a punk stick. She wanted *boplin*. Cute babies who looked like their father.

Back to Jacob.

"Hey."

Martha closed her eyes and opened them. As if her thoughts were enough to make him appear. That low, sandpaper-rough voice would not affect her. Mind over heart. In other words, *don't be addled.*

Martha inhaled and turned. "Hey, yourself."

Jacob pushed his straw hat back. His face had turned a deep bronze that served to highlight eyes the same color as the lake as the sun set on it. He bit his lower lip and let his gaze wander to the water and back. "I know what you think."

"You do? You read minds now?"

By unspoken agreement they moved toward the water, away from curious gazes. Martha lifted her warm face to a breeze made a few degrees cooler by the lake. The sound of birds chattering and the distant buzz of boat motors soothed her. The water lapped among huisache and mesquite brush along the shores with a peaceful regularity. She tried not to be hopeful. She tried not to think about Jacob's broad shoulders and the way his upper arms bulged against the cotton of his blue shirt. She tried not to inhale his woodsy scent.

Trust. Trust him. Trust Me.

The words sounded so clear, she glanced around to see if someone other than Jacob stood nearby. No one.

Jacob stopped on the path beaten by the many bare feet that had walked, run, strolled, and trudged along the lake, enjoying its beauty. "We sold the car."

She breathed and took a second to let it sink in like her bare feet in the warm soil under them. Trust would be so simple, so restful. Somewhere along the line she'd forgotten how to do it. Jacob's offering fanned the flame of hope. "You sold it for me?"

"We sold it because it was time, and we're not *kinner* anymore, and it's a heap of junk." He shrugged. "I'm a Plain man. Next week I'll start preparing for baptism. That's my plan."

"It's a *gut* plan." She liked it a great deal. "The others were okay with it?"

"All of them. It will be a nice-size baptism class."

"That's wonderful news."

"The other night, I did the right thing." Jacob's tone was firm but somehow respectful. "A man has to do what he thinks is right. Even if it means losing something."

"That's true." Something about his tone was different and no matter how difficult for her, he had a point. A man had to do what was right. She wouldn't respect a man who didn't. Or love him. How could she make him choose? "I understand what you're saying. I just worry that I might have to . . . It's hard to explain."

"Care for me like you do the *kinner*?" He slapped at a swarm of gnats and mosquitoes buzzing around them. "I won't be a burden or a responsibility. I will be a *mann* to my *fraa*. Someone to be counted on. Someone you can trust." He edged closer. "Take a walk with me."

"We tried that and it didn't work out."

"If at first you don't succeed, try, try again."

"I read somewhere that insanity is doing the same thing over and over again and expecting a different result."

"Plain folks aren't allowed to be insane."

Martha couldn't help herself. She laughed. His deep chortle sent goose bumps scurrying up her arms. "I talked to Jolene about Amanda and Simon."

He edged yet closer. "You're changing the subject, but that's okay. I talked to Leroy about Simon and Amanda."

They were on the same page about at least one important thing.

His long fingers brushed hers. She inhaled and tried to think. "Jolene has no problem with them passing the time together."

"Leroy neither. He seemed happy at the thought."

"Jolene too."

"Then we should—"

"*Jah*, we should."

Martha raced to find Amanda while Jacob tracked down Simon. Ten minutes later they met back at the same spot on the water's edge where it ebbed and flowed, sparkling in the last little bit of sun in the dusky beginnings of evening. Amanda clapped her hands, giggled, and covered her mouth when Jacob approached with Simon. "We're all together again." Simon's ears turned red. "We take another walk?"

"*Nee*. It's getting dark and you'll trip over something or get lost. I'll put a blanket down here so you can sit together and talk." Martha shook out a blanket and laid it on the grass close to the narrow shore but far enough away that the water wouldn't reach them. She turned and studied Simon's face to make sure he heard and understood. He seemed entranced by Amanda. "Does that sound good, Simon?"

He nodded but didn't look at her.

After making sure they were settled in, Martha faced the lake. What now? Did Jacob's offer to take a walk still stand? It really was getting too dark.

"We might not be able to take a walk, but we can stand on the pier where it's less crowded." Jacob took her hand. Goose bumps ran up her arm and tickled her neck. "That way Simon and Amanda can have their privacy, and so can we."

"Okay." She couldn't manage much more.

Martha followed Jacob to the short, narrow wooden pier a

few yards from where Simon and Amanda sat cross-legged, side by side, looking as if they weren't sure what to do next. She and Jacob were far enough they could talk softly without being heard, but close enough to come back if Amanda or Simon decided they needed some help with conversation. Like every couple in the world, they would figure it out. Another couple, this one English, sat at the end of the pier, dangling their feet over the water, their laughter loud and exuberant over the soft rustle of the cattails in the breeze. Jacob squeezed Martha's hand. "I meant what I said about being able to count on me."

Shyness strangled her for a second. She cleared her throat. "Ever since my *mudder* died, I've felt such a burden—no, that's not the right word . . . such a joy of responsibility for the *kinner*. It's like they're mine. They filled up my life when *Mudder* left it. I don't know what I would've done without them."

"It was different for me because I was the youngest. *Aenti* Susan took over when *Mudder* passed. But I understand." Jacob studied a flock of ducks floating on the lake as if he would find answers to life's secrets in the way they bobbed and floated in the water. "You had a hole that needed to be filled. They filled it. Now Susan is in their lives. She's really good at being an *aenti* and a *mudder*. She's like my *daed*. She knows what to say and when to say it."

"I know. I've seen it over and over again."

"Then you know they're safe with her. You don't have to look for excuses to say no to me."

"They aren't excuses."

"Are you sure? I work hard. I put faith first, then family. I'm an obedient *suh* to my *daed* and to *Gott*. Yet, you push me away. You're scared."

She *was* scared. "I don't ever again want to feel like I felt after *Mudder* died."

"Me neither. I don't know how long *Gott* intends for me to be here, so I can't make any promises on that score, but I can tell you I want to spend those days with you. As many as there are."

"That sounds nice." The future stretched, flower petals opening to the sun. "I will learn to trust."

Jacob leaned closer. "Take all the time you need."

She stood on tiptoes to meet him.

"Jacob, dude, there you are!" Dwayne's holler from the shore had its usual slur. "Dude, come over here. I got Black Cat 'crackers, and a chunk of raw meat."

CHAPTER 10

❧

Timing was everything. Jacob groaned. Martha jerked back and snatched her hand from his. Her fierce frown said it all. Everything rode on how he handled this. He forced himself to look over her shoulder to the shoreline. Dwayne stood in front of Amanda and Simon, a cane pole over one shoulder anchored by a package of meat in one hand, and a bundle of firecrackers with the familiar snarling cat on the red-and-yellow picture in his other hand. He dropped the meat on the ground next to his feet, laid the cane down, and proceeded to pull a lighter from his jeans pocket.

"Don't do that here," Jacob yelled as he strode double-time toward Dwayne. Martha followed, her bare feet slapping on the pier's wood as if punctuating his statement. "Everyone is having a good time. We don't want any part of your so-called fun."

"Chill out, dude. It's gonna be wild. A thousand 'crackers all at once."

Grinning, Dwayne lit the fuse and tossed the bundle to the ground directly in front of where Simon and Amanda sat on their blanket.

Explosion upon explosion ripped the air in a *rat-a-tat-tat* like gunfire. The acrid smell of gunpowder burned Jacob's nose. Sparks flew.

Dwayne pumped his fist and held it out for a bump with an imaginary friend. "Yeehaw! Woo-hoo! God bless America!"

Simon leaped from the blanket and planted himself between the exploding firecrackers and Amanda. Her face scrunched up in fear, she ducked her head. Her hands went to her ears.

"Stop-p-p it. S-s-stop it! Amanda doesn't like it."

Jacob sped up to a run. Martha kept pace at his side. "Are you crazy? You threw them right in front of Amanda and Simon. Didn't you see them?"

"Hey, I'm sorry, man." Dwayne threw up both hands as if in surrender just as the noise died away. "I thought they would like their own personal fireworks."

Hissing like a rattlesnake preparing to strike filled the sudden silence.

A mammoth alligator sat in a few inches of water, its long snout raised, only feet from where Dwayne stood on the sandy bank. It flapped its tail in a sharp rap that sounded like a slap. Its eyes shone in the dusk.

Sobbing now, Amanda scrambled to her feet. "I don't like it. I don't like it."

The alligator, at least fourteen feet long, hissed again and bared rows of pointy teeth. Its tail slammed the water again. Waves rippled around him.

"Hush! Hush, Amanda, hush." Jacob careened to a stop less than a yard from her and Simon. He didn't want to rile up the alligator with any sudden movements. The reptile could give chase up to thirty yards or more. He lowered his voice to a yell-whisper. "It's okay. It's okay."

"It's not okay." The pitch of her voice rose. "He'll hurt Simon. He'll hurt you and Martha."

"We'll be fine, I promise." His back to them, Jacob edged between his friends and the alligator, his feet sinking into the sandy, wet soil that led to the water. Dwayne seemed frozen, hands in the air, mouth open, his eyes wide in surprise. "Dwayne, back away. Slowly."

"Dude, this is crazy." Suddenly, Dwayne moved. The guy never did what he was told. He lowered himself in to a squat, his gaze on the gator, his hand patting the ground, searching for something. "I need the meat. This is perfect. Perfect, man."

"*Nee*, it-it-it is not." His face contorted in a fierce frown, Simon shoved between Jacob and Martha. He shook his finger at the alligator. "Don't you-you-you hurt-hurt my Amanda."

"He won't hurt her if you back away slowly." Jacob put his hand on Simon's shoulder and squeezed, tugging him back. He kept his voice soft, gentle. "You're in his playground. He wants this space all to himself. You have to back up."

"Please, Simon, back up like Jacob says." Martha grabbed Simon's hand as if to draw his attention from the alligator. "You too, Dwayne. We don't want to make the alligator mad."

"What if-if-if he comes after Amanda?" Simon's voice trembled. "What if he hurts her-her or you?"

"I'll help Amanda. You do what Jacob says, okay?" Martha let go of Simon's hand and sidled toward Amanda, one slow step at a time. "We'll be fine."

She put her arm around Amanda. "Can you walk backward?"

"Sure I can." Amanda's tears disappeared. "Like a game?"

"*Jah*, like a game." Martha smiled. "One step, two steps, three steps."

The alligator raised its enormous trap and hissed again.

"We need to move a little faster." Jacob backstepped. "He seems impatient. Come on, Dwayne."

"Nah, I'm fine."

Dwayne knelt in the sandy loom, a big grin replacing his earlier surprise. "The guys won't believe this stuff."

Jacob couldn't worry about a guy acting like an idiot as usual. He and Martha had to get Amanda and Simon away from the danger zone. Then he would deal with cotton-candy-for-brains.

One step. Two steps. Three steps.

Another hiss. Jacob froze. So did Martha. "What now?" she whispered. "Stay or go?"

Sweat ran down Jacob's temples. His shirt was soaked under his arms. "Keep going."

Together, they retreated.

"I don't even have to bait my pole." Dwayne scooped up his package of raw meat and ripped off the wrapper. "I knew that son of a gun was right there. I heard him."

"Be quiet." Contained fury lighted Jacob's words. Dwayne was about to do something stupid and he would have to stop him. "You need to get out of there."

"We have to keep him here until I get my rifle." Dwayne straightened. "I should've brought it. I don't know what I was thinking—"

The crocodile's tail slapped. His mouth opened.

Now or never. Jacob hurled himself forward, reaching for the meat. Simon moved at the same time. He flopped forward, stretching with both arms.

Jacob snatched the meat from Dwayne's hand and tossed it to the crocodile's left in one headlong motion. He lost his balance and hurtled toward the ground with an *oomph*.

Simon teetered. He fell next to Jacob.

Jacob face-planted in the ground. He rolled and sprang to his feet next to Dwayne, who gaped, empty hands still in the air.

The alligator snapped up the raw meat in its massive jaws and glided away.

With the salty taste of blood in his mouth, Jacob tugged Simon to his feet. They raced away from the water. "Go! Go, everyone, go."

Dwayne followed, cussing up a storm. "Aw, man, why'd you do that? We had a great excuse to snag us a gator! He threatened us."

"Only because you riled him up." Jacob tried to breathe through the ache that had once been his nose. His ribs hurt and a back muscle complained. "Someone could've been hurt bad. You have to stop. Stop drinking. Stop acting like a kid. Stop breaking every rule just because you can. You're not a kid anymore."

"Whoa, chill out, man. I didn't mean for anyone to get hurt."

In the light of the nearby fire-pit flames, Jacob whirled and faced the other man. "That's the thing. You don't mean to hurt other people. But you are. You're hurting your friends and your wife and your little ones. And you can't see it, but you're hurting yourself too."

"Aw, man, you're seriously killing my vibe."

"The alli-alli-alligator could've hurt A-A-Amanda." Simon slapped at dirt on his shirt and pants. "That's not nice. You're not nice."

"He's right." Jacob eyed Simon. Aside from the dirt on his clothes and face, he didn't look any worse for wear. *Praise* Gott. "We're men now with responsibilities. Time to act like it."

"Jacob and Simon are right." Rory Chapman stepped from the shadows beyond the fire. Her baby girl slept on her shoulder, curls hiding her face. Dark circles under her mom's eyes said she, too, was tired. "Am I not enough? Are your babies not enough? You have to drink or chase gators or race trucks on backroads to get your jollies? Do you have to kill someone before you stop?"

"What she said." Jacob planted himself in Dwayne's space. "You have to stop. For your babies' sakes. For your wife's sake." His gaze collided with Martha's. She nodded, her eyes bright. "For your friends' sake."

"I don't mean nothing." Dwayne ducked his head, the words a mumble. "I just like to have fun. Why does everybody have to be so serious all the time?"

"You gotta take responsibility." Jacob took a step closer. "You have to want help. Seek help. Go talk to Jesse. He helped you before. He will again."

Dwayne raised his head. He let out a gusty sigh. His gaze went to Rory. "I'm sorry, baby."

"I know you are. But sorry isn't enough anymore."

"Okay, okay. I'll do it."

"Say it, baby. You have to say it."

"I'll go see Jesse first thing Monday morning. I'll quit drinking."

Rory trudged across the grass and stopped short of her husband. She smacked his shoulder with her free hand. "Don't do it again. I mean it. No more chances."

"I won't, baby."

Smooching ensued. Followed by giggles from Amanda and Simon. They seemed to be holding hands, fingers entwined, all grown-up with their special friends.

Without a word, Martha turned and walked toward the fire. Jacob followed. Amanda and Simon slipped closer to the fire where Isabella offered them sticks with marshmallows ready for toasting. Jolene assembled the s'mores on the graham crackers and handed them out. The sound of chatter reached a comforting crescendo.

Light-headed with relief, Jacob eased his head back and pinched his nose, trying to staunch the *drip, drip* of blood.

"There's ice in the ice chest. I can get you some." Martha threaded her way between the clusters of folks visiting who were blissfully unaware of the earlier commotion. "It'll smell like fish, but it's clean."

"I reckon I won't be able to smell it anyway."

Martha chuckled. "Such a big honker is bound to bleed a little."

"I don't have a big nose."

"If you say so." She scooped up ice and wrapped it in a white handkerchief. "Take a seat."

Jacob glanced around. No one seemed to notice their exchange. *Gut.* He followed her to a picnic table out of reach of the light of the fire-pit flames. She dabbed at his face with a napkin and then handed him the make-do ice pack. "Looks like you'll live."

"Ouch." He held the pack to his nose. "Do you think Amanda and Simon will recover?"

The words were muffled, but Martha nodded. She eased onto the bench next to him. "Simon was brave. Amanda was scared, but she got to see her friend protect her. It was *gut*. What do you think will happen to them?"

"That depends on *Gott*'s plan for them, I reckon." He laid the ice pack on the table. "We can't see ahead so we have to trust. Amanda and Simon even more so. Their families have to trust He has a plan for them. I don't know if that means marriage or *kinner*.

But right now they're enjoying each other's company. That's a special gift to them. And they're special gifts to us. It all works out."

She nodded. "Because we can trust *Gott* to be there, no matter what happens."

"We can. And you can trust me to do everything I can to protect you, just like I did with Amanda and Simon."

"I saw that."

"What do you think of it?"

"I think it's *gut*. I think you've shown me you can be trusted. *Gott* can be trusted." She smoothed her apron. "I like what you said to Dwayne too. You sounded like Mordecai."

"If I were to sound like *mei daed*, I would tell you a man has a plethora of choices, but only one is right." He laughed, but she only looked confused. "A lot of choices, is what I'm saying. I'm joking. I hope to sound like him one day—to be like him."

"Like your *daed*, you did what a real friend does. You called Dwayne out and helped him see the error of his ways." She slid a little closer. "That's what a grown-up man does."

"So you really think I'm grown-up?"

"I do."

She lifted her face. He leaned in. This time no one intervened. The delays only made the kiss all the sweeter. She tasted of chocolate. Her lips were warm and soft. He raised his hands to her face, afraid she might stop. He didn't want to ever stop.

After a few minutes, he opened his eyes. She smiled. "I thought fireworks weren't allowed at a state park."

He laughed and kissed her again.

EPILOGUE

❧

A Sunday afternoon in November at Choke Canyon Lake was a far cry from a July holiday weekend. The camping spots were empty. The pavilions looked lonely. The only sounds were bluebirds scolding each other and a warm, damp wind whistling through thickets of mesquite. The lake had lost its shimmer in the metal-gray clouds that hung overhead. The pond grass and rushes that lined the shores had turned brown. Autumn dressed for the approaching winter.

Martha glanced up at Jacob. She couldn't read his face. He was one stubborn man. He refused to tell her why he'd gone to the trouble and expense of paying the van driver Mr. Martinez to give them a ride to the lake. From the time he'd picked her up at the farm until they arrived at the lake, he'd chatted about everything under the sun except this unusual foray away from home on a Sunday afternoon. Not even a hint. Mr. Martinez seemed happy with the situation. He brought a fishing pole and hiked off on his own the second they hopped from his ancient blue minivan.

"*Now* can you tell me what we're doing here?" She liked the feel of Jacob's hand in hers. He'd been holding her hand a lot in the months since the Fourth of July alligator-infested weekend. They walked and talked on Saturday nights. He took her home after every singing. They stared at each other during baptism classes. They stood in front of their families and friends and declared their faith, joining the church together. But they hadn't traveled before. "What's the big secret?"

He tugged her out onto the wooden fishing pier. "I like it here."

"That can't be why we drove an hour and you coughed up the money for a van and admission to the park."

"*Nee*. I decided I wanted to finish what I started here."

"What you started?"

"I was in a big hurry back in July. I thought we were ready. Maybe you were, but I wasn't. Now I am."

He let go of her hand and planted both of his around her waist. Before she could take a breath, he leaned down and let his mouth cover hers. She curled her fingers around his suspenders and hung on, determined never to let go.

His hands moved up, reaching for her face, cupping it. He leaned back. "I feel a little faint, ma'am."

"I think I'm supposed to say that." Her voice sounded like someone else's. High and quivering. "You brought me all the way out here to kiss me? We did that in July, as I recall."

And many times since.

"I haven't forgotten. This is for starters." And he proceeded to kiss her again. *Please* Gott, *don't let me do something silly like faint. And* danki, danki, danki.

This time, he raised his head and let his hands drop. "I have some questions for you."

Gott, *please don't let me faint. And praise You, praise You, praise You.* "You brought me all the way out here to ask me a question? You could've asked me on the front porch at home."

"With your *daed* watching my every move? Now you're just

being contrary." His blue-green eyes mesmerized her. He traced her lips with one long finger. She shivered. He smiled. "Do you trust me?"

"I do."

"Do you trust *Gott*?"

"You saw me profess my faith."

"So I did." He took a deep breath and let it out. His gaze locked with hers. "Will you marry me?"

It would've been humanly impossible to hold back her smile. "I will."

"You will?"

"I said *jah*."

He whooped like a little boy. He hooted and hollered. All the while looking like the grown man she knew him to be. The blue jays and the sparrows and the mockingbirds took flight.

"I don't know." She pretended to look around him. "Are you sure Dwayne isn't lurking in the weeds over there, waiting to interrupt? Are you sure you're grown up enough to marry me?"

"Dwayne is working at the auto shop and saving to take his family to Disney World." Jacob grabbed her around the waist and lifted her off the ground, twirling her until she was breathless with laughter. "Like me, he is all grown-up now. I want you to know, you'll never have to worry about taking care of me. We'll take care of each other and our *kinner*. Lots of *kinner*."

"I look forward to caring for our *kinner*." She swallowed tears, wishing she could tell her *mudder* about this important day in her life. Someday she would. "I trust you. And I trust *Gott*."

"Then it's settled."

They sealed the promise of a shared future with another kiss. And another.

DISCUSSION QUESTIONS

1. Have you ever had friends who pressured you to participate in "fun" that you knew to be wrong? How did you handle it? How do you think God expects you to handle it?
2. It was hard for Martha to trust after what happened to her mother. What would you tell her about God's love and His plan for her?
3. Dwayne was doing something against the law. Martha thought he should experience the consequences of his actions in order to learn a lesson from them. As a friend, Jacob wanted to help him and keep him from harm. Who do you think is right? Why?
4. Martha and Jacob both experienced the loss of their mothers as children. How did their losses change them? How did they respond differently?
5. Do you believe God has a plan for you even when events occur in your life that are painful or tragic? What does Scripture say about suffering?

ABOUT THE AUTHOR

 KELLY IRVIN IS THE AUTHOR OF SEVERAL Amish series including the Bliss Creek Amish series, the New Hope Amish series, and the Amish of Bee County series. She has also penned two romantic suspense novels, *A Deadly Wilderness* and *No Child of Mine*. The Kansas native is a graduate of the University of Kansas School of Journalism. She has been writing nonfiction professionally for more than thirty years, including ten years as a newspaper reporter, mostly in Texas-Mexico border towns. A retired public relations professional, Kelly has been married to photographer Tim Irvin for twenty-nine years. They have two children, two grandchildren, and two cats. In her spare time, she likes to write short stories and read books by her favorite authors.